THE *Italians*

ANGELO, ROCCO & STEFANO

THE

Italians

COLLECTION

August 2015

September 2015

October 2015

November 2015

December 2015

January 2016

THE *Italians*

Angelo, Rocco & Stefano

SARA CRAVEN
CHANTELLE SHAW
CHRISTINA HOLLIS

Published in Great Britain 2015
by Mills & Boon, an imprint of Harlequin (UK) Limited,
Eton House, 18-24 Paradise Road, Richmond, Surrey, TW9 1SR

ISBN: 978-0-263-91569-3

026-0915

Harlequin (UK) Limited's policy is to use papers that are natural, renewable and recyclable products and made from wood grown in sustainable forests.The logging and manufacturing processes conform to the legal environmental regulations of the country of origin.

Printed and bound in Spain
by CPI, Barcelona

WIFE IN THE SHADOWS

SARA CRAVEN

Sara Craven was born in South Devon and grew up in a house full of books. She worked as a local journalist, covering everything from flower shows to murders, and started writing for Mills & Boon in 1975. When not writing, she enjoys films, music, theatre, cooking and eating in good restaurants. She now lives near her family in Warwickshire. Sara has appeared as a contestant on the former Channel Four game show *Fifteen to One* and in 1997 was the UK television *Mastermind* champion. In 2005 she was a member of the Romantic Novelists' team on *University Challenge—the Professionals*.

CHAPTER ONE

April

THE EAR-RINGS WERE the most exquisite she had ever seen.

Nestling in their bed of black velvet, the single diamond drops glowed with a fierce inner fire that made her wonder if her fingertips would burn as she touched them.

But, in fact, they were cold, she thought with a small ironic smile as she fastened them into her earlobes.

Cold as the rest of the jewellery she had been given over the last endless months.

Cold as the chill in the pit of her stomach when she envisaged the evening ahead of her. And its possible aftermath.

She took the pendant, which had been the previous gift, from its case, and handed it to Donata, her maid, to fasten round her throat.

Then she rose from her dressing table, walked to the full-length mirror on an adjacent wall, and stood, straight and silent, subjecting her reflection to a critical, almost clinical examination.

The prescribed outfit for the evening was black, a simple full-length column of silk jersey, long-sleeved, and gathered in soft folds under the bust, its deep neckline revealing the first swell of her breasts, as well as setting off the pendant.

The dress was not in a colour or a style she particularly cared for. It made her look older than her twenty three years, she thought objectively. Conveyed a sophistication she certainly did not possess. But, like so much else in life, it was not her choice.

And, anyway, she asked herself with irony, when had a puppet ever picked its own costume?

Her hair had been swept up into an artfully arranged topknot, with just a few careless strands allowed to brush her cheeks and the nape of her neck.

She had never really warmed to Donata—the girl was too closely involved in the hollow sham that was her life, and probably saw altogether too much, she thought bitterly—but she could not fault her talent for hairdressing. Or, it seemed, her discretion. Whatever she might think of her employer's marriage, she appeared to keep it to herself.

She had learned to apply her own cosmetics. Practised with shadow, liner and mascara to make the most of the grey-green eyes that were her one real claim to beauty, so that they gleamed almost mysteriously under their fringe of heavily darkened lashes.

Her mouth wore the warm flush of a wild rose, and the same shade was echoed in the polish that enhanced her manicured nails.

And in her ears and at her throat, the diamonds glittered like ice in winter sunlight.

She heard a warning cough from Donata, and saw her glance significantly at her watch.

Time, it seemed, for another performance to begin. Reaching for her evening purse, she walked to the door and out along the gallery to the head of the stairs, hearing from the opposite direction the sound of another door closing.

She paused, as always, watching him walk towards her, tall and lean in the elegance of his evening clothes, and moving as lithely as a panther, as if hinting that the formality of his appearance might only be a façade.

And he halted too, his dark gaze sweeping her in one unhurried, comprehensive assessment.

He gave a swift curt nod indicating that her appearance at least had won his approval, then they began to descend the stairs, side by side, but far enough apart to ensure that not so much as his sleeve would brush her arm.

Then, as they reached the marble floored hall below, she was aware of him turning towards her. She heard his voice say quietly, 'Tonight,' and felt the word shiver across her senses until it became dread.

June the previous year

He had, of course, been ambushed. He realised it as soon as he entered the *salotto* and saw that his grandmother was not as he'd hoped, waiting to receive him alone. Instead, her daughter, Signora Luccino, her plump face set in disapproving lines, was seated beside the Contessa Manzini.

'Dearest Nonna.' He went gracefully to his grandmother's chair, and kissed her slender fingers. 'And Zia Dorotea.' He acknowledged his aunt's presence with a polite inclination of the head that was not quite a bow. 'What a pleasant surprise.'

Well, at least in one respect he was telling the truth, he thought drily. He had certainly not expected to come face to face with his late father's older and least favourite sister, the imposing matriarch who ruled her large family as an absolute despot. But he doubted very much if either of them would derive much pleasure from the encounter.

'*Caro* Angelo.' Cosima Manzini indicated that he should take the sofa opposite. 'You are looking well, dearest.'

He thought he heard his aunt give a quiet snort, but continued to smile pleasantly.

'Thank you, I am in the best of health. Probably more by good fortune than good judgement as I am sure Zia Dorotea wishes to remark.'

'I do not think that riding in a private horse race, when you were still recovering from the shoulder you dislocated in a polo match shows any kind of judgement, my dear Angelo,' said the Signora.

Angelo's smile widened. 'But I had been heavily backed to win—not least by yourself, *zia*, or so my cousin Mauro tells me,' he pointed out softly. 'It would have been most discourteous to let people down, so I did not do so.'

The expression on the Signora's face said plainly that Mauro would suffer for his indiscretion.

'You took a great risk, *caro*,' his grandmother added, her arched brows drawing together.

'A calculated one, Nonna.'

'*Tuttavia*, Angelo *mio*, there is a matter you must now seriously consider.'

His mouth tightened. 'You are again referring, I presume, to marriage.'

'Dear one, I must do.' Cosima leaned forward, her eyes pleading. 'I have no wish to interfere, or to make you angry, but it is over two years since your beloved father died, and you became Count Manzini. You need a son and heir to inherit the title in his turn.'

He said bleakly, 'I am aware of my obligations, Nonna. None better, I assure you. But I do not find them particularly appealing.'

'No,' said his aunt. 'You prefer to trifle with other men's wives rather than find one for yourself. Oh, do not defend him, Mamma,' she added sharply as the Contessa tried to speak. 'It is the truth and Angelo knows it. There are plenty of single girls for him to choose from, but until he stops behaving like a tomcat all over Rome, he will never find a bride.'

He said between his teeth, 'How good of you to take such an interest in my private life, Zia Dorotea.'

'If only it were private,' she retorted. 'But I fear that it is only a matter of time before one of your liaisons becomes a public scandal. And I tell you, Angelo, you will have no-one to blame but yourself if the Galantana brand suffers as a result.'

'We make clothing for the fashion industry, *zia*,' he returned coldly. 'Not church vestments. I hardly think any stories about me as the chairman of the company will affect whether a girl buys a skirt with our label on it or another's.' He shrugged. 'It might even boost sales. Who knows?'

'Oh, you are impossible.' She reached for her bag and rose. 'I have not the patience to reason with you.'

'As I am fast running out of patience to listen to you,' Angelo said crisply. 'Busy yourself with finding a wife for Mauro. That should occupy you for the next several years.'

She gave him a look of concentrated fury and swept to the door. When it had closed behind her, the Contessa said mildly, 'That was neither kind nor polite, *mio caro*.'

'Yet it had the ring of truth she allegedly admires so much. However, I will send her some flowers and make peace.' He was silent for a moment, then sighed irritably. 'She did not come here today, I am sure, just to lecture me on my sins. No doubt she has a suitable candidate in mind as a wife for me.'

'*Davvero*, she mentioned—someone.'

Angelo's face relaxed into faint amusement. 'But of course,' he said softly. 'And are you going to tell me her name?'

'She is called Elena—Helen in her own language.'

'An English girl?' He didn't hide his surprise.

'With Italian blood,' the Contessa nodded. 'Her grandmother Vittoria Silvestre was a dear friend of mine and Dorotea also had affection for her. She married an Englishman, and one of her daughters did the same, a man called Blake. They eventually settled near Genoa, but sadly were killed one winter in an accident on the *autostrada*. Elena, their only child, now lives in Rome, and works as a translator for the Avortino publishing company.'

'She works?' His brows lifted. 'So she is "not just a pretty face" as the English say.'

'You would be a better judge of that than myself.' The Contessa played with her rings. 'It seems you have met her.'

'I have?' Angelo frowned. 'I do not recall.'

She said expressionlessly, 'She was at a dinner party you attended at the house of Silvia Alberoni.' She paused. 'A name that is familiar to you, I think. And certainly a pretty face.'

Under his breath, Angelo cursed his Aunt Dorotea, wondering at the same time how she came by her information.

I shall have to be more careful in future, he thought grimly.

Married to the wealthy but dull head of a firm of top accountants, Silvia was as bored as she was young and beautiful, and also ripe for mischief as he'd swiftly detected at their first meeting. Subsequent and more private encounters had proved her just as ardent and inventive as he'd conjectured, and their *affaire* had prospered.

Until then, he had also believed it to be a secret, which was why he'd risked accepting her invitation to dinner. Most of the other guests had been from the world of finance, so he had found the evening instructive as well as entertaining, but he seemed to remember there had been a girl, quiet and essentially nondescript, seated at the other end of the table. The fact that he'd barely noticed her, he thought, said it all.

He said coolly, 'It is kind of my aunt to bring her to my attention, but I believe I require at least a modicum of personality in the woman I marry. Signora Alberoni's guest seemed—a complete nonentity—a girl without looks or significance.'

'I am sorry to hear it,' his grandmother said after a pause. 'I would not have thought Vittoria's grand-daughter could be so signally lacking in appeal. But any decision must naturally be yours—when you choose to make it.' She paused. 'Now ring the bell, *mio caro*, and Maria will bring coffee.'

And the conversation, to Angelo's relief, turned to other topics.

But that did not mean he was off the hook, he thought, as he drove home later. And in many ways his grandmother and interfering aunt were right. He should be married, and if this might be possible to achieve without having to abandon his bachelor pleasures, he would propose to the first suitable girl who took his eye.

But the experiences of some of his married friends whose submissive doe-eyed brides had turned into control freaks before the honeymoon was over had proved an active deterrent. True, they seemed more philosophical than crushed, but Angelo knew it would not do for him.

But, at the same time, he could not envisage what he might find acceptable either.

He enjoyed women, and the pleasure of women, always making sure that he gave back the delight that he took, but he had never fallen in love with any of the girls who'd shared his bed, or considered that they might also share his future on a long-term basis.

He offered no promises and made it clear he expected none in return.

In addition, there was a kind of inner reserve in him which seemed to warn him when each liaison had run its natural course, and could be safely ended, with charm, generosity—and finality.

And he suspected with a trace of regret that his *affaire* with Silvia Alberoni might already be reaching those limits.

She was a passionate and insatiable mistress, but that reliable antenna of his had recently picked up that she might have begun to foresee a different role in his life for herself, if the worthy Ernesto could be conveniently sidelined.

The word 'annulment' had even been mentioned, lightly and amusingly, it was true, and solely in the context of her failure to become pregnant during the two and a half years of her marriage.

'I was told once that a woman's body can reject the seed of a man she does not truly love.' One crimson-tipped finger had drawn an enticing pattern in the curling dark hair on his chest. 'Do you think that is true, *mi amore*?'

He had curbed his instinct to dismiss the idea as ludicrous nonsense but in much pithier terms, and, instead, murmured some meaningless platitude about a woman's sensitivity which appeared to satisfy her. But the exchange had raised a red flag in his consciousness just the same. As did her use of the word 'love' which he'd always deliberately avoided in his *affaires*.

But even more alarming was the possibility that rumours might be circulating about them. That if Zia Dorotea had learned of their relationship, then others might also have done so, and that the stories might eventually reach Ernesto Alberoni.

Angelo would deny them, of course, but he had to ask himself if Silvia could be trusted to do the same, or if she might see this as an opportunity to escape from a disappointing marriage, and find a husband more to her taste. And there was a real danger she might want it to be him. Could insist that having destroyed her marriage, he had an obligation towards her. Had even once expressed disappointment that she had not met him while she was still 'free'. Another word to set alarm bells ringing.

Because Silvia, though beautiful and entertaining, was hardly the material from which good wives were made. After all, she'd had no compunction about putting horns on the unfortunate Ernesto, and who was to say she would not do the same to another husband, given the opportunity?

Suddenly he could see the precipice yawning in front of him and knew that, for safety's sake, he needed to step back, and fast, while he still could.

For there was another reason why any kind of open scandal should be avoided, particularly at this moment. The quality of the Galantana brand of clothing had saved the company from the worst effects of the global recession—indeed, they were planning expansion—but for that they needed extra finance for more new machinery at the Milan factory, as well as buying another site for workshops near Verona.

Which was principally why he had accepted Silvia's dinner invitation, because he'd learned that Prince Cesare Damiano, head of the Credito Europa bank would be present, and not because he liked to live dangerously.

He and Prince Damiano had spoken briefly but constructively, and negotiations were now proceeding. And while the banker was a charming, cultivated man with a passion for rose growing, he was also known to be a stickler for old-fashioned morality.

Any overt lapse on Angelo's part could well blow the

deal out of the water, and delay would be costly in all kinds of ways.

So a period of celibacy was indicated. Irritating, he decided cynically, but a necessity. As, it now seemed, was his marriage, which would provide a safeguard as well as an expedient.

He drove into the security parking of his apartment block, and rode the lift up to the top floor. As he stepped through his front door, his manservant, Salvatore, was waiting to take his briefcase and discarded jacket.

'There have been two phone calls for Your Excellency,' he announced, lowering his eyes discreetly. 'Also a note has been delivered.' He paused. 'Will your *signoria* be dining out this evening?'

'No,' Angelo returned, looking moodily at the unmistakable pale mauve envelope on the hall table. 'I shall eat here. Something light, Salvatore. I am not very hungry.'

The other's eyes lit up. 'I have some good veal—which I will cook in a little Marsala, perhaps?'

'With a green salad,' Angelo agreed. He ran a weary hand round the nape of his neck. 'In the meantime, I think I'll take a sauna. Get rid of some of the kinks of the day.'

In his bedroom, he stripped then walked into the bathroom, grabbing a towel on the way, to the wooden cabin that opened off it. He poured a dipper of water scented with aromatic herbs on to the coals and, spreading his towel on the slatted wooden bench, stretched out, closed his eyes and let his mind drift.

If he was going to marry, he mused, there were a number of practical matters to take into consideration, the most urgent being living accommodation, because, convenient as it was to the Via Veneto and the Rome headquarters of Galantana, this apartment was also his bachelor pad, and due to its past associations, not a suitable place to bring his bride, although he had no intention of getting rid of it.

No, he thought, she would be far happier living on his estate in the hills just outside the capital, and it would be a better environment for the son he hoped for. Or it would be once the air of melancholy following the loss of his mother, which had dulled his own memories of a happy childhood and caused him to avoid the place in recent years, had been banished forever.

His father, turned by grief into a virtual recluse, had suddenly and quite unexpectedly begun a refurbishment programme on the villa itself three years before. It had gone into abeyance on his death, but the time had come, Angelo decided, for it to be revived and completed.

It was odd, he admitted to himself, to be making plans for a woman he didn't even know as yet, but, as the Contessa Manzini, she would soon learn the duties and responsibilities of her new status and, he hoped, the pleasures of it too as he had every intention of being both generous and considerate.

She might not have his love, the sweet and passionate emotion that had held his parents steadfastly in thrall to each other, because he doubted whether he was capable of such feelings, but he could and would offer her, at the very least, respect along with every material comfort she could wish for. And a decent show of ardour should not be too difficult to feign. Besides, if she was pretty enough, he might not have to pretend, he told himself, grimacing inwardly.

He'd stayed with friends in Tuscany the previous weekend, and partnered a girl called Lucia in an impromptu tennis match. Good legs, he thought judiciously, a figure that curved in all the right places, and dark eyes that had gleamed in his direction more than once. He had not asked for her telephone number but that was an omission that could easily be rectified with an email to his host.

On the other hand, each time she'd played a bad shot, she'd giggled and he'd begun to find this irritating. The thought of having to listen to it morning, noon and even night was not appealing.

He sat up abruptly, cursing under his breath. He was hardly perfect husband material, so why should he expect to find the perfect wife? And what made him think Lucia would even want him?

For once, and perhaps understandably, he was finding relaxation difficult, so he abandoned the sauna, showered briskly, pulled on jeans and a polo shirt and went to the *salotto*.

As he'd anticipated, both phone messages were from Silvia, requesting him to call her. And her letter proved to be in similar vein but rather more demanding, he noted, his lips tightening. Clearly his absence in Tuscany and his omission to contact her immediately on his return had not pleased her. She was becoming distinctly proprietorial, and although he would have his regrets at terminating their association, he realised he had no choice.

He did not belong to her, he thought coldly, pouring himself a whisky. To her, or any other woman, and he never would. He had seen what that could do. Had seen his father become a silent stranger, the heart and spirit torn out of him after his wife's death—little more than a sad ghost in a house which had once been filled with sunshine and laughter.

Had found himself, scarcely out of boyhood, excluded from his own grief in the face of his father's desolation.

And without the tenderness and support of Nonna Cosima, who had taken him into her own home, he would have been left very much alone.

As he emerged from the darkness of that time, he'd sworn that he would never allow anyone to make him suffer like that. And nothing had happened since to persuade him to change his mind.

His marriage would be a practical arrangement without illusions, he vowed silently, and he would set himself to make it work.

Therefore, as a beginning, he would decline Silvia's suggestion that as Ernesto would be away the following weekend, they should take advantage of his absence at some discreet *albergo* in the wilds of Umbria or Reggio Calabria.

Instead, he thought, crumpling the note in his hand, I will be spending the time in close consultation with the builders at Vostranto, so I shall call her tomorrow and make my excuses.

And after that, I shall also ask Ottavio for Lucia's phone number.

'No,' said Ellie. 'It's very kind of Madrina to invite me, but I've already made my plans for that weekend. I'm sorry, Silvia.'

'You don't sound it.' Her cousin leaned back in her chair, pouting. 'I suppose you're off to bury yourself at Nonna Vittoria's shack as usual.'

It might only be a small house, but it was hardly a shack, Ellie thought drily. And Silvia clearly hadn't thought so when she discovered that their grandmother's will had left Ellie in sole possession of what could be an eminently desirable property in a charming fishing village on a beautiful coastline. She had raged about the total unfairness of the bequest for weeks if not months, accusing Ellie of wheedling her way into Nonna Vittoria's good graces.

By which Ellie supposed she meant visiting her grandmother regularly and remembering her at birthdays and Christmases. Something Silvia's busy social life had overlooked most of the time.

'And how can you even think of it when you could be staying in the lap of luxury at the Villa Rosa?' Silvia went on.

'Perhaps I don't find the lap of luxury particularly comfortable,' Ellie said drily. 'Especially when I'm aware that I'm the only person present who's actually an employee instead of an employer.'

Silvia waved a languid hand. 'Oh, you're far too sensitive, *cara*. Besides Madrina adores you, and you owe her a visit. She has said so, and will be so upset if you refuse.' She paused. 'And you could do me the most enormous favour too.'

Ellie's hand stilled in its task of refilling their coffee cups. Ah, she thought, without surprise. Now we're coming to it.

She said, 'Oh God, Silvia, you haven't been losing money at bridge again, not after the things Ernesto said last time.'

'Oh, that.' Silvia looked down, playing with the emerald

and diamond ring on her wedding finger. 'I've hardly touched a card for months. Truly. Anyone will tell you.'

'Except that I don't know anyone to ask,' Ellie returned, scenting an evasion. 'And I have no money to bail you out, so don't even think about it.'

'That's not what I'm asking,' Silvia denied swiftly. 'It's just that—well—Ernesto is being a little silly at the moment about my going away without him, even to see my own godmother, and if he knew you'd be there too, I'm sure he'd change his mind.'

Ellie brought over the fresh coffee, placing the cup on the table beside her cousin's chair.

She said slowly, 'It's not like him to play the heavy husband. Silvia, you're sure that you're not the one who's being silly?'

Silvia flushed angrily. 'And what makes you an authority on married life? I wasn't aware that you even had a boyfriend.'

Ouch, thought Ellie, remembering at the same time that attack had always been Silvia's favourite form of defence. Also, that it had been several weeks since her cousin had sought her company—and then only at the last minute to make up the numbers at a dinner party, where, to add to her usual shyness, she'd felt badly dressed and totally out of her depth.

Especially when Silvia had been at her sparkling best, eyes gleaming like her jewellery, and her mouth curved on the edge of a smile all evening, and the centre of everyone's attention. As if, Ellie thought, a fire had been lit inside her.

In fact, on that occasion, Ellie had taken her godmother's place, as the Principessa Damiano had been suffering from a heavy cold. But at least she'd only had to give up a few hours—unlike this new request, where she'd be committed from Friday evening until late afternoon on Sunday. Not a prospect she relished, however fond she was of her tiny, exquisite godmother fluttering like a butterfly in the pale draperies she affected.

Although that, Ellie had always suspected, was just a façade, concealing a will of reinforced steel. Which was why she'd probably used Silvia to back up her invitation.

But Ellie was always conscious that Madrina inhabited a

world where Silvia belonged, but she herself did not. They might be first cousins, but chalk and cheese didn't even come near it.

Silvia, the elder by almost a year, was silvery fair, with green eyes that looked at the world from the shadow of extravagant lashes, a small straight nose and a frankly sexy full-lipped mouth. Her chief ambition from childhood had been to marry a rich man and she'd achieved it effortlessly, although Nonna Vittoria had frowned and tutted over her choice, murmuring that *cara* Silvia needed to be held in check, and that her *fidanzato*, though estimable, might not be the man to do it.

Ellie, on the other hand, had often thought, without rancour, that she resembled the negative of a dramatically coloured photograph. Her own hair was the shade generally known as dirty blonde, and she was pale-skinned and slender. Nonna Vittoria always told her she had unusual eyes, but the rest of her features were nothing to admire. Nose too long, she thought. Mouth too serious.

However, on the plus side, she enjoyed her work, liked most of her colleagues and had a small group of friends of both sexes with whom she ate out and attended films and concerts.

She supposed it was a relatively sedate existence, but it suited her. Yet so did her own company, and the times when she could escape to the coast and the waiting Casa Bianca were among her happiest.

She couldn't let the opportunity to spend the weekend there pass. Could she?

Yet, as she drank her coffee, she sent a covert glance at her cousin. Something was wrong. She knew it. The shining brightness of a few weeks ago had become restive—even edgy.

She said quietly, 'Silvia, I don't want us to fall out but I need you to be honest with me. Why do you want me to accept Madrina's invitation?'

Her cousin looked sulky. 'It is nothing. An absurdity. A man Ernesto feels has paid me too much attention. He has even started to think that I am meeting this man and not going to

Largossa at all. But if he knows that you and I will be at the Villa Rosa together, his mind will be at rest.'

Ellie frowned. 'Wouldn't it be simpler if he accompanied you himself?'

Silvia spread her hands. 'He cannot. There is a client—an important man—with tax difficulties which must be settled *pronto.* So Ernesto must handle the case personally, even if he has to use the weekend.'

Ellie could sympathise with the client's needs. Italy's labyrinthine tax laws were not for the inexperienced or the faint-hearted.

And yet—and yet…

She recalled suddenly that she'd thought she heard the name of Alberoni mentioned in a low-pitched conversation by the water cooler at work a few weeks ago, only to find when she joined the group that they were talking about something completely different.

Now she found herself wondering uneasily if the subject had been deliberately changed at her approach and just what they'd been discussing.

If the stolid Ernesto had been stirred to a seething mass of jealousy, might he have reason? Whatever, he seemed to be taking steps to keep Silvia in check at last, and maybe, as her cousin was all the family she had left, she should help, besides having no wish to hurt her godmother's feelings by a refusal to attend her house party.

'Who else will be there?' she asked cautiously.

Silvia shrugged. 'Oh, Fulvio Ciprianto and his wife.' She added casually. 'Plus one of Madrina's elderly cronies, the Contessa Manzini.'

Manzini, thought Ellie. The name was vaguely familiar, but in what context? Then her mind went back to that wretched dinner party, and she remembered. A man, she thought, tall, very dark, and lethally attractive even to her untutored gaze, who'd been pointed out to her as Count Angelo Manzini. Not, she'd reflected at the time, that he looked even remotely like an angel. The lean saturnine face, amused dark eyes and mobile, sensuous mouth suggested far more sin than sanctity.

However, no playboy apparently, but the successful chairman of the Galantana fashion group, or so she'd been informed by her neighbour during a brief lull between courses.

Which, considering what she'd been wearing, was probably why the Count had totally ignored her.

'A few others, perhaps,' Silvia went on, twisting the emerald on her finger again. 'I am not sure. But if you get bored,' she added with renewed buoyancy, 'you can always ask Zio Cesare to show you his roses. You like such things.'

Ellie had never addressed her godmother's august husband as 'uncle' in her life, and Silvia knew it. Another reminder of the wide gap in their circumstances.

'Thank you,' she returned ironically.

'So I can tell Madrina that you will be coming with me, Ella-Bella?' Silvia was watching her almost eagerly.

But, thought Ellie, there was another element in her expression that was not so easy to fathom, and which sparked a faint *frisson* of concern.

'Only if you swear never to call me that stupid name again, Silly-Billy. We're no longer children,' she retorted crisply. 'And I'll telephone her myself.' She paused. 'Shall we go in my car?'

Silvia looked as horrified as if Ellie had suggested they trudge to Largossa, pushing their luggage in a wheelbarrow. 'You mean that little Fiat? No, I will arrange for Ernesto to lend us the Maserati with Beppo to drive us.'

Ellie frowned. 'He won't want them himself?'

'He has the Lamborghini.' Silvia pursed her lips. 'Or he could walk. The exercise would do him good, I think.'

'Poor Ernesto,' said Ellie.

And poor me, she thought when her cousin had departed, leaving a delicate aroma of Patou's 'Joy' in the air. Although that, she admitted, was rank ingratitude when she would be staying in a superbly comfortable house, with magnificent food and wine, and being thoroughly indulged with her godmother's unfailing affection.

But it was simply not the kind of visit she was accustomed to. Usually she was invited to keep Lucrezia Damiano company while her husband was away attending meetings with other European bankers. Sometimes, but not always, Silvia came too.

But Ellie could not imagine why her cousin was so keen for them both to attend what seemed to be a distinctly middle-aged party.

Oh for heaven's sake, she adjured herself impatiently, as she carried the coffee pot and used cups into her tiny kitchen. Stop worrying about nothing. It's not a major conspiracy. It's simply a couple of days out of your life, that's all.

And when they're over, you'll be straight back to the old routine again, just as if you'd never been away.

Then she paused, as she began to run water into the sink, staring into space as she wondered exactly what it was that Silvia wasn't telling her. And why she should suddenly feel so worried.

CHAPTER TWO

'*CARISSIMA!*' Lucrezia Damiano embraced Ellie fondly. 'Such a joy.'

Ellie, partaker of a largely silent drive from Rome in the back of the Maserati, with Silvia, face set, staring moodily through the window, had yet to be convinced of the joyousness of the occasion, but her godmother's welcome alleviated some of the chill inside her.

The Villa Rosa had begun its life at the time of the Renaissance, and, with additions over the centuries, including a small square tower at one end, now had the look of a house that had simply grown up organically from the rich earth that surrounded it. The Damianos possessed a much grander house in Rome, but Largossa was the country retreat they loved and regularly used at weekends.

The *salotto* where the Principessa received her guests was in the oldest part of the house, a low-ceilinged room, its walls hung with beautifully restored tapestries, furnished with groupings of superbly comfortable sofas and chairs, with a fireplace big enough to roast a fair-sized ox.

The long windows opened on to a broad terrace, and offered a beguiling view of the grounds beyond, including the walled garden where Cesare Damiano cultivated the roses that were his pride and joy.

But her host, Ellie learned, would not be joining the party until the following day.

'My poor Cesare—a meeting in Geneva, and quite

unavoidable,' the Principessa lamented. 'So tonight will be quite informal—just a reunion of dear friends.'

She turned to her other god-daughter, who was standing, her expression like stone. *'Ciao, Silvia mia. Come stai?'*

'I am fine, thank you, Godmother.' Silvia submitted rather sullenly to being kissed on both cheeks, causing Ellie to eye her narrowly.

She didn't look fine, she thought. On the contrary, since she entered the house, Silvia appeared to be strung up on wires. Nor had it been lost on Ellie that, on their arrival, she had scanned almost fiercely the cars parked on the gravel sweep in front of the villa's main entrance as if she was looking for one particular vehicle before sinking back in her seat, chewing at her lip.

'And now there are people you must meet,' the Principessa decreed, leading the way out on to the terrace.

An elderly lady, dressed in black, her white hair drawn into an elegant chignon, was seated at a table under a parasol, in conversation with a younger, plumper woman with a merry face, but they turned expectantly at the Principessa's approach.

'Contessa,' she said. 'And my dear Anna. May I present my god-daughters—the Signora Silvia Alberoni, and Signorina Elena Blake. Girls, allow me to make the Contessa Cosima Manzini and Signora Ciprianto known to you.'

The Contessa extended a be-ringed hand to both, murmuring that it was her pleasure. Her smile was gracious, but the eyes that studied Ellie were oddly shrewd, almost, she thought in bewilderment, as if she was being assessed in some way. If so, it was unlikely that her simple button-through dress in olive-green linen, and the plain silver studs in her ears would pass muster. And nor, she imagined, would her very ordinary looks.

The Contessa, by contrast, was not only dressed in great style, but her classic bone structure still suggested the beauty she must have been in her youth.

They took the seats they were offered, and accepted glasses of fresh lemonade, clinking with ice. Silvia seemed to have come out of sulky mode and was talking brightly about the journey, the warmth of the day, and the beauty of the gardens, her smile expansive, her hands moving gracefully to emphasise some point, while Contessa Manzini listened and nodded politely but without comment.

Under the cover of this vivacity, Ellie found herself being addressed quietly and kindly by Anna Ciprianto, and asked, with what seemed to be genuine interest, about her work at the Avortino company, so that she was able to overcome her usual shyness with strangers and chat back.

After a while, Lucrezia Damiano went off to greet more guests, a couple called Barzado, also middle-aged, the wife bright-eyed and talkative, whom she brought out to join the party.

So what on earth am I doing here? Ellie asked herself in renewed perplexity. And, even more to the point, what is Silvia?

On the surface, her cousin was brimming with effusive charm, the very picture of the lovely young wife of a successful man, but Ellie could see that her posture was betrayingly rigid, and the hands in her lap were clenched rather than folded.

I want to help, she thought, wondering why, when she and Silvia were together, she so often felt like the older one. But how can I—if she won't talk to me—won't tell me the problem?

And at that moment she saw the Contessa look down the terrace, a hand lifting to shade her eyes, as the faint austerity of her expression relaxed into warmth and pleasure.

'Mio caro,' she exclaimed. *'Alla fine.* At last.'

Ellie did not have to look round to see who was approaching, and whose tall shadow had fallen across the sunlit flagstones. Because one glance at Silvia, her eyes wide and intense, her natural colour fading to leave two spots of blusher visible on her cheekbones, suddenly told her everything she needed to know, making her realise at the same time that it was information she would far sooner have been without. And that all her concerns about this weekend were fully justified.

Nor did she need to wonder further about the whispers round

the coffee machine, either in her workplace, or probably any other.

'Oh God,' she whispered under her breath, dry-mouthed with shock. 'I don't believe this. Silvia—you complete and utter fool.'

'My dearest one.' Count Angelo Manzini, contriving to look elegant in chinos and an open-necked white shirt, bent to kiss his grandmother's hand, then her cheek. 'Ladies.' A brief, charming smile acknowledged everyone else at the table, but bestowed no special attention anywhere.

Ellie had the curious sensation that the air around them had begun to tingle, and hastily drank some more lemonade, keeping her eyes fixed firmly on the ground, as he pulled up a chair and joined the group.

In daylight and close up, he was even more formidable, she thought, taking a deep steadying breath, and wishing with all her heart that she was back in Rome. Or that Silvia was.

She wondered if she could invent some emergency to provide her with an excuse for leaving, only to remember, with a sinking heart, that she had inadvertently left her mobile phone on charge back at her apartment, and that any landline calls to the villa would be answered by Giovanni, the major domo, and relayed through the Principessa herself.

So it appeared she was stuck here for the duration.

Lucrezia was speaking. 'My dear Count, I know you are acquainted with Signora Alberoni, but I believe you have not been introduced to her cousin, my other god-daughter, the Signorina Elena Blake.'

'No, I have not had that pleasure. I am charmed, *signorina*.'

Ellie sat up with an alarmed jolt, forcing herself to look at him, and murmur something polite and meaningless in return. His mouth was unsmiling, but his dark gaze that met hers held a faint glint that might have been amusement. Or—equally—anger.

Though what he had to be angry about defeated her, she thought, glancing away, her own expression stony. After all, she was the one who'd been manipulated into providing cover for his affair with Silvia. But if he imagined she'd have come within miles of the Villa Rosa if she'd known the truth, then the glamorous Count Manzini could think again. And, she told herself almost grinding her teeth, if he actually thought it was funny…

As soon as she could do so, she excused herself on the grounds she needed to unpack and went indoors, feeling as if she'd escaped.

There was never any question about which room she'd be using. Since her first childhood visit, when she'd gazed entranced at the little tower, telling her amused godmother that it was like something out of a fairy tale, that had been where she'd slept.

But as she climbed the spiral staircase leading up to it from the little sitting room below, she reflected that, mercifully, the Principessa no longer teased her that she was waiting for some princely hero to leap up the other steep flight of exterior steps from the garden to the small balcony outside her window and carry her off.

On the contrary, in recent years, she'd come to regard the tower room in much the same light as the Casa Bianca—as something of a refuge, and probably it would never be more so than this time, she thought with a troubled sigh as she contemplated the afternoon's developments.

Unlike Silvia, Ellie had only brought one small case, so her unpacking was soon completed, but she had no intention of returning to the terrace, even though it would probably be expected of her.

Instead, she used the tiny adjoining bathroom to shower away the stickiness of the journey, and, she vainly hoped, some of its subsequent tensions. Then, wrapped in her white cotton robe, she curled up in the small deeply cushioned armchair in front of the open window and resignedly gave full rein to her uneasy thoughts.

She would be having severe words with Silvia, once the opportunity presented itself, she promised herself grimly. Her cousin had no right—no right at all—to implicate her even marginally in whatever was going on between herself and that diabolically good-looking bastard who'd just swanned in.

Not that there were any real doubts in her mind about the situation—how could there be?—which suggested that, if Silvia wasn't careful, other people including Madrina, would be drawing the same conclusions.

And Silvia must be mad if she thought her godmother, or, more particularly, the austere Prince Damiano would tolerate any possibility of open scandal under their roof.

And while she could admit that maybe Ernesto was not the most exciting man in the world, she remembered how Silvia had insisted she wanted to marry him and no-one else. Or was it more the status of being a rich man's wife she'd actually hankered for?

Whatever—there was a limit to Ernesto's placidity, and if he even suspected that Silvia had been unfaithful to him, there'd be trouble bordering on catastrophe.

How could her cousin take such a risk—especially when it did not seem to be making her happy? Ellie asked herself in bewilderment. But remembering her original assessment of Count Manzini, she doubted whether bestowing happiness would be a priority in his relationships anyway.

Here today, she thought, biting her lip, and gone tomorrow. Not that she was any real judge of such matters, of course, but instinct warned her he was the kind of man anyone with sense should cross a busy street to avoid.

But there were no busy streets at the Villa Rosa, as Ellie discovered several hours later when, to her horror, she found she'd been placed next to Count Manzini at dinner.

It was punishment, she thought, for fibbing to her godmother that she'd stayed in her room with a slight headache instead of rejoining the party.

Nor was it any consolation that the Count seemed no more pleased at having her as a neighbour than she was.

Because Madrina had emphasised an informal evening,

Ellie had kept back the long dress she'd brought in deference to the Prince's known wishes, choosing instead a pretty georgette skirt in white, patterned with sunflowers, which floated around her when she moved, and a scooped-neck silk top, also in white. Neither of them were from the Galantana line, as she was sure one quick glance had told him.

She had no idea who'd made his expensive suit either, but decided it was probably Armani.

At the other end of the table, Silvia was resplendent in a royal blue cocktail dress, made high to the throat in front, but plunging deeply at the back. She seemed to have recovered her equilibrium—in fact she looked almost glowingly triumphant—and was chatting with animation to her neighbours as if she didn't have a care in the world.

Leaving me free to do the worrying for her, Ellie thought, serving herself from the dishes of *antipasti* which began the meal.

She'd not yet had the chance for a private word with her cousin who'd been missing from her room at the other end of the villa when she went in search of her, leaving Ellie to wonder where she was and decide that she'd probably prefer not to know.

'May I offer you some tomato salad?' Count Manzini enquired with cool politeness, and she looked up from her plate with a start.

'No,' she said, stiltedly. 'No, thank you.'

'I seem to alarm you, *signorina*,' he went on, after a pause. 'Or do you simply prefer to eat in silence?'

'I think—neither.'

'I am relieved to hear it.'

He smiled at her for the first time, and she felt her throat tighten nervously as she reluctantly experienced the full impact of his attraction. The government, she thought shakily, should issue a warning, and felt something like a grudging sympathy for Silvia.

'I believe we have encountered each other before, but were

not formally presented to each other,' he continued. 'One evening at the home of Ernesto Alberoni, I think.'

'Perhaps.' Ellie stared rigidly down at her food. 'I—I don't remember.'

'Che peccato,' he said lightly. 'Also, I was not aware that our hostess had more than one god child. Do you visit her a great deal?'

'As often as I can, yes.' Her tone was faintly defensive.

'And this weekend—it is an engagement of long standing?'

She wanted to say 'Hasn't Silvia told you how she dragged me down here at the last minute as a cover story?' but decided against it. On the other hand, she didn't see why she should answer any more of his questions.

She shrugged. 'I can't really remember when it was arranged,' she returned, deliberately casual. 'Does it matter?'

'Not at all,' he said. 'I am just a little curious about your presence at a party where the other guests are so much older.'

'But I'm not the only one.' She was careful not to glance in Silvia's direction. 'The same could be said of you, Count Manzini.'

'I am here because I have business with Prince Damiano,' he said softly. 'And when it is concluded, I shall be gone.'

Let it be soon, thought Ellie, helping herself to more anchovies and wondering at the same time if her cousin was aware of his plans.

When he resumed the conversation, he turned to rather more neutral topics, asking if she played tennis—she didn't—and if she liked to swim, at which point she claimed mendaciously that she hadn't brought her bathing costume.

He was being perfectly civil, yet Ellie was thankful when his attention was claimed by Signora Barzado, seated on his other side, and she was therefore able to relax a little and enjoy the *gnocchi* in its rich sauce, and the exquisite veal dish that followed.

It occurred to her that even if she'd been unaware of his involvement with Silvia, she would still not have felt comfortable with him. There was arrogance beneath the charm, she thought, suggesting that he regarded women as just another facet of his success.

Besides, he was in orbit round some sun while she remained completely earthbound.

Not that it mattered, she told herself, as she ate her *panna cotta* with its accompanying wild strawberries. Tomorrow he would leave and, with luck, she would never have to set eyes on him again. All the same she wished that Prince Damiano had not been detained in Geneva.

It was a long meal with strega and grappa to accompany the coffee which ended it, but when it was over and they drifted back to the *salotto*, Ellie's need to talk to Silvia was thwarted again by her cousin immediately opting to play bridge with Signora Barzado and the Cipriantos.

Count Manzini, to her relief, took himself off to the billiard room with Carlo Barzado, while his grandmother and the Principessa occupying a sofa by the fireplace had their heads together in low-voiced and plainly confidential conversation.

Ellie found a magazine in a rack beneath one of the side tables, and took it to a chair on the other side of the room. It was mainly concerned with the fashion industry, and, inevitably, had a feature on Galantana praising its success and detailing its anticipated expansion. This was naturally accompanied by a photograph of Angelo Manzini seated at his desk, his shirt sleeves rolled back over tanned forearms and his tie loose. He looked tough, business-like, and, as even Ellie could appreciate, sexy as hell.

The camera, she thought, drawing a breath, was no doubt being operated by a woman.

At the bridge table, one rubber followed another and Ellie was forced to accept that Silvia was avoiding any kind of *tête à tête* between them, and she might as well go to bed.

'So soon, *cara*?' The Principessa regarded her with concern. 'It is not still the headache?'

'Oh, no,' Ellie assured her swiftly and guiltily. 'That seems to have gone.'

In her room, the bed had been turned down and her white lawn nightgown prettily fanned across the coverlet, but the helpful maid had also closed the windows for some abstruse reason, turning the room into a temporary oven.

Sighing a little, Ellie opened them again, drew the curtains, and switched on the ceiling fan. She took a quick cooling shower, cleaned her teeth, then folded back the coverlet to the bottom of the bed, deciding for once to dispense with her nightgown before sliding under the cover of the sheet.

She'd arranged to leave the Avortino office early that day, so she'd brought some remaining translation work with her to finish off. It was a simple enough task, and normally she'd have whizzed through it, but this time she found it well-nigh impossible to concentrate, and after struggling for almost an hour, she gave up.

If I go on, I'll have a genuine headache, she thought, putting the script back in its folder, then switching off her lamp and composing herself for sleep instead.

She lay for a while, staring into the darkness, listening to the soft swish of the fan above her, while the events of the day played through her mind like a depressing newsreel. And most disturbing of all was the number of unwanted images of Angelo Manzini that kept intruding upon her.

She tried to tell herself it was hardly surprising, considering that blinding moment of unwelcome revelation about Silvia and its possible repercussions. But it was troubling nevertheless.

On the other hand, there was no point in losing sleep over it, so she turned on to her side, closing her eyes with resolution.

He should not, Angelo told himself grimly as he glanced at his watch, be contemplating this.

Having made the break, he should adhere to his decision and not be lured back, even if it was for 'one last time' as she'd breathed to him in that secluded corner of the garden before dinner. When she'd stood so close that the shape of her untrammelled breasts under the cling of her dress were clearly revealed, the nipples standing proud. So close that the familiar perfume she wore filled his senses, reviving memories that commonsense told him were best forgotten.

Although he knew of her relationship with the Principessa, he'd been frankly astonished and certainly not best pleased to find her here. In view of the serious purpose of his visit, she was a complication he did not need.

And yet when she'd looked up at him wistfully, touching her parted lips with her little pointed tongue, reminding him of its delicious artistry, and whispered, 'Don't you want me, *mio caro*?', in spite of himself, he had found his body responding to her enticement with all its former urgency.

All the same, he would have drawn the line at traversing unfamiliar corridors to reach her, in the hope that the other members of the house party—his hostess in particular—would be safely asleep.

But as this would not be necessary, the promise of 'one last time' seemed worth the risk.

No-one, he told himself, would be likely to see him descending from the *loggia* outside his room, especially now he'd changed his white shirt for a thin dark sweater.

But if the worst happened, he could always explain he'd been unable to sleep, and decided to get some air.

Or, he could take the infinitely wiser course of resisting temptation altogether, and staying where he was. However disappointed his former *innamorata* might be, she could hardly make a scene over his dereliction. Not in this company.

And afterwards, he would be careful to avoid any encounters with her until she had found the inevitable someone to take his place.

Counsels of perfection, he thought cynically. Which he had, *naturalmente*, no intention of following. Not while that gloriously rapacious body was waiting to welcome him on this hot, starlit night.

Earlier, he'd fetched the flashlight from his car, and sliding it into his pocket, he went noiselessly out to the *loggia* and down the steps to the grounds below.

* * *

Ellie was never sure what woke her. For one sleepy moment, she wondered why, on such a still night, the pale curtains at her window seemed to be billowing into the room? Only to discover, with blank terror, that she was no longer alone. That a tall shadow, darker than all the rest, was standing beside the bed and a man's voice was whispering teasingly, 'Were you asleep, *mia bella*? Then I hope you were dreaming of me.'

Then before she could move or force her paralysed throat muscles to scream, the mattress beside her dipped under a new weight, and strong arms reached for her, drawing her against bare and aroused male flesh while a warm mouth took hers in the kind of deep and sensual kiss wholly outside her experience.

And for one brief, appalled instant, she felt her ungiven body arch against him in a response as instinctive as it was shocking.

Then, as sanity came racing back, she tore her lips from his and tried to push him away, raking her nails down the hair-roughened wall of his torso.

He swore and his grasp slackened fractionally, giving her the chance to fling herself across the bed away from him, her hand reaching desperately for the lamp switch.

And as light flooded the room, Ellie's horrified, incredulous gaze met that of her assailant.

Angelo was the first to speak. He said hoarsely, 'You? But I don't understand…'

'Get out of here.' She was blushing from head to foot, burning with shame, as she delved for the sheet, dragging it up to cover her naked breasts. Trying at the same time not to look at him. 'Just—go. Now. For God's sake.'

But it was too late. There was a sharp knock at the door, followed by her godmother's voice saying, 'Is all well with you, Elena? An intruder has been seen in the garden.'

Angelo muttered something soft and violent under his breath, and dived for the sheet in his turn. And before Ellie could answer, think of some reassurance to send her latest visitor away, the door was flung wide, and the Principessa came in, swathed in an ivory silk dressing gown. And behind her, dignified in grey satin, the Contessa Manzini, with Carlo Barzado beside her, and Giovanni bringing up the rear.

Lucrezia Damiano stopped, a hand flying to her throat, her eyes widening in shock and dismay. There was a long and deadly silence, which the Contessa was the first to break, turning to request Signor Barzado and the gaping major domo to leave before she too stepped into the room, closing the door behind her.

She said, '*Cosa succede*, Angelo. What is happening here? Have you lost your mind or simply all sense of honour?' She looked at Ellie, her face like stone. 'Is my grandson here at your invitation, *signorina*? The truth, if you please.'

Angelo answered for her. 'No,' he said. 'From first to last, Nonna, it was my own idea.' He glanced down at the scratches on his chest, his mouth twisting wryly. 'But clearly, I should have thought again—for several reasons.'

'You are saying you have disgraced our family name—forced yourself on this girl—on a whim?' The Contessa closed her eyes. '*Dio mio*, I cannot believe it.'

It occurred to Ellie that hoping to wake up and find she'd simply been having a nightmare wasn't working. Neither was praying for death.

Clutching the sheet so tightly that her knuckles turned white, she said huskily, 'Contessa—Godmother—I know how this must look but—really—nothing happened.'

'I presume because he was interrupted.' The Principessa's voice was colder than her god-daughter had ever heard it, as she looked pointedly at Ellie's nightgown lying on the floor beside the bed.

No, Ellie thought painfully. Because he discovered he was in the wrong room, with the wrong woman.

Thought it, but realised she couldn't say it because it would only make matters a thousand times worse.

Angelo indicated his own clothing. He said coolly, 'Perhaps, before anything more is said, I might be permitted to dress myself.'

'*Tra un momento*. My god-daughter's needs come first.' The Principessa took Ellie's robe from the chair and advanced to the bed. 'Put this on, my child, then come with us to the *salotto*.' She added, 'You will have the goodness to join us there, Count Manzini, when you are ready.'

Back turned to him, and seated on the edge of the bed, Ellie huddled awkwardly into the robe and fastened its sash, her fingers all thumbs. She was suddenly aware that she was trembling, and on the verge of tears.

It's all so ridiculous, she thought, like some dreadful bedroom farce. Except that on this occasion there can be no last act explanations to make everything right again. Because they would have to involve Silvia, and that can't happen.

As she followed the two older women downstairs, her mind went into a kind of overdrive as she struggled to make sense of what had happened.

It went without saying that Angelo Manzini had expected to find her cousin waiting for him, but Silvia's room was at the other end of the villa, so what could possibly have made him think she was sleeping in the tower?

And what was all this about an intruder in the grounds? Who had seen him?

Every question she asked herself seemed to throw up another, and she didn't like any of the answers that were suggesting themselves to her.

Giovanni was just leaving the *salotto* as they arrived. His face might be expressionless, but he radiated disapproval just the same and Ellie, who'd known him all her life, found herself avoiding his glance.

He'd lit the lamps and brought a tray of coffee to the room, and the Principessa poured a measure of brandy into a glass and brought it to Ellie.

'I have instructed Giovanni to have another room prepared for you,' she said. 'You will not wish to return to the tower.'

No, thought Ellie, with a swift pang. Never again for as long as I live.

Any stupid fairy tale dreams I still had finally crashed and burned tonight.

Aloud, she said, 'Thank you,' and swallowed some of the brandy, feeling its warmth pervade the chill inside her. 'But I swear to you—both of you—that nothing happened.'

'You regard my grandson's shameful conduct—this outrage to your godmother's hospitality as nothing?' The Contessa's question was icy. 'Are you saying, *signorina*, that you are accustomed to share your bed with strangers? That this unforgivable insult should be—laughed off in some way? Treated as one of the aberrations of modern life? If so, I doubt if Prince Damiano will agree with you.'

Ellie flushed again. 'No,' she said, her voice constricted. 'No, of course not.' She hesitated, 'Does he—have to be told?'

'I think so,' said the Contessa. 'Before the story reaches him from another source.' She paused. 'It is unfortunate that Carlo Barzado witnessed what had happened, because he will tell his wife, and she will immediately tell the whole world.'

Ellie's lips parted in a soundless gasp. 'Oh—surely not.'

The Contessa shrugged. 'It is inevitable.'

The Principessa sat down beside Ellie, and took her hand. She said more gently, 'We must suppose that Count Manzini gave some indication—at dinner, perhaps—that he found you attractive, my child, and you were flattered by his attention. Gave him reason to think that you would welcome him later. Is that how it was?'

Ellie bit her lip. The truth was impossible, she told herself, so she would have to rely on prevarication.

She said quietly, 'If I did, it was—unintentional.'

'But I think we must accept that was the case and act accordingly.' Her godmother's tone was firm. She looked towards the door. 'I am sure Count Manzini will agree.'

Coming into rooms silently must be one of his talents, Ellie thought bitterly because she'd been totally unaware of his arrival—yet again. But there he was, leaning against the doorframe, the lean body apparently relaxed, his dark face impassive as he listened to what was being said.

But Ellie wasn't fooled. The anger in him might be dammed back, but she could still sense it. Feel it reaching her across the room.

But why, she demanded silently, when I'm the innocent party in all this? And you know it.

Angelo walked slowly forward. 'I deeply regret, Signorina Blake, that I completely misunderstood the invitation I thought I had received.' His mouth twisted harshly. 'It was an unforgivable error, and *naturalmente*, I wish to make amends for my behaviour in any way that is suggested.'

'My dear Angelo,' said his grandmother. 'In view of Prince Damiano's known moral stance, you have only one course of action. Tomorrow, *mio caro*, to prevent further scandal, you will announce that you and Signorina Blake are engaged to be married.'

CHAPTER THREE

ELLIE'S HAND JERKED and the remains of her brandy splashed down the skirt of her robe.

She said in a voice she hardly recognised, 'No. I can't—I won't do it. It—it's crazy. I tell you—nothing happened.'

'I believe you.' Lucrezia Damiano took the glass from her hand. 'And if only you had been seen by no-one but the Contessa and myself, there would be no problem.' She sighed. 'But my dear Cesare, I fear, will adopt a very different attitude.

'Promised lovers carried away by their feelings, he might accept, although he would certainly not approve. But a casual encounter based on a passing attraction, and conducted in his house?' She shuddered. 'That he would find intolerable.' And paused, adding, 'Unforgivable.'

Ellie could feel the tension in the room crackling around her like an electrical storm.

'I'll talk to him,' she said wildly. 'Somehow make him understand…'

'But, dear girl,' said the Principessa. 'What could you possibly say?'

And in one thunderstruck moment, Ellie realised that both her godmother and the Contessa knew perfectly well exactly where and with whom Angelo had really planned to spend the night.

That they'd probably been aware of the situation for some time.

But that, even if it was not a secret, it would still not be spoken of openly, because discretion had to be observed at all costs.

Which, in the short term, she was being called upon to pay. And her silence was only the first instalment.

She bent her head. 'Nothing,' she said wearily. 'I suppose.'

'You show good sense,' the Contessa remarked. She looked calmly at her grandson. 'You have not spoken, Angelo *mio*.'

His tone was icy. 'Perhaps I am lost for words.'

'*Tuttavia*, I am sure you appreciate the necessity. Your negotiations with Prince Damiano will go more smoothly if you undertake them as Signorina Blake's *fidanzato*, rather than her attempted seducer. I am certain you must agree.'

'Under the circumstances, it seems I have little choice,' he said with an undisguised bitterness that made Ellie send him a surprised glance from beneath the veil of her lashes. He added with chilling clarity, 'And an engagement is not a marriage.'

Excuse me, Ellie wanted to say indignantly, but just who is doing the big favour here and to whom? Because, Count Angelo Manzini, I wouldn't want you if you came gift-wrapped.

And tried to put out of her mind the sudden searing memory of the way his mouth had moved on hers with such devastating sensual purpose, and her own shocked, aching reaction.

'Then the matter is settled,' the Principessa said briskly, and rose. 'Now I suggest we try to get some rest for what is left of the night.' She paused, then added pointedly, 'Let us hope there will be no further alarms to disturb us.'

Ellie did not find the remainder of the night particularly restful. Her belongings had already been transferred to her new room, thanks to the supremely efficient Giovanni, whom, she thought shuddering, she never wanted to look in the face again. She had to admit that the accommodation was more luxurious than the tower room and possessed a very much larger and very comfortable bed for its occupant to sink into.

But she could not relax. She had far too much to think about, little of it pleasant. For one thing, it was clear that she and Angelo Manzini had been deliberately set up, and almost certainly by Silvia, but what she couldn't figure was—why?

For another, as she'd turned at the door of the *salotto* to say 'Goodnight', she'd found him watching her go with an expression of such scornful resentment that she'd felt her skin burn under his regard.

Anyone would think, she'd thought angrily, as she went upstairs, that I was the one having the illicit *affaire*, instead of him. But whatever problems he's having, he's brought entirely on himself, and he has no-one else to blame.

Plus he must know the last thing I ever wanted was to become involved with him or any of his sordid little games, so a touch of gratitude wouldn't come amiss.

Nor could she escape the terrible irony that the first time she'd found herself in bed with a man was only as a result of mistaken identity. She supposed it was almost funny, yet she had never felt less like laughing in her life.

The entire situation had been total humiliation, she thought as pain twisted inside her, turning rapidly into complete disaster.

She lay in the darkness, her mind revolving wearily over the same well-trodden ground, trying to make sense of it all and failing miserably.

Wondering too how she would get through the horrific difficulties of the day ahead, pretending to be engaged to a man who appeared to despise her.

She could find no answer to that and there were already pale streaks in the eastern sky when she eventually fell into an uneasy sleep.

It was mid-morning when she was woken by one of the maids bringing her a breakfast tray of tea with lemon, warm rolls, ham and cheese. At least she was being spared the gauntlet of the dining room, she thought, as the memory of Signor Barzado's face, goggle-eyed with shock, invaded her shuddering mind. But that had to be the least of her worries.

She ate what she could, then showered quickly and dressed.

She paused to look at herself in the full-length mirror before venturing downstairs, scrutinising her ordinary dark green linen skirt and very ordinary white tee shirt. That said it all, she thought, grimacing at her reflection. And no-one in their right mind would ever believe that a man like Angelo Manzini would ask her to marry him, or steal through the darkness for a secret night of passion in her arms.

However, that was the story, and she would somehow have to stick to it. But only for a strictly limited period, she told herself, lifting her chin. Which was probably the sole aspect of the situation that she and Count Manzini were likely to agree on.

Giovanni was waiting as she descended the stairs, inclining his head respectfully as he told her the Principessa wished her to be shown to her private sitting room.

No real surprise there, Ellie thought drily. It was a charming retreat, furnished in shell pink, a shade her godmother described as 'most calming to the nerves', and where no-one else would dare to go unless specifically invited, so their conversation would be undisturbed.

When they reached the door, Giovanni tapped deferentially, then ushered her in. Ellie walked in, a smile nailed firmly in place, only to stop dead as the room's sole occupant turned from the window to face her.

He was wearing charcoal pants this morning, and a matching shirt open at the neck. Against the sunlit pastel background, he looked as dark as a moonless night, making Ellie feel, absurdly, that this pretty room was no longer a sanctuary but a panther's den.

It was all she could do not to take a step backwards, but she recovered herself and said quietly and glacially, 'I thought I was here to speak to my godmother, Count Manzini.'

'She felt we should have an opportunity to meet alone.' His tone was casual. 'And as we have to convince the world we have been doing so quite intimately over the past weeks, it might be better if you addressed me as Angelo. And I shall call you Elena.'

It was all said without smiling, but at least he wasn't looking at her as if she was a slug in his salad. Cool indifference seemed an appropriate description. And she would match it.

She lifted her chin. 'Then you really intend to go on with this—ridiculous pretence?'

'Unfortunately, yes.' He paused. 'It was mentioned last night, I think, that I am here to negotiate an important financial deal for Galantana with Prince Damiano. There is a great deal at stake, and I will not allow my plans for a major expansion of the company to be wrecked by the malice of an angry woman.'

She said quickly. 'Angry?'

'You were aware, I suppose, that your cousin had been my mistress?'

'No, I wasn't,' she snapped. 'Not until you arrived yesterday and I saw her reaction.'

'Ah,' he said. 'Then you also will not know that I ended the relationship two weeks ago.'

'Ended it?' She stared at him. 'That wasn't the impression you gave last night.'

'It was to be the last time,' he said, shrugging. 'And one doesn't wish to disappoint a lady.'

'Really?' Ellie's tone bit. 'Maybe you should have remembered the risk you were running a little earlier and stayed in your own room.'

'Hindsight,' he said, 'is a miraculous gift. Besides, the invitation I received was—most pressing.'

Her face warmed as she recalled just how sure he'd been of his welcome. 'I—I really don't want to hear about it.' She took a deep breath. 'And I still can't believe that Silvia's done this. I—I had no intention of spending the weekend here. I only came because I was concerned about her.' She spread her hands. 'Even if she wanted revenge by setting you up, why did she have to involve me? It's unbelievable.'

His voice was expressionless. 'She may have had a reason.'

'Well, I can't imagine what it could be.' Ellie paused. 'Anyway, how did she know you'd be here?'

He frowned. 'I probably mentioned it, when it seemed not to matter. I forget.'

'A costly lapse.'

'As you say.' His mouth hardened. 'But, believe me, I would have remembered if she had said she was also to be a guest—and changed my plans accordingly.'

Ellie said slowly, 'Once she'd talked me into it, of course, her scheme just—fell into place. I can see that now. After all, you'd have no means of knowing that the tower room was always given to me.'

'No.' He gave her a considering look. '*Infatti*, its isolation seemed to make it ideal for a place of assignation.' He paused. 'How did she persuade you to come with her?'

She bit her lip. 'She said Ernesto was becoming foolishly jealous and she needed me to be a kind of chaperone.'

'*Dio mio.*' His mouth tightened. 'And instead she made you her *ingenuo*—her fall guy.'

'Yes.' She hesitated. 'I presume she was also the one who gave the alarm about the supposed intruder.'

'But of course,' he said. 'And with impeccable timing.'

She swallowed. 'If you say so.' Her flush deepened. 'But surely you—you must have known that you weren't—that I wasn't…?'

'Not until you drew blood.' His smile was sudden and mocking. 'And maybe not even then, although it is usually my back that suffers.'

If she blushed any more, she would probably burst into flames, Ellie thought, setting her jaw. 'Then it's a pity you didn't realise your mistake at once,' she said icily. 'And spared us both some hideous embarrassment as well as this present ghastly mess.'

'How true,' he said. 'But a man with a warm, naked girl in his arms does not always think clearly, you understand.'

No, thought Ellie. She did not understand, but she did not intend to cause him further amusement by saying so.

She said stiffly, 'You seem to be taking this very lightly, Count Manzini.'

'Do I?' There was an edge to his voice. 'You would be entirely wrong to think so, Signorina Blake. I accept the situation we have been forced into because I must. But, believe me, I shall not forget the cause.'

He paused. 'Tell me something. Why, last night, didn't you tell the truth about my presence in your bed?'

She said in a low voice, 'Perhaps if Madrina had been alone, I'd have done so, and the whole thing could have been—hushed up. But there were other people there—your grandmother—Signor Barzado. I couldn't let them know that you thought I was really Silvia.'

His mouth curled cynically. 'Your loyalty is as touching as it is misplaced.'

She said stiltedly, 'What you don't realise is that she's been—good to me. Generous too with things like—clothes.'

'And the scent you wore last night,' he said softly. 'Was that also a gift from her?'

'Why, yes. It was almost a full bottle. She said she no longer cared for it.' She gave him an uncertain look. 'How did you know?'

'A fortunate guess,' he said. 'Pour the rest away, *signorina*. It does not suit you, as I am sure she knew.'

'But it wasn't just Silvia,' she added unhappily. 'There were her parents to consider as well. They've always been so kind to me.' She hesitated. 'And—Ernesto, too, in his way. He doesn't deserve to be hurt like this.'

He shrugged. '*Prima o poi*. Sooner or later, it will happen, but I, *grazie a Dio*, shall not be the cause.'

He moved away from the window, walking towards her, and this time she did step back, her eyes meeting his defensively. He halted, the dark brows lifting in hauteur.

He said, 'Perhaps I should remind you that we are supposed to be passionately in love. So much so that we forgot everything in our need to be together.'

'Who on earth is going to believe that?' she muttered defensively.

'No-one—if you intend to flinch each time I come near you,'

he returned tersely. 'Everyone—if you stand with your hand in mine and smile at me while our engagement is announced. And, most importantly, Prince Damiano will believe it.'

'But is that really so important? There must be other banks you could approach if Credito Europa turns you down,' she protested.

'In the financial world, a rejection by Cesare Damiano would be taken very seriously,' he said. 'It would be a black mark not just against me but Galantana too. I cannot permit that to happen.'

He added harshly, 'This trick that Silvia has played on us is like a stone dropped into a pool. The ripples are already beginning to spread. I discovered this at breakfast when I encountered Signora Barzado's prurient gaze. She cannot wait to leave, I think, and tell all Rome how we were caught *in flagrante*.'

Ellie looked down at the carpet. 'Your grandmother believes that too.'

'*Bene*. It follows that we must give the lady another less interesting story to spread.' He added sardonically, 'One with a happy ending.'

'It can hardly be called that.' She swallowed. 'More a tissue of lies.' She hesitated. 'And just how long will we have to maintain this deception?'

'For as long as it is necessary.' He shrugged. 'Believe me, *signorina*, you are not the only sufferer.'

He glanced past Ellie as the door opened to admit the Principessa, her smile a little fixed.

'You must excuse me. I have been welcoming another guest. Silvia's husband, *caro* Ernesto, has been able to join us. Such a pleasure.' Ignoring Ellie's gasp of disbelief, she paused, playing with the bracelet she was wearing, her glance flickering from one impassive face to the other, now flushed with anger as well as embarrassment.

'And by now you have arranged everything between you, I am sure,' she went on. 'The Prince has telephoned to say he will be here for lunch, so I suggest the announcement is made then.'

But nothing happened…

The same desperate words echoed and re-echoed in Ellie's head, but remained unuttered. There was no point, she thought numbly. A course of action had been agreed, and would be adhered to. Ernesto's sudden arrival had guaranteed that. But what had brought him? Had he come of his own accord, or had it already been arranged with Silvia? And had the important client who needed his advice ever existed?

She felt too weary to think any more, as she watched Angelo Manzini bow slightly, kiss her godmother's hand then leave.

The Principessa came over to her, studying her with critical eyes. 'You look a little worn, dearest girl. If you go to your room, my maid will bring you this wonderful concealer that I have discovered and show you how to use it. You must look radiant for your *fidanzamento*.'

Ellie gave her an anguished look. 'Godmamma—I…'

Lucrezia Damiano kissed her on the cheek. 'And do not worry, my little one.' She gave a determined nod. 'All will be well. All will be very well. You will see.'

Consolata was deft and clever with cosmetics, Ellie was forced to admit. The face that looked back at her from the mirror was no longer as pale and strained as it had been. Her lashes had been darkened with mascara, and her mouth defined by a soft coral lipstick.

The older woman had frowned and sighed, however, over the limited choice of clothing in the wardrobe and reluctantly agreed that the skirt and top Ellie was already wearing would have to do.

But the *signorina* was not to go immediately to the *sala da pranzo*, she added. The *Principe* had returned and wished first to speak to her in the garden.

Ellie's heart sank, but she supposed the interview with Cesare Damiano was inevitable.

She found him as usual in the walled garden among his

beloved roses, a tall man with iron-grey hair, treading slowly along the graveled walks, his gold-rimmed glasses on his nose as he scanned the beds for signs of disease or pests.

As Ellie reached him, he turned from his scrutiny of a magnificent display of blooms so deeply crimson they seemed almost black.

'The *Toscana*,' he said meditatively. 'As beautiful as when it was first grown here six hundred years ago. It gives one a sense of stability—of the rightness of things. Do you not think so, Elena?'

'Yes, Your Highness.'

He studied her gravely. 'Your godmother tells me that you and Count Manzini wish to be married, my child.'

That, thought Ellie, startled, is the last thing either of us wants.

Aloud, she said hesitantly, 'We—we have agreed to become engaged, sir.'

He pursed his lips. 'An engagement is a solemn promise and, in this case, made not before time, according to what my wife has told me.' He sighed. 'And while I deplore the way your courtship has been conducted, I believe I must give you both my blessing.

'I have spoken to Count Manzini,' he went on more briskly. 'And he has assured me there will be no more unseemly incidents before the ceremony. Nevertheless, young blood runs hot, and the Principessa and I agree that you should at once take up residence in our house in Rome, and be married from there. That should remove temptation and at the same time dispel any unfortunate rumours.' He allowed himself a faint smile. 'I shall allow myself the privilege of giving you away, my dear child.'

The world seemed to recede to some far distance. She was aware of the sun beating down on her head, and the hum of bees. And from somewhere, her voice saying hoarsely, pleadingly, 'But there's no need for so much hurry—surely.'

The austere look returned. 'I hope not indeed. But at the

same time there is also no reason to delay.' He glanced past her. 'As I am sure your *fidanzato* will wish to assure you.'

Ellie turned apprehensively to see Angelo Manzini approaching unhurriedly down the path.

Prince Damiano patted her shoulder. 'I will leave you together. But first—this.' He reached out and picked a long-stemmed red rose from a nearby bush. 'A flower for lovers,' he said, handing it to her, then, bowing slightly, walked off towards the house.

She watched him go, almost in despair, then turned to face Angelo, her slim body rigid, her eyes blazing accusation.

'You seem disturbed, *mia bella*,' he commented coolly as he reached her.

'I'll say I'm disturbed,' she said shakily. 'This engagement is quite bad enough, but they seem to be planning our wedding as well. What the hell is going on?' She drew a breath then added furiously, 'And I'm neither yours, nor am I—beautiful.'

'Not when you are glaring at me, perhaps. And your choice of clothing hardly does you justice either.' He paused. 'But you have possibilities, as I observed last night when you were wearing no clothes at all.'

For a moment she was lost for words, then she said chokingly, 'How—how dare you?'

He shrugged. 'You chose to turn on the lamp. And I am not blind.'

'No,' she said fiercely. 'And you also have the power of speech, so go back to the house right now and tell them it's all off. That I've turned you down.'

'That would be foolish,' he returned unmoved. 'Particularly as we have the Prince's approval—in addition to our other well-wishers.'

'What do you mean?' Ellie demanded huskily.

His smile did not reach his eyes. 'Come, *signorina*. You cannot be that naïve. Or that stupid. You must know that Silvia is not the only conspirator at Largossa this weekend.'

She said, 'And I tell you that I haven't a clue what you're talking about. Now will you do as I ask?'

'No,' he said. 'Because it would solve nothing. *Infatti*, it would simply make matters infinitely worse. I have already explained to you why I need the Prince's goodwill. Can you afford to have it withdrawn? You are fond of your *madrina*, I think. Do you really wish to be barred from her house and denied her affection? Because that would follow.

'More than that,' he added grimly. 'How will you like being known as my discarded lover? Is that the kind of notoriety you desire? And do you truly want your cousin to enjoy her unpleasant victory and laugh at us both? Because I do not.'

'But—marriage.' She pronounced the word with something like revulsion.

'Grazie,' Angelo returned coldly. 'However, I have no more wish than you to put my head in that noose. For the moment, there will be an engagement only.' He paused. 'But engagements can be easily broken. It happens every day. We have only to choose some convenient moment.' His mouth curled. 'And I will make certain that the fault is mine. Some flagrant act of infidelity, perhaps, to make the world think you have had a fortunate escape.'

Ellie took a breath. 'Count Manzini, you have the morals of an alley cat.'

'While you, *signorina*, have the tongue of a shrew. Shall we agree that we are neither of us perfect? *Nel frattempo*, in the meantime, I offer you this.' He produced a small velvet-covered box from his pocket and opened it.

Ellie looked down at the square antique sapphire set amidst a blaze of diamonds and swallowed.

'I—I can't wear that.'

'You are allergic to precious stones?' He sounded mildly interested.

It would have been childishly rude to retort, 'No, only to you,' so she refrained.

'I simply couldn't accept anything as valuable,' Ellie said, and frowned. 'How come you're carrying something that expensive around anyway?'

'It belongs to my grandmother,' he said. 'She promised that

when I planned to marry, she would allow me to choose a ring from her collection for my *fidanzata*. I picked this one.'

'But you did not pick me,' Ellie said. 'And you have no plans to marry—anyone. As the Contessa knows perfectly well. So this is sheer hypocrisy.'

'No,' he said. 'It is part of our agreement. Now give me your hand.' He met her defiant eyes, and added, *'Per favore.'*

She stood in silent reluctance as he slid the ring over her knuckle. She wore little jewellery at the best of times and none at all on her hands, and it felt heavy—even alien.

She was still holding the rose that the Prince had given her, and its fragrance, exquisitely sweet and sensuous, drifted upwards in potent contrast to the bleakness of the moment.

'Do you have any further instructions for me?' she asked bitterly.

'Instructions, no,' he said. 'But perhaps—a suggestion.' And took her in his arms. For a moment, sheer astonishment held her still as his lips plundered hers in a hard, draining kiss without tenderness or, she recognised with shock, any real desire.

Then, as she began to resist, he let her go. He said softly, 'Your mouth is the colour of that rose, *mia bella*. At last you look as if you know a lover's touch. So, now let us do what we must.'

CHAPTER FOUR

AFTERWARDS, IT WAS the faces she remembered. The Contessa, impassive; her godmother beaming but with anxious eyes; Signor Barzado trying to hide his astonishment and his wife her disappointment that a potential scandal had been overtaken and diluted by convention; the Cipriantos, astonished too but pleased.

And above all Silvia, seated beside her clearly bemused husband, her lips stretched in a smile, but her eyes burning with anger as Prince Damiano made the announcement with grave pleasure, and Angelo took Ellie's hand, glowing with the blue fire of his sapphire, and raised it formally to his lips.

The lunch had been sumptuous, but she'd eaten like an automaton, hardly tasting a mouthful. Then there'd been the toasts to be got through, her mouth aching in an effort to smile and acknowledge the good wishes, whatever their level of sincerity.

Standing rigidly to receive Silvia's air kiss on both cheeks, then watching her turn to Angelo with the husky murmur, 'Congratulations, *mio caro*. How truly clever you are.'

Being lost for words as Ernesto, after wishing her joy without the slightest conviction in his voice, had said, 'This is very sudden, Elena. I wasn't aware you were even acquainted with Count Manzini.'

And discovering Angelo at her side, smiling as he replied, 'But I have you to thank, Signor Alberoni. I saw her first at a dinner party at your house. Now—here we are.'

Later, feeling her face warm in a blush of sheer embarrassment as she again listened to Angelo courteously parrying the jovial demands to know when the happy day would be. Asking herself why she should be surprised, when talking himself out of dodgy situations was probably an everyday occurrence for him?

Now, at last, finding solitude in her room, with the shutters closed against the profound afternoon heat. And the door locked. An unnecessary but instinctive precaution. Because she was still trembling inside from the unexpected brush of Angelo's lips on hers as he escorted her to the stairs and his whispered, 'Soon we will be sharing the siesta, *mia carissima*.' And knowing his remark had been pitched at the world at large and that he didn't mean a word of it hadn't affected her reaction in the slightest. Which, in retrospect, worried her a little. Or rather more than a little.

Telling herself not to be stupid, Ellie turned restlessly on to her side and tried to relax. Her rose had been rescued from the lunch table by Giovanni and was now in a slim glass vase beside her bed. Something else she could have done without, she thought, as its evocative perfume reached out to her again, bringing with it unwanted and frankly dangerous memories.

Warning her that the coming days and weeks—she prayed it would be no longer—might well be some of the most difficult of her life.

Her most immediate problem, she realised sombrely, was the suggestion, fast turning into a decree, that she take up residence in the Damiano *palazzo* in Rome in order to prepare for her wedding. And, of course, to avoid any further sexual temptation before the legalised union of the wedding night.

It was almost funny, but she'd never felt less like laughing.

She could only hope that the Principessa would come to her rescue and use all her considerable powers of persuasion to convince her husband that such precautions were quite unnecessary, without stating precisely why this was so.

I just want my own life back, she told herself with a kind of desperation. My apartment, my work, my friends, and, more than anything, Casa Bianca, my house by the sea. If I'd only stuck to my guns and spent the weekend there, I'd have been spared this nightmare.

But even this won't last forever, and then I can start to be happy again.

And tried to ignore the small insistent voice in her head warning her that her life had changed forever, and, however hard she tried, nothing would ever be the same.

The dress she'd brought to wear for dinner that evening was new, ankle length in a dark blue silky fabric, with cap sleeves and a crossover bodice, the slenderness of her waist accentuated with a narrow band of blue and gold silk flowers. As she put it on, she realised, to her annoyance, that its colour matched the Count's sapphire almost exactly. As if it had been planned in advance, she thought with an inward groan.

She wished with all her heart that she could change it for something crimson—or magenta, or even bright orange—but she didn't possess as much as a scarf in any of those colours. Nor could she bring herself to wear the sunflower skirt two nights running.

The concealer that Consolata had left for her did its work again, and her freshly washed hair shone as it curved gently round her face, so, in spite of her inner confusion and anxiety, she looked relatively composed when she went down to the *salotto.*

Giovanni was waiting in the hallway to open the door for her, and she paused, drawing a deep breath, feeling as if she was about to walk onstage without knowing what play she was in, let alone any of the lines she was supposed to say. But the major domo's discreet smile and nod of approval helped launch her into the room, even if the sudden hush that met her appearance was disconcerting enough to induce a wave of shyness to sweep over her.

For a moment, she wondered if she was late, but one swift glance told her that she was not the last arrival. That neither Ernesto nor her cousin were yet present. No doubt Silvia was waiting as usual to make a last minute entrance in something by Versace that would knock everyone sideways.

I just wish I could do the same to her, she thought grimly.

'My dear.' Prince Damiano walked towards her. 'How charming you look.' He turned to Angelo who had accompanied him. 'You are a lucky man, Count.'

'I am well aware of exactly how fortunate I am,' Angelo returned silkily. His lips were smiling, but there was no accompanying warmth in the dark eyes as he took Ellie's unresisting hand and kissed it lightly. '*Mia bella*, Nonna Cosima is anxious to be better acquainted with her future grand-daughter. May I take you to her?'

His choice of words made her heart miss a beat. 'Yes,' she said huskily, recovering herself. 'Yes, of course.'

The Contessa was seated on a sofa, chatting to Signora Ciprianto, who rose to make a tactful retreat at Ellie's approach.

'I have brought you my treasure, Nonna,' Angelo said lightly. 'I am sure you will be as delighted with her as if you had chosen her yourself.' He paused as the Contessa bit her lip and changed colour slightly, then turned, smiling, to Ellie. 'May I get you something to drink, *mia cara*?'

There was something going on here, Ellie decided. Something she didn't know about, and probably wouldn't like.

Sudden anger shook her, and with it a desire to be perverse. She met Angelo's gaze limpidly. 'Oh, just the usual, please.' And being rewarded with a swift flash of annoyance in his eyes, she added, 'Darling,' as he turned to walk away.

The Contessa leaned forward and took her hand. 'Elena—I may call you that, I hope, and you must say Nonna Cosima. We have met in difficult circumstances, but we must now put them behind us and look instead to the future, and to happiness. Do you agree?'

Ellie was taken aback. The Contessa was speaking as if there'd been a slight glitch, now sorted out to everyone's satisfaction, when she knew—she must know—that the contrary was the case.

She said quietly, but with emphasis, 'The whole thing can't be forgotten too quickly as far as I'm concerned. And please believe that is something I absolutely look forward to.' She added stiltedly, 'I hope that's the reassurance you want.'

There was a glint in the dark eyes that struck Ellie as far too reminiscent of the lady's grandson. 'Not precisely,' said the Contessa. 'But it will serve for now.'

And then she began, with great charm, to ask questions. If Ellie had ever thought it was only the Spanish who had an inquisition, five minutes with Angelo's grandmother would have convinced her that the Italians weren't far behind.

She found herself speaking with total candour about her parents, her friends, her work at the publishing company, revealing, she realised, probably more than she wished. And, finally, she told the Contessa about her apartment.

When she mentioned she lived there alone, the Contessa's delicate brows rose. 'Then the sooner you accept the invitation to move to the Palazzo Damiano the better, dear child.'

Ellie sat up very straight. 'I see no need for that. Besides I love my apartment. It's my home.'

'But not for much longer. After all, you are going to be married, and you will share your husband's home.'

Ellie's hands clenched together in her lap. 'And—when I get married, I will do so.' *Or if…* 'But until then, I'll stay where I am.'

'Yet surely you must see that is impossible.' The Contessa sounded almost coaxing. 'Angelo could not be permitted to visit you there.' She gave a resolute nod. 'From now on, there must not be as much as another whisper of scandal about your relationship with my grandson.'

And as Ellie's lips parted to tell her without mincing her words that visits from Count Manzini did not feature on her personal agenda, and that there was no relationship with him—neither past, present nor future—she heard Angelo's voice saying coolly, 'Your drink, Elena *mia*. Campari with a splash of soda.' Adding softly, 'Just as you like it, *carissima*.'

Of course, Ellie thought, almost grinding her teeth. He'd have asked Madrina. As I should have known.

Accepting the glass from him, with a murmured, *'Grazie,'* she wished very much she could throw the drink at him, drenching the open mockery in the dark face and staining, perhaps irrevocably, his immaculate dress shirt as well. Before, that is, she left the room, screaming.

As it was, she took immediate refuge behind a wall of reserve, returning only monosyllabic replies to any remarks made to her, and thankful to her heart when the Prince, his wife and the rest of the party came to join them, and conversation became general.

It was when Giovanni announced respectfully that dinner was served that she realised that the group was not complete.

She said in an undertone to the Principessa, 'But, Madrina, Silvia and Ernesto haven't come down yet.'

'They are not here, *mia cara*.' Her godmother conveyed the news almost casually. 'Silvia felt that she was developing a migraine—so painful, so debilitating—therefore Ernesto took her back to Rome. Such a good and caring husband.

'But do not concern yourself about your own return,' she added brightly. 'Cesare has already said that you will travel with us. At the same time, arrangements can be made to bring your things from your *appartamento*. Which makes everything so very convenient, don't you agree?'

No, Ellie didn't agree, but she knew, through experience, that there was no point in saying so. Not once Prince Damiano had spoken. And since when had Silvia suffered from anything like a migraine?

It's like trying to find your way out of a maze, she thought bitterly as she made her way to the dining room. Every way you turn, you come up against a blank wall.

But later, when she looked up and found Angelo watching her across the silver and crystal of the polished dining table, his dark gaze frankly speculative, it occurred to her that blank walls might be the very least of her troubles.

As an object lesson in discovering how the other half live, Ellie soon realised, residence at the Palazzo Damiano could hardly be bettered.

She walked on marble floors from one massive, high-ceilinged room to another. She slept on the finest linen sheets, and her delicious food was served on delicate porcelain.

Her little flat would have fitted easily into the bedroom she'd been given alone, quite apart from the small but comfortable sitting room which led to it, and the luxurious bathroom which adjoined it.

And her second-hand Fiat screamed 'poor relation' when parked beside the Prince's limousine and her godmother's elegant Alfa Romeo on the gravelled sweep in front of the *palazzo*…

But when all this nonsense is over, she told herself staunchly, unlike so much else, it will be still around and still reliable.

And so, she hoped, would her job, even though her engagement had proved to be a nine day wonder at the office, to her acute embarrassment, while the sidelong looks from certain people had confirmed beyond doubt that rumours of Silvia's affair with Angelo Manzini had indeed reached the public domain.

In addition, one of the directors had called her in and asked outright at what point prior to her marriage did she plan to resign. Totally taken aback, she had flushed and stammered that she loved her work, and had no intention of abandoning it, and been answered by sceptically raised eyebrows, and the comment that her *fidanzato* might have very different ideas.

If I have to go on biting my lip each time he's mentioned, she thought savagely, I shall soon have no mouth left.

Even more galling was having to endure his actual physical presence at the *palazzo*, where he'd become a regular visitor, dining with them several times a week. And telling herself that his visits were only part of the pretence and that it was Prince

Damiano whom he really came to see made the situation no easier to bear.

He sent her flowers, too. Her sitting room was full of them.

And he kissed her. Mainly on the hand and the cheek admittedly, but sometimes on the lips—invariably when it was impossible for her to take evasive action.

Ellie supposed that nine out of ten women would have asked why on earth she would wish to avoid being kissed by one of the most attractive men in Italy, and found it difficult to explain, even to herself.

After all, she couldn't say that it was because she knew his kisses were prompted by duty rather than desire, when the last thing she wanted was for Angelo Manzini to desire her. Those brief moments in bed in his arms when she'd suddenly turned into a complete stranger had taught her that. And the memory of them still had the power to dry her mouth and make her tremble in a way that was totally outside her experience.

Which was where, she thought resolutely, she wished it to remain.

I must be one of nature's spinsters, she told herself, and derived no great comfort from this prosaic reflection.

She had not bargained either for being introduced to his relations. His Aunt Dorotea had been one of their earliest callers, a formidable matron who had given Ellie a searching look from head to toe then given an abrupt nod as if expressing satisfaction. Though what all that was about defeated Ellie entirely.

On a more positive note, Signora Luccino had brought her daughter Tullia with her, a girl with a sweet, merry face, married to a lawyer the previous year, and Ellie thought with regret that, under different circumstances, they might have been friends.

The Contessa Cosima, too, was a frequent visitor, alarming Ellie with a gentle flow of chat about churches and wedding dresses. That, she thought, was carrying pretence too far, and wished she had the nerve to say so.

In fact clothing had become an issue altogether. Her

wardrobe might be basic, she thought defensively, but it was perfectly adequate—a view that her godmother clearly did not share. The large *guardaroba* in her room was beginning to fill up with skirts, pants and tops in linen and silk, and a growing selection of evening wear in clear jewel colours and floating fabrics. And each outfit seemed to have its own shoes and bag in softest leather.

As if, she thought, scowling, it was not the done thing for Count Manzini to see her wearing the same thing twice.

She had tried to protest more than once that she was not a clothes horse, but the Principessa had waved these contentions away, smiling. It was her pleasure to see her dear Elena looking so lovely—and so happy too, she added brightly as Ellie's jaw dropped.

But there was no visit from Silvia. At first Ellie had thought that her cousin was quite understandably steering clear of her, only to be told by the Principessa that Ernesto, presumably in his role as good and caring husband, had taken Silvia for a little vacation on Corfu where his family had a house.

The days at the *palazzo* became weeks, and as they approached a month Ellie wondered how much longer the negotiations between Galantana and Credito Europa could possibly drag on, and when the deal would finally be done.

Because until that happened, she couldn't calculate how soon she'd be able to escape from this gilded cage, no matter how luxurious and loving it might be, and begin to reclaim her own life again.

More than anything, as the city heat increased, she missed the Casa Bianca and the breezes that blew from the sea, but her suggestion that she should spend some of her weekends there had been kindly but firmly declined. While her supposed engagement endured, it seemed she was going nowhere.

Surely it can't last much longer, she told herself each night with increasing desperation as she lay in bed staring up at the painted ceiling where gods and goddesses cavorted with unfeeling cheerfulness at some woodland banquet.

Worst of all, she'd noticed that one of the gods—probably

Mars—was black haired and dark eyed, his lean muscular body hardly concealed by the lion-skin thrown across one shoulder, and bearing a disturbing resemblance to Angelo Manzini. Or was that simply her over-active imagination?

Whatever, it wasn't an image she wished to find invading her bedroom all over again, but found to her acute annoyance that it still lingered in her mind, even when she turned over and buried her face in the pillow. Rendering her still more tongue-tied when she encountered the Count in the flesh, as it were, although he was always elegantly covered in some designer suit or other.

Another potent suggestion that the quicker she got out of there and back to sanity, the better it would be for her.

And each night she breathed the silent prayer. 'Oh please—please—let it be soon.'

Angelo stepped out into the heat of the Roman morning, as the automatic glass doors of the Credito Europa Bank whispered shut behind him. His face was calm as he walked to his car, taking his seat in the back with a murmured acknowledgement to the driver holding the door open for him, but this outward appearance was deceptive.

Because, underneath, he was blazingly, wickedly angry.

'Does Your Excellency wish to return to the office?' Mario asked with faint bewilderment as the silence lengthened.

Angelo pulled his thoughts away from the meeting he'd just attended, and met the chauffeur's enquiring gaze in the driving mirror. He said curtly, 'No, take me to my apartment.'

If Mario found this a strange request in the middle of a working day, it was not his place to argue. He dropped his employer at the main entrance, was told he would not be required again, then watched with a puzzled frown as Angelo strode inside.

The apartment was cool and silent, Salvatore as usual doing his marketing at that time of day. Which was good because Angelo wanted to be alone.

He walked into the *salotto*, impatiently stripping off his

jacket and tie, and tossing them over a chair. He unbuttoned his waistcoat, tore open the neck of his shirt, then poured himself a large Scotch, swallowed it, and poured another, even larger. He'd come home with the intention of getting blind, roaring drunk and wasting no time about it.

The news—no, the ultimatum—that he'd just received at the bank called for nothing less.

He could still hardly believe it. He thought he'd dealt with the trap that had been set for him at Largossa. Believed that simply going through the motions of courting the girl who'd been used in the snare—this Elena, Silvia's cousin and so much unlike his former mistress that she might have come from a different planet—would be enough to get him what he wanted, and he could then walk away. And that she would be equally grateful to see the back of him.

Dio mio, he thought. He'd almost felt sorry for her, recognising the reluctance of her co-operation. But no longer.

He walked to the sofa, flinging himself back against the cushions, taking another mouthful of Scotch, eyes narrowed, mouth compressed as he stared into space.

Now, too late, he recalled someone telling him when he was younger that Cesare Damiano had been nicknamed the Crocodile in banking circles.

Today the Prince had more than lived up to his name.

'My wife cares deeply for her god-daughter, Count, and is naturally concerned for the immense harm to her reputation if there were—consequences resulting from your liaison with her.'

He had sat on the other side of his polished desk, hands together, fingertips forming a kind of steeple, his expression grave as he studied the younger man. 'I am sure you understand me.'

And I, thought Angelo bitterly, fool that I am, I never saw it coming. Never understood that another trap had been set and was waiting for me. And while, if I'd used an atom of commonsense, I might have avoided the first, there is nothing I can do about the second.

Holy Madonna, I couldn't tell him there'd be no consequences as I'd simply been tricked into the wrong bed, or I'd have found myself lying on the pavement outside, thrown there by his security staff. And the consequences of that would be truly horrendous.

Therefore if I want his money, I have to bite on the bullet by accepting the eternally damned terms he spelled out to me with such care, and somehow persuade the little Signorina Milk and Water to become my wife. With the assurance that, once the knot is tied, the finance will become immediately available.

He punched the arm of the sofa with his clenched fist.

Dear God, what a prospect, he thought despairingly. To have to marry a girl who looks at me as if she'd come across a snake sleeping in the sunshine. Who shrinks from my lightest touch and answers me in monosyllables from surely the coldest mouth in Rome.

But I know quite well it's not the Prince pulling the strings. That I have his charming wife, plus my own grandmother, and, of course, Zia Dorotea to thank for this current horror. All they needed was the opportunity I was stupid enough to give them, and my fate was sealed.

I must have been insane to think that an engagement would be enough to satisfy them, he told himself. And perhaps I should have asked myself too if their chosen candidate for the post of my wife was really only the scapegoat she appeared to be.

And, for a brooding moment, found himself remembering a slim body warm against his and soft lips that had briefly trembled beneath his kiss. Very briefly, he thought, because the next moment, she had scratched him like a tigress.

Restively, he finished the whisky in his glass and set it aside. Well if there was no other way to secure the promised loan, and they all wished to transform Elena Blake into the Contessa Manzini, he would oblige them.

But, he decided with icy resolution, she would have the title and the status—nothing more, because she was the last woman in the world he would have chosen for himself, and he had no intention of making her his wife in any real sense.

In fact, he told himself harshly, he would continue to seek his pleasures where he found them, though with rather more discretion in future, and he hoped they would all—the girl Elena included—be satisfied with the result of their machinations.

And as he had the phone number of an enchanting creature he'd met at a reception the previous week, instead of drinking himself into oblivion, he would call her right now and see if she was free for lunch, and whatever else the afternoon might suggest.

Starting, he thought with sudden grimness, as he meant to go on.

At first she couldn't quite believe what she was hearing. Didn't want to believe it, yet found herself listening numbly to what Madrina was saying so gently but with such total finality.

At last, she said, her voice shaking, 'I didn't even want to be engaged. You know that. But—marriage—to him! I couldn't—not possibly. And he—he doesn't wish it either. I know it.'

The Principessa patted her hand. 'But after what happened between you, the Count has to make reparation. Surely, you understand this.'

She sounded like the voice of sweet reason, Ellie thought, aghast.

'Your engagement must now be followed by a wedding,' her godmother went on. 'Quite apart from other considerations, our families bear two ancient names, and his own sense of honour as well as ours demands it. Besides it is high time he was married.'

She added with a note of reproof, 'You cannot have forgotten, dearest child, the exact circumstances under which you were discovered.'

'No,' Ellie said bitterly. 'Or the reason for it.'

The Principessa pursed her lips warningly. 'Put whatever you imagine out of your mind, Elena. It is of no use to dwell on something that cannot be altered.' She paused, then went on more briskly. 'Do not forget that Angelo Manzini is one of Rome's most eligible bachelors, and many young women would be glad to take your place at his side.'

Ellie wanted to say 'And they'd be welcome to him,' but something in the set of Madrina's mouth warned her against it.

Although that did not mean she was going to meekly submit to this new and frankly terrifying plan for her future. Far from it.

All this family honour stuff is like something left over from the Renaissance, she thought, seething. But I'm not a Damiano, and I have no intention of becoming a Manzini. My name is Blake and I make my own decisions.

So, I wouldn't have his glamorous Nobility as a husband, even if he came gold-plated and loaded down with sapphires.

He's well and truly off the hook, and so, thank God, am I.

CHAPTER FIVE

ON HIS ARRIVAL at the *palazzo* the following day, Angelo was informed by the butler that the Signorina was in the courtyard, and that it would be his honour to conduct the Count to her side.

So the purpose of his visit was clearly no secret, he thought grimly, as he followed in Massimo's stately wake, aware that his elegant silk tie seemed to be on the point of strangling him, and realising that, probably for the first time in his adult life, he was nervous about a meeting with a girl.

Although, of course, it was not just any meeting, as he swiftly reminded himself. So much—too much—depended on his ability to persuade her to his way of thinking, his personal reluctance notwithstanding.

The courtyard, at the rear of the *palazzo* was only small but pleasantly shaded by a lemon tree. The ideal setting, he supposed cynically, for such an encounter.

Elena, he saw, was sitting on the broad stone rim of the goldfish pond, her head bent, trailing her fingers through the water.

When Massimo announced him, she got to her feet in one hasty, almost clumsy movement, and Angelo realised that his own tensions at the coming interview were shared, if not exceeded.

At the same time, he saw that she was even paler than usual, her eyes shadowed and her lips pressed together as if to stop them trembling. She was more than tense, he thought with a jolt of shock. She was actually scared, and suddenly the wave of simmering resentment that had carried him here ebbed a little under the need to reassure her.

To explain, as well as he could, that the union being proposed between them would not include any of the usual physical obligations of being his wife. In fact, few constraints at all, if he could only make her believe him. And that she would spend their time together in all the comfort she could wish.

He walked slowly towards her, halting at what he hoped was a safe distance, unwilling to intimidate her further.

He said quietly, '*Buona sera*, Elena. *Come sta?*' He paused, and when she made no reply, continued, 'I think you have been told why I am here.'

'Yes.' Her voice was husky, her hands curling into fists in the folds of her very ordinary navy skirt. The plain white shirt she wore with it demonstrated she had not thought it necessary to adorn herself for the occasion, he thought sardonically.

She went on quickly, 'And I need you to know that I—can't. That what you ask is—quite impossible.'

'But you do not yet know what I want.' He kept his voice gentle. 'And that is what I wish to discuss with you now—alone and privately. An arrangement between the two of us that no-one else will hear of. Are you willing at least to listen to me?'

'There's no point.' She shook her head. 'I—I have to stop it now while I still can. They may have made you ask me, but they can't force me to say "yes" in return. Not in this day and age. It would be—barbaric. Even Prince Damiano would have to accept that.'

He said drily, 'I think, *mia bella*, that you overestimate the Prince's degree of tolerance. He expects us to be married. *Ecco*, a wedding ceremony will take place.'

'No,' Ellie said. 'It can't. I—I won't.'

'There is another man in your life perhaps?'

'No,' she said raggedly. 'But that's not the point.'

Sighing, Angelo walked over to her and sat down on the pond's stone surround, indicating with a brief gesture that she should join him. She obeyed mutinously, maintaining a more than decorous distance between them, making him suppress a flicker of irritation.

He said, 'Neither your wishes nor mine are the only consideration here, Elena. That is the real point, as I believed I had made clear to you.

'I have already committed myself to serious expenditure on my company's behalf on the basis of the financial package agreed in principle with Credito Europa. But unless you now become my wife, the package will be withdrawn and my dealings with the bank, which are already public knowledge, will be cancelled altogether with potentially disastrous results.

'Please understand that I have no intention of allowing such a thing to happen. Galantana provides a living for too many people in these difficult times, and I will not jeopardise my company's current success or the future of my workforce and suppliers while I have the power to avoid such a catastrophe.'

He looked at her, his mouth twisting wryly. 'You clearly do not want me as a husband. *Bene*. Let me be equally frank and say that I do not desire you as a wife.

'I suggest therefore that we regard our marriage as nothing more than a business deal—a temporary inconvenience that can be speedily concluded once Galantana's expansion has been paid for.

'As we shall be sharing no more than a roof, a discreet annulment can be arranged, and you will receive a generous settlement in return for your co-operation.' He smiled at her coaxingly, willing her to soften. 'So—what do you say?'

Stormy colour warmed her face. 'That it's the most flagrantly immoral idea I've ever heard, and you must be mad to think I'd ever agree.'

Angelo stayed silent for a moment, irritation warring with disappointment within him. She might be quiet, he thought, but she was certainly not biddable. He would have to be more direct in his approach.

'I think madness will be waiting for us if you refuse.' He allowed a grim note to enter his voice. 'If the deal with Credito

Europa fails, I shall have no reason to hide the truth about that night at Largossa. I shall tell Prince Damiano about the trick your cousin Silvia played on us both, and why, and point out that there is no reason for our engagement to each other to continue. I believe you can imagine what might follow.'

He bent and picked up a pebble from the ground, then dropped it into the water.

Ellie stared down as the ripples began to spread slowly but surely, becoming wider all the time.

It did not need any great exercise of the imagination, she thought bitterly. The consequences of Silvia's reckless behaviour had always been there, like shadows on the edge of a room. A very public divorce from Ernesto would probably be the least of it. The shadows would touch them all.

She said, 'This is like—blackmail.'

'Call it rather a matter of expediency.' His voice was level. 'If there is no marriage between us, the Barzados would no longer be silent, but rush to add their own embellishments to the existing gossip. Do you truly wish to be the centre of stories of midnight orgies at the Largossa estate, Elena? Be responsible for the damage to the Damiano reputation?'

'No.' She almost choked on the word. '*Certo che no.* Of course not.'

He shrugged. 'Then it can all be quite simply avoided. There will be a wedding ceremony and, after it, life will go on much as it does now, except that you will live at my house at Vostranto.'

He ignored her faint gasp and continued, 'It is quite large enough to accommodate us both without awkwardness. In any case, I intend to remain at my apartment in Rome during the week, so you will have little more of my company than you endure at present.' He smiled coldly. 'Perhaps less. And your nights you may spend alone with my goodwill. Let that be clearly understood.' He shrugged again. 'Then after an interval—a year, two years perhaps—we can set about dissolving the marriage, and you will be rich and free.'

As she hesitated, he added quietly, 'Elena, I beg you to

think how much we both and others have to lose if you persist in rejecting me.' He paused. 'Believe me, if there was another choice to be made, I would take it.'

For a long moment, dizzy with uncertainty, she stared down at the flagstones at her feet, imagining them cracking apart, herself falling through the gap helplessly into some abyss.

In a voice she barely recognised, she said, 'You promise—you give me your word that you'll leave me alone. That you won't…' She broke off in embarrassment, not knowing what to say.

'I guarantee you will have nothing to fear from me.' His mouth twisted. 'I think our previous encounter was enough for us both.'

'Yes.' Her voice was small, stifled, as she tried hard not to think about those brief shocked and shocking moments, and the greater nightmare that had so swiftly followed. That still enveloped her in spite of his assurances.

And yet…

I do not desire you as a wife.

Words that were, perhaps not quite as comforting as they should have been. That—if she was totally honest—stung a little in their indication that she had somehow fallen short of a standard that was none of her making. That she had not even known was required of her.

'So may I tell the Prince that you have consented to be my bride?'

She lifted her head and looked at him, her eyes enormous in her pale face. 'If there is no other way, then I suppose—yes.'

His brows lifted mockingly. 'You are graciousness itself.'

'If you wanted a more generous reply,' she said, 'you should have asked a more willing lady.'

'On the contrary, Elena,' he said softly. 'I think you will suit my purpose very well.'

He reached for her hand and made to raise it to his lips, but Ellie snatched it back, flushing.

'Perhaps you'd restrict your overtures to those times when we have an audience to convince, Count.'

There was a pause, then he said courteously, 'Just as you wish, *signorina*.'

But Ellie knew that in that moment's silence she'd detected anger, like a flare of distant lightning, and even though she wrote it off as a typical male reaction to a dent in his machismo, she found the discovery oddly disturbing just the same.

They were married two weeks later at a very quiet ceremony held in the *palazzo*'s private chapel.

Ellie refused outright, despite all persuasions, to wear a conventional white gown and veil, and chose instead a silken slip of a dress, high-necked and long-sleeved in a pretty shade of smoky blue.

Signora Luccino looked at it askance, but her brows lifted in open disapproval when she heard that the pressure of work currently being experienced by the bridegroom had caused the postponement of the tradition *luna di miele*. Indefinitely.

'You astonish me, my dear Angelo,' she said majestically. 'I would have thought your new bride should take precedence over any matter of business.'

Angelo gave her a cool smile. 'You concern yourself without necessity, Zia Dorotea. Vostranto will provide us with all the peace and seclusion we could ever wish. Is it not so, *carissima*?' he added, turning to the new bride in question, who was silently praying for the entire farce to be over and done with, and as soon as possible.

The one bright spot in a hideous day, she reflected, had been the absence of Silvia, who was, it seemed, accompanying Ernesto to a conference in Basle.

But even that was small comfort as she stood before the ornate gilded altar listening to herself say the words that, in the eyes of the world, gave her to Angelo Manzini.

Now she could only blush vividly and murmur something incoherent that might have been assent to his question. Her awkwardness, however, did her no disservice either with Signora Luccino or any of the other guests. Indeed, her obvious shyness at the prospect of being alone with her glamorous husband was seen as charming.

Yet in an odd way Vostranto had become the least of Ellie's concerns about her unwanted marriage. The first time Angelo had taken her there, she'd sat beside him in the car, staring at the back of the driver's head, taut and unhappy as if she was on her way to jail.

The house itself was a surprise, an impressive pile of pale golden stone against the folded greenery of the foothills. It was roofed in green terracotta tiles and two massive wings reached out from the central building like arms outstretched in welcome, enclosing a gravelled courtyard where a fountain played in front of the lavishly carved doors of the main entrance.

Ellie stepped out of the car, and stood for a moment, relishing the warmth of the sun after the air-conditioning of the limousine, and watching the sparkle of the drops as a marble Neptune, his head thrown back in smiling triumph, endlessly poured water from an urn shaped like a shell.

To her own astonishment, she found her inner tensions begin to dissipate a little, even if the idea of the house welcoming her was clearly a figment of her imagination, and allowed herself to be escorted inside with more composure than she'd anticipated.

The entrance hall seemed vast and directly ahead of her a wide staircase made from the same marble as the floor led up to a broad half-landing carpeted in crimson, where it divided with two shorter flights of stairs leading up to twin galleries on either side.

'Your rooms will be in the West Wing,' Angelo informed her almost casually, nodding in that direction. 'Mine, in the East.' His smile was brief and did not convey much amusement. 'I hope that will provide enough distance between us to put your mind at rest.'

It occurred to Ellie suddenly—almost bleakly—that even if he'd said he'd be sleeping in the adjoining room to hers, there would still be a space like the Sahara Desert between them.

And had to catch at herself with faint bewilderment—because that was a good thing. Wasn't it?

Aloud, she said woodenly, 'You are very considerate.'

'I cannot take the credit.' He shrugged. 'The arrangement is a tradition.'

A pretty chilly tradition too, like all that insistence on family honour, Ellie decided silently as she followed him to the *salotto*. And could surely be dispensed with in this day and age. Although not on her account, naturally, she added hastily.

But one day, when they were free of each other, he would no doubt marry again, this time to a girl who would persuade him to rethink the sleeping arrangements because she wanted him close to her all night and every night.

And once more felt something she did not totally understand stir in the pit of her stomach.

The *salotto* was long and low-ceilinged, with a fireplace even bigger than the one at Largossa, suggesting how cosy the room could become in the depths of winter. But for now, the French windows at the far end stood temptingly ajar, inviting the occupants to step out on to the sunlit terrace beyond, and drink in the green lawns and flower beds she could only glimpse.

She'd been told the workmen engaged on the refurbishment had only left the previous day and she was aware of the scent of paint and fresh plaster in the air, and how the walls seemed to glow. She listened in silence to Angelo's cool and impersonal account of how the wiring had been replaced through the house, and all the plumbing modernised.

As if, she thought, he was delivering a lecture on the renovation of old houses to a not very interesting audience, instead of describing her future, if temporary, home.

From the *salotto*, they went to the dining room, with its superb frescoed ceiling, but by-passed altogether the room he referred to as 'my study' on their way to the kitchen quarters.

Which meant, she thought, that there were no-go areas for her too.

It was something of a relief to be delivered over to Assunta, his plump and smiling housekeeper, for the remainder of the tour, which, of course, included the rooms intended for her in the West Wing.

The bed, she supposed, swallowing, was also traditional, a huge canopied expanse of snowy linen, piled high with pillows, and a wonderful crimson coverlet with the Manzini coat of arms embroidered in gold.

But Ellie was aware of a swift jolt at Assunta's confidential disclosure that His Excellency had been born in that bed, accompanied by a twinkling glance to remind her where her own duty lay.

In the adjoining *stanza di bagnio*, as well as a deep, sunken bath, there was a semi-circular shower cabinet that would easily have accommodated the entire bathroom in her flat on its own.

And she would never, in a hundred years, have sufficient clothes to fill that panelled dressing room with its wall of wardrobes.

The entire set-up made her feel overwhelmed and even a little off-balance with the weight of its obvious expectations, especially when she'd realised from the first moment that almost everyone who worked in the house or on the estate was lurking in the vicinity in an attempt to catch a glimpse of her, and that the smiles that greeted her held unalloyed goodwill.

But then it was a long time, as Assunta had told her, the brown eyes suddenly a little anxious, since Vostranto had a mistress.

They're all going to be so disappointed in me, Ellie thought, as she returned downstairs to the unsmiling young man who was about to reluctantly bestow all this grandeur upon her.

She thought he'd be waiting for her in the *salotto*, glancing impatiently at his watch, but the room was deserted and she stood for a moment quite alone, relishing the quiet, reminding herself that this was how life was going to be for the foreseeable future, but also that she was used to it—accustomed, most of the time, to her own company both at her apartment and the

Casa Bianca—so that shouldn't, wouldn't be a problem. That really it was what she preferred.

And even as that thought took shape in her mind, everything seemed to change, as if, for a moment, this room into which she'd walked as a stranger only an hour or two before had become suddenly familiar and somehow—enfolded her.

So that when Angelo strode in from the terrace a few minutes later, looking preoccupied and asking if she was ready to leave, she agreed quietly and calmly, knowing that, when the time came, she would be even more contented to return. And that at least part of her life as the Contessa Manzini, while far from perfect, would at least be endurable.

But not all the issues within the marriage were going to be as easy to deal with. There was, for instance, the vexed question of her employment.

'My wife,' Angelo told her icily when she'd asked how soon after the wedding she could return to Avortino, 'does not work.'

Ellie gasped indignantly. 'But that's ludicrous,' she protested. 'Just what am I supposed to do all day—sit around twiddling my thumbs? Thank you, *signore*, but no thanks. I love my job, I'm good at it, and I've promised my boss that I'll be back at my desk—*pronto*.'

'Then you should have consulted me first, when I would have told you it was out of the question.' His expression was like stone. 'The matter is closed.'

'Like hell it is.' Her voice shook. 'I've agreed, much against my will and better judgement, to this pretence of a marriage. A little compromise on your part might be good.'

His lips tightened. 'If you think I am being unreasonable, Elena, consider the practical difficulties. Travelling into the city each day is only one of them.'

She lifted her chin. 'I have a car.' And I also had an apartment I could have used, she added silently, which you've made me get rid of, while keeping your own.

'I have seen your car,' Angelo said dismissively. 'Old and unreliable. A potential death trap, which will have to be replaced.'

He paused. 'But that changes nothing. You will have no time to spend at Avortino once you become the Contessa Manzini. Your predecessors have found that in itself a full-time job with a household to run. New duties to learn.'

'Well I can't speak for a long line of downtrodden women,' Ellie returned with equal coldness. 'But the household in question seems to have been managing perfectly well without either of us for some considerable time.'

'But that will change once we are married,' he said flatly. 'I intend to use Vostranto far more, and you will have to accustom yourself to being the hostess when I entertain friends—business acquaintances. That, I think, will take time.'

In other words, Ellie thought, slashed by a pain as sharp as it was unexpected, I'm not up to the job. As if I needed any reminder.

She said quietly, 'Then perhaps you should postpone your social whirl, Count Manzini, until I've gone back to the real world and you've acquired someone more suitable to welcome your guests.' She paused. 'I'm sure you'll be spoiled for choice.'

There was a silence, then he said slowly, 'Allow me to apologise. I did not intend how that must have sounded.'

Ellie looked past him, biting her lip. She said remotely, 'It really doesn't matter.' And wished with all her heart that her statement were true.

But, she told herself in silent defiance, if he thought the question of Avortino had been settled, he was entirely wrong. When this so-called marriage was concluded, she would need to work, having no plans to accept the proposed settlement however generous.

When it's over, I want it to be over, she thought. Which does not include being under any kind of obligation to him, legal, financial or otherwise.

However, she had not anticipated that Casa Bianca would prove yet another bone of contention.

The Principessa had mentioned it casually over dinner one

night. 'Your little seaside retreat, Elena. What will happen to that when you are married?'

Ellie hesitated, uncomfortably aware that Angelo, who had been talking to the Prince, had turned his head and was looking at her, brows raised in enquiry.

He said softly, 'A retreat for a new wife. That sounds a little alarming, *mia cara*. Also unnecessary. What is this place, and where?'

Ellie met his gaze, concealing her unease at the challenge in his voice. 'My grandmother left me a little cottage at the coast in a place called Porto Vecchio.' She added coolly, 'It's only a small fishing village, and not a bit fashionable, so I don't suppose you've heard of it.'

'No, but I have learned of it now, and the fact that you own a house there, which I was also unaware of.' He paused. 'It must involve you in considerable expense. I therefore presume you will wish to sell it?'

'On the contrary,' said Ellie. 'I have no intention of parting with it, although I may possibly rent it out in the holiday season.' *When hell freezes over.*

Angelo inclined his head courteously. 'All that is something we will naturally have to discuss.'

Ellie widened her eyes into a limpid stare. Allowed her voice a note of amusement. 'But, *mio caro*, what is there to talk about, when my decision has already been made?'

Besides, she added silently, Roman dictators went out with Julius Caesar, or hadn't you heard?

But the set of Angelo's jaw as he turned his attention back to the plate of *osso buco* in front of him, coupled with a long, thoughtful look from Contessa Cosima, warned her that she had probably not heard the last on the subject.

However, there was no way she was giving up the cottage, she vowed inwardly, no matter what objections her reluctant husband might have to her possession of it. It was her own special place and it meant too much—held too many memories to be abandoned on his say-so.

Nonna Vittoria had left a sum of money to cover immediate

maintenance costs and local taxes, but this, of course, would not last forever. And as Ellie had no intention of asking Count Manzini for a cent towards Casa Bianca's upkeep, retaining her job and its salary was becoming even more essential, she thought grimly.

But lying sleepless that night, an idea came to her that could solve that particular problem, although its accomplishment would probably not sweeten Angelo's temper.

On the other hand, there went a man far too used to getting his own way—especially with women. Maybe it was time he got his comeuppance, even in a minor way.

There was a room at Vostranto, not large but with good light, and not currently being used for very much, although there was a small kneehole desk under the window which, Ellie had been told, was where Count Angelo's late mother had written her correspondence and overseen the household accounts.

But if her laptop was installed there, she'd be able to receive translation work from Avortino by email, and return it, completed, by the same method. So commuting would not be necessary, and if she continued to use her maiden name for professional purposes, no-one need ever know that the new Contessa Manzini was gainfully employed, with or without her husband's goodwill.

She would need Assunta's help, but her instinctive response to Vostranto and the spell it had worked on her seemed to have established her firmly in the housekeeper's good books, so she did not foresee major problems from that direction at least.

Or, she reflected, turning over and punching her pillow into shape, just as long as there weren't too many references to the nursery accommodation on the second floor, also unoccupied.

But a week later, with the toasts drunk, the wedding cake distributed and the alien gold of Angelo's ring gleaming on her hand, Ellie was no longer so confident about winning the necessary concessions. After all, she reminded herself, she had basically been hired to do a job, so her status at Vostranto would be little more than that of an employee. And as she drove with her husband to her new home, this time without the chauffeur's presence, she could feel her inner tensions building again.

Glancing sideways, she saw that the tanned face with its sculpted mouth looked strangely austere, and realised he too must have reservations about the immediate future, and the sterile bargain it contained.

But it was all his own doing, she reminded herself stonily. I was just caught up in the subsequent storm. So whatever regrets he's having, he fully deserves.

And Silvia, of course, had got off scot-free as she'd done so many times in childhood when retribution threatened, proving that there was no justice. But Ernesto seemed to be keeping a close eye on her, so perhaps her wings had been clipped.

'Is something wrong?' Angelo asked suddenly, and she jumped.

'No. Why do you ask?'

'You seem a little restless.'

'Recent events,' she said, 'are hardly conducive to calm.'

There was a silence, then he said, 'I do not know what else I can say to assure you…'

'That I am of no interest to you?' Ellie lifted her chin. 'Believe me, *signore*, that is probably the least of my concerns.'

'Then what troubles you?'

She took a breath. 'There's something I have to tell you. I've decided to go on working—but from home—your home—from Vostranto.'

'How do you propose to do so?' His tone was not encouraging.

'By email. I—I've had a room your mother once used fixed up as an office.' She paused. 'It won't disturb you or get in the way of the household duties that seem so important to you. I'll work all the hours I need to for that. However, you must see that I need my career and my future.'

'You do not trust me to support you adequately?' He rapped the question at her.

'Yes—for the time being.' She swallowed. 'But try to understand that I also value my independence. Which will last a great deal longer than this—pretend marriage.'

He said something under his breath. Then: 'And you did not think to consult me before putting these arrangements—in place?'

'I thought of it—yes.' She stared rigidly ahead through the windscreen. 'But I decided I knew what you would say. And if you now countermand my instructions, then your staff will know that—as well as everything else—my wishes do not matter to you, which will make it difficult for me to gain their respect, and run Vostranto as efficiently as you seem to wish.'

There was another silence, then he said softly, 'I see I have underestimated you, Elena. On this occasion, I shall allow your orders to stand. But make sure—make very sure—that you do not underestimate me. I am still the master of Vostranto.'

'Of the house—yes.' Her heart was thudding wildly. 'But you're not my master, Count Manzini, and you never will be.'

He jerked the wheel suddenly, and Ellie cried out as the car veered to the side of the road, coming to rest on the grass verge.

'You like to challenge me, it seems, *mia bella*.' His voice bit. 'But you have done so once too often.'

He reached for her almost negligently, pulling her hard into his arms. His mouth was hard too, and sensually explicit, inflicting a kiss without mercy which left the softness of her lips bruised and burning when at last he raised his head.

His gaze was mocking, cynical, as he looked down at her.

'So, now you know, Elena, what it means to make me angry. You would be well advised not to risk it again. *Capisce*?'

She said in a voice she did not recognise, 'I—I understand.' And did not speak again for the remainder of the journey.

CHAPTER SIX

ELLIE STOOD, her arms wrapped almost protectively across her body, in the middle of the room she would now have to learn to call hers. Which made it, she thought, swallowing, no less imposing. Or daunting.

Besides being the only place in the house where she still felt like a stranger—an interloper.

That great canopied monolith was so obviously a marriage bed that she found herself wondering how many Manzini wives had lain there in the past waiting to perform their marital duties—something which, at least, she would be spared.

At the same time, her fingers strayed momentarily to her mouth, still tender and slightly swollen from the ravishment of his kiss.

She recognised, of course, that it had been foolish to provoke him, but his high-handed manner was enough to try the patience of a saint.

But, to her relief, he had not so much as glanced in her direction again until their arrival at the house, when he'd escorted her between the two rows of happily applauding staff to the door, lifted her into his arms and carried her across the threshold to more cheers and laughter.

And she'd forced herself to smile as if she was a real bride, and that this traditional ritual, ensuring she did not inadvertently trip or stumble on entering her new home, would actually bring her marriage good luck.

Good fortune, however, was the last thing on her mind. The

previous few days had been a strain, and now that it had all stopped, she felt tired and almost on the verge of tears.

She had been served coffee and delicious lemon-flavoured biscuits in the *salotto*, after which Angelo had excused himself with cool politeness and gone off to his study to read his emails.

Ellie, in her turn, was whisked upstairs by Assunta. She found, to her astonishment, that her cases had already been unpacked and their contents put away in the dressing room by someone called Donata, who was, it seemed, her personal maid, and who would return later to help her bathe and change for the evening ahead.

'But I don't want a maid,' Ellie protested. 'I wouldn't know what to do with one.'

'She will know,' Assunta said firmly. 'Besides for the wife of Count Manzini, it is most necessary. You will see.' She paused. 'And now, Contessa, you should rest before dinner.' However, her discreet twinkle as she departed suggested that it was the hours following dinner for which her young mistress should principally be refreshed and ready.

I'm such a fraud, Ellie thought wearily as the door closed behind the good woman. But, all the same, she had to admit the idea of a rest was appealing, although not on that enormous bed with all its implications which she would deal with when she had to.

However, there was a couch shaped like a particularly luxurious *chaise longue* by the shuttered window which would answer her requirements perfectly.

Ellie removed her shoes, her tights and, carefully, her dress, revealing the exquisite lingerie—bra, briefs and half-slip—also in soft blue silk, that she wore beneath it, just part of the *corredo da sposa* that the Principessa had firmly insisted on providing.

All of it far more glamorous than anything I'd have chosen for myself, she thought with a sigh, as she stretched out on the cushions, and, under the circumstances, a total waste of money.

As were the wages of this maid who'd been hired for her, of course, but she realised that this was an issue where it might be wiser to give way, as a nod in the direction of some kind of marital harmony.

After all I can't fight him about everything, she acknowledged dispiritedly. So I should save my ammunition for the battles that really matter. Whatever they turn out to be.

And found herself sighing again.

Angelo surveyed the information on his computer screen with tight-lipped satisfaction, and a certain relief. It seemed as if the finance deal with Credito Europa was going through without the last-minute hitches and prevarication that he had half-expected.

Apparently the Crocodile is a man of his word, after all, he thought cynically. And I, may God help me, am now married.

He pushed back his chair and stood up. He would have to return to Rome at some point to sign the necessary documentation, but that would not be a problem.

After all, his new bride was hardly likely to regret his absence, he thought coldly. *Al contrario*, having turned a once charming room into an efficient and characterless workspace as he'd recently observed, she would probably welcome his departure. See it as an opportunity to further the career that meant so much to her.

He wondered why the idea of her continuing to work for Avortino was irritating him so much. Surely he should welcome anything that would occupy her attention and keep her from enquiring too closely into his own activities.

And he should not have allowed his annoyance over her stubborn resistance to his wishes—or her apparent assumption that she was the only sufferer in their present situation—to get the better of him and goad him into inflicting on her that travesty of a kiss.

The holy saints knew it was the last thing he'd ever intended, he thought moodily. He'd planned to be kind and courteous, putting her at her ease in difficult circumstances, and instead he'd acted like the worst kind of boor.

His behaviour had been unbelievable, he told himself, besides creating an awkwardness between them that he knew he must somehow put right before it became unforgivable too.

Because, however rarely it might be, they were still committed to sharing a roof, and it would be helpful if they were able to do this with some degree of accord, even if it was only in public.

Mouth twisting, he took the Credito Europa's letter of confirmation from the printer. At least he could show her that there had already been some benefit from this unwanted marriage. That their mutual sacrifice was partially justified at least.

But it was by no means certain that he could persuade her to see it that way. He accepted ruefully now that it had been a serious error of judgement as well as unkind to describe her as 'a nonentity'. She had a mind and a will of her own, the little Elena, and, it was clear, no very high opinion of him either.

So perhaps it was time, he told himself wryly, that he tried to make amends of some kind. Establish at least a working relationship. And try to end this strange day on better terms than its beginning.

If that was possible, he added silently, and sighed.

Ellie was drifting in and out of a light sleep when she was disturbed by a firm rap at the bedroom door, followed by the sound of the door itself opening.

Pushing her hair back from her face, she lifted herself on to an elbow, expecting to see the threatened maid. But, instead, to her shock, it was Angelo who came striding briskly into the room.

'What are you doing here?' Ellie, hideously aware that she was in her underwear, looked round vainly for a rug or even a shawl to put round her shoulders as a cover-up. 'What do you want?'

He too looked taken aback, a tinge of colour emphasising the sculpted cheekbones as his dark gaze scanned her then hurriedly turned to the paper in his hand. 'I came to share some news with you.'

'Couldn't it have waited?' she asked tautly.

'Yes,' he acknowledged, mouth tightening. 'But I thought it would please you to know that Prince Damiano has today agreed the deal with Galantana, and therefore our days together can be considered as already numbered.'

'Oh,' she said. 'I—I see. Well, that's—good.'

'I imagined you would think so.' He paused. 'However, there is also another matter that perhaps we should discuss.'

'If it's about the maid you've hired for me,' Ellie said quickly, 'Assunta's already told me.'

'The maid?' His brows lifted. 'No, it concerns the other staff.' He hesitated. 'I learned just now that a celebration dinner is being prepared for us tonight. The *sala da pranzo* has been specially decorated with flowers, and the Manzini *calice* taken from its cabinet and cleaned. I should warn you that at some point in the evening, it will be filled with wine and various herbs and tradition demands that we drink from it while the household applaud.'

Ellie frowned. 'Is that a problem?'

'Not for me.' Angelo shrugged. 'But to share the *calice* will also signify our hope for a blissful wedding night and many babies to follow.' He gave her a sardonic look. 'It figures, therefore, that they will not expect us to sleep apart on such a meaningful occasion.'

Ellie sat up, embarrassment forgotten. She said crisply, 'Then they'll have to be disappointed.'

'You said in the car that you needed to gain their respect,' he reminded her softly. 'I must tell you, Elena, that to reveal yourself so soon as a wife who is no wife at all will not win that respect for you. *Infatti*, it could have the opposite effect.'

'That's a risk I'll just have to take.'

'Even when it could so easily be avoided?'

'You mean if I let you sleep with me?' She shook her head. Her voice sounded stifled. 'Never. Oh God, I knew I couldn't trust you.'

'I mean,' he said coldly, 'if I spend tonight in this room rather than my own. Nothing more.' He glanced around him. 'As you can see, it could easily accommodate half a dozen people.' He added more gently, 'Believe me, Elena *mia*, you would not wish them to think you displease me. Your life here will be much easier if it is thought we are truly man and wife, and that there is at least affection between us.'

She stared up at him. 'And you—being here tonight will be enough to convince them of that?'

'It will probably be necessary to pay you other visits in the future,' he said. 'But they will be few and I will make them brief. I shall not again stay all night.' His mouth twisted. 'If I wait until you are asleep, you will not even be aware of my presence.'

He watched her as she sat head bent, staring down at the floor. At last, she sighed.

'Yes, then—if I must. But you have to promise that you'll keep your word. That you won't try to—to...'

'The world is full of willing women, *mia cara*,' Angelo drawled, his voice faintly derisive. 'I have never forced my attentions on a reluctant girl yet. Believe me, you will not be the first.'

He paused. 'However, once we have drunk from the *calice* tonight, I shall be expected to kiss you. Perhaps, in return, you could smile at me? Is it agreed?'

As she nodded unwillingly, there was a tap on the door, and he turned. 'Ah, Donata.' He spoke pleasantly to the plump dark girl hesitating awkwardly in the doorway. 'The Contessa has been waiting to meet you, is that not so, *carissima*?' He took Ellie's hand and raised it fleetingly to his lips, adding huskily, 'Until later then, *mi amore*. I can hardly wait to be alone with you at last.'

And Ellie watched him go, in the furious knowledge that she was blushing to the roots of her hair.

Her day did not improve as it proceeded into evening.

Donata was polite and efficient, and sighed openly over the

handmade silk and lace underwear that she laid out for Ellie to put on after her bath, but at the same time there was just the faintest suggestion in her manner that her new employer probably needed all the help she could get.

Or am I being over-sensitive? Ellie asked herself drily.

Whatever, it made no real difference, she decided, shrugging mentally. She was not, as the maid clearly assumed, dressing to be undressed later by her bridegroom. Merely forcing herself to do what was expected of her.

Just as later in the *sala da pranzo*, she disguised her total lack of appetite by making herself eat at least some of all the delicious food set in front of her at a candle-lit table, garlanded with pink and white roses, and gleaming with silver and crystal.

And when the *calice* was ceremoniously borne in—beaten gold, no less, and engraved with the Manzini coat of arms—she rose, laughing, to her feet and stood in the circle of Angelo's arm as they drank, even managing to endure the firm, warm pressure of his mouth on hers when he bent to claim his kiss.

After which, as he had warned her, she was required to retire demurely to her room, and await her husband's pleasure.

'Are there any other embarrassing medieval customs I should know about?' she'd asked him stonily, aware that her skin was warming again. 'I hope they won't want to inspect the sheets to prove that I was a virgin.'

His mouth had hardened. 'And I hope there may come a time, Elena, when you may appreciate their pleasure in having you as their Contessa and respond more graciously.'

When she got to her room, the officious Donata had already been there to turn down the bed on both sides, and lay across its foot the faintly austere white satin nightgown and the matching robe, tying at the waist with ribbons in which Ellie was supposed to entrance her bridegroom, then, her duty done, had discreetly and thankfully departed.

Ellie hung away the pretty primrose dress she'd worn at dinner, put her discarded underwear in the clothes basket, and slid the slender length of satin over her head. As she turned to reach for the robe, she caught a momentary glimpse of herself in the long wall-mirror and paused, arrested, aware that for the first time that day she actually looked like a bride.

And found herself wondering suddenly what it would have been like if her marriage had been a real one to a man she loved and who loved her in return, so that she'd be waiting here with delight and anticipation for her husband to come to her and take her in his arms.

And was assailed by a wave of such bleak loneliness that she almost cried out in despair.

Biting her lip, she put on the robe, fastened it, then sat down at the dressing table and began to brush her hair with slow rhythmic strokes, in an attempt to restore herself to calm, so that she could meet Angelo's arrival with the necessary cool and unemotional indifference.

Or at least his eventual arrival, she thought when an hour had passed with no sign of him. She rose from the *chaise longue*, where she'd been perching nervously, retrieved the book she'd brought with her from the *palazzo*, a detective story set in Florence, removed her robe and, getting into bed, began to read.

Somewhere in the house, she heard a clock strike yet another hour and she paused, glancing at the door. Perhaps he'd changed his mind, she thought hopefully, having decided that their public performance with the loving cup was quite enough to fulfil the hopes of their well-wishers.

She closed her book and turned to switch off the lamp on her night table only to realise that her bedroom door was opening once again to admit Angelo. He came in quietly, and halted, looking at her across the room, brows raised quizzically.

He said, 'I thought by now you would indeed be asleep.'

He was wearing, she saw with a sudden thud of the heart, a black silk knee-length robe and apparently nothing else. And for a devastating moment, found herself remembering the night in the tower room and the touch of his bare skin against hers.

'I—I was reading,' she returned, her mouth suddenly dry.

'It must be a fascinating book to keep you awake until this

hour.' He began to walk slowly towards the bed. 'Perhaps you should lend it to me to provide me with a suitable diversion for the next week or so. Just as a precaution, you understand.'

He reached the other side of the bed and began to untie the sash that fastened his robe at the waist.

Ellie said hoarsely, 'What are you doing?'

'Getting ready to sleep, *naturalmente*. Or is that perhaps a *trabocchetto*—a trick question?'

'But you can't,' she protested. 'At least—not here.'

'If you imagine, *mia sposa*, that I intend to spend the night on that penance of a couch, then you are quite mistaken.'

'But it's perfectly comfortable.'

Angelo shrugged gracefully. 'For you, perhaps, for an hour during the siesta. Not for a man of my height at any time.'

'Then I'll sleep there myself,' she flared, pushing away the covers and swinging her legs out of the bed.

'And I prefer that you remain where you are.' He spoke quietly but there was a note of steel in his voice. 'I advise you to accede to my wishes in this, Elena. Do so, and we shall both pass a peaceful night. But to defy me and force me to bring you back to this bed might have consequences you would not care for.'

He paused. 'Now I suggest you turn your back, switch off the light and relax. You will soon forget that I am here.'

For a rigid, disquieting moment, she remained where she was, mentally weighing the possible repercussions of disobedience and realising reluctantly that she could not afford to take the risk.

Slowly she slid back under the covers and reached again for the lamp switch, plunging the room into darkness. As she did so, she felt the faint dip in the mattress signalling that he was now lying beside her, even if it was at a safe distance.

But there is no real safety, she thought, resting her hot cheek against the cool of the pillow. I'm in uncharted territory here, and I'm scared. As for forgetting that he's here—how impossible is that?

By contrast, however, Angelo seemed to have little difficulty in ignoring her presence. In a matter of minutes, or so it seemed to Ellie, his quiet even breathing revealed that he had fallen asleep, leaving her to lie awake and restive, but unable to show it, her only alternative to gaze unseeingly into the shadows, counting the long minutes as they turned slowly into hours and thinking of all the other nights ahead of her when she would have to do the same, until the time when this strange—even incredible—non-marriage finally came to its end.

And hoping, with something approaching desperation, that it might be soon.

Three months later

Ellie closed her laptop, and stretched gently, easing her back. At the same time, she allowed herself a faint smile of satisfaction. Because of a colleague's illness, she'd just completed the translation of a lengthy scientific handbook, crammed with the kind of technical jargon known only to the initiated.

The inherent difficulty of the task, too, had demanded total concentration, which meant that she had less time to focus on other, more personal problems. Such as the equally inherent difficulty of presenting a convincing performance to the world in her ongoing role as the young Contessa Manzini, she thought unhappily.

Something which was preying on her mind more and more as her marriage began to turn from weeks into months, although she was at a loss to know why.

On the face of it, she had little to complain about. As she'd suspected it had not taken her long to become familiar with the household routine, which ran like clockwork anyway without any real intervention from her.

And, she had to admit, Angelo had scrupulously kept his word as to how their lives together would be conducted, which was quite simply—apart. That since their wedding night, he had paid precisely three visits to her room, and those only for the sake of appearances, during which they'd slept on strictly opposite sides of that gigantic bed.

And he had never even attempted to lay a hand on her.

Not that she wanted him to, of course, she reminded herself swiftly. So, it was a relief to know that he clearly shared—maybe even exceeded—her own reluctance.

Because there had been no repetition of that burning savagery of a kiss either. His greeting and leave-taking invariably consisted of the merest brush of his lips across her cheek and her fingers, and that only when others were present.

And if there were moments when she wondered whether the marriage was setting a pattern and that she was destined to spend the rest of her life alone and undesired, she kept such thoughts strictly to herself, pretending that the possibility was not as hurtful as it sometimes felt.

And that, of course, there would be someone—someday—when this was over and life became real again.

So there was really nothing for her to be uneasy about. Or not where Angelo was concerned, anyway, she amended swiftly.

Because she could not deny she was being subjected to pressure of a different nature and from another source entirely. Something she had never expected, and found increasingly difficult to deal with.

She got up from her seat and walked restlessly over to the window, staring out at the sunlit landscape with eyes that pictured another scene entirely.

It had begun some six weeks after the wedding. Her godmother had invited her to a lunch party at Largossa—'A very small affair, *mia cara*, and all female.'

She'd been delighted to find Nonna Cosima present, but less pleased to see Signora Luccino, whom she was learning to call Zia Dorotea. For some reason, the older woman had seemed convinced from the start that Ellie's marriage was entirely her own design, and that she deserved the credit for bringing it about.

And how wrong was it possible for anyone to be? Ellie thought bitterly. But at least the Signora had brought Tullia with her, which promised some alleviation.

It was during the *aperitivos* before lunch that the first blow fell.

'You look well, *cara* Elena,' Zia Dorotea pronounced magisterially. 'Almost blooming, in fact. Is it possible you have good news for us all?'

Ellie set down her glass of *prosecco* with immense care, controlling the silent scream building inside her. She was aware of Madrina and Nonna Cosima exchanging glances of faint anguish and Tullia's open glare at her mother, but it made no difference. The words had been spoken. The question 'Are you pregnant?' was out there, and awaiting an answer.

Only she had none to give.

She forced a smile. 'I spent the weekend at Porto Vecchio. If I have colour in my cheeks, it's probably thanks to the sun and sea breezes.'

'I hope Angelo has also benefited from the break,' said Signora Luccino. 'The last time I saw him, I thought he looked a little strained.'

Ellie bit her lip. 'He wasn't able to accompany me. He had—engagements.' *And please don't ask me where or with whom because I didn't ask him, and I don't want to know anyway.*

'Besides,' she added. 'It wouldn't be his kind of place. It's altogether—too basic.'

'You are saying he has never been there?' The Signora sounded scandalised. 'That you go alone when you have been married less than two months?'

'Oh, Mamma,' Tullia intervened impatiently. 'Husbands and wives do not have to live in each other's pockets.'

'Then perhaps they should,' was the austere reply. 'Particularly when the future of an ancient dynasty is involved. Angelo needs an heir, and perhaps he should be reminded of the fact.'

Nonna Cosima intervened gently. 'I think, my dear Dorotea, that we should allow the children to conduct their own lives, and enjoy the freedom of these first months of marriage together. I am sure the nurseries at Vostranto will be occupied soon enough.'

'But hardly when Angelo spends all week in Rome and Elena disappears to the coast without him at weekends,' the Signora returned implacably. 'I gave birth to my own son within the first year of my marriage, because I knew what my duty was.'

Ellie looked down at the gleam of her wedding ring, her face wooden, thankful that no-one in the room knew the entire truth about her relationship with her supposed husband.

At which point, Giovanni had arrived to announce that the Principessa was served, and Ellie was off the hook.

But not permanently, of course. Ever since there'd been little hints, little nudges, often growing into far more pointed enquiries about her health each time she encountered the Signora.

If things had been different with Angelo, she thought, if they'd been something approaching friends instead of strangers whose paths occasionally crossed, then she could have mentioned it to him—perhaps made a joke of it—but asking for it to stop at the same time.

As it was, she had to endure in a silence that was actually becoming painful in some strange way.

Now, she found she was watching her reflection in the glass panes, studying without pleasure the set of her mouth and the guarded wary eyes. If she'd ever bloomed, she thought with a sigh, there were few signs of that now.

She was startled to hear the distant clang of the bell at the front door. Visitors at Vostranto were rare during the week, and did not usually call without an appointment or an invitation. Perhaps the caller had come to the wrong house, she thought.

Yet a few moments later, there was a tap on the door heralding Giorgio's arrival.

'The Signora Alberoni has called, madam. I have shown her into the *salotto*.'

For a moment she stared at him, initial incomprehension turning into disbelief. Silvia—*Silvia* here? It wasn't possible.

'No, I won't see her. Tell her to go.'

The angry impetuous denial was so clear in her head that she thought she'd already spoken it aloud, until she realised

Giorgio was still waiting for her reply, his expression faintly surprised. Her hands had balled into fists in the folds of her denim skirt and she made herself unclench them, forcing a smile.

'*Grazie*, Giorgio. Will you please ask Assunta to bring coffee and some of the little raisin biscuits? And perhaps Bernardina has made some almond cake?'

Going through the motions of hospitality, she thought, when what she really wanted was to run away screaming.

Then, mustering her composure, she walked down the hall to the *salotto* to confront the cousin who, in one tumultuous night, had brought about the ruin of her life.

CHAPTER SEVEN

ONE LOOK AT Silvia told Ellie that her cousin was not there to apologise. She was standing in the centre of the room, a dark red silk dress clinging to every curve, her eyes narrowed as she surveyed her surroundings.

'You've done well for yourself, *cara*,' she commented, sending Ellie's elderly skirt and collarless white blouse a derisive look. 'Strange how things sometimes turn out.'

She walked over to the fireplace and studied the coat of arms carved into its stonework. 'This is the first time I have been here. Did you know that?'

'No,' Ellie returned quietly. 'I didn't know.'

Silvia tossed her head, making her blonde hair shimmer. 'I tried several times to persuade Angelo to invite me, but he always made some excuse.'

'I see.' Ellie lifted her chin. 'So, what excuse do you have for making this visit now?'

Silvia spread her hands gracefully. 'Do I need one—to see my own cousin?' She paused. 'I didn't send you a wedding present, because what can one possibly give someone who's scooped the equivalent of the Euro-lottery? It was really very clever of you.'

She walked to a sofa and sat down crossing her legs. 'Or was it?' Her tone was meditative. 'Maybe it was all the idea of that old witch, his grandmother and her daughter, the Luccino woman. God knows that precious pair have been trying to force him into an unwanted marriage for years. Did I supply them with the chance they wanted?'

She laughed harshly. 'How ironic. How truly ironic.'

Ellie took a step forward. 'Silvia—how could you do such a thing?'

'Why wouldn't I?' Silvia's eyes flashed. 'Did he think—did he really think that I would allow him to throw me aside as if I was nothing? No-one treats me like that—ever. I knew the importance of his deal with Zio Cesare and how damaging its failure would be. Therefore, I decided to teach him a lesson.' Her smile was calculating. 'I knew I could still make him want me, and that he would not be able to resist my invitation.'

Ellie said in a low voice, 'I meant—how could you involve me? As you've just said—your own cousin.'

Silvia shrugged negligently. 'Because I knew you were the last girl in the world that Angelo would ever find attractive, so that when he was found in your room, he would look and feel a complete fool. It was the final perfect touch.'

Ellie turned away. She said in a stifled voice, 'You must be mad.'

'He made me suffer,' Silvia retorted. 'I wanted him to suffer too. To realise what he had lost when he ended our affair.'

'But it couldn't have continued,' Ellie protested. 'What would have happened if Ernesto had found out?'

Her cousin shrugged again. 'He would have divorced me, *naturalmente*, and I would have been free to marry Angelo, who must now be wishing every day of his life that he had not been so hasty and thrown away our happiness.'

Happiness? thought Ellie with disbelief. What happiness could possibly grow from such a selfish obsession—or from inflicting misery on others?

She took a deep breath. 'If that's all you came to say, maybe you should leave.'

'When I'm enjoying all this fabulous hospitality?' Silvia gave a little, tinkling laugh. 'I think I'll stay for a while so we can chat—woman to woman.' Her voice sank intimately. 'I'm dying to know, *carissima*, how you like married life. Does Angelo fulfil every lonely little fantasy you ever had?'

Her gaze swept mockingly over Ellie's shrinking body. 'I must tell you that you do not seem the picture of rapture, *mia cara*.'

'You can think what you wish.' Ellie lifted her chin. 'However, I have no intention of discussing my relationship with…' She hesitated. She could not bring herself to say 'Angelo' because she never used his given name. On the other hand she could hardly say, 'Count Manzini' to Silvia of all people.

So she compromised with 'my husband'—a description totally lacking in accuracy, too, she reminded herself with a faint stab of unexpected pain.

Although she'd always known that she would have to see her cousin again one day, she'd imagined an occasion when others would be present, obliging her to find a way to smile, be civil and pass on.

She had not bargained for this one-to-one confrontation, or that it would take place so soon—or here—on territory that should have been taboo.

She was surprised that the Count had not given private orders that Signora Alberoni was not to be admitted, but perhaps he'd not believed she would have the gall to simply—invite herself like this.

She was thankful that he was not returning to Vostranto until the following evening. She could only imagine his reaction if he'd arrived back to find his former mistress comfortably ensconced in his *salotto*.

That unaccountable pain stirred inside her again. She'd tried very hard not to think about Angelo and Silvia as lovers, but the gloating expression in her cousin's eyes had said more loudly than any words that she hadn't forgotten a thing about sharing his bed and his body.

That Silvia was able to recall all the kind of intensely intimate details about him—how it felt to be kissed by him, touched, taken in passion—that Ellie would never know.

That she didn't want to know, she corrected herself hastily, but which put her at a terrible disadvantage just the same.

She was aware too that she wasn't handling the situation particularly well, and that Silvia would be enjoying her discomfiture.

And the knowledge that Angelo had never brought his former mistress here in spite of some pretty heavy-duty wheedling was somehow very little comfort.

It was almost a relief when a tap on the door heralded the arrival of Assunta, with a maid following her, pushing a trolley laden with coffee and a lavish selection of biscuits, cakes and pastries.

'Dio mio.' Silvia's laugh sounded melodiously again. 'But how delicious! I am being so spoiled today.'

But you always have been, Ellie wanted to say. From birth, according to Nonna Vittoria. The baby visited in your cradle only by good fairies bringing you beauty, charm and uncritical love from all those around you. Making you believe that you could have anything you wanted, and live for yourself alone. And that, whatever you did, you would be forgiven.

And I signed up to that too, went along with it for all these years, even though Nonna—and later Madrina—tried to warn me gently to be careful. Because, even if I was always on your side, there was no guarantee you'd always be on mine. Why couldn't I see that?

Maybe that was why Nonna bequeathed the house at Porto Vecchio to me—because she knew that, some day, something you'd do would make me need a refuge.

Aloud, she said quietly, 'Assunta, please make sure that the Signora's driver is looked after.'

'Oh, I drove myself, *cara*,' Silvia informed her, shrugging. 'As I often do these days.' She turned a brilliant smile on the housekeeper. 'So you are the wonderful Assunta. Count Manzini has sung your praises to me so often.'

Assunta inclined her head in a manner that managed to be polite and sceptical at the same time, then withdrew leaving the maid Rosaria to pour the coffee into the exquisite bone china cups, and hand round the plates of delicacies, giving Silvia the opportunity to fuss with wistful sweetness over the calorific content of each offering.

'I have to be so careful of my figure for *caro* Ernesto's sake,' she sighed. 'A woman owes it to her husband to make the best of herself, don't you think so, Elena *mia*?' A comment which accompanied another disparaging look at what Ellie was wearing, and also took in the fact that her hair was drawn back and crammed into an elastic band at the nape of her neck.

I don't think Angelo would care particularly if I starved myself to death or ate until I burst, she thought, suppressing a silent sigh, and deliberately selecting a choux pastry oozing cream.

Even when Rosaria left and they were alone, there were thankfully no further inroads into the subject of Ellie's marriage, and Silvia reverted to talking about herself—parties she had attended, film premieres where she had been a guest, a fabulous new boutique, a miraculous new hairdresser.

'Such a pity you do not spend more time in Rome, *cara*. I could show you a whole new world.' Silvia delicately wiped some crumbs of almond cake from her fingertips and put down the linen napkin. 'But for now you can show me your world,' she added, a little smile playing around her lips. 'So—the full guided tour, if you please.' And paused before adding, 'Including, of course, the bedrooms.'

Ellie replaced her cup carefully on its saucer, swallowing down the silent scream rising inside her.

She said levelly, 'I'll ring for Assunta. She knows far more about the house's history than I do.'

Silvia pouted. 'If you wish, but I would rather hear it from you, the mistress of all this magnificence. And of its master, too.' She shook her head, as she rose, smoothing her dress over her hips with a languid gesture. 'Ella-Bella, the little mouse. Who would ever believe it?'

Well, I wouldn't for one, Ellie thought as she crossed the room and tugged at the embroidered bell pull beside the wide hearth. Because I know it couldn't be further from the truth. And so, I suspect, does she.

And wondered again why Silvia was there.

He still could not believe what he had done. It was ridiculous—impossible—almost making him doubt his own sanity.

Because all the arrangements had been in place. The carefully chosen flowers delivered that morning. The lunch reservation in the eminent restaurant of an exclusive hotel, with coffee served privately and discreetly in a suite on the first floor when the meal was over.

And he had talked to her and smiled, and let his eyes caress her, watching her lips part on a small indrawn breath as the first flush of overt desire warmed her smooth skin.

Beautiful, sexy and much more than willing, he'd thought pleasurably. Exactly the kind of recreation he needed after the long hours he'd been working to finalise the Galantana project, and a glorious end to the past weeks of celibacy.

Even now he couldn't be sure of the moment when it first occurred to him that it was not going to happen. Wasn't aware of having made the decision, or why he'd done so. He only knew, without a shadow of doubt, that when lunch concluded, there would be no delicious consummation between silk sheets, accompanied by five star brandy. That, in fact, he would be making an excuse and leaving. Regretfully, *naturalmente*, but quite definitely.

He'd seen her shock, her disbelief as she realised the promised seduction was not going to happen after all, then pride had come swiftly to her rescue—and to his. Even so, he'd gone out into the heat of the afternoon calling himself every kind of bastard.

He'd told his secretary that he would not be back in his office that day, so a return to his apartment seemed the obvious choice. And possibly a cold shower, he'd thought in self-derision.

Yet, for some reason, here he was, driving towards Vostranto.

Now I know I'm crazy, he thought bitterly. Because what kind of a welcome can I expect there?

He pulled the car over on to the verge, switching off the engine and staring ahead through the windscreen, his dark eyes moody. The image of a girl's face rose up in front of him, pale and strained, her soft mouth unsmiling, her eyes sliding nervously away from his. It had been the same each time they'd been together since the wedding, and the truth was that he was at a total loss to know how to ease the unhappy situation between them.

She was, he told himself, unreachable. At least by him. Not, of course, that he had wanted to reach her, he reminded himself swiftly. Not at the beginning when he'd dismissed her so contemptuously as a potential bride.

He'd soon realised, however, that his description of her as a nonentity had been unfair and unjustified. That she'd quickly demonstrated that she had a mind—and a will—all her own which she was prepared to pit against his.

Now, for the first time, he found himself wondering if there'd perhaps been someone else in her life. If his unwelcome intrusion had actually robbed her of a lover, for whom she was still grieving, and if that was why she continued to shrink from him—particularly on those few nightmare occasions when they shared a bed, and she lay a few feet away from him in a trembling silence that had nothing to do with sleep.

But no, he decided, his mouth twisting. If Elena had been in love, had given herself to another man, she would not have been considered by Zia Dorotea or his grandmother as a suitable candidate to become the Contessa Manzini. Which, for some unfathomable reason, she undoubtedly had been, long before Silvia Alberoni's machinations had forced them together so ludicrously.

Leaving him stranded in the unenviable position of being a husband but without a wife.

Although she was hardly to blame for that, he thought ruefully. In the time leading up to the wedding had he made any real attempt to woo her? To alleviate for her the humiliation of knowing that she was being married only to preserve a business deal and persuade her instead that, even if they could not expect marital bliss, they might achieve a working relationship with perhaps some attendant pleasure?

Then proved it by stealing her away from the *palazzo* and coaxing her somehow into letting him make gentle lingering love to her.

Yet, in reality, furious at being manipulated into such a proposal, he had instead stressed that their union was a strictly temporary arrangement which would be dispensed with swiftly and efficiently at the appropriate time. And that there would be no physical intimacy between them.

That was what he'd promised, and what, it seemed, he now had to live with.

Because there seemed little chance of any alteration in the *status quo*, he thought flatly. Indeed, the available evidence suggested that she was not even marginally attracted to him. That she might even dislike him or, which was worse, fear being alone with him.

It should never have come to this, he told himself bleakly. I should not have allowed it to happen. And I cannot let it go on.

With an abrupt sigh, he re-started the car and pulled out on to the road.

As he approached the next long bend, he heard the sound of another vehicle's horn, blowing in warning, and, with that, a lorry came round the corner in the act of being overtaken by a dark blue Maserati.

Angelo was already braking, his mind filled with a confused impression of the lorry driver's white face and a fist being shaken, as he swerved, swiftly and urgently, hearing the crunch of metal as his wing made glancing contact with a concrete block lying in the grass at the side of the road.

He stopped a few yards further on, and sat for a moment aware that he was shaking, his heart going like a trip-hammer. He'd had near misses before, but that was the closest he'd ever come to total disaster.

Santa Madonna, he thought. If I'd been doing any real speed…

He saw that the lorry had also come to a halt, and the driver and another man were running back to him.

The Maserati, however, had vanished.

As if on auto-pilot, he assured his anxious questioners that he was not injured, and that the damage to his car was slight. An annoyance only that could have been so much worse.

'And I did not even get the number of the car, *signore*.' The lorry driver shook his head in disbelief as he prepared to depart. '*Dio mio,*' he added from the heart. 'Women drivers!'

'Yes,' Angelo returned softly and grimly. 'Women drivers.'

Because he had recognised the car, so he already knew its number, and who had been at the wheel, and cold, burning anger was building inexorably inside him as he resumed his journey towards Vostranto, as well as a sense of grim determination.

Ellie watched Giorgio close the massive door, and listened with a sense of almost overwhelming relief as the car roared away down the drive, taking her unwanted guest away at last.

Feeling as if she'd been wrung out, mentally and emotionally, she turned to the major domo. 'I have a slight headache, Giorgio. I'm going to rest for a while.'

She refused his concerned offers of tea, painkillers or a cold compress for the forehead, and returned upstairs to the room she'd left only a few minutes before.

It hadn't changed in any material sense, but it was different all the same. Silvia still seemed to be there, scrutinising everything, insisting on seeing even the bathroom and the dressing room, where her eyes had narrowed at the display of clothes on the hanging rails.

'At least you will look the part in public, *cara*, if he ever allows you to be seen there with him,' had been the first comment to grate across Ellie's nerve endings.

No detail seemed too small to be spared a remark.

But the focus of her attention had been the bed. She'd stood, unmoving, staring at it in silence, a smile playing about her full lips until Ellie had wanted to scream.

She'd said at last, 'I am trying to imagine you in the act of surrender on this bed, but strangely I find it quite impossible. You still look so innocent—so sadly untouched, it makes me wonder if he has ever taken the trouble to consummate the marriage. He will have to do so eventually, *naturalmente*,' she continued musingly. 'It is his duty to his family to have a son, as I am sure Contessa Cosima has told him, so you can be of use for that, if nothing else. I wonder what has been holding him back? Maybe he still thinks of what might have been—with me.'

Ellie forced herself to meet Silvia's mocking gaze. To speak levelly, 'Why don't you ask him?'

The smile widened, and became laughter. 'I shall not have to, Elena *mia*. He will tell me himself soon enough.'

She'd gone to the door, then suddenly paused and walked back, bending to run a caressing hand across the magnificence of the bedcover.

Her voice had been quiet but very distinct. 'It isn't over yet, *cara*. You have to understand that. Because I still want him. And I shall have him, just as I would have done that night. Except he had to be punished. But now I think he has suffered enough—don't you?'

And she had smiled again and left, hips swaying in her red dress, her hair a golden coronet in the late afternoon sun, while Ellie followed, numb with disbelief and some other emotions not quite so easily defined.

Now looking at the bed, seeing again Silvia's possessive fingers stroking its cover as if they were someone's skin, she felt as if she'd been somehow coated in slime. And, for a moment, terribly afraid—as if the sun had gone out forever, leaving her in darkness.

Oh come on, she adjured herself impatiently. You've just had an unpleasant hour or so, and it's thrown you because your own cousin's become someone you only thought you knew.

But for the moment at least, she found she did not want to lie down on the bed, and having tried and failed to get comfortable on the *chaise longue*, she decided to attempt a different ploy.

She walked into the bathroom, shedding her clothes as she went, and turned on the shower, gratefully allowing its powerful cascade to stream over her, washing away the foam from the scented gel she'd applied to her skin and with it some of the tensions and sense of unease left in Silvia's wake. And, if she was honest, some of the pain too.

Some, but not all, she thought as she stepped dripping out of the cubicle, reaching blindly for a towel.

Only to find herself being firmly enveloped in a bath sheet, then carried, swaddled and helpless, back into the bedroom where she was set on her feet.

'*Buona sera*, my sweet wife,' Angelo said softly. 'Does a shower cure a headache? I did not know that.'

Her lashes felt gummed together by the water, but she prised them open somehow staring up at him with mingled anger and shock.

'What are you doing here?' she demanded breathlessly, stepping back and trying not to trip on the trailing bath sheet. Trying, too, not to blush and failing miserably. 'How dare you—walk in on me like that?'

The sculpted mouth curled. 'And how dare you invite your *sciattona* of a cousin here in my absence?' he retorted coldly. 'Did you think I would welcome such a guest—or simply hope I would not find out? I am waiting to hear.'

She'd had a rotten afternoon and now this—this hideous embarrassment of knowing he'd seen her naked for a second time. She longed for the floor to open and swallow her, but it was clearly not going to do so, so she lifted her chin defiantly. 'I do not have to explain myself to you, *signore*.'

'Think again,' he invited crisply.

'Most of your family have visited us here.' She was hardly able to believe she was saying these things. That she was being such an idiot. Almost as stupid, she thought mutinously, as he was arrogant. What right had he to—turn up out of the blue like this and challenge her? 'Am I not allowed to see my only living relative in return?'

'I am astonished you should wish to do so.' The dark gaze narrowed. 'Or do you have more in common than I thought? Did the pair of you perhaps work together to fool us all that night at Largossa?'

She wanted to slap him hard across the face for that, but her arms were confined inside her wrapping, and she dared not try to free them in case the beastly towel slipped or fell off altogether.

'Believe whatever you want,' she snapped. 'It makes no difference to me. Now will you please go and allow me some privacy.'

'Privacy?' Angelo queried derisively. '*Santa Madonna*, what has there ever been in this marriage but privacy?'

She stiffened defensively. 'I'm sorry if you're not satisfied with your bargain.'

'And you are?' He looked her over in such a way that the sheltering towel seemed, disturbingly, no longer to exist. 'Perhaps I no longer believe that.'

'As I said before—think what you wish.' She was beginning to shiver in the damp folds, and did not want him to conclude that she was trembling. That she feared him in any way.

But—there was something different about him today. His unannounced arrival in her room was not the kind of aloof, courteous behaviour to which she'd become accustomed. Besides, his whole attitude seemed edgy—challenging, and this change in him bewildered her. Made her—anxious.

She added in a low voice, 'Angelo—please go.'

'When I am ready,' he said. 'Also when you have told me the truth about your cousin. Why was she here? What did she want?'

The bald answer to that was—'You,' but Ellie hesitated to return it, instinct telling her that these were dangerous waters when she was already out of her depth.

She said quietly, 'She wished to see the house. And, of course, to laugh at me.'

Oh God, she thought, I didn't intend to say that.

His gaze sharpened. 'For what reason?'

She swallowed. 'Because I'm completely out of place here. And everyone must know this.'

He said slowly, 'Elena, you are the Contessa Manzini. There is not a soul beneath this roof who does not regard you with affection and respect.'

Except yourself…

Dismissing the thought, Ellie bent her head. 'How can you say that when they know—they all must know that we're only pretending to be married.' *And Silvia in particular…*

'Forgive me, but I did not think you would be concerned.' His voice was level. '*Dopo tutto*, you have never given that impression.'

She stared at the floor. 'Perhaps it was today—seeing Silvia here—looking again at the portraits of the previous Contessas in the *salotto* and the dining room and seeing how beautiful they were, just as she is.' She added bitterly, 'How they would all have known how to behave—what was expected of them all the time—instead of being a fish out of water like me.'

The hardness of his mouth relaxed a little, and he spoke more gently. 'Elena, let me assure you that you do not resemble any fish known to the mind of man.'

'I'm being serious!'

'I am glad to hear it, because it is time we spoke seriously.'

She still didn't look at him. She said with faint breathlessness, 'Is that why you're suddenly here in the middle of the week—to tell me that you've decided to end the marriage?'

For a brief instant, Angelo was sorely tempted to tell her the whole truth—that he'd been on the brink of spending an enjoyable afternoon in bed with a beautiful girl he'd met at a dinner party two nights earlier, but had suddenly changed his mind for reasons he could not explain even to himself.

That he'd decided to return home on another apparent whim, but that the incident on the road which could so easily have left him seriously injured or dead had turned an impulse into resolution.

Which now prompted him to offer her honesty along with the new beginning which had now crystallised in his mind.

Starting with the moment he had seen her standing naked in the shower, the tendrils of soaked hair hanging round her face, the droplets of water running down over the pale skin of her breasts to her midriff and the slight concavity of her belly, and glistening on her slender thighs.

Recalling too how his body had stirred under his sudden sharp desire to lick each tiny trickle from her flesh and watch her rosy nipples lift and firm to hard peaks under the glide of his tongue.

Had he forgotten, he wondered in astonishment, or had he simply not noticed on that far off night just how lovely she looked without clothing?

Then paused, just in time as he realised the exact nature of his prospective confession.

'Sciocco,' he apostrophised himself silently. *'Idiota.'*

Dio mio, his near-miss must have affected his brain if he imagined for one moment that might be what she wanted to hear from him.

No, he thought, it would be far better—wiser to use the opportunity she had given him, and, leaving all other issues aside, start by answering the question she had asked.

'No,' he said quietly. 'That is not why I am here. *Al contrario*.'

She looked up at that, her eyes widening, but, he thought, in apprehension more than pleasure, and took a swift mental step backwards.

He went on, 'I regret if my displeasure at your cousin's visit caused me to speak roughly to you.'

'It doesn't matter.' The grey-green eyes slid past him as if she was looking at the bed. 'Although you couldn't possibly imagine I would actually invite her here.'

'Perhaps, *mia bella*, I was not thinking too clearly. But I am a little more lucid now, and I have a proposition to put to you.'

He paused. 'Elena, I would like you to reconsider the terms of our marriage.'

She repeated 'Reconsider?' as if she had never heard the word before. Then: 'In what way—reconsider?'

'You said earlier that the other Contessas knew what was expected of them, and that is true. They were aware, *per esempio*, that a priority in their lives was to provide an heir for the Manzini dynasty, to ensure our ancient name did not die.'

She did not move. It was as if, he thought, she'd been turned to stone inside the towel that swathed her.

'And I have the same wish—the same dream of a son to follow me. I am asking you, therefore, to make our marriage a real one. To live with me as my wife, and become, in time, the mother of my child.'

She stared at him, lips parted, her gaze almost blank and he continued hurriedly, 'I do not require you to answer me now, Elena. I realise you need time to think.' He paused. 'I hope we can discuss the matter later—over dinner *forse*.'

He smiled at her swiftly and, he hoped, reassuringly, then turned and walked to the door.

Ellie watched him go, with a sense of total unreality, as Silvia's mocking words buzzed in her head. *'His duty to his family to have a son,'* her cousin had said. And *'You can be of use for that, if nothing else...'*

This is crazy, she thought. It cannot be happening to me. I must be having a bad dream while I'm sleeping off my headache.

And even if it was all true—if he'd really been here asking her to change her entire life, her hopes for the future—her answer, now and for all time, was 'No.'

What else could it possibly be? she asked herself. And felt tears, harsh and wholly unexpected, burn suddenly in her throat and blur her startled eyes.

CHAPTER EIGHT

WHEN SHE WAS calm again, Ellie washed the tearstains from her face, dried her hair, placed her discarded clothing in the linen basket, and put on her robe.

As she tied its sash, her attention was attracted by the noise of some heavy vehicle in the courtyard below. When she went to the window, she was surprised to see Angelo's car being loaded on the back of a transporter. As the truck departed with its load, there was a rap on the door, and Assunta entered carrying a pile of clean towels.

Ellie turned. 'Is there something wrong with the *signore*'s car, Assunta?'

The older woman stared at her, astonished. 'But it was damaged in the accident, Contessa. You must know that.'

'Accident?' Ellie queried, startled. 'I—I don't think I understand.'

Assunta shook her head. 'There was nearly a collision with another car overtaking when it should not have done so.' She crossed herself. 'The *signore* escaped without injury, may God be praised, through his own swift action. Otherwise he might have been killed.' She paused. 'Did he not tell you this?'

'No,' Ellie said slowly. 'He—didn't mention it.'

'Perhaps he did not wish to cause you concern.' Assunta's warm, inquisitive gaze scanned Ellie's slim figure, as if seeking for a reason for the Count to show such consideration to his young wife.

'Yes,' Ellie agreed quietly. 'Perhaps.'

'The Count wishes me to say that dinner will be served at eight o'clock this evening,' Assunta continued. 'After his ordeal, he will need an early night, *senza dubbio*.'

'Sì,' Ellie said after a pause. 'No doubt he will.'

When Assunta had delivered her towels to the bathroom and left, Ellie wandered back to the *chaise longue* and sat down, staring into space.

He might have been killed…

An uncontrollable shiver ran through her. Yes, she'd have had the promised freedom but at what kind of terrible cost? Didn't they say—Be careful what you wish for, because it could be granted?

She suddenly had an image of him standing in front of her, as he had been so short a time before. Could see the lean, long-legged body, his powerful shoulders undisguised by his elegant suit, the dark incisive face, the fathomless eyes and the swift, slanting smile as if they'd been etched on her brain.

Was aware of a tug of something which was almost like yearning, secret and unbidden, and which she had never experienced before. And could not afford to experience again.

A real marriage…

His words seemed to take on the impact of a siren song, with the power to beckon her to disaster, and she knew she could not allow that to happen.

He had married her from necessity not desire, and necessity was still driving him. It would be futile and dangerous to think otherwise.

At the same time, maybe she should re-think the bluntly negative response she'd been planning. Find some other way to tell him what he asked was impossible.

Silvia had said that she could not imagine her surrendering to Angelo on that bed. Well, she could not do so either. Could not, she told herself as her heart thundered against her ribcage. And would not.

Or not in the way he would undoubtedly have in mind.

Because she was simply a matter of expediency to him—as she always had been and always would be. And having his baby would be no different either. She would be little more than a surrogate mother. Stories in the papers suggested that women were well paid to use their bodies for such a purpose, but under strict terms and conditions.

She could formulate her own, she told herself. Rules to be strictly observed which would also safeguard her against harbouring any absurd fantasies about him, or about her role in his life.

And the price of her compliance would be her eventual escape from this meaningless existence that had been forced on her and the regaining of her freedom. That would be made totally clear.

For a moment, she quailed inwardly at the prospect of telling him, then rose, squaring her shoulders. After all, she thought, as long as he gets the heir he wants, why should he care? It may even be a relief.

She waited until it was almost eight o'clock before she ventured downstairs. To Donata's obvious disapproval, she'd insisted on wearing her plainest dress, a simple crossover style in white silk, and left her hair loose.

She found Angelo standing by the open windows in the *salotto*, looking broodingly over the gardens, a glass of his usual whisky in his hand. He turned as she entered, his brows lifting. '*Mia bella,*' he said softly. 'You look like a bride again.'

Ellie was taken aback. She'd meant to indicate that she hadn't taken any particular trouble with her appearance. That, for her, this was just—any evening. She said with constraint, 'That was not my intention.'

He clicked his tongue, his smile glinting. 'You disappoint me. Would you like a drink?'

'*Sì, grazie*. Some fresh orange juice.'

'You do not think the circumstances call for something stronger?' He added ice to the tumbler and brought it to her.

She took the drink with a word of thanks. 'I suppose you mean the circumstances of my learning from Assunta that you'd apparently escaped death by inches?' She kept her voice cool and level.

'*Sì*—among other things.'

The juice was sweet and refreshingly cold against her dry throat. 'Is that why you suddenly decided you needed a child to carry on your name? Why you no longer wanted to wait for the day when you'd be rid of me at last and able to find a wife more to your taste?'

His tone was reflective. 'It reminded me, *certamente*, how unexpected life can become—and how fragile. And that it is by no means certain that the future Contessa you describe even exists.'

'But you'll never know,' she said. 'Unless you try to find her.'

'Ah,' Angelo said softly. 'But that could take forever, and I also realised how unwise it is to allow time to—waste.' He paused. 'Besides, my decision was not as sudden as you may think.'

She said huskily, 'And if I say I still find it—unacceptable.'

'Then I shall try to persuade you to change your mind. I have not forgotten, *carissima*, how sweet your lips once tasted.' His gaze travelled slowly from her mouth down to the slender curves now hidden by the discreet vee of her neckline. 'I believe, with your permission, that I could make you happy.'

'A practical demonstration of your famed skill with women?' Ellie lifted her chin. 'I don't think so.'

There was another silence, then he said, 'I would not have described my intentions in those terms.'

'Then we must agree to differ. In any case, it hardly matters.' She took a deep breath. 'The truth is you wish me to have your child. We do not have to be—lovers in the usual sense to achieve this.'

He said, frowning, 'Perhaps I sustained some blow on the head this afternoon, for I find myself singularly stupid tonight. Have the goodness to explain what you mean, *per favore*.'

'You told me earlier you wished me to—live with you—as your wife.' She stared down at the melting ice in her glass.

'But I—I wouldn't find that acceptable. However, if you simply wanted to change the manner of your—visits to me at night in order to make me pregnant, I would agree to that. But only that.'

There was a further, more ominous silence, then Angelo said quietly and courteously, 'I am still not sure I understand you. At least,' he corrected himself, 'I hope I do not. Are you saying, *effettivamente*, that you will allow me occasional access to your body solely for the purpose of procreation?'

'Yes.' She did not look at him.

He said hoarsely, '*Santa Madonna*, Elena, you surely cannot mean that.'

'I do mean it,' she said. 'Those are my conditions for having your child, and ensuring the Manzini succession. They won't change.'

He took a step closer, his hand reaching out as if to stroke her cheek, and Ellie recoiled, her heart skipping a beat as she retreated a step. He must believe, she thought, that he would only have to touch her…

Angelo halted, the dark brows snapping together as he studied her. He said at last, 'So am I never to hope that we will spend our nights sharing a bed together—sleeping in each other's arms after we have made love?'

She bit down on her lip. 'Why not hope instead, *signore*, that I waste none of the time you mentioned, and give you a son very quickly.' She paused. 'And I'm quite sure your nights won't be lonely without me, so you could be getting the best of both worlds.'

'How curious you should think so.' He drank the remainder of his whisky with an angry jerk of the arm, then walked to the door, holding it open for her with exaggerated politeness. 'And now, my dear wife, shall we have dinner? After which, I shall, of course, avail myself of your unparalleled generosity. Or do I perhaps need your consent in writing first? No? Then—*avanti*!'

* * *

In spite of some formidable past competition, it was quite the most difficult meal she had ever eaten in his company.

Except that she didn't really eat it, but merely pushed the food round her plate as if doing so.

Angelo, however, much to her resentment, ate everything placed in front of him as though he did not have a care in the world, or a thought in his head besides the enjoyment of his cook's delicious food.

Afterwards, in the *salotto*, he swallowed his coffee as if his throat was lined with asbestos, then offered her a smile which did not reach his eyes.

'I think it is time to retire, *carissima.* I shall inform your maid that her services will not be required tonight. I look forward to joining you *prima possibile*.'

'As soon as possible.' The loaded words tormented her all the way upstairs to her room.

She undressed and washed, before slipping into one of the chiffon and lace nightgowns provided in her trousseau. Then, sitting at her dressing table, she began to brush her hair, just as she had done on her wedding night, seeking once again a tranquillity which was beyond her.

Maybe, she thought, swallowing, she should simply settle for courage instead. Or at least the ability to conceal she was trembling inside.

She had just put the brush down and got to her feet when Angelo came noiselessly into the room, wearing his usual black silk robe. He paused, looking her up and down, his mouth twisting.

'Is it not a little late for such modesty?' he asked ironically. 'Particularly when your virginity is about to be sacrificed.'

Colour burned in her face. 'Please,' she said in a low voice. 'Please don't say things like that.'

'Ah,' he said. 'I see. You may treat me as if I were the dirt on your shoe, but I must still behave with consideration. Is that it?'

Ellie stood where she was, looking wretchedly down at the floor, and heard him sigh, quickly and sharply.

He said, 'It is still not too late, Elena. We can forget everything that has been said today—put the last months behind us, if you will come to me now as my bride on our marriage night.' His voice was low and very gentle. 'Trust me, *mia cara*, with your innocence and, this first time, give yourself to me completely so that we can remember it with joy for the rest of our lives.'

Ellie walked to the bed, and slid under the covers, remembering with a stab of pain how Silvia's hand had touched them in possession. Had in the past touched *him*...

She kept her tone cool. 'I think you have enough memories, *signore*. I have no wish to add to your tally.'

For a moment, he was very still. When he spoke, his voice was harsh. 'I shall not ask again. Let it be as you wish.'

He flung off the robe and got into bed beside her, propping himself on an elbow as he looked down at her. He muttered what was undoubtedly an obscenity under his breath, then drew her towards him, under him, his hand stroking the skirts of her nightdress away from her body as he did so, before parting her thighs.

Eyes closed, Ellie experienced the first intimate touch of a man's fingers. She had quite deliberately made him angry, yet this initial exploration was gentler than she'd expected—or probably deserved—and she felt sudden shame mingled with another emotion, less easy to decipher.

Angelo sighed again, very quietly this time, and his other hand lifted to cup one small pointed breast through its veil of chiffon, his thumb moving softly, rhythmically against the nipple until Ellie pushed it fiercely away.

'Don't!'

'Carissima,' he whispered urgently. 'I am not some brute. Must I be denied one caress—or even a kiss?'

Yes, she thought, you must. Because I want to be able to protect myself by hating you, so that I'll never be tempted to allow you near me in any way or to want more than this.

But she said nothing and, after a brief hesitation, he reached for one of the pillows, and slid it under her hips, raising her towards him. He lifted himself above her, and she felt the velvet hardness of him in stark and powerful arousal between her thighs, and a shiver of apprehension ran through her at what she had invited.

She thought wildly—This can't happen. It's not possible. Then Angelo moved unhurriedly and with great precision, taking himself *there* to the hidden centre of her womanhood and beginning slowly and carefully to enter her, resting his weight on his clenched fists on either side of her body.

She heard his terse whisper warning her to relax.

Yet there was no pain. What disturbed her most was the total strangeness of the sensation—and the way her untried, unbidden flesh seemed so ready, even eager to yield in order to accommodate him and further his total possession of her.

She had not, she thought dazedly, bargained for that particular danger.

Although her eyes were still shut tight, some instinct told her that he was looking down at her, the dark gaze searching her face for signs of discomfort or fear, and she had to fight an almost overwhelming impulse to reassure him in some way. To touch his face, or his hair, maybe even to slide her arms round his neck.

Which, of course, was sheer madness, but, then, nothing that was happening seemed to be real. Except, she thought, for his body, which with one last measured thrust, was now completely sheathed inside hers. His voice saying quietly, 'Is it well with you, Elena? I need you to tell me.'

And her whispered, 'Yes.'

In spite of everything, he was trying to be kind, she thought, bewildered, even as some female instinct she'd not known she possessed told her that, if she had let him, he could have been so much more than that.

He began to move inside her, gently at first, then more forcefully, withdrawing a little, then pushing back ever more deeply, awakening new and threatening feelings. Making her realise with alarm she would have to fight her body's wish to respond to the imperative drive of his loins as their force increased.

That there was an unfamiliar tide rising in her bloodstream, her bones, her skin, nudging at every atom of her consciousness that threatened to overwhelm her, urging her to lift her hips in answer to each warm and silken thrust. To make demands that were all her own.

And then—it was over. She heard his breathing change, quicken. He threw back his head, his voice crying out harshly almost bitterly and she felt a spurt of scalding heat far within her. Then he was still and there was silence.

For a moment or two, Angelo remained where he was, head bent, chest heaving, sweat slicking the bronzed shoulders, then, with the same care he'd shown her when it began, he lifted himself away from her, lying supine at her side, one arm resting across his closed eyes.

Ellie lay still too, her heartbeat going crazy as she attempted to adjust to what had happened. The words, 'It could have been so much worse,' were running through her brain like a ribbon unwinding, but she was not sure she believed them. Instead, and with even greater difficulty, she had to face what might have been…

He had done exactly what she'd told him she would accept, she thought. No more, no less. She had faced him and won, so why did she suddenly feel as if she had lost? Because that made no sense—no sense at all.

She turned her head slowly to look at him just as Angelo sat up abruptly, swinging his legs to the floor, and reaching down for his discarded robe.

'Congratulations, Elena.' He tossed the words over his shoulder. 'You have survived your ordeal with great fortitude. Let us hope for both our sakes that you will soon have good news for me, so that you are never called upon to endure it again.'

She watched him walk to the door. Her lips parted to say something—she wasn't sure what, it might have been just his name—then the door closed behind him, and she realised it was too late.

Too late, she repeated silently, and turned over, burying her face in the pillow.

The following April

She had learned long ago how to conduct herself at all these social events which Angelo required her to attend at his side.

Had mastered how to walk in with her hand resting lightly on his arm, and her smile already nailed securely in place. To offer all the appearance of a cherished young wife blissfully approaching the first anniversary of her wedding to one of the most glamorous men in the city. And to dazzle them with the diamonds and other jewels that would be regarded as an overt sign of Count Manzini's satisfaction with his marriage.

Knowing that none of the eyes watching them—friendly, inimical, admiring or jealous—must be allowed to catch even a glimpse of the reality of her abject failure and his bitter disappointment. Their mutual ongoing nightmare.

Tonight—a charity reception which Contessa Cosima was helping to host in aid of an orphanage—was an occasion like any other. She moved slowly round the room, slender in her black dress, the drink in her hand virtually untouched, pausing to greet acquaintances, to laugh and talk for a while before moving on, her timing immaculate, her appearance serene.

But underneath it all, her stomach was churning as she contemplated the end of the evening, the return to Vostranto and, later still, the promise of her husband's brief, monthly visit to her bedroom, conducted as always with cool efficiency and dispatch. Her terms strictly adhered to in every respect. The only verbal exchange between them Angelo's polite enquiry about her physical comfort as he took her.

Also just an occasion like any other, she told herself, her throat tightening. That was how she had to look at it, anyway, even when it could mean going to him eventually to tell him she had not conceived this time either. Just as she'd done every month up to now.

But maybe it wouldn't be like that, she thought. Maybe tonight, Nature would relent and her magic trick would work, as it had done only a few weeks ago for Tullia.

And if Ellie's delighted congratulations to her friend had

concealed different emotional strata, she was the only one who'd known it.

'And you, too, must have a baby very soon, Elena,' Tullia had declared buoyantly, hugging her. 'Then the children can play together.'

Zia Dorotea had sniffed and looked on the verge of launching some tart remark, but subsided after meeting Nonna Cosima's steady look.

Tonight, Angelo's grandmother was seated in a high-backed chair at the side of the room, and she smiled and beckoned when she saw Ellie.

'*Mia cara*, I wish you to meet my dear friend, Mother Felicitas. She is the superior of the Daughters of the Nativity who run the orphanage for us.'

The woman beside her was small and rosy-cheeked with sparkling dark eyes, wearing an ankle-length grey dress and a crisply starched white headdress and veil.

'This is a great pleasure, Contessa.' An appraising glance accompanied her handshake. 'We have always been blessed by the support of the Manzini family, and your godmother, the Principessa Damiano is another benefactor.'

She smiled. 'I am told that, unlike the Count's late mother and grandmother, you are a working wife, but I hope that in the future we can also persuade you to find time in your busy life for us. It would be an honour.'

Ellie coloured faintly. 'I—I'd really like that. Although I've never had a great deal to do with children.'

'But all that will change for you soon, I expect.' Mother Felicitas's glance was kind as she rose to her feet. 'That is life's way.'

'Yes,' Ellie agreed quietly. 'I—I hope so.'

'I must go now,' the nun added. 'Good night, my dear Cosima, and thank you for all you do for our children. Please bring Count Angelo's charming wife to visit us soon. We would be so delighted.'

'Come and sit with me, my child,' Nonna Cosima said when

Mother Felicitas had gone. 'You look a little pale this evening. You are not working too hard?'

'I don't think so.'

'Angelo is spending longer hours at Galantana than anyone can remember,' his grandmother continued musingly. 'And still using his apartment in the city while he does so, it seems.' She paused. 'I hope you are making time for each other in all this ceaseless industry. That is what a marriage needs, dearest girl, in order to succeed.'

Ellie bent her head. 'It also requires a couple who love each other,' she said in a low voice. 'And who weren't forced together for the sake of some outmoded convention.'

'Is that how it still seems to you?' Cosima Manzini queried softly. 'I am sorry to hear it.' She gave a faint rueful smile. 'I would not deny that my grandson has serious flaws, but I had hoped that, by now, he might have found a way of recommending himself to you as a husband, Elena. That you would be building a life together.'

Whereas, thought Ellie with a pang, we've never been further apart. And the fact that Angelo spends so much time in Rome should be a relief, but in another way it's sheer torture.

Because I know the way we live at Vostranto—the fact that there's no real intimacy in our lives and that the time we've spent in bed together since we were married can probably be measured in hours—and I realise that can't possibly be enough for him.

Because he's a man who has needs that I wouldn't know how to fulfil, even if I wanted to, and when I'm with him at a function like this, or at a dinner party and I see how the women look at him, I find, in spite of myself, that I'm wondering where he really spends his nights in Rome—and with whom.

Whether any of the girls who smile and chatter to me are really laughing at me behind my back—the dull wife, not only betrayed but apparently barren too.

And I'll wonder tonight, as I always do when he comes to me, if he's secretly glad not to have to pretend a desire he doesn't feel. Then I'll close my eyes and dig my nails in the palms of my hands and keep very still trying not to think of anything at all—or feel anything at all which is getting more and more difficult each time. And when he goes back to his own room and I'm alone, I'll lie awake for hours, trying not to cry, or—even worse—to follow him and ask—beg…

She looked down at her hands, clasped tightly in her lap. 'I don't think that's really feasible. We just aren't—suited to each other.'

'I am grieved to hear you say it.' Nonna Cosima's voice was very quiet. 'You see, *mia cara*, we thought long before that night at Largossa—your godmother and I—Dorotea too—that you would make Angelo an ideal wife. That you would find your match in each other.' She sighed. 'It seems we were not as clever as we thought.'

Ellie was silent for a moment, then she said, stumbling a little, 'Did Angelo also know what you thought—what you wanted?'

The older woman hesitated 'Dear child, it was no secret that his family—his friends felt it was high time he was married.'

'But I—I'd been—suggested?'

'Mentioned, perhaps, no more.'

'I see.' Ellie rose, smoothing her dress. 'It—explains a great deal.' *And makes me understand why there was really no escape—for either of us…*

'Elena.' Nonna Cosima took her hand, her eyes anxious. 'Promise me that Angelo is not unkind to you.'

'No,' Ellie returned after a pause. 'Under the circumstances, he's very—considerate. And generous too.' She touched fleetingly the diamonds in her ears and at her throat, forcing a smile. 'I really have nothing to complain about.'

She bent and kissed the scented cheek, smiled again in what she hoped was reassurance, then walked away.

Her circuit of the room completed, and her duty done, she looked round for Angelo and saw him several yards away, head slightly bent while he listened with rapt and smiling attention to what was being said to him. As she started towards him, the groups of people around him moved slightly, giving her a clearer view and she realised that his companion was Silvia, standing so near him that their bodies were almost touching as she looked up into his eyes, lips pouting, and one crimson tipped hand resting on his sleeve as if to emphasise the closeness of their association.

Ellie halted, shocked and turned away abruptly, nearly cannoning into a waiter carrying drinks. She muttered an apology then tossed the remaining wine in her glass down her throat before grabbing another from the tray, and swallowing a third of its contents in one gulp before heading for one of the long windows that had been opened on to the balcony beyond.

It had rained earlier, and there was a freshness in the air to combat the traffic fumes from the streets below. Ellie leaned on the wrought iron rail, aware of a trembling sensation in the pit of her stomach.

Her husband, she thought, with Silvia—as if time had somehow rolled back and they had regained their former intimacy. But how could it have happened?

Since her unexpected descent on Vostranto the previous year, and the quarrel that it had provoked, her cousin's name had not been mentioned. Nor had she been encountered at any of the social events that Ellie had attended, largely, she'd supposed, because Silvia would not find the company sufficiently entertaining.

Yet here she was at the kind of function she would normally have avoided. Unless, of course, she had good reason to be there…

Ellie took another mammoth swallow of wine, feeling the jolt of it curl down to her toes, although it didn't totally dispel that strange inner shaking as she'd hoped.

It was one thing to tell herself that Angelo would not feel obliged to remain faithful, and quite another to face the reality of his betrayal of his marriage vows—and with Silvia.

Did her cousin simply have to crook her little finger and watch him come running? she asked herself, anger building inside her. Was Angelo's desire for her so overwhelming that he could now overlook everything else that had happened—the selfish, vengeful trick she had played on both of them?

'Well,' she said aloud. 'If so, I don't have to wait around and watch.'

She finished the last of her wine, left the glass on a convenient ledge, and, feeling oddly empowered, walked back into the room and headed for the door.

A hand fell on her arm, halting her. 'Where have you been?' Angelo demanded. 'I have been looking for you.'

'I've been playing the part of your wife,' she said. 'And now I'm going to have the car brought round and go home.'

'Without a word to me?' His brows lifted. 'How was I supposed to get back to Vostranto?'

'I intended to leave a message. And I imagined you would spend the night in Rome,' she said. 'As you so often do.'

He said silkily, 'Not when I have one of my rare appointments with you, *mia bella*. An occasion not to be missed, believe me.'

'Indeed? Then I'm afraid, for once, you'll have to excuse me.'

His mouth curled. 'You are developing a headache, perhaps? The usual reason for a wife to evade her husband's attentions.'

'No,' she said, forcing her voice to speak coolly, dispassionately. 'Nothing like that. I've simply decided I just can't do this any more. And therefore I'd prefer to be alone tonight.'

'And if I wish to adhere to my own preferences?'

There was a note in his voice she'd never heard before, but her eyes were steady as they met the anger in his. Her tone was level too. 'Then your *signoria* will have to use force. Or accept that we're better apart.'

'Yes,' he said. 'Perhaps that would be safer—for tonight at least. So, I shall not detain you further.' He stepped back, making her a slight formal bow. *'Arrivederci, carissima.'*

'Goodnight,' Ellie whispered, and went to the door, fighting an impulse to look back and see if he was watching her leave.

Or whether he had already turned away in search of Silvia.

Because that was something she found she could not bear to know.

CHAPTER NINE

SHE AWOKE SLOWLY, and lay for a moment totally disorientated, staring at plain white walls and spring sunlight lying slatted across the polished boards of the floor, wondering why the bed was so much narrower, and why Donata was not here opening the shutters and bringing her morning coffee.

Of course, she thought. I must have been having a dream about Vostranto. That's what threw me. But I'm actually at Casa Bianca. I drove down to Porto Vecchio yesterday. And I'm not going back.

A week had passed since the night of the reception. Seven days and nights had come and gone without a word from Angelo. He was in Rome, and she was at his house in the hills, but the real distance between them covered continents rather than miles.

'Better apart' she had told him, and it seemed that he now agreed with her, she'd told herself as she roamed restlessly round Vostranto. That he accepted that they should put an end to this ill-assorted marriage and start their lives again.

After all, she reasoned, there was nothing to keep them together, not even the hope of a baby, and she would agree without argument to whatever means he chose to achieve their mutual freedom.

She had her work—almost more than she could handle if she was honest—and she would find another apartment somewhere in the city. Re-start her life as it had been, and find some peace. Regard the last months as a mistake—serious but not irretrievable.

She'd tried very hard during his absence not to think about him. Not to wonder where he was and what he did once the working day was over. Above all, she worked on not speculating who he might be with, especially now that she had the image etched on her mind of Silvia's hand curling possessively round his sleeve to go with that other memory of her standing smiling at the bed she planned to share with him, as she'd done from the first.

Angelo must have decided that, in spite of everything she'd done, her cousin was the woman he really wanted. That she was too deep in his bloodstream for him to turn away again, and he would forgive her as everyone had always forgiven Silvia, because beauty was its own excuse.

He must genuinely love her, Ellie thought. And, in the end, that was all that mattered. Wasn't it? She had to believe it was true, anyway.

And she—she would be Ellie Blake again, instead of this strange manufactured creature masquerading as the Contessa Manzini. She'd always felt that she was filling someone else's shoes, and, no matter how she'd been dressed up, she'd never looked the part as Silvia, beautiful, stylish and totally single-minded, undoubtedly would.

She could only hope that her cousin would love Vostranto as much as she'd done and be content there, rather than regarding it as just another glamorous Manzini asset and hankering for the hectic social life of the city.

But that, she thought, would not be her problem. And perhaps, because she'd won as she always insisted on doing, Silvia's attitude would change.

Whatever, there was nothing now to hold Angelo back from pursuing her again. He'd got his investment and the Galantana expansion was forging ahead, so the prospect of scandal over her divorce from Ernesto would no longer be of any great concern.

And Ellie resolved that she would play her part—assuring

her godmother and Prince Damiano that her marriage to Angelo would never have worked in a thousand years. Making it clear that it was no-one's fault, that as a couple they would always be chalk and cheese, oil and water, so that bringing the whole unfortunate fiasco to an end had to be the best solution for all involved.

That she herself found the decision an actual relief.

All the same, there would be anger, she knew and disappointment. She could imagine Nonna Cosima's sadness, and Madrina's bewilderment, while Zia Dorotea would have a field day, apportioning blame indiscriminately, and hoped they could understand why she had gone without saying goodbye to them.

Because she could never, ever explain why it had all become so impossible. Why she could no longer endure the dutiful ritual that might lead to conception from a man whose desires and passions had always been focussed elsewhere.

She could not even define to her own satisfaction why it had been so necessary for her to be the one to put an end to it all and walk away, and told herself it had to be pride.

Or perhaps it was the terse communication she'd eventually received from him by email, informing her that he would be returning at the weekend, because matters could not continue in this way between them and there were things that must be said.

She had sat staring at it, scanning the message over and over again, before pressing the delete button, because she knew these would be things she could not bear to hear.

Even if their marriage had been doomed from the outset, she'd played her part in its failure, she'd thought, as she went upstairs to begin preparations for her departure. And she could give no hint to anyone—Angelo least of all—that the prospect of Silvia's triumph was like the intolerable pain of a knife being turned in an open wound.

When she'd come down with her travel bag, smiling cheerfully, she'd told a concerned Assunta merely that she intended to have a little holiday, but her plans were fluid, and she was not sure when she would return. Which, she thought, was her only untruth.

And there had, of course, only ever been one place to come to.

She sat up slowly in the bed, pushing back her hair, looking round the familiar room. The cottage had always been her refuge, and never more so than now. It was her own space, she thought, with no disturbing resonances of anyone else.

As she pushed back the covers, she saw the faint pale mark on her finger where her wedding ring had been. She never wore it when she came down here, anyway, because it belonged to another life, which, for a short while she was leaving behind her.

But, this time she was going for good, so she'd left it in Angelo's bedroom with all the other jewellery he had given her, and her handwritten letter telling him simply that in view of the disaster their marriage had become, she was leaving in order to save them both further embarrassment and unhappiness. She added in conclusion that she wanted nothing from him except the legal dissolution of their relationship, and that she wished him well for the future.

She'd brought away little more than the clothes she stood up in. The designer gear on the padded silk hangers had never been her choice anyway, so she wouldn't miss it, and besides there was plenty of stuff here in the cupboard and drawers that suited her purpose far better—cotton skirts, pants and tops and some swimwear, although, admittedly, it was rather too early in the year for sea-bathing.

She padded barefoot out of the bedroom in her brief cotton nightshirt, and walked to the kitchen. Signora Alfredi, the stout elderly widow next door, who kept an eagle eye on Casa Bianca when Ellie was not there, had left a bag of groceries on the kitchen table, including some bread, sliced ham, eggs and a pack of coffee, so breakfast was taken care of.

Later, she would supplement her supplies at the local shops, and, for lunch, she would probably see what the fishing boats had brought in. Then, tonight, she would eat as usual in the little *trattoria* on the quayside, where Santino and Maria would welcome her back.

My routine, she thought, spooning coffee into the machine. Sweet and reassuringly familiar. As if I'd never been away and the last wretched months had never happened. This is what I need. And it's all I need.

Yet in spite of her resolution, it was a couple of days before Casa Bianca began to work its usual magic. She slept poorly for one thing, and was glad she could not remember her dreams. Also she found it difficult to concentrate on her work, making elementary and annoying mistakes.

After one particularly trying session, she decided to close down her laptop and get some fresh air to see if that would get rid of the cobwebs in her mind.

On the way out, she called at Signora Alfredi's house to pick up her dog, Poco, who was her usual companion on such walks. He was an odd-looking little animal, with a round amiable face, drooping ears, a long body and short legs, and he possessed seemingly boundless energy. However, the Signora's health and increasing girth meant she could not give him the exercise he needed, so this had become a task which Ellie gladly assumed when she stayed at the cottage.

He scampered happily beside her along the promenade and down the shallow flight of wooden steps to the almost deserted beach, then took off like a rocket along the sand with a bark of sheer joy, eventually returning with a piece of stick that Ellie was required to throw for him. A game, experience told her, that she would tire of long before he did.

In spite of a breeze from the sea, there was real heat in the sun today, and she moved her shoulders pleasurably inside her thin shirt as she walked along the edge of the water, watching the golden light dance on its ripples.

When Poco returned from his umpteenth foray, once more dropping his stick expectantly at her feet, she picked it up and, slipping off her espadrilles, ran laughing into the shallows, splashing along regardless of the soaking of her white cut-offs as the dog chased her, yapping excitedly, leaping up to retrieve his treasure which she was holding teasingly just out of reach.

Suddenly she felt exhilarated, the sense of freedom she'd longed for actually within reach as she danced in and out of the water, singing to herself.

When eventually, she turned to run back the way she'd come, something made her glance up at the promenade, and, in the blinding dazzle of the sun, she seemed to catch a glimpse of a man's dark figure standing there motionless, as if watching her. Blinking, she put up a hand to shield her eyes, but when she looked again there was no-one there.

I can't sleep, she thought in self-derision, and now I'm seeing things. Time to get a grip, Ellie my dear.

She threw the stick for Poco one last time, then called him to heel and went home.

The *trattoria* was busy that evening, enjoying its usual brisk local trade. Ellie made her way to her corner table, acknowledging the smiling greetings from other diners, and sat down, in the comfortable certainty that Santino would soon appear with her Campari and soda.

The plate of mixed meats that would precede her asparagus risotto had just been placed in front of her when she became aware that the hum of conversation around her had suddenly stilled—that something like a *frisson* had run through the crowded room.

She looked up and saw the reason, her eyes widening involuntarily.

He was standing in the doorway, glancing round him, relaxed and faintly smiling as he took in his surroundings. Assured and undeniably good-looking, she summarised him objectively, as if completing some mental check list. Casually but expensively dressed. And sexy in a way that transcended mere looks. Even across a crowded room.

Someone she'd never seen at Santino's before—or anywhere else in Porto Vecchio for that matter, otherwise she'd have remembered, along with every other woman in the room.

But however memorable, he was simply not her type, she told herself, dismissively. Experience, it seemed, had the distinct advantage of conferring immunity.

Although, to give him his due, the newcomer seemed oblivious to the effect he was having on the female clientele at large.

Ellie decided that he must be staying at the big white hotel on the promontory, which was pricey and fairly formal and had just re-opened for the summer. Quite a few of its residents, especially the foreign tourists, eventually found their way down to the port in search of less stuffy surroundings. But not usually so early in their stay, she thought drily, then realised with shock that he was strolling towards her corner.

Oh, no, she thought with sudden breathlessness. This couldn't be happening. It wasn't possible…

'Buona sera, signorina.' The swift charm of his smile touched her like a finger stroking her cheek as she looked up, stiffening defensively. 'As we are both unaccompanied tonight, I hope you will allow me to join you.'

'No! I mean—I don't think so.' She set down her glass with something of a jerk. 'I'd prefer to be alone, thank you.'

His shrug was graceful. '*Che peccato.* I am desolated.' He paused. 'Do you think you might relent by the time coffee is served?'

She swallowed. 'I'm afraid I won't be staying that long, but—but have a pleasant meal,' she added almost wildly.

'I am sure I will,' he returned. 'But it could have been a delight.'

Very smooth, Ellie thought stonily, as he walked away and she addressed herself to the Parma ham on her plate. But cuts no ice with me.

All the same, she'd found the incident disturbing, even though she felt she'd handled it well, letting him see that any approach was unacceptable. But it was annoying that the only free table was right in her sightline against the opposite wall, so that she only had to look up to see him there. And to find that, most of the time, he was looking right back at her, his gaze intent, even considering.

He has no right to do that, she thought smouldering. No right at all. Why couldn't he have stayed where he belonged—up at the hotel or—wherever?

However, she was careful to complete her meal without undue haste, choosing *panna cotta* served with a fruit *coulis* for dessert, then paid her bill and left, staring rigidly ahead to ensure there was not one more atom of eye contact. Safely outside, she was almost tempted to run, but told herself she was being ridiculous.

For one thing, the newcomer was far too occupied with Santino's *pollo Milanese*, while, for another, and more importantly, he had almost certainly got the message by now. For his kind, making a beeline for any single woman in his orbit was a mere reflex action like breathing, and she'd be stupid to read any more into it than that.

It was just that it had been—so unexpected. Nothing like it had ever happened to her before. And she could not risk getting involved.

The wisest course would be to pretend it had never happened at all. Anyway, if he began to be a real nuisance, she would only have to tell Santino, and he would be instantly warned off. Porto Vecchio, after all, was full of people who remembered Nonna Vittoria with deep affection.

But it would not come to that. He was probably not used to rejection, especially in public, she thought as she let herself into the house, but it would do him a world of good. So, tomorrow night, with luck, he would eat back at his hotel, giving up as a bad job any random thoughts he might still be harbouring about her.

Although she hadn't the least idea why he should, she thought, examining herself critically in her bedroom mirror. She hadn't changed and suddenly become a beauty—an object of desire to an attractive man. And it wasn't as if she'd looked affluent wearing an old blue dress, much loved but faded by the sun, and with plain silver studs in her ears. So there'd been no reason for him to wish to spend even five minutes with her.

It makes no sense, she told herself. No sense at all. But it's over, so what does it matter?

She considered eating at home the following night, but told herself she'd be stupid to allow herself to be pressured out of her favourite restaurant on the off-chance some visiting glamour-boy might be present. And even if he did dine at Santino's, he would be unlikely to try again and risk a further snub.

And, in the event, he did not turn up, so she'd been worrying—if that was the word—about nothing. Though that had not prevented her looking up nervously each time anyone came into the *trattoria*.

Behaving like a cat on hot bricks, she derided herself, over someone who'd probably moved on by now to look for more excitement.

But she was mistaken as she discovered the following morning when she was on the beach with Poco and saw him walking towards them, long muscular legs and bronze arms displayed in shorts and a polo shirt.

'Buongiorno,' he greeted her pleasantly as he halted, looking up at the sky. 'They say it will rain later. Do you think so?'

'It's unlikely,' Ellie said shortly and would have walked on, except he'd crouched down, snapping his fingers and Poco, the treacherous mutt had gone straight to him and was lying across his sandaled foot, waving his paws in the air.

'Your dog at least seems to like me, *signorina*,' he commented as he gently rubbed the proffered tummy. 'What is his name?'

'He's my neighbour's dog,' Ellie said coldly. 'And his name is Poco.'

'An odd choice. He is hardly as small as all that.'

Ellie bit her lip. 'She told me she called him that because when he was a puppy, she asked his breed and they told her "A little of this and a little of that."'

'I think they told the truth.' He got lithely to his feet, tucking

Poco under his arm. 'My new friend and I are going to the *caffe* by the church. Would you care to come with us?'

'No, of course not!'

He said briskly, 'Then you had better tell me where you live so I can deliver Poco safely home when we have finished our refreshments.'

'But you can't do that,' Ellie said stormily.

'What is to prevent me? I wish it.' He gently pulled one of Poco's ears, and had his hand licked. 'And he is perfectly willing.'

'He's not your dog.'

'Nor yours, it seems. And I need my coffee,' he added. 'If you are so concerned for Poco's welfare, I suggest you join us.'

He set off across the sand to the promenade, and Ellie followed, angry to feel so helpless but knowing she had no choice, because there was no way she would allow him near Casa Bianca, whatever the excuse.

When they were seated at a table on the pavement, and she'd been served with a filter coffee while he chose espresso and a sweet roll which he shared with Poco who'd been brought a bowl of water, Ellie said tautly, 'Are you doing this to punish me?'

His brows lifted. 'For what?'

She met his gaze defiantly. 'For refusing to have dinner with you, of course.'

'Is the coffee here so bad it ranks as punishment?' He sounded faintly amused. 'I don't think so.'

'Then—why?'

'It is quite simple. The other morning, I saw a girl laughing and dancing in the sea as if she did not have one care in the world. I wanted to find out what could have prompted such happiness.'

So, she had not imagined that she was being watched. It was a disturbing thought and she made herself drink some coffee before she answered. 'I think—realising that I didn't have to be unhappy any longer.'

'What made you so sad?'

She looked away, her heart hammering. 'I don't want to discuss it.'

'Ah,' he said softly. 'Then it is a man.'

'No,' she denied swiftly. 'Or—not in the way you think.'

This is dangerous, she thought with a kind of desperation. I shouldn't be here. I shouldn't be doing this. I ought to leave the coffee, grab Poco—and go. Talking to him like this—being with him—is madness that I can't afford.

'How do you know what I think, *signorina*?'

'I don't,' she said. 'I don't know you, *signore*, or anything about you. And I'd prefer to keep it that way.' She rose. 'Now, Signora Alfredi will be wondering where we are, so if you'll excuse me...'

'On one condition,' he said. As she passed his chair to retrieve the dog, he put a hand on her arm. 'That you have dinner with me tonight.'

'That's quite impossible.' She looked down at the darkness of the tanned fingers against the comparative pallor of her own skin, her throat tightening uncontrollably. 'And don't touch me—please.'

His hand lifted immediately, unquestioningly. 'But we both have to eat,' he said. 'Shall we meet at the *trattoria* at nine, or should I collect you from your house?'

'No!' The word sounded almost anguished, and she paused, taking a deep breath. Be careful, she thought. Be very careful. 'Anyway, you don't know where I live.'

'It would not be hard to discover.' He smiled faintly. 'Maria at the restaurant has a romantic heart, I think.'

Romantic... The word seemed to judder in her mind.

She said, her voice taut, 'Please understand, *signore*, that there is no possibility of—romance between us, and there never will be.'

He leaned back, the dark eyes speculative. 'But, *signorina*, how can you be so sure?'

She scooped up a wriggling Poco. 'Because I am married,' she said stonily. 'And one bitter experience is quite enough in anyone's lifetime. Does that answer your question? Now please leave me alone.'

And she walked away, without looking back.

She was restless all day, unable to settle to the translation work awaiting her attention, or, if she was honest, to very much at all. And she didn't need this kind of distraction, she told herself angrily. She'd come here for peace and quiet. To find herself again. Perhaps even—to heal…

Not to engage in a reluctant battle of wits with someone she didn't know—and didn't want to know.

She was tempted to pack her bag, lock up Casa Bianca, walk up to the square where her car was parked—and go.

But where? Not back to Vostranto, that was for sure. And turning up at the Palazzo Damiano would involve a lot of questions she would prefer not to answer—or not immediately.

Besides, why should she be the one to leave? She belonged here and he most certainly didn't. So, he had no right to intrude like this and turn her small private world upside down. Amusing himself at her expense by this—totally meaningless pursuit.

A man, she thought, fuelling her resentment, who'd never learned to be kind, because he hadn't found it necessary. Who was accustomed, instead, to using his surface attraction in order to gain easy favour. And wasn't used to taking 'no' for an answer.

Only, it wasn't going to work. Not with her. So he could just—pack his designer luggage and move on. Go back to playing his games with people who knew the rules.

But until he did so, she was damned if he was going to turn her into a prisoner in her own home. Or a fugitive.

Yes, she would eat at the *trattoria* tonight, she decided, squaring her slender shoulders, because that was how she lived when she was here, and his presence would not deter her, or the probability that he would manoeuvre her somehow into sharing his table.

And if that prospect, and the memory of their previous

encounters, was preventing her concentration on the job in hand, she would find something else to occupy her.

With a suggestion of gritted teeth, she embarked on a heavy-duty clean of the living room, moving furniture, scrubbing the floor and even washing walls, before moving on to the kitchen, the shower room and finally her bedroom. The two empty rooms at the rear of the cottage which in Nonna Vittoria's day had provided the accommodation for family holidays she decided to leave for another day.

When evening came, she showered and washed her hair, drying it to hang casually loose and shining round her face, then dressed in slim white cotton pants, and a dark red top even more elderly than the blue dress. She reached for her scent spray only to put it back, unused, together with her cosmetic bag.

This rendezvous was not of her choosing, she reminded herself, viewing herself with indifference, so there was no compulsion to make an effort. Exactly the opposite, in fact.

She walked slowly to the restaurant, her hands clenched into fists in her pockets as she strove for an appearance of composure.

He was there, as she'd known he would be, seated at a table set for two with flowers, candles lit, and chilled white wine, while Maria, of the romantic soul, waited, eyes dancing to usher her there.

He got to his feet, relaxed in chinos and a white shirt, its cuffs rolled back over his forearms, his smile glinting.

He said softly, 'So you came. I was not sure that you would.'

'Really?' She took her seat. 'Now I'd have said you'd never suffered a moment's uncertainty in your entire life, *signore*.'

'Then perhaps you should not judge by appearances, *signorina*.' He paused. 'But must we be so formal?' He offered her a swift smile. 'My name is Luca. And yours?'

Her hesitation was palpable. 'It's—Helen,' she said at last. The English version of her name, she thought, that only her parents had used. Something to hide behind.

He inclined his head. '*Buonasera*, Helen. It is good to meet you.'

She looked down at the white cloth. 'It's hardly the first time.'

'Then let us make it so.' He signalled to Santino, who came to pour the cold, sparkling wine into the waiting flutes. He added softly, 'To your good health,' as he raised his glass.

The wine tingled against the dryness of her mouth and throat. She said huskily, 'I don't know what I'm doing here. This is such a mistake.'

'Why do you say that?'

She stared at the bubbles in her glass. 'You—you already know.'

'Ah,' Luca said. 'Because you are married.' He reached out and took her hand, his thumb smoothing the pale band of skin where her wedding ring had been. 'But it is not an easy thing to remember.'

His touch was infinitely light, but it seemed to rip through her, making her heart pound unevenly, and she pulled her hand away, flushing. 'You've also forgotten that I—asked you not to touch me.'

'But that, I think, is impossible.'

She swallowed. Her voice was a thread. 'Then let me tell you this. Whatever you think is going to happen between us—you're wrong.'

'So, I shall have to live with disappointment,' he said lightly. 'However, we can still enjoy our food, I hope. I ordered for us in advance, *mia bella*—linguine with mussels and roasted sea bass. Do you approve?'

She bent her head. 'It sounds—delicious.'

'Good.' He raised his glass again, the dark gaze intent, almost reflective in the candlelight. 'Then, *buon appetito*, Helen—for this—and whatever else tonight may bring. Even if it is—nothing.' And he drank to her.

CHAPTER TEN

'SO,' LUCA SAID, sampling the *zabaglione* which he'd chosen for their dessert. 'Tell me about your husband.'

Ellie put down her spoon, startled. His behaviour over the meal had been impeccable, keeping the conversation general, light and amusing, encouraging her to relax and enjoy each excellent course, even to smile and respond shyly to his practised banter. Yet now he'd suddenly switched to the personal again. The much too personal. And she wasn't sure how to handle it.

She took a breath. 'There's nothing to tell,' she countered.

'Nothing?' he queried lightly. 'So, does he even exist, I wonder, or is he an invention to keep unwanted lovers at bay?'

She made herself eat some of the frothy concoction in front of her. 'He's real enough,' she said eventually. 'But I can't describe him, because I don't know him, or anything about him and I never have.'

His brows lifted. 'You married a complete stranger?'

'It was an arrangement,' she said. 'Forced on us both by circumstance.'

'I believe such arrangements can sometimes turn out well,' he said, after a silence. 'With a little goodwill on both sides.'

'Perhaps.' Ellie couldn't eat any more and put down her spoon. 'But—not in this case.'

'You seem very sure.'

'I've had plenty of time to decide.' *And now, because of*

Silvia, I have a convincing reason too… 'And concluded that I should leave.'

'And came here.' His tone was reflective. 'Will you tell me why?'

'Because I knew it was the last place that he—my husband—would ever come to.'

Luca frowned. 'What is wrong with it?'

Ellie shrugged. 'Oh—it's not vibrant—or glamorous—or full of the beautiful people—like those he went ski-ing with last winter,' she added.

'But you did not accompany him.' A statement rather than a question.

She shook her head. 'I don't ski.'

'You could learn. Or you could simply enjoy the air and the beauty of the mountains as many do without venturing on to the slopes.'

That, she thought, was what Tullia had said. 'Oh, do come with us, Elena,' she'd appealed. 'We can find a nice terrace and sit with our hot chocolate and wonderful cakes while Angelo and Domenico and the others go off on their black runs.

'Besides, Mamma was saying the other day that you and Angelo have still not had a honeymoon.' She'd looked at Ellie with dancing eyes. 'Perhaps in such a romantic place, he will wish to treat this as one.'

And she'd replied, forcing herself to smile back, her heart pounding, even though the prospect of sharing a room and a bed with him for the duration had been one of the main deterrents, 'A little too public, don't you think? Anyway I'd probably do something silly—slip on the ice and break something and spoil his plans. Believe me, I'm far better off staying at Vostranto.'

Tullia had pouted, but when she returned, she had little to say about the trip other than Ellie was probably right not to have gone, and would have been bored.

Angelo had said even less.

Now, striving for lightness, and a way to bring the conversation and the evening to a speedy end, she said, 'Maybe I'm just the indoor type.'

'And yet you spend part of each day on the beach.'

'That's quite different. When I'm here, I'm alone—and free.'

He looked at her unsmilingly. 'Is that what I saw that first morning—a dance of freedom?'

'I—I don't know.' Had it been freedom, she wondered, that inexplicable, overwhelming sense of irresistible joy that had so unexpectedly assailed her, as if some locked door had suddenly opened on to a new and hopeful world? And all she had to do was hold out her hand to claim it for her own?

Before, of course, she realised what was awaiting her...

Hurriedly, she pushed back her chair and reached for her bag. 'Anyway, I must be going,' she said.

'You do not wish for coffee and some strega, perhaps, or sambucca?'

'*No, grazie.* But it was a wonderful meal,' she added politely. 'So, if you will excuse me, *signore*.'

He rose too. 'May it not be Luca?'

She swallowed. 'If that is—really what you want.'

'Indeed it is,' he said. '*Buona notte*, Helen. I wish you pleasant dreams.' He paused. 'And I look forward to meeting you on the beach tomorrow.'

'I—I may not be there. I have—things to do.'

'Then Poco and I will both be disappointed.' He walked round the table, took her hand and raised it to his lips. 'And as I am now convinced you are married,' he said softly, 'what can you possibly have to fear?'

And that, thought Ellie as she gave him a taut smile before heading for the door, was the six-million-dollar question.

She lay for a long time that night staring into the darkness, her mind endlessly reviewing every word that had been spoken between them, her inner vision possessed by images of him in almost frightening detail—the turn of his head, the length of the black eyelashes, the shape of his mouth. As if, she thought, she'd been gazing at him all evening, committing him to some private corner of her memory, instead of trying to avoid glancing at him at all.

Under her nightshirt, her body was tingling, her nipples hard against the thin fabric, scalding heat between her thighs.

Oh God, this is so wrong, she told herself, turning over to bury her flushed face in the pillow. Wrong and crazy. I don't recognise myself any more, or know what I'm doing, and that scares me. Because there are so many reasons why I shouldn't be thinking about him—ever, and the fact that I'm still technically a married woman is probably the least of them.

'Luca,' she whispered under her breath. 'Luca—why did I have to meet you now? Why couldn't it have been long ago when everything was different? When I was different?'

She fell asleep at last, but woke again at sunrise. She showered, put on her robe, then worked doggedly for several hours, drinking cups of black coffee and not allowing herself to think of anything else while she caught up with her schedule.

This was her real life, she thought, as she finally closed down her laptop, and she must never forget that. Must take care to ignore any temptation to wonder if it could ever have been otherwise.

She did some washing and hung it in the small courtyard at the back of the house. It was going to be the warmest day yet, she realised, looking up at the sun, high in an almost cloudless sky. A foretaste of summer heat, and there was little breeze so the sea would be like a millpond.

She fought with herself as she tidied an already tidy house, repeating over and over again that she would be a fool and worse than a fool to go anywhere near the beach today whatever the weather. But, as she'd known from the first, it was a losing battle, so she changed into a bikini, covered it with shorts and a cheesecloth shirt, put sun lotion, a towel, some bottled water and an apple in a canvas bag and headed for the shore.

She had just reached the steps when Luca's hand descended lightly on her shoulder. *'Buon giorno,'* he said. 'Where is your little friend today?'

She said stiltedly, 'The Signora's niece is taking her out for the day, and Poco is going too. The children adore him.'

'Ah.' His brows lifted. 'So, is it possible for you to tolerate my company alone?'

He was wearing khaki shorts, and espadrilles, his sun glasses pushed up on top of his head, and the rest of him was bare bronze skin. The faint amusement in his dark eyes was also playing round his firm mouth, and every inch of him spelled danger.

She said huskily, 'I thought I might swim.'

'I thought so too. I was only waiting for you.'

'And if I'd stayed away?' *As I should have done…*

He shrugged a shoulder and she tried not to notice the play of muscle under the smooth skin. 'Then I would have come to find you.'

He had already spread a towel in the shelter of a rock, and she arranged hers beside it, fumbling a little as she felt tension building inside her.

He said gently, 'There is no need to be afraid.'

Now how did he know that? she wondered wildly. Aloud, she said, 'I—I don't understand what's happening. Why you are doing this, when you know—when I've told you the situation.'

'You have told me certain things.' The dark gaze held hers. 'But not all of it, I think.'

Ellie bit her lip. 'All that is possible, anyway.'

'At least until you begin to trust me,' he agreed, unzipping his shorts to reveal black swimming trunks.

Feeling absurdly self-conscious, Ellie discarded her own shorts and shirt, thankful that her dark green bikini was cut on lines more demure than strictly fashionable, but aware, just the same, of the frank appreciation in his expression.

Then he took her hand, and began to walk down the beach, his pace quickening until he was running with Ellie laughing and breathless at his side as they reached the water's edge, and splashed into the softly curling shallows.

For a moment the sea felt so cold it made her gasp, but Luca's arm was round her, urging her forward, making her forget her initial recoil as the water deepened.

And when the lean, brown body beside her dived forward into the waves, she followed, the chill suddenly becoming—exhilaration.

It had been months since her last swim, and all the bleak unhappiness and uncertainty she'd experienced during that time seemed to fall away from her, leaving her buoyant as the sunlit air as she cut through the water in her smooth, efficient crawl.

When she began to feel the pull on her muscles, she turned and swam back slowly to where Luca was waiting for her, treading water, his dark hair gleaming in the sun.

'You swim very well,' he said. 'Where did you learn?'

'Here,' she said. 'My father taught me when we came to stay with my grandmother.' She wrinkled her nose. 'I used to go to the public baths sometimes when I lived in Rome, although they were always so crowded. Several of my colleagues went to the big hotels to swim in their pools, but I found that too expensive.'

'Che peccato,' Luca said softly. 'Because I often did the same. We might have met much earlier.'

'I think I'd have been lost in the crowd.' *In so many ways...* She forced a smile. 'But that's why I'm out of practice and out of condition.'

'It is not apparent. You came here often as a child?'

'Whenever it was possible. We all loved it.' She paused. 'Nonna Vittoria's other daughter, my aunt and—and her family were never as keen.'

Now why, she wondered vexed, did I need to mention that?

She added hurriedly, 'And I love it still.'

'That is evident. But it is a pity that you come here alone.'

'I don't see it that way at all.' She began to swim back to the shore using a sedate breast-stroke. 'I'm quite happy in my own company.'

His voice reached her quietly. 'And that is an even greater

pity. A woman with such a gift for happiness should not prefer solitude.'

Once out of the water, Ellie walked quickly up the beach, aware of Luca keeping pace at her shoulder and the unruly hammering of her heart as she headed for the freshwater shower sited at the edge of the promenade to rinse the salt from her skin. She stepped into the shallow basin, and reached for the control lever only to find his hand covering hers as he joined her under the shower head, pulling her towards him.

She said in a voice she didn't recognise, 'No, please, you mustn't. It's not right…'

'Are you throwing your marriage in my face again, Helen?' His tone was harsh. 'The fact that you belong to another man? Do you wish he was here with you now instead of me—this husband?'

And this time her whispered 'No' was in acceptance, not denial, as Luca turned on the water and stood, holding her close against him so that she breathed the cool, salty fragrance of his skin as the cascade covered them both. She could feel the thud of his heart echoing through her own bloodstream, and leaned into him, resting her forehead against the muscularity of his chest, her legs shaking under her, waiting for what would be.

When the gush of water stopped, Luca put his hand under her chin, tilting her face up towards his. He said gently, 'I will say again—you have nothing to fear, I promise you. Nothing.' And let her go.

Afterwards, when they had gone back to the rock and dried themselves, Ellie produced her sun lotion and Luca lay, propped up on an elbow observing her, his dark gaze candidly intent, as she applied the liquid to her slender legs, her arms, her midriff, and, having carefully removed the halter strap, the faint swell of her breasts above the bikini top.

She said with a catch in her breath, 'Why are you watching me?'

'You know why, *mia bella*.' There was a smile in his voice, as he stretched out a hand for the bottle. 'So there is no need to play games. Permit me to attend to your back, *per favore*.'

She turned over, lying face downwards on her towel, her body rigid, hands clamped to her sides, trying to subdue the uncertain clamour of her pulses.

Luca began with her shoulders, his touch as gentle as she had hoped—or perhaps dreaded. As he smoothed the lotion into her heated skin with light, circular movements, Ellie found her fists slowly beginning to unclench and the tension in her muscles relaxing.

His hand moved downwards, and she flinched instinctively as he released the clip that fastened her bra.

'No—please.'

'Will it also please you to have a mark across your back?' he asked softly, as his fingertips anointed the delicate, untrammelled contour of her spine.

There seemed no answer to that, and the lingering stroke of his hands on her body was making her so breathless she probably couldn't have spoken anyway, she thought, closing her eyes and giving herself up to pure sensation.

He did not hurry, finishing his ministrations decorously about a centimetre above the band of her bikini briefs. 'Now you will not burn.'

But she was scorching already, every fibre of her being, each bone, each drop of blood in her starved body coming alive, its long-suppressed hunger crying out for appeasement—for a satisfaction that had up to now only existed in her imagination. That she had tried so hard to teach herself to live without, while struggling at the same time to endure those brief, unhappy encounters in the marriage bed. Until endurance threatened to turn into heartbreak and became utterly impossible.

A voice she did not recognise mumbled *'Grazie.'*

'Prego,' Luca returned and she felt the swift brush of his lips on the nape of her neck before he turned away to stretch out on his own towel.

She pretended to doze, keeping her eyes closed, letting her breathing slow to a quiet rhythm, but her body was wide-awake, in thrall to this delicious agony of need that his touch had engendered. Which he must realise, she thought unhappily. He was an experienced man who'd know exactly what effect even the most casual caress would have. Who intended it to arouse and incite. To make her want him.

Because—hadn't seduction been his purpose ever since he'd walked into the *trattoria* some forty eight hours earlier and seen her there? She swallowed. After all, he'd hardly made a secret of it. Had he? And her rejection of him had only made him more determined, if only to heal his damaged male ego.

I should never have let this begin, she thought desperately. I should have gone while I had the chance. Headed south. Found a small *pensione* somewhere equally unfashionable and played the waiting game until I could call Santino and check that Luca had gone and it was safe to return.

But it was pride that kept me here. Wanting to prove to myself that I could cope with the situation and keep him at arm's length. That very same pride that took me away from Vostranto. The need to convince myself that I was in charge of my own destiny and needed to take the initiative. To jump before I was pushed.

Yet how could I have imagined that something like this could ever happen? That he could suddenly appear like this, turning my life upside down, so that I no longer know what to do—or even who I am any more?

But it's left me with only one certainty—that if I let him any closer to me, I'll be lost forever, faced with a lifetime of regret. And I cannot afford that, especially when all he wants is a few hours' entertainment. Because there can't be any more to it than that and he has to know that. Has to…

And she went on lying silently there, only a few inches away from him, the ache of desire in her body fighting the turmoil in her mind. Knowing she would only have to stretch out a hand to touch him while reciting all the very real and cogent reasons to do no such thing.

Recalling another time when the urge to touch a man—to offer him her body—had almost overwhelmed her and reminding herself, too, of the unhappiness that would inevitably have followed if she'd given way. The shame she would have felt after revealing her innermost feelings and needs to someone whom she knew neither loved nor cared for her in the ways that mattered. The misery of discovering where his desires were truly centred.

Luca was the opposite of the husband she had left, but he was equally an enigma, his motives inexplicable. Which made him even more dangerous.

And the feelings he'd so effortlessly awoken in her—the longing to be touched as a woman, taken—would, in the end, lead only to disaster because there could be no lasting commitment from him either.

Caught up as she was in these mental struggles, she was suddenly jolted by the touch of his hand on her shoulder and rolled away from him with a gasp, remembering too late that her top was unfastened.

A wave of heated crimson swept up from her toes as she hastily covered her bare breasts with her hands, but Luca merely picked up her bikini bra and handed it to her without comment.

Once she was safely covered again, he said, glancing at the sky, 'It is becoming hotter than ever, so I suggest we look for somewhere with shade to have lunch.'

She took a deep breath, words of polite but resolute denial forming in her head that would finally and inexorably convince him he was wasting his time, only to hear herself say huskily, 'Yes—that seems a good idea.'

They chose a bar at the end of the promenade, sitting at a table under its striped awning to eat large prawns grilled on skewers accompanied by rice salad and fresh bread, and drink cold local beer. It was delicious, messy and relaxed in a way she wouldn't have dreamed it could be.

And he talked to her—asking her tastes in music, books, and the theatre. Making her laugh with his frankly cynical comments about the political situation. Seeking her views on topics like the global economy and climate change. Avoiding the questions she knew she would have found impossible to answer.

At the same time, at every moment, she was aware of his eyes on her, sometimes smiling, sometimes searching, always brilliant in their intensity. Aware of the proud lines of his nose and cheekbones—and how that lord-of-creation look softened when his mouth curved in amusement. Found herself watching him as if mesmerised. As if to gaze forever would not be enough.

Felt the ache of forbidden necessity deep within her. The helpless, shameful thrust of her hardening nipples against the confines of her bikini.

And when the meal was over, the bill paid, and Luca stood up, saying softly, 'Helen, *mia carissima*, I think it is time for a *siesta*,' she went with him willingly, her hand clasped in his, back to Casa Bianca. Her retreat. Her own very private space, shared with no-one. Until this moment.

Her hand shook as she tried to fit the key in the lock, and Luca took it from her and opened the door, then picked her up in his arms and lifted her over the threshold as if she was a bride.

Too late now to listen to the voice in her head telling her to step back because this was all wrong—so very wrong. That there could be no future with this man who was offering her only the transient pleasure of the moment. And—most of all—that she didn't do things like this—and never had. That there would be a price to be paid which she could not afford…

Then his lips took hers and the voice was silenced.

They were lying together on the bed, naked, in the warm golden light slanting across the bed from the shuttered window. The few clothes they'd been wearing had been tossed aside like leaves in a breeze as Luca had undressed her and then himself between kisses, his hands moving over her uncovered skin as if he was touching the delicate petals of a flower.

He pulled her closer, his kiss deepening as his tongue sought hers, thrusting into the sweetness of her mouth with sensual urgency, astonishing her with the swift glory of her response, her hands clasping his shoulders, twining round his neck, stroking his thick dark hair. Learning every smooth, supple line of him. Unable, it seemed, even in those first moments, to get enough of him as if a lifetime's waiting was ending at last.

Knowing, too, that, whatever pain still waited for her, there could be no turning back.

His hands moved downwards, his fingers moulding the swell of her breasts, teasing the rosy peaks to lift to the voluptuous caress of his mouth, making the breath sigh from her parted lips as he suckled her gently.

She had not known until now that her entire body could sing to the slow, languorous glide of a man's hands and lips exploring her. That there would be excitement to be discovered in the arch of her throat, the softness of her underarms and the inner hollow of her elbow. That his slow traverse of her spinal column would make her rear blindly against him, gasping, or that she would moan with pleasure as he cupped her small, firm buttocks and traced the slender line of her flanks.

But then no-one had touched her like this before, or whispered soft words of desire against the newly awakened eagerness of her untutored flesh.

Nor had she experienced the tip of a tongue seeking the whorls of her ear, or teeth nibbling gently at its lobe.

Her thighs had never parted, as they were doing now, welcoming the heated arousal of her lover's erection pressed between them. She reached down to find him, her fingertips stroking the silken length of the engorged male shaft in a kind of wonderment, as she felt his whole body quiver in responsive delight, making her realise that her need was shared—equalled.

And that it was too late to remind herself that it was only a temporary delight. That there could be no future in this. None.

His fingers were moving on her too, gently, exquisitely igniting new sensations, as he sought her tiny hidden pinnacle, bringing it to aching, swollen, delicious life, making her whimper, wordlessly, pleadingly against his shoulder as her body lifted to the delicate torment of his caress.

She was instantly aware of his touch changing, intensifying, drawing her inexorably into some blind, mindless region of the senses. Holding her there on an unknown brink for a breathless eternity before releasing her into a throbbing, soaring agony of pleasure.

And her body was still shaking from the last lingering tremors of rapture when he lifted himself over her, entering her, filling her with total completeness, then sliding his hands under her hips and raising her towards him in a silent command to lock her legs round his waist.

As he began to move slowly and rhythmically inside her, Ellie found herself remembering another time, another place, another man.

Recalling the feelings, the instincts she'd so deliberately denied herself then, but allowing them free rein now because it was all so incredibly, indescribably different.

Letting herself mirror every strong, powerful thrust, answering his demands with her own, her entire being alive and enthralled by the unexpected potential of her awakened sexuality. Feeling her inner muscles close round him then release. Hearing him groan in husky satisfaction at her response—at this mutual and glorious attuning of their bodies. Clinging to his sweat-slicked shoulders, as her mouth drank from his with eager, entranced delight.

I never dreamed… The only coherent thought that came to her as their bodies rose and fell together. *I never dreamed…*

Yet this was no dream. This was stark and beautiful reality, as inevitable as her next flurried breath. *What I was born for…*

Luca was moving faster now, driving more deeply into her hot, wet sheath, and Ellie could feel a strange, sweet tension building within her like a fist slowly clenching. A small, aching sound was forced from her throat as she stared up, eyes widening, at the man above her, dark against the sunlight, the sensations he was creating spiralling relentlessly out of control. Carrying her away on the scalding tide of his desire.

Then, as the first harsh spasm tore through her and she dissolved into shuddering helpless ecstasy, she cried out, her voice breaking on his name and heard him answer her.

CHAPTER ELEVEN

WHEN THE WORLD finally stopped reeling, Ellie found she was lying in his arms, her head pillowed on his chest, as he gently stroked the damp hair back from her forehead. There were a thousand questions teeming in her mind, but the warm aftermath of passion was being superseded by a sudden agony of shyness at the memory of her abandoned surrender, and she knew she could ask none of them.

He must have sensed her growing tension because he said softly, 'Is all well with you, *mia bella*? I did not—hurt you?'

'No—oh, no.' She hesitated then said on a little rush of words, 'I just—didn't realise—didn't know...'

'And now that you do?' He tilted her chin, raising her face for his kiss. Caressing her lips with his until she relaxed back into his embrace. 'You have no regrets I hope?'

'No,' Ellie said slowly. 'I'll never have those—whatever happens.'

'Even when I have to leave you?' His hand slid down to clasp the curve of her hip.

There was a heartbeat of silence, then she said, 'Are you planning to go?'

'At some moment, *sì*.' There was a smile in his voice. '*Naturalmente*, I have to return to my hotel to change my clothes, *mia cara*, in order to take you to dinner.' He kissed her again. 'But not immediately,' he murmured against her lips, his hand moving with quiet purpose.

'No,' she whispered back. 'Not immediately.' And gave

herself up to the renewed joy of his touch. The slow delicious establishment of a need as passionate as it was mutual. A reaching out to each other that somehow transcended the purely physical, as it carried them to the sweet agony of orgasm, and as Ellie rested in its honeyed aftermath, she realised there were tears on her face.

Afterwards, she made coffee, black and strong, and as she carried the cups into the living room, she found him, fresh from the shower, a towel draped round his hips, studying her laptop and the files beside it.

He turned to look at her, his slow smile reminding her of what had just happened between them under the warm cascade of water, and a wave of heat enveloped her.

'You work here?' His brows lifted.

'Of course.' Ellie kept her tone light. 'Just as I would in any other place. I have my living to earn.'

'Ah, yes,' he said softly. 'And you do—what precisely?'

'I translate from English for a publishing house called Avortino.'

'Love stories, *mia bella*?' His tone teased her.

Ellie shook her head. 'Nothing like that. Mostly non-fiction. Often quite technical stuff.' She opened the top file and handed him a couple of pages. 'You see?'

He drew her to him, his arm lightly round her waist, and read, grimacing slightly. 'You find this—interesting?'

'Not this particular assignment perhaps. But, on the whole, it's a job I love,' she said. *And it demands a high level of concentration—something which has proved a lifeline in the past and may do so again.*

She added quietly, 'In future, I may go back to working in-house. I haven't quite decided yet.'

'No,' he said softly. 'In your situation, there must be so many decisions to be made.'

As well as many more that will be made for me…

He drank his coffee, and put down the cup. 'Now, I must go.' He picked up his discarded clothes still lying with hers on the floor, mute evidence of how eagerly they'd stripped each other as soon as the front door closed behind them.

As he dropped his towel, Ellie moved closer, running a tantalising finger down the length of his strong spine. 'Do you have to—really?' she whispered.

He grinned at her over his shoulder. '*Sì, carissima*. We have to eat, *dopo tutto* and I think even Santino would draw the line if we arrived tonight like this.' He caught his breath as her hand strayed lower. 'However, the sooner I leave, my little witch, the sooner I shall return. And after we have eaten, we shall have the entire night to please each other so do not tempt me now.'

'You mean I could?'

He dragged on his shorts, zipped them and turned to pull her into his arms. 'Always,' he muttered unevenly against her lips.

Alone, Ellie pressed a hand to the soft tingle of her mouth, aware that her entire body was aglow, singing with fulfilment.

I'm a different person, she thought wonderingly. I've been re-born—and nothing will ever be the same again.

And she whispered his name, yearningly, achingly, into the silence.

But it can't last…

That was what Ellie had to keep telling herself, over and over again as each blissful day and night slid past and a measure of sanity began to return. It just can't…

However warm and passionate it might be, however sweet the madness, it was still only an interlude. It had no future and when the real world intervened again, which at some point it must, she would have to learn to be alone again.

Even the mark on her finger where her wedding ring had been had now faded as if it had never existed—rather, she thought, like the marriage itself. A few months that had involved a different lifetime and a different girl. A place to which she could never return. A time for her to begin her life again.

Once or twice Ellie had wished that she still had some of the designer clothes and sexy lingerie that had filled the closets at Vostranto, so that she could wow him when he arrived to pick her up each evening.

On the other hand, as she reminded herself, none of those glamorous garments had done much for her in the past, so instead she'd visited Porto Vecchio's only boutique and bought herself a new and very inexpensive dress, in a soft and floating fabric with dark green flowers on a cream background, and watched with delight his face light up when he saw her.

'How very lovely you are,' he'd whispered as he kissed her, his hands sensuous as they moulded her slender shape through the thin material. Making them, as she recalled, very late for dinner even by Italian standards.

Although they spent most of their waking hours—as well as the time they slept—together, he had never asked if he might move out of the hotel and join her at Casa Bianca as she'd half-expected, and Ellie had hesitated to suggest it herself. After all, it was hardly a necessity, she thought, when they were so happy with life just as it was.

Also, it seemed that he had totally accepted her need to work because he never intruded on her after he'd left for the hotel each morning, generally timing his return for around noon. It occurred to her that perhaps he also had matters to attend to in the interim period, although he never mentioned them directly.

All that, she thought, savoured too much of the real world rather than the idyll they were sharing, and maybe he thought so too.

The warm weather continued, drawing them each afternoon to the beach and the shade of their rock, usually accompanied by Poco. The Signora was clearly intrigued by her young neighbour's new human companion, her eyes twinkling at him in undisguised appreciation, but she nobly forbore to ask any questions. And if she saw him leave in the early mornings, it was never mentioned.

When, at last, she did sound a note of caution, it concerned the weather rather than personal relationships.

'No more beautiful days.' She peered at the sky frowning. 'Tomorrow, or perhaps tonight there will be rain. Perhaps a storm.'

'Oh,' Ellie said, dismayed. 'I hope you're wrong.'

'Never,' the Signora exclaimed superbly. She pressed a dramatic fist to the shelf of her bosom. 'I know this place the whole of my life. I know how quickly things can change. So make the most of today, Elena, because it cannot last.'

And as Ellie walked back to Casa Bianca, she heard the echo of her own inner warnings, and felt herself shiver as if the threatened rain had already begun to fall.

By evening, the clouds were already gathering and a chilly wind had sprung up making the candle-flames dance and flicker under their glass shades at the *trattoria*.

'The Signora was right,' Ellie said as they ate their chicken *puttanesca*. 'All good things do come to an end.'

He took her hand, and she saw him looking down at her bare wedding finger. He said quietly, 'But other things can take their place.'

She said with faint breathlessness, 'Perhaps I don't want anything to change.'

'Yet I think it must.' His voice was gentle. 'Because we cannot continue as we are. Surely you see that.'

'Yes.' She withdrew her hand from his clasp. 'Yes, I do. I—I accept that totally. I mean—when you came down here, you can't have foreseen or planned for this to happen. For us to meet as we did.'

'No,' he said. 'You are right. I did not anticipate—any of it.'

'And if you'd simply stayed in your hotel like most of the other guests, it would have been entirely different.'

'I cannot deny that either.' He picked up his glass and drank, the movement jerky.

She looked down at the table. 'So I need you to know that I—I didn't expect it either.'

His mouth twisted. 'As you made clear, *mia cara*. You were not easy to convince.'

'Then let me make this clear too.' She took a deep breath. 'I don't expect nor want anything more either.'

He was silent for a moment. 'You cannot mean that,' he said at last. 'Are you saying these things because of the past? Because of your marriage—the way it was?'

'I'm saying that we have our real lives—our actual commitments—far away from here.' She lifted her chin. 'We've had this—time together, these few days and nights, and they've been wonderful, but that's all. There's nothing else, and there never can be.'

She paused. 'So maybe a change now is appropriate, even necessary. Isn't there a saying—quit while you're ahead?'

'I have heard it used,' he said slowly. 'But is that truly what you wish?'

'Yes, *signore*.' Her gaze met his without wavering. 'It is.'

But I'm lying, she thought, pain twisting inside her. I want to hear you tell me that in spite of everything, we have a future. I want you to say that you love me. I wish for the impossible.

And, instead, saw him glance towards the window, hit by the first spatter of drops.

He said lightly, 'It seems that, in any case, we will not be going to the beach tomorrow. What will Poco do?'

'Stay indoors with the Signora.' She made her tone match his, carefully masking the agony of loss. 'He loves going in the sea, but he hates the rain. He doesn't seem to recognise that they're both water.'

He even managed to look amused. 'Well, he is not alone in that, *mia cara*.' He paused. 'Have you always liked dogs?'

'We had a golden retriever when I was a child.' She drank some wine. From somewhere managed to produce a reminiscent smile. 'He was called Benji, and he was big and soft and sweet.' She added with faint huskiness, 'I missed him terribly when he died.'

And this—this is like another death…

'He was not replaced?'

She shook her head. 'It wasn't possible. My father had a new job and we were moving to an apartment without a garden.'

'Che peccato,' he said. He leaned back in his chair, surveying her with narrowed eyes. 'I am trying to imagine,' he said, 'how you looked when you were a little girl.'

Oh God, don't do this to me—please.

She shrugged. 'Scrawny. Hair in plaits. Big eyes.' She grimaced. 'Only the hairstyle has really changed.'

He gave a despairing glance at the ceiling. *'Dio mio*, how many times do I need to say how beautiful you are before you believe me?'

At least once a day, she thought, for the rest of my life. One of so many things I can never tell you in return.

Santino lent them an ancient umbrella for the walk back to the Casa Bianca, its shelter precarious as the wind threatened to turn it inside out.

At the door, she halted. 'Perhaps we should say *"Addio"* here.'

'A clean break?' he queried derisively. 'No, *mia bella*. Never in this world.'

And as he had done that first time, he unlocked the door himself, carrying her into the house. Once inside, he put her on her feet and stood for a long moment, looking down into her face.

She tried again. 'Believe me, please. This—is so unwise.'

'I agree,' he said. 'But it is also far too late for wisdom.'

He took her gently in his arms and began to kiss her slowly and very deeply, his mouth moving on hers in insistent demand, making her moan softly with the aching need of arousal before he lifted her again, shouldering his way into the bedroom.

His hands were deft as he undressed her, his mouth tender and seeking on her uncovered body and she held him, hands clasping his shoulders, offering herself for his possession, gasping a little as he filled her and made her complete. As they moved together in the unison that they had learned, knowing every nuance of each other's responses.

Yet even as she began to dissolve into delight, Ellie could feel that he was holding back, concentrating on her pleasure, her satisfaction rather than his own. But it was too late for protest or to lure him into equal abandonment because her senses were already spiralling giddily out of control, her body shuddering in the first fierce spasms of climax.

And even after she had cried out, her voice lost and wondering, he had not finished with her, his lips performing a sensuous traverse down the length of her trembling sweat-dampened body, his hand parting her thighs for the voluptuous caress of his fingers and his tongue.

She tried to tell him that it was too soon—that it was impossible—but she couldn't speak, caught once more in the irresistible rush of desire. Carried away almost inexorably. Convulsed—drained by its culmination.

He said her name hoarsely and took her again, his strong body driving her to limits she'd never guessed at. Urging her towards some dangerous edge and holding her there for a breathless, agonised eternity before permitting them both the harsh, pulsating tumult of release.

Sated, exhausted, Ellie lay beneath him, treasuring the relaxed weight of his body against hers, stroking the dark head pillowed on her breasts.

The calm, she thought, after the storm. Then, hearing the rattle of the wind against the shutters and the low rumble of thunder in the distance, she thought of all the other storms still to come. And how they could so easily tear her life apart.

And wondered how she would ever bear it.

It was just after dawn when she woke with a start, and sat up, wondering what had disturbed her. And in that same moment, discovered she was alone.

At first, she remained still, listening intently for the sound of the shower, trying to detect the aroma of coffee in the air. Searching for the normality of morning, but there was nothing.

And as her eyes grew accustomed to the dimness of the room, she saw that his clothes were missing too.

Ellie bit her lip, tasting blood. She wasn't accustomed to this, she thought. She'd become used to waking in his arms, his warm mouth coaxing her to desire. Later, to showering with him, running her fingers laughingly over the stubble on his chin and the faint marks it had left on her skin.

Yet at some moment, it seemed, he'd decided that a clean break was best after all. And gone. Without a kiss. Without a word.

She flung back the covers and got up, reaching for her robe. With last night's memories crowding in on her—his hands, his lips, the scent, the taste of him—it was impossible to stay where she was, or try to sleep again.

In the living room, she paused, looking round her in a kind of desperation. This little house—her refuge for so long—suddenly felt bleak and empty, as if it no longer belonged to her, but to some stranger. As if the heart had been ripped out of it. Or was it the dark hollow that had opened up inside herself that she was sensing?

She took a deep, steadying breath, then padded into the kitchen and put the coffee to brew, before toasting some bread to go with the ham and cheese she'd taken from the fridge for breakfast.

Knowing she needed to keep herself occupied far more than she required food.

She ate what she could, then showered and dressed in denim jeans and a dark blue sweater, grimacing at the pallid face which looked back at her from the mirror.

She sat down at her work table with gritted teeth, but her usual ability to concentrate had deserted her. She found she was staring at the rain-lashed window, wondering where he was, what he was doing, what he was thinking. Then endlessly repeating everything that had been said between them the previous night. Telling herself as she did so that she had done absolutely the right thing. That she hadn't cried or begun a sentence with 'Can't we…' so that at least she could emerge from this extraordinary situation with some semblance of dignity.

And one day she'd be able to look back and be proud—maybe even glad that she'd had the strength to behave so well.

At last, she gave up on the current translation, and deciding that struggling against the wind and rain was better than fighting her unhappy thoughts, she took the ancient hooded waterproof cape that had once belonged to her grandmother from the cupboard, and went for a walk.

Under the leaden sky, a grey sea hurled foam-tipped waves at the beach, the hiss and roar of its ebb competing with the noisy gusts that whipped at Ellie's cape, and stung her face with whipped up particles of sand.

Head bent, she battled along the deserted promenade, her imagination telling her that at any moment she would hear him say her name—her real name—and she would look up and see him there, on his way to find her and say all the things she longed to hear.

Last night in the *trattoria* she'd let fear and pride get the better of her, but now there was only her need for him. Her longing to be his in any way he wanted. However little he could offer.

She stopped, gazing up at the bulk of the hotel above her on the headland, determination building inside her. What she was planning was probably the height of stupidity, but, as he'd said last night, it was too late for wisdom.

I have to see him, she thought. Even now. Talk to him. I can't let it end like this—not without knowing—being certain…

She made for the long, steep flight of steps cut into the cliff, and began to climb. When she reached the top, breathless and dishevelled, she cut across the gardens to the hotel's main entrance, and the wide glass doors opened at her approach.

The foyer was almost empty, but there was a buzz of laughter and chatter from the bar where the guests were enjoying their pre-lunch drinks.

Ellie went straight across the wide expanse of marble floor to the reception desk, water dripping from her cape. A man in a formal dark suit raised his eyes from the computer screen he was scanning and stared at her as if he could not believe the presence of such a scarecrow in the hotel's sophisticated surroundings.

He said with hauteur, 'I may help you, *signorina?*'

Pushing back her hood, she said quietly, 'I wish to speak to Count Manzini, if you please. I believe he is staying here.'

'He was a guest, *signorina*, but no longer.' The man offered a thin smile. 'He left two hours ago to return to Rome.'

The world seemed suddenly to recede to a great distance. Ellie leaned against the edge of the desk. She said, 'I didn't realise he was leaving so soon. Did he say—why?'

She received a disparaging look. 'His Excellency gave no reason for his departure, *signorina*. He is not obliged to explain himself. But I believe he received a telephone call.'

'I see.' Ellie paused. 'Do you know if he is planning to come back?'

'He did not say so, *signorina*. He was clearly in a hurry to be gone.'

Ellie lifted her chin. 'Well, I'm sorry to have missed him, but no doubt we'll meet up when I too return to Rome.'

'Indubbiamente, signorina.' He inclined his head with insincere courtesy. 'Is there any other way in which I can assist you?'

'No,' she said. 'Thank you. I should also have telephoned instead of wasting a journey.'

As she walked back towards the entrance, she realised that her legs were shaking and prayed it did not show. She did not dare risk the steps again, but made her way carefully down the winding hill, half dizzy with the questions teeming in her mind.

As she reached Casa Bianca, the Signora's door opened, and the good woman appeared under an umbrella, brandishing an envelope. 'This came for you, *cara*.' She gave her a shrewd look. 'A boy was knocking at your door—a *fattorino* from the hotel, I think.'

The envelope was cream, thick and expensive, bearing the single word 'Elena'.

'Grazie.' Ellie forced a smile and took the letter into her own house to the Signora's evident disappointment. She removed her cape and hung it in the shower to dry, then sat down and opened the envelope.

'Circumstances force my return to the city,' the letter began abruptly. 'And perhaps it is better this way, even though so much still remains unsaid between us.

'You were right, of course. I did not come to Porto Vecchio in order to become your lover. On the contrary, my original purpose was to agree terms for the separation you requested when you left Vostranto.

'I allowed myself to become sidetracked, but the ridiculous pretence, which should never have begun, is now over. Luca and Helen no longer exist, and should be forgotten. I accept too that the marriage between us is over.

'In conclusion, let me say that I intend to make full financial provision for you in the divorce settlement, and you may use this or not as you wish.

'This will be a matter for discussion at our next meeting.'

His signature 'Angelo' was a dark slash at the foot of the page, and Ellie felt the anger in it like a slap across the face.

She sat staring down at the words in all their bitterness and finality until the tears she could not hold back made them first blur and, eventually, vanish altogether as she wept for everything that might have been, but was now lost forever.

CHAPTER TWELVE

RIDICULOUS PRETENCE…

Those were the words which haunted Ellie for the rest of the day, and the greater part of the night.

Of course that was all it had been, she told herself over and over again. She'd known that from the first, but, somehow, she'd allowed herself to forget for a while. To let herself be drawn into this crazy charade that he'd initiated. And, almost, in some incredible way, come to believe it.

To actually think that Angelo Luca Manzini was the lover she'd only dared to imagine in her wildest dreams. And, in the most dangerous kind of wishful thinking, to suppose that some of these dreams might even come true.

Just how many kinds of a fool was it possible to be? she wondered in quiet anguish as she contemplated what she had done. What she had allowed him to do.

After all, she knew that he didn't care for her—that it was Silvia he really wanted. That evening at the reception, she'd seen with her own eyes that, in spite of everything, the passion still burned as brightly as ever between them.

Dear God, wasn't it the knowledge of that, with all its attendant humiliation, that had made her leave Vostranto? Leave him, as she'd thought, forever?

Yet, somehow, he'd made her think she was beautiful—desirable—when all the time he'd simply been amusing himself. Or, which was even worse, perhaps taking his revenge for all those past rejections of his lovemaking.

Making a deliberate nonsense of her avowed indifference to him. Demonstrating that she was just the same as any of the other women who'd shared his bed. As easy to seduce. As easy to walk away from when he wished it to end.

And he had wished it, she reminded herself painfully, as she read once more the letter that she already knew by heart. He'd come to Porto Vecchio to offer her a divorce—the first one in the entire history of the Manzini family and bound to set tongues wagging in conjecture all over Rome.

But giving her the freedom she'd asked for was no simple act of altruism on his part, she reminded herself stonily. He had his own reasons for wanting their sham of a marriage to end, no matter what scandal that might provoke.

She had little doubt that Silvia was one of the topics for discussion still not touched upon, and she could only be thankful to have been spared the pain of that. Because her cousin had to be the motivation driving him to seek his liberation, no matter what the consequences.

That, she thought wretchedly, and the fact that I've totally failed to give him the child he asked from me.

She remembered Silvia standing greedy-eyed in the bedroom at Vostranto, already planning the change in her future. Supremely confident in her beauty, and the power of her sexuality to win Angelo back. To become the Countess Manzini as she'd always intended.

Between the two of them, they've wrecked my life, Ellie thought, pain wrenching at her heart. And I can't deal with that rationally. It's impossible.

And yet, having come all this way, making this specific journey in order to administer the *coup de grâce*, some obscure passing whim had caused him to postpone his decision. Instead, hiding behind other names, other identities, in the process messing with her head and destroying her power to reason or to be on her guard as she should have been, Angelo had played his own private game with her.

A game that was now over.

But at least she had not given him the opportunity to finish it. The moment he'd hinted that they could not continue as they were, she'd acted swiftly, decisively. She could always be proud of that if nothing else. Proud that she hadn't waited for sentence to be pronounced.

And if she'd changed her mind a short while later and gone to find him—well, he would never, ever know that she'd yielded to such pathetic weakness. Or be aware that, without him, she felt only half alive, pacing the floor since his departure, unable to settle or think of anything but him.

She'd stripped the bed and re-made it so that there would be no lingering trace of the cologne he used to act as a reminder of his presence tempting her to reach for him across the empty space beside her.

But, as she soon discovered, it made little difference, because he was not just in the bedroom, but everywhere.

She found him in the shower, stroking scented gel into her skin. At the stove in the kitchen, creating the best carbonara sauce she'd ever tasted to go with the pasta. In the living room, sharing the old sofa with her, his hands and lips caressing her in the preliminaries to love, before pulling her, laughing, down on to the soft rug for his possession.

She couldn't even stand at the sink without recalling how he would appear behind her, his arms sliding round her waist as he pushed her hair away in order to nuzzle the nape of her neck.

Forcing her to the realisation that the freedom she'd demanded was just another illusion. That in her heart and mind she was still chained to him. And that her precious Casa Bianca was no longer a sanctuary but a prison.

She tried to pinpoint the time—the day—the hour when she had begun to want him, aware that it was well before she'd admitted as much to herself, ashamed to recognise how long ago it truly was. Certainly before the living nightmare of her marriage had been imposed on her.

I was like a child crying for the moon, she acknowledged sadly, knowing full well that it was unattainable. That I was still just as I'd always been—Silvia Alberoni's younger, plainer cousin.

Yet, I built every possible defence I could against him. Insisted he keep his distance. Threw myself into work as if my life depended on it. Tried desperately not to wonder where he was and who he might be with when he stayed in Rome. Fought each lift of the heart when he returned to Vostranto, each quiver of the senses when I was alone with him and all the other small, secret self-betrayals in case he picked them up on some inner male radar and guessed the truth.

And then I ran away, believing I was escaping from the humiliation of being set aside as the failed, unwanted wife. Thinking I could somehow avoid a broken heart. When it was here waiting for me all the time.

Oh, why did he have to follow me? Why couldn't he have left it all in the hands of his lawyers?

Even after another three days she was unable to find answers to those or any of the other questions tormenting her, enclosing her in a kind of limbo.

On the surface, her life went on as usual. She forced herself back to work, relying on her strict professionalism to get her through her assignments.

The weather was still blustery, but fine enough to enable her to escape at some point from the four walls that used to be her safeguard. She took Poco for long walks, evading the Signora's coy queries about 'the return of your handsome friend'.

At the *trattoria*, which she continued to brave each evening, Santino and Maria were more discreet, but she could sense their brimming curiosity too—and their disappointment.

On the morning of the fourth day, she had just cleared away breakfast and was on her way to her laptop, when there was a loud rap at the front door.

Her heart seemed to lurch, and for a stunned instant, she stood staring across the room, aware what she was hoping and despising herself for it.

A second impatient knock and a rattle at the door handle prompted her into action, reaching for her keys.

She flung the door open, her lips parting in a soundless gasp as she saw who was waiting for her.

'So you are here.' Silvia walked past her into the living room. 'I had begun to wonder.' She began to unbutton her white trench coat. 'Aren't you going to ask me to sit down, *cara*? Offer me coffee? I am sure I can smell some.'

Ellie remained where she was. She said quietly, 'Why have you come here?'

Silvia's eyes widened in assumed surprise. 'But, Elena *mia*, to talk to you, of course. To deal with the kind of detail that men somehow find so difficult.' She shrugged. 'But let us examine the broad picture first. You have, of course, agreed that your marriage to Angelo is finally and irretrievably over.'

Ellie said stonily, 'I think that is my business and his. No-one else's.'

'On the contrary, as the other person most nearly involved in this, I have a right to know what is planned. And to help the matter reach a rapid and satisfactory conclusion.' She draped her coat over the arm of the sofa, and sat down, crossing her legs. 'I presume this is also your wish.'

Ellie walked over to the table and leaned against it, the hard, polished edge biting into her hands. 'And what about Ernesto?' she queried tautly. 'Does he have a view in all this?'

Silvia examined her nails. 'Of course, shut away in this forgotten corner, you cannot know what is happening in the wide world. Let me enlighten you. Ernesto and I are no longer together and will very soon be divorced.'

'How convenient,' Ellie returned bitingly.

Silvia laughed. 'More of a necessity, *cara*, once he had heard the news. When I told him I was having Angelo's child. Even he knew then he could not keep me with him.'

Ellie's heart seemed to have stopped beating. She stared at Silvia, knowing she would never be able to forget the triumph in the glowing eyes, or the faint mocking smile that curved her cousin's mouth.

She said in a voice she didn't recognise, 'I don't believe you.'

'You mean because in the past I have never been drawn to the idea of having babies?' Silvia nodded. 'It is true. I admit it.' She paused. 'But who should know better than you, Elena, how much Angelo needs an heir? And I have come to realise that, when you love a man, you wish to give him everything he wants.' Her smile widened. 'So that is what I have done, and you cannot imagine his delight.'

Ellie looked down at the floor, biting the inside of her lip until she tasted blood. Fighting one pain with another.

'Naturally we wish to be married as soon as possible,' Silvia went on brightly. 'So I suggested that Angelo should come down here in person and talk to you. Put his powers of persuasion to good use rather than issue an ultimatum from a distance. When his heart is set on a thing, he becomes quite impossible to resist, don't you find?

'And as he is now instructing his lawyers, his methods were clearly successful.' She gave a little gurgle of laughter. 'He has always believed that the end justifies the means and I understand he had you eating out of the palm of his hand.'

She paused again. 'But we now feel that for his grandmother's sake—and to spare Madrina's feelings too—it would be better if your marriage was quietly annulled. After all, *cara*, neither of you wished to marry the other, so it should be quite simple to arrange.'

'I know very little of these things.' Ellie was astonished to hear the steadiness of her own voice. 'But I'll sign whatever paperwork is necessary, if that's what you came to hear. And now I'd like you to go.'

Silvia rose unhurriedly, smoothing her skirt. 'You seem a little disturbed, *cara*.' Her gaze searched her cousin's white face. 'The situation is awkward, perhaps, but there is no real need for embarrassment between us. Whatever Angelo felt obliged to do was for my sake and the sake of our future together. I know this, so please believe that I do not begrudge the time he spent with you, or how it was spent. And I wish you well.'

Ellie did not reply. Somehow she managed to get to the door without stumbling, and hold it open for her unwanted visitor. Somehow, she managed to close it and lock it behind her.

Then she bolted to the bathroom and was instantly and violently sick.

'You are selling Casa Bianca?' The Signora stared at Ellie in disbelief. 'Your grandmother's house where you have known such happiness for so long? No, it is impossible. You could not do such a thing.'

'I'm afraid that I must.' Ellie gave her neighbour a strained smile. 'Coming here for all these years has been wonderful, but nothing lasts forever, and my life is going to be very different from now on. In fact I'm probably going to get a job in England and live there, so it—it's time to sell.'

She added, 'Someone from the property company is coming to give a valuation this afternoon. I wanted to tell you myself before he arrived.'

'But why—why do you do this? Italy is your home. Your friends are here. Also your family.'

Ellie winced inwardly. 'But I'm going to find another home, somewhere else. I—I need to make a change. I've been thinking about it for a while.'

'I know this while,' the Signora said darkly. 'It is since your handsome man went away. You cannot deceive me, Elena.' She made an impassioned gesture. 'So if he comes back, and you are no longer here—what then? How will he find you?'

Ellie took a deep breath. 'There's no question of that. I have my own life to deal with. No-one else is involved.'

'But you were happy with him,' the Signora said gently. 'All the world could see it. Now it is different—as if a light inside you has gone out.' She paused. 'And there will be sadness here too. You will be much missed by myself and many others. Poco will grieve.'

Ellie bent to fondle the little dog's ears. 'Perhaps your new neighbours will like walking too,' she whispered to him.

Detaching herself would not be easy, Ellie thought when she was back in her own living room. But it had to be done. She could neither stay here nor return to Rome.

She had to find some other place where she could hide until the wounds Silvia had so contemptuously inflicted had healed. Somewhere her cousin would never find. Or Angelo either…

Our next meeting…

It was those casual words from his letter, now torn up and burned, which had forced this drastic action from her. Because the thought of having to see him again, even briefly in the formality of a lawyer's office, was totally, and hideously unbearable.

His betrayal of her was worse than she could ever have imagined, leaving her hollow with pain and shock. It was also incomprehensible because he already knew from the note she'd left she was willing to divorce him. There was no need for any extra 'persuasion' from him with or without Silvia's sanction, so why had he gone to those lengths to seduce her? To lure her into a fantasy world and pretend such tenderness—such desire. She shuddered, her throat tightening with renewed misery. It was cynical, wicked, unforgivable.

But the person she most needed to forgive was herself—for allowing it to happen. For letting him indulge his sexual ego at her expense.

If he'd needed to make sure she'd meant what she said, why hadn't he been honest with her—told her that he had resumed his affair with her cousin and that Silvia was pregnant? It would have hurt terribly, but it would hardly have been any great surprise. A blow she'd been expecting to fall. Besides, the raw and monstrous pain now tearing her apart was far worse.

Yet that was not her only torment. Because even hating him as she did—as she must do—could not confer any kind of immunity from him. On the contrary, she had to face the humiliating truth that she dared not risk another confrontation. That her anger and misery over his treachery might not be sufficient protection. That if he smiled at her, moved towards her or—dear God—touched her, she might not be able to trust herself to turn away.

She needed another refuge and fast. A place where no-one would dream of looking for her. Not Nonna Cosima, Madrina or even Tullia, she thought with a pang. And once they learned the reason for her sudden disappearance, as they soon would, none of them could really blame her.

A place where she would be safe, she told herself with a sigh. And where she might one day forget that she was also running from herself.

'And they lived happily ever after.' The story drawn to its proper conclusion, Ellie closed her book and smiled down at the semi-circle of entranced faces in front of her.

'More, *signorina*, more,' a chorus of small voices petitioned, but she shook her head.

'It is almost time for the lunch bell. If you are late, Mother Felicitas might say there must be no more stories.'

However far-fetched the threat, the children accepted it and trooped off.

Ellie slid the book into her bag, and rose, preparing to follow them, then paused, walking instead to the sunlit window. It was a wonderful view of rolling green hills, shimmering in the haze of summer heat, interspersed with fields of yellow mustard and scarlet poppies. The nearest town was a mere smudge on the horizon.

Directly below was a small paved courtyard with a mulberry tree, its canopy shading a wooden seat, which had become one of Ellie's favourite places.

The convent was the perfect sanctuary, she thought. And she would never be able to sufficiently repay Mother Felicitas for offering it to her. Or for asking so few questions.

When Ellie had told her haltingly that her marriage was over, she had simply expressed quiet concern. And she had also acceded to Ellie's request that no-one should be informed of her presence—with one proviso.

'I understand that you need time and privacy to consider your future, my dear child, and they are yours. But if anyone asks me directly at any point if you are with us here, I will not lie.'

Ellie bent her head. 'That—won't happen.'

Nor had it. Six weeks before, while she was still at Casa Bianca, she had written to both Angelo's grandmother and the Principessa stating that she was well and happy but needed to be alone, and asking them to understand and not worry about her.

Her room in the part of the convent that housed the orphanage and school was pleasant if a little Spartan, its bed too narrow to encourage forbidden dreams.

On the practical side, Mother Felicitas had arranged an extra table and chair so that she could continue to work as usual. She paid for her board and lodging, but in addition she helped out in the school, giving informal English lessons to some of the older children and reading her own translations of popular children's stories to the younger ones.

Her mail was being sent on by arrangement from the property company selling her house in Porto Vecchio, but so far there was no sign of the documentation which would begin the legal dissolution of her marriage.

Clearly Angelo's lawyers did not share Silvia's sense of urgency about the procedure, thought Ellie who found the delay bewildering. Apart from anything else, surely Angelo's pride would demand his heir should be born in wedlock.

She found the whole situation becoming seriously unsettling. How could she begin again, or even plan positively for the future, with this cloud still hanging over her?

In spite of the convent's almost tangible air of peace, the strain of waiting was taking its physical toll of her. The food was good and plentiful, but her appetite had temporarily deserted her, and she had lost a little weight. She felt weary much of the time too, yet had trouble sleeping. In addition, and not too surprisingly, she found herself often on the verge of tears. She'd taken her troubles apologetically to the Infirmarian,

Sister Perpetua who, in her quiet noncommittal way, had recommended fresh air and exercise.

She'd followed her advice, yet, this morning, she'd woken with a slight headache and vague queasiness as if she was coming down with a virus.

I can't afford to be ill, she told herself. I've too much else to cope with, and I don't want to be a liability to the nuns either.

Being with the children had lifted her as it invariably did, and the headache at least had faded. But the thought of food was totally unappealing, Ellie admitted with a sigh, resting her forehead against the glass. Maybe she would forget the mid-day meal and rest on her bed for a while.

As she turned from the window, Mother Felicitas came into the room, an envelope in her hand.

'This came for you, dear child.'

It was from the property company in Porto Vecchio, Ellie saw listlessly. Perhaps they'd sold Casa Bianca, which would be gratifying, of course, but still wasn't the news she was expecting.

She slit open the envelope and extracted the single sheet, scanning the typewritten contents.

There had been, she read, a lot of interest in Casa Bianca, but they had accepted on her behalf an excellent cash offer well above the asking price from Count Angelo Manzini.

Ellie gave a gasp, her hand straying to her lips as the words swam in front of her incredulous gaze. She turned to Mother Felicitas. Her voice barely audible, she said, 'My home. He's bought my home—for her…' and felt herself slide down into impenetrable darkness.

CHAPTER THIRTEEN

'THERE'S NOTHING WRONG with me,' Ellie protested. 'I shouldn't be in the Infirmary. I—I just had a shock, that's all, and that's why I fainted. I—I'm not ill.'

'No, no.' Mother Felicitas patted her hand. 'Sister Perpetua assures me that the symptoms of early pregnancy are often uncomfortable, but only rarely do they become serious.'

If a bomb had gone off in the quiet Infirmary, Ellie could not have been more horrified.

When she could speak: 'A baby? She says I'm having a baby? But I can't be. It's impossible.'

'She nursed in an obstetrics hospital before she joined our Order,' Mother Felicitas said gently. 'She told me what she suspected over a week ago.' She paused. 'Whatever has happened in the past, Contessa, this is news that you must share with your husband.'

'No.' Ellie sat up, icy with sudden alarm. 'I can't do that.'

'But you may carry the heir to an important name, my child. This cannot remain a secret. Count Manzini has to know he is to be a father.'

'That's the last thing he'll want to hear,' Ellie whispered. 'Please believe me, Reverend Mother, and don't ask me to explain.' And as the realisation of everything she had lost overwhelmed her, she began to weep silently and hopelessly.

Worn out emotionally, she slept better that night, aided by a tisana of Sister Perpetua's making, and woke the next day calmer, and filled with a new sense of resolution.

She would close her mind to the past, and use the money that Angelo had paid to take Casa Bianca from her to fund her new life in England.

He had everything now, she thought, pain twisting inside her. Her pride, her memories, her little house—and the love—the need she'd tried desperately to deny, and which he had also taken so carelessly, because he could.

At lunchtime, she made herself eat a bowl of soup and a little pasta, then, encouraged by Sister Perpetua, went to sit out under the mulberry tree. It was a hot, drowsy day with little breeze when even the birdsong seemed muted, and not ideal, she thought wryly, for the making of serious plans. For looking forward instead of back as she must do.

And at first, when she heard the excited yapping of a dog disturbing the stillness, Ellie thought she must be having a waking dream.

But bundling across the courtyard towards her was total reality with a round face and drooping ears, his tail wagging furiously and his barking changing to squeaks of excitement.

She jerked upright, staring in disbelief. 'Poco?' she whispered. 'Poco, what are you doing here?'

And then she realised who was following him, standing in the archway, tall and lean in cream denim pants and a black polo shirt, watching her in silence.

Oh, no, she wailed inwardly. It can't be true. This can't be happening to me.

She knew what she must look like—washed out with scared eyes and lank hair in a faded cotton dress—and as she jumped to her feet, she folded her arms defensively across her body.

Angelo halted, brows lifting almost resignedly as he saw the gesture. He said quietly, '*Buona sera*, Elena. *Come sta?*'

'I was all right,' she said. 'Until now.'

He was thinner, she thought with a wrench of the heart, the lines of the dark face more clearly marked, his eyes shadowed, his mouth bleaker. But she could not let herself see these things. Feel the ache of them.

She said tautly, 'I'm told you've bought Casa Bianca. If you mean it as a gift for Silvia, you've wasted your money. She never liked Porto Vecchio even as a child. She always preferred places with glitz and glamour.'

'I bought it for myself,' he said. 'Do you wish to know why?'

'I presume because it's a way of providing for me that I can't refuse. But it doesn't really matter.' She lifted her chin. 'The house is gone, and soon I shall be gone too.'

She paused. 'So, how did you find me? Did Mother Felicitas contact you—even though she promised…?'

'No,' he said. 'She did not. No-one did. I saw some mail on a desk at the property company addressed to the Daughters of the Nativity, and remembered that I'd seen you talking to Mother Felicitas at that last reception we'd attended together.'

His mouth twisted. 'Suddenly, after all the fruitless days and weeks of searching, everything fell into place. So, I came here asking for you, and she sent me here.'

Poco was lying on his back at Ellie's feet, waving ecstatic paws in the air and she knelt to scratch his tummy, her hair falling across her flushed face, her stomach churning weakly.

'You were looking for me? But why? We—we'd said—goodbye to each other.'

'We said a great deal,' Angelo returned abruptly. 'But I am not sure how much of it was true.'

'Well, I know the truth now.' She did not look at him, concentrating fiercely on Poco.

'If you are speaking of the letter I sent you,' he said harshly. 'I wrote it because I was hurt and angry. I regretted it at once and tried to prevent it being delivered, but I was too late. And by the time I was able to return to Porto Vecchio, you had disappeared.'

'What possible right had you to be hurt and angry?' She did look up then, her eyes accusing. 'Or are you going to deny that you went back to Rome because of my cousin Silvia?'

'I deny nothing. I answered a cry for help from my grandmother.' Angelo strolled forward. 'Silvia had appeared at Nonna Cosima's house in hysterics, screaming that I had destroyed her marriage and that honour demanded I should offer the protection of my name to her and the child she was expecting by me.' He paused, smiling faintly. 'It was something of an emergency, you understand. I had to go.'

Ellie gasped. 'You find it amusing?'

'Most absurdities are laughable, *mia cara*.'

Her voice shook. 'And poor Ernesto's broken heart—his humiliation at knowing his wife is having another man's baby—that's also a joke?'

'Ernesto,' he said, 'knows no such thing, and I doubt he would care anyway. He ended the marriage himself, Elena *mia*, by leaving your cousin very publicly for his secretary, Renata Carlone. They have been lovers for some time and I understand that when he has obtained his freedom, they will be married. I fear Silvia is the one to be left humiliated.'

'But he adored her,' Ellie protested. 'He was desperately jealous of every other man who came near her.'

'Once, perhaps,' Angelo said grimly. 'But his passion for her now, like the baby she claimed to be expecting, exists only in her imagination.'

Ellie took a breath. 'You mean—she's not pregnant?'

'Not by me. Nor by anyone else,' he said tersely. 'Once I confronted her, demanding that she should submit to the usual tests, and warning her that I would insist on DNA evidence in due course, she became first evasive—then sullen—before finally admitting she could not be sure of her condition. In other words, she was lying.'

'But she came to see me,' Ellie protested. 'She—she told me that you were still her lover, and thrilled about the baby, which was why you needed the quickest possible divorce or annulment.'

'And you believed her?' Angelo's tone was incredulous. 'In spite of everything she has done? And in spite of everything that you and I have been to each other?' He closed his eyes. '*Santa Madonna*, how is it possible?'

'But she knew—about us,' Ellie insisted desperately. 'She knew everything. She said you'd simply been doing what was necessary, for her sake, to persuade me to agree to whatever you wanted.'

'And so I did, *carissima*,' he said quietly. 'But for my own sake, not hers.'

Ellie lifted Poco into her arms. Held him like a shield. 'But how could she know what had happened between us unless you told her?'

'Quite easily, *mia bella*. I have suspected for a while that I was being watched, and at Porto Vecchio, I became certain of it. There was a woman staying at the hotel who somehow contrived to be on the beach—at the *trattoria*—everywhere that we went.

'I spoke to Ernesto and he told me he had found fees for a private detective agency on Silvia's credit card, and thought wrongly that he was their target.'

He shrugged a shoulder. 'Clearly, she was hoping for evidence of my infidelity in order to make trouble between us. Instead, she discovered only that I was having an affair with my own wife.'

Ellie looked away. She said in a low voice, 'Or pretending to do so.' She rallied. 'But you still wanted her. I—I saw you together at that reception, remember. Saw the way she looked at you and how you smiled back at her.'

'Body language can be deceptive, *carissima*,' he said. 'To an onlooker, it may well have appeared a pleasant conversation. But what a pity you cannot read lips instead, or you would have known that I was telling her with great frankness that she was wasting her time. That it was over between us long ago. That she would never have any place in my life, and I wished her not to approach me again.'

'Oh.' Ellie swallowed, trying to steady the turmoil in her mind. 'Where is Silvia now?'

'She has thrown herself on the mercy of your godmother,' he said drily. 'But I understand Prince Damiano is already tired of scenes and tantrums and has delivered an ultimatum, ordering her to leave.'

She said bitterly, 'And the Prince's orders are invariably obeyed, as I know to my cost.'

'Do you mean that?' he asked gently. Another long stride brought him dangerously close. 'Has our life together always been so unbearable? Can you look into my eyes and tell me so?'

She didn't dare look at him at all. She said huskily, 'Don't—please. You never wanted to marry me. We both know that. Why didn't you just let me go? Why did you come after me?'

Angelo was silent for a moment. 'I must be completely honest, *carissima.* And the truth is that I did not wish to be married at all. I resented the family pressure being exerted upon me to—do my duty, and furiously angered by the trick Silvia played on us both.

'But once you became my wife, Elena, things changed. *I* changed. Vostranto was a house I loved, but, with you as its mistress, it became more. It turned into a home—a place that I cherished and was glad to return to, even though you treated me like a stranger each time I did so,' he added wryly. 'Keeping always at a distance and barely speaking to me.'

He sighed abruptly. 'I told myself I should find comfort elsewhere. I even went looking, but still spent my nights alone.

'When you finally agreed to share your bed with me, I accepted your terms because, in my arrogance, I believed I could eventually persuade you to surrender—to enjoy being in my arms.

'Only it never happened. Each time we lay together, you shrank from me. Withheld the slightest response, even a kind word.

'I was once told some nonsense about a woman's body rejecting the seed of a man she did not truly love, but I began to wonder if it could be true. If you hated me too much to make a baby with me. And I realised the hell our marriage must have become for you.

'And when you ran away rather than submit to me again, I knew I could not go on torturing you like this.

'So I followed you to Porto Vecchio to tell you not to be

afraid any more. That I would not make you more unhappy than you already were by persisting with our marriage.

'But, seeing you—watching you on the beach that first morning, I saw a girl I did not recognise. No longer withdrawn and reticent, but someone who sang and laughed and danced in the waves. Someone I longed to know in every way.

'And I began to wonder if we had met as strangers in a distant place, without outside interference, whether things could have been different between us. If we might have fallen in love and found we wanted to spend the rest of our lives together.

'I decided there and then that I had to know. That I must discover if it would ever be possible to win you for my own, so, perhaps mistakenly, I became Luca, and courted you as my Helen.'

He took Poco from her arms and set him gently on the ground. Took her hands and drew her down beside him on the bench.

'I bought Casa Bianca, *mi amore*, because it was there I experienced the only true happiness of my life. Where I learned the enchantment of making love to the woman I loved. Of enjoying life's simplicities in her company. Of becoming a real husband to my adorable wife, the other half of myself.

'I believed what we had created there would go with us when we became Angelo and Elena once more, as, eventually, we would have to do. Instead, I faced the worst rejection of all and realised I had failed. That you *might* have learned to welcome my lovemaking but you did not want my love, because your freedom was far more important to you than any future we might have together. As if we had been playing some game, which had now ended.'

She tried to say his name and he put a quiet finger on her trembling lips.

'One moment more, *carissima*. I returned to Rome feeling defeated—empty. In a way, I welcomed your cousin's ludicrous intervention because it gave me a focus for my anger, and made me realise that I too would go to any lengths to get you back, even when I found you had run away again, and all hope seemed lost.'

He took a deep breath, his hands tightening on hers.

'And this is why I have come to find you, Elena *mia*. To ask you to come back to me and learn, if you can, to love me as I love you. To be my wife forever.

'I told Mother Felicitas that I had come to take you home, and even if you send me away again, *mia bella*, I shall not give up. Ah, my sweet one, will you not even look at me?'

She met his gaze, saw the uncertainty that haunted its tenderness and hunger.

She said quietly, 'Don't you see—I had to keep you a stranger. I thought it was the only way I could avoid a broken heart. I knew Silvia still wanted you—was obsessed with becoming your Contessa. She came to Vostranto and told me so. Told me she could get you back, and I believed her.'

She took an uneven breath. 'All my life, it seemed, I'd been the shadow to her sun, and I told myself that would never change. That I'd never be more than the girl who'd been forced on you, and, therefore, keeping you at a distance would be my only salvation. Because I couldn't bear to be touched, knowing you wished I was someone else. And I was scared that one night I would let you see how I really felt, and that you might laugh at me or, even worse, pity me.

'Then—seeing you with her that night at the reception, I realised this half-life I was living had become impossible. That if you wanted Silvia in return, I'd have to go away—somewhere I wouldn't have to see it. Wouldn't wonder every moment of the day and night if you were with her. Imagining you…'

Her voice broke. Angelo took her in his arms and held her close, his cheek against her hair, his voice murmuring words she had never believed she would hear.

'So,' he said at last, using his handkerchief carefully to blot away the tears she'd been unable to contain. 'I cannot kiss you as I wish to do, *mia bella*, because once I start, I will not be able to stop and I have no wish to offend Mother Felicitas who has kept you safe for me.'

He ran a finger down the curve of her cheek. 'You will come back with me and our dog to Vostranto and make it a home again instead of an empty shell?'

'Our dog?' Ellie glanced down at Poco, peacefully snoring under the bench, and gave an involuntary giggle. 'My God, you mean you've kidnapped him again?'

'No, no, *carissima*. The Signora is going to live with her son, whose wife does not care for animals, so she offered me Poco—as a wedding present. It seemed a good omen.'

He paused. 'Is it, Elena? Will you now say the words I most want to hear, and tell me that you love me? That we will be man and wife forever?'

Ellie said softly and simply, 'I love you, Angelo, with all my heart. I always did and I always will.'

She smiled into his eyes, all shadows fled. 'What is more, my darling, I can prove it.'

She took his hands in hers, kissed them gently, then carried them to her body, holding them to the place that sheltered his child, her shining face telling him all he needed to know.

A DANGEROUS INFATUATION

CHANTELLE SHAW

Chantelle Shaw lives on the Kent coast, five minutes from the sea and does much of her thinking about the characters in her books while walking on the beach. An avid reader from an early age, school friends used to hide their books when she visited, but Chantelle would retreat into her own world and still writes 'stories' in her head all the time. Chantelle has been blissfully married to her own tall, dark and very patient hero for over twenty years and has six children. She began to read Mills & Boon® romances as a teenager and throughout the years of being a stay-at-home mum to her brood, found romantic fiction helped her to stay sane! Her aim is to write books that provide an element of escapism, fun and of course romance for the countless women who juggle work and a home life and who need their precious moments of 'me' time. She enjoys reading and writing about strong-willed, feisty women and even stronger-willed sexy heroes. Chantelle is at her happiest when writing. She is particularly inspired while cooking dinner, which unfortunately results in a lot of culinary disasters! She also loves gardening, taking her very badly behaved terrier for walks and eating chocolate (followed by more walking—at least the dog is slim!).

Chantelle is on Facebook and would love you to drop by and say hello.

CHAPTER ONE

SNOW had been falling across Northumbria all day, burying the moors beneath a thick white blanket and icing the peaks of the Cheviot Hills. Picturesque it might be, but it was no fun driving on slippery roads, Emma thought grimly as she slowed the car to a crawl to negotiate a sharp bend. With the onset of dusk the temperature had plummeted to well below freezing, and most of the minor country lanes had not been gritted, making journeys treacherous.

The north-east of England often saw snow in the winter, but it was unusual to last this late into March. Thankfully, her battered old four-by-four, which had once seen service on her parents' Scottish hill-farm, coped well with the conditions. It might not be the most stylish vehicle, but it was practical and robust—rather like her, Emma acknowledged, with a rueful glance down at the padded ski jacket she was wearing over her nurse's uniform. The jacket made her resemble a beach ball, but at least it kept her warm, and her thick-soled boots were sturdy and sensible.

The narrow road wound uphill, bordered on either side by the walls of snow that had been piled up when a farmer had cleared the route with a tractor earlier in the day. Nunstead Hall was still three miles ahead, and Emma was growing concerned that even if she made it to the isolated house she was in danger of being stranded there. For a moment she contemplated turning back, but she hadn't visited Cordelia for two days, and she was anxious about the elderly lady who lived alone.

A frown furrowed her brow as she thought of her patient. Although Cordelia Symmonds was in her eighties she was fiercely independent. But six months ago she had fallen and broken her hip, and then recently she had had an accident in the kitchen and badly burned her hand. Cordelia was becoming increasingly frail, and it was no longer safe for her to live alone at Nunstead, but she had refused to consider moving to a smaller house closer to the village.

It was a pity Cordelia's grandson did not do more to help his grandmother, Emma thought darkly. But he lived abroad, and always seemed too busy with his high-powered career to have time to visit Northumberland. She had heard the pride and affection in Cordelia's voice on the many occasions when she had spoken of her grandson, but sadly the old lady seemed to have been abandoned by her only living relative.

It wasn't right, Emma thought fiercely. The subject of care for the elderly was close to her heart—particularly after the terrible event at the beginning of the year when she had visited a ninety-year-old man and discovered he had passed away in his armchair in a freezing cold house. His family had gone away for Christmas and had not arranged for anyone to check on him. The thought of the poor man dying alone still haunted her.

Remembering Mr Jeffries, Emma knew she could not allow the situation with Cordelia to continue. Perhaps she could somehow contact Cordelia's grandson and persuade him that he needed to take some responsibility for his grandmother? she brooded.

The car slid on the icy road, and she concentrated on driving through the increasingly heavy snowfall. It had been a long and difficult day, due mainly to the weather. Just this last visit, she thought wearily, and then she could collect Holly from the childminder, go home to the cottage and light a fire before she started cooking dinner.

She chewed on her lip as she recalled how her daughter had been coughing again when she had dropped her at nursery that morning. Her flu virus had been particularly severe, and the long winter wasn't helping the little girl to pick up. Spring couldn't come soon enough. Warm sunshine and the chance to play outside in the garden would do Holly the world of good, and hopefully put some colour back on her pale cheeks.

Rounding the next bend, Emma gave a startled cry when she was faced with car headlights blazing in front of her. Instantly she braked, and let out a shaky breath when she realised that the other car was not moving. A quick inspection of the scene told her that the car must have skidded on ice, spun around and then hit the bank of snow at the side of the road. The back end had actually crashed through the snow wall, and was partly submerged in the ditch.

There only seemed to be one occupant—a man—who flung open the driver's door and climbed out, apparently unhurt.

Halting her car beside him, Emma leaned over and wound down the window.

'Are you all right?'

'*I* am, but that's more than can be said for my car,' he replied tersely, his eyes on the sleek silver sports car half buried beneath a mountain of snow.

His voice was deep-timbred, with a faint accent that Emma could not immediately place but sent a tiny frisson down her spine. It was a very sexy voice—as rich and sensuous as molten chocolate. She frowned at the unexpected turn of her thoughts. A practical and down-to-earth person, she was not prone to wild flights of fancy.

The man was standing to one side of his car, out of the glare of the headlights, so she could not make out his features. But she noted his exceptional height. He was easily several inches over six feet tall. His superbly tailored sheepskin coat emphasised the width of his broad shoulders. Although she could not see him clearly, she sensed his air of wealth and sophistication, and she wondered what on earth he was doing in this remote area. The nearest village was miles back down the road, whilst ahead stretched the vast Northumberland moors. She glanced down at his leather shoes, which were covered in snow, and immediately dismissed the idea that he might be a hiker. His feet must be freezing.

Even as the thought came into her head he stamped his feet, as if to get the blood circulating, and pulled a mobile phone from his pocket.

'No signal,' he muttered disgustedly. 'Why anyone would choose to live in this godforsaken place is beyond me.'

'Northumbria is renowned for its unspoilt beauty,' Emma felt compelled to point out, feeling a tiny spurt of irritation at his scathing tone.

In her opinion, anyone who chose to drive across the moors in a snowstorm should have the sense to pack a spade and other emergency supplies. Personally, she loved Northumberland's dramatic landscapes. When she had been married to Jack they had rented a flat in Newcastle, but she hadn't enjoyed living in a busy city and had missed the wildness of the moors.

'There are some wonderful walks through the National Park—although it is rather bleak in the winter,' she conceded. Sensing the man's impatience, she continued, 'I'm afraid my phone doesn't work out here either—few of the phone networks do. You'll have to get to a village before you can call a garage, but I doubt anyone will send a truck to tow your car out until tomorrow.' She hesitated, instinctively wary of offering a complete stranger a lift, but her conscience nagged that she could not leave him stranded. 'I've got one more visit to make and then I'll be going back to Little Copton, if you want to come with me?'

He had no choice but to accept the woman's offer, Rocco realised as he walked around his car and saw that the back wheels were submerged in three feet of water. Even if he could clear the mound of snow that had collapsed on top of the roof, it would be impossible to drive up the side of the ditch; the wheels would simply spin on the ice. There was nothing for it but to find a hotel for the night and arrange for his car to be rescued in the morning, he concluded, reaching over to the back seat to retrieve his overnight bag.

He glanced at the bulky figure of the woman in the four-by-four and guessed that she was from one of the farms. Maybe she had been out to check on livestock: he couldn't imagine why else she would be driving across the moors in the snow.

She was certainly well built, he thought, as he climbed up into the car and squashed himself into the small space on the seat beside her. But her woollen hat was pulled low over her brow, and a thick scarf covered most of the lower half of her face, so it was impossible for him to guess her age.

'Thank you,' he murmured, closing the door and feeling a welcome blast of warm air from the car's heater. It was only now sinking in that he was lucky not to have been injured in the crash, and that he could have faced a long, cold walk to find civilisation. 'I was fortunate you were driving this way.'

Emma released the handbrake and carefully pulled away, her hands tightening on the steering wheel when she felt the car slide. She rammed the stiff gear lever into second gear, and tensed when her hand brushed against the man's thigh. In the confines of the vehicle she was even more aware of his size. His head almost brushed the roof, she noted, darting him a lightning glance. The collar of his coat was pulled up around his face, hiding his features, so that all she could really see of him was the dark hair which fell across his brow.

In the warm car the spicy scent of his cologne teased her senses. It was an evocatively masculine smell and stirred an unbidden memory of Jack. Her mouth tightened as the image of her husband's handsome face, his shock of blond hair and his lazy grin, flooded her mind. Jack had been a natural-born charmer who had loved the finer things in life, she remembered bleakly. She had bought him his favourite, ruinously expensive aftershave the last Christmas they had spent together, naively unaware that he probably wore it when he slept with other women.

She slammed a brake on her thoughts and became aware that the stranger was staring at her.

'What did you mean when you said you have to make one last visit? It's not a good night to be out socialising,' he said, glancing through the windscreen at the snowy lane illuminated by the car's headlights.

The area was familiar to Rocco. He knew there was only one more house ahead before the road dwindled to a track that wound across the moors. It was a stroke of good luck that his rescuer was heading in the direction of his destination, but he was puzzled as to where she was going.

Once again Emma felt a little quiver run down her spine

at the man's husky, innately sexy accent. Definitely not French, she decided, but possibly he was Spanish or Italian. She was curious to know why he had been driving along a remote Northumbrian country lane in a snowstorm. Where had he come from and where was he heading? But politeness and her natural diffidence prevented her from asking him.

'I'm a district nurse,' she explained. 'One of my patients lives out here on the moor.'

Beside her, she felt the stranger stiffen. He snapped his head towards her and seemed about to say something, but at that moment a stone gateway loomed out of the darkness.

'Here's Nunstead Hall,' Emma said, relieved to have arrived in one piece. 'Enormous, isn't it? The grounds are beautiful, and there's even a private lake.'

She turned onto the driveway and stared up at the imposing old house that was in darkness apart from one window, where a light was shining, and then glanced at the forbidding stranger, wondering why he made her feel uneasy. His brows were drawn into a deep frown, and she was puzzled by his tangible tension.

'Does your patient live here?' he demanded tersely.

It was too dark to see the expression in his eyes, but something about his hard stare unnerved her.

'Yes. You can probably phone the garage from the house,' she told him, assuming that he was frowning because he was anxious about his car. 'I have a door key so that I can let myself in. I think it would be better if you stay here while I ask Mrs Symmonds if you can use the phone.'

She reached over to the back seat for her medical bag and seconds later felt a blast of cold air rush into the car. 'Hey!' Irritation swept through her when she saw that the stranger had ignored her instructions and climbed out of the four-by-four. He was already striding up to the front door of the Hall, and she hastily jumped out and ran after him, stumbling in the thick snow that covered the ground. 'Didn't you hear what I said? I asked you to stay in the car. My patient is elderly and might be frightened at the sight of a stranger on the doorstep.'

'Hopefully I'm not that terrifying a sight,' he drawled, sounding arrogantly amused. He brushed off the snowflakes that were settling thick and fast on his coat. 'Although if you don't hurry up and open the door I'm going to look like the Yeti that's reputed to stalk the Himalayas.'

'It's not funny,' Emma snapped. She did not care for the hard glitter in his eyes, and wished that instead of rescuing him from the roadside she had phoned Jim at Yaxley Farm, which was the closest neighbour to Nunstead Hall, and asked him to bring a tractor to tow the stranger's car out of the ditch. She gave a startled gasp when the man took the key from her fingers and slotted it into the lock. Her anger turned to unease. For all she knew he could be a criminal on the run, or a lunatic! 'I must *insist* that you return to the car,' she said firmly. 'You can't just stroll in as if you own the place.'

'But I do own it,' he informed her coolly as he pushed open the door.

For a few seconds Emma gaped at him, stunned, but when he stepped across the threshold into the house she regained the use of her tongue. 'What do you mean? Who *are* you?'

She broke off when a door leading off the hallway opened and tiny, silver-haired Cordelia Symmonds appeared. Desperately concerned that the old lady would be scared to find a stranger in her home, Emma spoke quickly.

'Cordelia, I'm so sorry—this gentleman was stranded in the snow and…'

But Cordelia did not appear to be listening. Her eyes were focused on the stranger and a beaming smile spread across her lined face.

'Rocco, my darling. Why didn't you tell me you were coming?'

'I wanted to surprise you.' The man's accented voice was suddenly as soft as crushed velvet. 'Unfortunately my car skidded on ice, but luckily the nurse here—' he flicked a sardonic glance at Emma '—offered me a lift.'

Cordelia did not seem to notice Emma's confusion. 'Emma, dear—what a wonderful girl you are for rescuing my grandson.'

Grandson! Emma's eyes flew to the stranger. In the brightly lit hall she could see his face clearly, and she recognised him now. Pictures of him frequently appeared in celebrity gossip magazines, alongside frenzied discussion about his tangled love life. Rocco D'Angelo was the CEO of a famous Italian sports car company—Eleganza—and a multi-millionaire playboy who was reputed to be one of Europe's most eligible bachelors. And Cordelia's grandson.

Why hadn't it clicked? Emma asked herself impatiently. The clues had been there—the flash car, his foreign accent and his indefinable air of *savoir-faire* that only the very rich possessed. She hadn't been expecting to meet him, of course. But why hadn't he explained who he was? she thought irritably.

'Come along in, both of you,' Cordelia invited, turning back to the sitting room.

Emma went to follow, but found her way barred as the stranger—she was still struggling with the shock news that he was Cordelia's grandson—stepped in front of her.

'Just a moment—I'd like a word with you. Why exactly are you here?' Rocco asked in an undertone, pulling the sitting room door half closed so that his grandmother could not hear their conversation. 'Cordelia looks perfectly well. Why does she need a nurse to visit her?'

It was there again—that faintly haughty tone in his voice that made Emma's hackles rise. Images flashed in her head of poor Mr Jeffries, who had died alone, and Cordelia's joyous smile at her grandson's unexpected visit. The elderly lady clearly thought her grandson was Mr Wonderful, and from his arrogant air Rocco D'Angelo seemed to share that opinion.

'If you took *any* interest in your grandmother you would know why I am here,' she said sharply, feeling a small spurt of satisfaction when his eyes narrowed. 'I don't know if you're aware that Cordelia fell and broke her hip a few months ago. She's still recuperating from hip replacement surgery.'

'Of course I know about that.' Rocco disliked the nurse's belligerent attitude, and the implicit criticism of him that was apparent in her tone. His voice iced over. 'But I understood that she was recovering well.'

'She's over eighty, and she should not be living here in this remote house all alone. Her recent accident when she burned her hand is proof of that. It's a great pity that you are too busy with your own life to pay Cordelia any attention.' Emma gave him a scathing look. 'From what I understand, you are her only living relative. You should be doing more to help your grandmother.' She pushed past him. 'Now, please excuse me. I need to see my patient.'

The sitting room was like an oven. At least Cordelia did not stint on heating the house, Emma thought, watching Rocco—who had followed her into the room—immediately shrug off his coat. Her eyes seemed to have a magnetic attraction to him, and she felt a peculiar sensation in the pit of her stomach as her brain registered that he was utterly gorgeous. His black jeans and matching fine wool sweater moulded his lean, hard body. Raven-dark hair was swept back from his brow, emphasising the perfect symmetry of his chiselled features, his sharp cheekbones and square chin giving him a harsh, autocratic beauty that took her breath away.

With his incredible looks he could be a film star, or a male model from one of those glossy magazines that were occasionally donated to the surgery's waiting room and featured articles about the rich and famous aboard their yachts in Monaco, she brooded.

He looked over at her, and she felt embarrassed that he had caught her staring at him. Her face grew hotter when he trailed his unusual amber-coloured eyes over her in brief assessment, before dismissing her with a sweep of his thick black lashes. Clearly he did not consider her worthy of a second glance. But why would he? she asked herself irritably. She was not a skinny, glamorous clothes horse like the stunning French model Juliette Pascal, who was reputed to be his current mistress. Emma had long ago accepted that even if she dieted permanently she would never be a fashionable and totally unachievable size zero, and she was painfully conscious that in her padded jacket she looked like a sumo wrestler.

Rocco was seething. The gratitude he had felt towards the nurse for rescuing him from the roadside had rapidly disappeared when she had voiced her opinion that he did not care properly for his grandmother. She knew nothing about his relationship with Cordelia and had no right to pass judgement on him, he thought furiously.

He adored his *nonna*, and the nurse's assertion that he was too wrapped up in his own life to pay her any attention was ridiculous. However busy he was, he always phoned her once a week. It was true he hadn't managed to come to England for quite a while—not since his brief visit at Christmas. He felt a pang of guilt when he realised that it was nearly three months since he had last been at Nunstead.

But Cordelia did not live alone. The nurse—Emma, he recalled his grandmother had called her—was wrong about that. Before he had returned to Italy he had employed a housekeeper to take care of the house *and* Cordelia.

Thoroughly riled, he glared at Emma, whose face was still half hidden beneath her scarf. Never in his life had he seen a woman wear such an unflattering hat, he mused, his eyes drawn with horrible fascination to the red woollen monstrosity on her head, which had slipped so low that it now covered her eyebrows. But she was no longer looking at him, and was staring down at Cordelia's feet.

'Cordelia, why is there snow on your slippers?' Emma frowned when she saw the elderly lady shiver. 'Don't tell me you've been outside in the garden? It's freezing, and you could have slipped on the ice.'

'Oh, I only went a little way down the path.' A worried look crossed Cordelia's face. 'Thomas has disappeared. I can't find him anywhere.'

'I'll look for him, and then I'll make some tea. You sit by the fire and warm up,' Emma instructed firmly, concern for her patient providing a welcome distraction from Cordelia's disturbingly handsome grandson.

In the kitchen she filled the kettle and then opened the back door. The garden was a white wilderness illuminated by the moonlight. She compressed her lips at the sight of footsteps across the snow-covered lawn. Thank heavens Cordelia hadn't fallen; hypothermia would have set in very quickly in the sub-zero temperature.

Gleaming green eyes caught her attention. 'Thomas, come here you little pest.' A ball of ginger fur shot past, but she managed to catch it, wishing she was still wearing her gloves when the cat dug his needle-sharp claws into her hand. 'It would have been your fault if Cordelia had slipped over,' she told the animal with mock sternness.

Her expression became serious. This situation could not be allowed to continue. For her own safety Cordelia would have to be persuaded to move closer to the village—or her arrogant grandson who had turned up out of the blue would have to be persuaded to take responsibility for his frail grandmother, and at the very least arrange for full-time staff to care for her at Nunstead Hall.

Rocco D'Angelo was in the kitchen when she went back inside. Although the room was a fair size it suddenly seemed claustrophobically small as he prowled around like a sleek, dark panther. Even his name was sexy, Emma thought ruefully, irritated with herself for the way her heart-rate quickened when he strode around the table and halted in front of her, his glittering golden eyes trapping her gaze.

'Who is Thomas?' he demanded curtly. 'And why are *you* making tea? Surely the housekeeper should do that?'

'This is Thomas.' Emma set the cat on the floor. 'He turned up on the doorstep a couple of weeks ago and Cordelia adopted him. We think he'd been abandoned and had been living wild, but sought shelter when the weather became colder. He's half feral and usually only goes to your grandmother,' she added, glancing at the scratch on the back of her hand and feeling a flare of annoyance when Thomas rubbed his head against Rocco's leg and purred. 'And there isn't a housekeeper, as I'm sure you know,' she continued sharply. 'To be honest, I don't know how you can have allowed Cordelia to remain here when there's no one to help with shopping and cooking, and generally keeping an eye on her. I'm sure you lead a very busy life, Mr D'—'

'I hired a housekeeper called Morag Stewart to look after the house *and* my grandmother the last time I was here at Nunstead.' Rocco interrupted the nurse mid-flow. It was obvious she had been itching to give him a lecture on his inadequacies, but he was in no mood to listen.

He was well aware of his failings, he thought grimly. As always, coming back to Nunstead Hall evoked memories of Giovanni. It was twenty years since his younger brother had drowned in the lake on the grounds of the house, but time had not erased the memory of his mother's hysterical screams, nor her accusation that it was *his* fault Gio was dead.

'I told you to look after him. You're as irresponsible as your goddamned father.'

The image of his brother's limp, lifeless body still haunted him. Gio had only been seven years old, while Rocco had been fifteen—old enough to be left in charge of his brother for a few hours, his mother had sobbed. He should have taken better care of Gio. He should have saved him. But he had failed.

Rocco's jaw tightened. The guilt he felt about Gio was now mixed with a new guilt that once again his actions had resulted in terrible consequences—although mercifully not in another death. But it had been a close call, he acknowledged grimly. A year ago a young actress, Rosalinda Barinelli, had swallowed an overdose of sleeping pills after he had ended their affair. It had only been by lucky chance that a friend had found her and called an ambulance. Rosalinda had survived, but had admitted that she had tried to take her life because she could not bear to live without *him*.

'I always wanted more than an affair, Rocco,' she had told him when he had visited her in hospital. *'I pretended to be happy as your mistress, but I always hoped you would fall in love with me.'*

To his surprise, Rosalinda's parents had been sympathetic when he'd explained that he had been unaware of their daughter's feelings, and that he had never made promises of marriage or commitment to her. They had revealed that Rosalinda had formed a similar strong attachment to a previous boyfriend. She had always been emotionally fragile, and they had not blamed Rocco for her suicide attempt. But, despite the Barinellis' reassurance, he still blamed himself.

Now, as he stared at Emma, his conscience pricked. Maybe she was right to be concerned about his grandmother. He could not understand why Cordelia was living alone at Nunstead Hall, but he was determined to find out what was going on.

CHAPTER TWO

EMMA switched the kettle onto boil and began to unravel her scarf. Glancing down, she saw that she had walked snow into the kitchen from the garden, and tugged off her boots before unzipping her jacket. Her mind dwelled on Rocco D'Angelo's assertion that he had arranged for a housekeeper to work at Nunstead.

'There's never been a housekeeper here since I've known Cordelia. I've never met this Morag Stewart, and your grandmother has never mentioned her. When did you say you hired her?'

'Just before Christmas.' Rocco's jaw hardened at the scepticism in Emma's voice. He was infuriated that she clearly did not believe him. He was not used to having his actions questioned—especially by a woman. In Rocco's experience women agreed with everything he said.

'Nonna was still frail after her hip replacement. I wanted to take her to my home in Italy, but she refused to leave Nunstead. You might be aware that I am the chief executive of the sports car company Eleganza?' he continued coldly. 'It is a demanding job and I have little spare time.'

The past four months had been manic. The death of his father after a short illness had been a shock, and his workload had been immense as he had continued to run

Eleganza at the same time as trying to sort out Enrico's affairs. What a tangled web his father had left behind, Rocco thought grimly.

He stared at the nurse through the cloud of steam that enveloped her as she poured water from the kettle into a teapot. 'I knew I would not have time to visit England regularly, so I contacted a staff agency and subsequently appointed Morag Stewart as housekeeper and companion to Cordelia.'

'Your grandmother didn't become my patient until the end of January,' Emma said slowly. The realisation was sinking in that she might have misjudged Cordelia's grandson. 'I took over caring for her from one of my colleagues after our rounds were reorganized, and I was immediately concerned that she lived on her own such a long way from the village. At first I only saw her once a week, to check her blood pressure, but since she burned her hand I've visited every couple of days.' She stared at Rocco, accepting that it was unlikely he had made up the story about hiring a housekeeper. 'Morag Stewart must have left Nunstead for some reason,' she ventured.

'I intend to find out *why* from Cordelia.'

But his intention to quiz his grandmother about her unsatisfactory living arrangements was not as imperative as it had been a few moments ago, Rocco discovered. Ever since he had watched Emma pull off her boots, to reveal a pair of surprisingly shapely legs sheathed in black hose, he had been intrigued to see the rest of the woman who had so far been hidden by outerwear that would not have looked out of place in the Arctic. The removal of her scarf had exposed a face far younger than he had expected, with creamy skin and a lush, full-lipped mouth that drew his gaze.

Now she pulled off her hat and shook her head, so that

her hair settled around her face in a chin-length strawberry blonde bob that shone like raw silk beneath the bright kitchen light. Her features were attractive rather than pretty, Rocco mused. There was strength in the firmness of her jaw, and her grey eyes, the colour of rain-clouds, were intelligent and coolly assessing. Finally she shrugged off her padded jacket. Her body was an even more pleasant surprise, he noted, skimming his eyes over her blue nurse's uniform and focusing on her slim waist, the gentle flare of her hips and the rounded fullness of her breasts.

The thought came into his head that this was how a woman *should* look. He was jaded by a diet of whippet-thin, glamorous models. Emma's curvaceous figure was a delightful contrast to his numerous high-maintenance mistresses. As he stared at her he was reminded of a Renaissance painting of Adam and Eve in the Garden of Eden. Like Eve, Emma's soft curves were sensual and tempting. He wondered what she looked like naked, imagined her breasts filling his hands like plump peaches…

The sharp stab of desire in his groin was unexpected and disconcerting. She wasn't his type, he reminded himself. To his surprise he found her physically attractive, but her brisk, no-nonsense personality reminded him of the strict headmistress of the English prep school he'd been sent to at the age of six, and her readiness to jump to conclusions without checking facts irritated the hell out of him.

Which brought him back to his grandmother and the case of the missing housekeeper, he brooded.

'I still think you should have found the time to visit between Christmas and now.'

The nurse's disapproving voice interrupted Rocco's thoughts.

'If you had, you would have known the housekeeper

wasn't here and that Cordelia was struggling to cope on her own. I appreciate that you lead a busy life, Mr D'Angelo, but I know for a fact that you aren't always working. Cordelia saves every newspaper clipping about you, and only last week she showed me a photo of you on the ski slopes at Val d'Isère.'

Emma opened a cupboard and took down three of the bone china cups and saucers that she knew Cordelia preferred to mugs before turning to face Rocco.

'In my opinion…'

'I'm not interested in your opinion,' he stated. 'Particularly in relation to my private life.' Rocco's mouth thinned as he struggled to control his anger. What would the sanctimonious, busybody nurse say, he brooded, if he revealed that the reason for the skiing trip had been an attempt to build a relationship with his father's illegitimate young son, Marco—a half-brother whose existence he had been unaware of until shortly before Enrico's death? 'My personal life is no concern of yours.'

'True,' Emma agreed tightly. 'But your grandmother's welfare *is* my concern. I'm worried about her safety, living on her own, and I'm sure she's not eating properly. I would be failing in my duty if I did not report my concerns to Social Services.'

She could tell from the dangerous gleam in Rocco's tiger-like golden eyes that she had angered him with her bluntness. In her job she had found that people often became defensive when reminded of their responsibilities towards a vulnerable relative. But it was too bad, she thought, lifting her chin to meet his intimidating glare. She had grown very fond of Cordelia, and dreaded the thought of her falling and lying unaided, because there was no one around to come to her rescue—just as no one had come to the aid of poor Mr Jeffries.

'Your grandmother needs help,' she told Rocco fiercely. 'It is unacceptable for you to abandon her while you gallivant around the world—whether for business or pleasure,' she added, thinking of the attractive blonde in the photo, who had no doubt been Rocco's companion both on and off the ski slopes.

Rocco muttered a curse under his breath, his patience finally snapping. 'I head a billion-dollar global company. I do not *gallivant* anywhere. And I have certainly not abandoned Cordelia.' He took a deep breath and sought to control his temper. Emma was a nurse, he reminded himself, and it was her job to ensure that her patient was safe and well cared for. 'I appreciate your concern, but it is unnecessary. I am perfectly capable of looking after my grandmother.'

'Really?' Emma's brows arched disbelievingly. 'I've seen little evidence of that. Cordelia has been struggling for weeks—the accident when she burned her hand was very serious. Your turning up out of the blue occasionally is simply not good enough. What she needs is for you to live here at Nunstead with her.'

'Unfortunately that is impossible. Eleganza is based in Italy and I need to live there.' Even more so now that he had Marco to consider, Rocco thought heavily. But he was damned if he would explain himself to Miss High-and-Mighty. All Emma needed to understand was that he intended to fulfil his responsibility towards his grandmother and take care of her—although quite how he was going to do that when Cordelia had always insisted that she would never leave Nunstead Hall was something he had not yet figured out.

It was not surprising that Rocco preferred to live at his luxurious villa in Portofino rather than on the windswept Northumberland moors, Emma thought, recalling the photos of his house in the Italian province of Genoa that Cordelia had once shown her. There had been other photographs of Rocco aboard his yacht, with the sea sparkling in the background and a gorgeous brunette in a minuscule bikini pressing her body seductively up against him.

'My grandson is a handsome playboy, just like his father,' Cordelia had said, her obvious fondness for Rocco mixed with a faint air of resignation at his pleasure-seeking lifestyle. 'But he says he has learned from his father's mistakes and has no intention of marrying and having children.'

Emma dragged her thoughts back to the present. 'Well, something has got to be done,' she said crisply, trying to dismiss the memory of the photo and Rocco's muscular, tanned torso from her mind.

She had finished making the tea and went to pick up the tray at the same time as he stretched his hands towards it. Heat shot up her arm at the brush of his warm skin against hers. Startled by the unexpected contact, and her reaction to it, she jerked her hand away as if she had been burned.

The kitchen door swung open and Cordelia walked in, seeming not to notice Emma's pink cheeks or the way she quickly stepped away from Rocco.

'I was wondering what had happened to the tea,' the elderly lady said cheerfully.

'I was just about to bring it in.' Nothing in Rocco's voice revealed that he was fighting a strong urge to run his fingers through the shiny bell of red-gold hair that framed Emma's face. He could not identify her perfume, but he liked the delicate lemony fragrance, which was so subtle compared to the cloying designer scents most women he knew chose to drown themselves in.

With an effort he dragged his mind from the sexual allure of his grandmother's nurse and fixed Cordelia with a stern glance. 'Nonna, where is the housekeeper I arranged to live at Nunstead with you?'

'Oh, I sacked Morag ages ago—after I discovered her stealing money from my purse,' Cordelia told him brightly. 'Dreadful woman—I'm certain she had been pilfering from almost the minute she arrived. I've realised since she left that several pieces of silverware have disappeared.'

Rocco exhaled heavily. 'Why didn't you tell me? You knew I did not want you to live alone after your fall last year.' His exasperation with his grandmother was mingled with a flare of satisfaction when he noted the guilty expression on Emma's face. She knew now that he had not abandoned Cordelia. Perhaps that would teach her to be a little less judgemental in future, he thought self-righteously. On the other hand, his conscience pointed out, Emma *had* been right when she had said that he should have found the time to visit Cordelia during the past three months.

'I didn't want to worry you,' his grandmother explained. 'You had enough to deal with, running Eleganza. And of course losing your father must have been such a shock.' She sighed. 'It's hard to believe that my one-time son-in-law is dead. Enrico can only have been in his early sixties, and he was still so handsome. He had just finished making another film when his cancer was diagnosed, hadn't he?'

Rocco nodded. 'At least he was not ill for very long. He would have hated that.' His father had not been an easy patient, he remembered heavily. Enrico D'Angelo had been one of Italy's most famous film stars. Fêted and adored all his adult life, he had expected his son, for whom he'd had little time during Rocco's childhood, to be at his bedside twenty-four hours a day. But there had been little that Enrico's doctors could do apart from keeping the dying man comfortable, and Rocco had felt a sense of helplessness that he could not save his father—just as he had not saved his brother, nor prevented his mother's fatal accident years before.

Dragging his mind from the past, Rocco recognised his grandmother's attempt to steer the conversation away from herself. 'But, Nonna, I wish you had told me about the housekeeper. I believed these past few months that you were being looked after.'

'I don't *need* looking after,' Cordelia argued hotly. 'You should know by now that I'm a tough old stick. And before you start—' she fixed her grandson with a sharp stare '—I will not move from Nunstead. I was born here, and I intend to die here.'

Emma glanced at Rocco and felt a reluctant tug of sympathy for him. His grandmother was barely five feet tall, and looked as though she weighed little more than a sparrow, but she was as strong-willed as an ox. Rocco would have a battle on his hands if he attempted to persuade Cordelia to move house, she thought ruefully.

He turned his head and their eyes met in a moment of mutual understanding. She knew she owed him an apology. It sounded as though he had done his best to arrange a live-in companion for Cordelia, and far from being too busy to come to England he had remained in Italy to be with his terminally ill father.

'Why don't we go back into the sitting room?' she murmured, addressing Cordelia because she felt embarrassed about how unfairly she had accused Rocco. 'I want to take a look at your hand.'

It was a relief to move away from the gorgeous Italian. She was shaken by her strong awareness of him. He made her feel flustered and on edge, and caused her heart to thud unevenly. But *why* did he have such an effect on her? she asked herself impatiently as she followed him along the hall, trying not to allow her eyes to focus on his muscular thighs and the taut buttocks outlined beneath his close-fitting black denim jeans. He was stunningly good-looking, but she knew of his reputation as an inveterate charmer, and she had sworn after Jack that never again would she be seduced by a handsome face and a ton of charisma.

As they neared the door to the sitting room she glanced at the portrait of Cordelia's daughter hanging in the hallway. Flora Symmonds had been exquisitely beautiful, she mused as she studied the painting of the world-famous actress who had died unfairly young and at the height of her career.

'She was stunning, wasn't she?' Rocco halted next to her and followed her gaze. 'My dear *mamma*—beautiful, talented, but unfortunately a lousy mother,' he said harshly.

Emma gave him a shocked look. 'You don't mean that.' She was glad Cordelia had walked ahead of them into the sitting room and could not hear her grandson.

'It's the truth.' Rocco's jaw hardened as stared at the portrait of his mother. 'Both my parents were selfish and self-obsessed. They should never have had children, and they quickly realised that fact and sent us away to school as early as possible.'

'Us?' Emma was puzzled. Cordelia had only ever spoken of Rocco, as if he was her only grandchild.

He was silent for so long that she thought he was not going to answer her, but then he said quietly, 'My younger brother and I attended boarding school in England. Cordelia was more of a parent to me than either my mother or father. I spent many school holidays here at Nunstead when my parents were both away making films.' He turned his head from his mother's picture and gave Emma an amused smile. 'I agree that the Northumberland National

Park has some great walks. I spent a lot of time exploring the moors when I was a boy.'

Emma felt her face redden at his reference to their conversation in the car, when she had been unaware of his identity. 'I didn't realise you were familiar with the area,' she muttered, adding a touch defensively, 'It's a pity you didn't explain who you were.'

He shrugged. 'I did not know you were on your way to visit my grandmother and saw no reason to introduce myself. I see now that your concern for Cordelia was justified,' he added honestly. 'If I had known she was living alone I would have immediately come to England and made other arrangements regarding her care.'

She believed him. The affection Rocco felt for his grandmother was evident in his voice, and Emma felt ashamed of the way she had been so quick to judge him. 'I'm sorry about your recent bereavement,' she mumbled. 'I hadn't made the connection, until Cordelia spoke of him, that Enrico D'Angelo was your father. He was a brilliant actor. I was shocked when I read about his death in the newspapers a few months ago.'

Although Rocco did not appear to have been close to his parents, it must be hard to have lost both of them, she thought. She guessed he was in his mid-thirties, which meant he would have only been a young man when his mother had driven her car along a clifftop road on the French Riviera and taken a hairpin bend too fast.

The accident had made headlines around the globe. Flora Symmonds and Enrico D'Angelo had been world-famous film stars whose tempestuous marriage, numerous affairs and bitter divorce had been played out in the media spotlight. It was little wonder that Rocco had preferred to spend his school holidays with his grandmother, in the peaceful surroundings of Nunstead Hall.

Her eyes strayed against her will to his sculpted face. He met her gaze, his golden eyes gleaming, and her heart gave a little flip when his mouth curved. She might have known that his smile would be devastatingly sensual. He was the archetypal alpha-male—good-looking, confident and oozing sex appeal. Just like Jack, and exactly the type of man she had vowed to avoid like the plague.

The timely reminder of her husband served as a cold shower, dousing her awareness of Rocco. He was a charmer, but she was determined not to be charmed, and her smile was distinctly cool as she murmured, 'I think you had better carry the tea in before it stews.'

Five minutes later Rocco grimaced as he watched Emma remove the dressing on Cordelia's hand to reveal a large patch of raw scarlet skin. 'That looks painful,' he said grimly. 'How did you burn yourself, Nonna?'

'Oh, the silliest thing.' Cordelia shook her head impatiently. 'I had heated up some soup for my lunch and somehow managed to spill it onto my hand while I was pouring it into a bowl. Those copper-based saucepans are terribly heavy. I shall buy some different ones the next time I go to Morpeth.'

'How have you been getting to the town, or even Little Copton, since Morag left?' Rocco frowned as he thought of how isolated his grandmother was here at Nunstead Hall. One of the reasons he had appointed Morag Stewart had been because she had assured him she would be happy to drive Cordelia around the local area.

'I haven't been able to go anywhere since Dr Hanley said that my eyesight is too poor for me to be able to drive. I'm sure he's wrong,' Cordelia said indignantly. 'I was perfectly safe. I used to drive ambulances in London during the Blitz, you know.'

'I know you did, Nonna. You were—and are—amazing,' Rocco said softly.

Cordelia's spirit was as indomitable as ever, but her reference to the part she had played in the Second World War was a reminder of her advancing years, he thought heavily. Once again he felt guilty that he had not checked to see that all was well at Nunstead Hall, but he had been so focused on his father in the weeks before he died, and also on searching for Enrico's mistress, who was the mother of his young son.

'I'm very lucky to have such a wonderful nurse,' his grandmother continued. 'Emma has been bringing me my shopping. I don't need much—just milk and bread mainly—but I must have cat food for Thomas. He does like his three meals a day.'

'He's the best fed cat in the whole of Northumberland,' Emma said dryly. 'I only wish *you* would eat three meals a day, Cordelia.'

There was genuine affection in her voice, and the smile she gave his grandmother was notably warmer than the frosty glances she occasionally directed his way, Rocco noted. Although he hated to admit it, his curiosity was piqued by Emma's coolness. It was fair to say that it was not the sort of response he usually received from women, he thought self-derisively.

He acknowledged his luck in having been blessed with an athletic build and facial features that had drawn attention from the opposite sex since he was a youth. A degree of cynicism, developed over the years, warned him that his status as heir to his grandfather's billion-pound company added greatly to his appeal. Mistresses came in and out of his life with mundane regularity, and it was rare for any woman to hold his interest for more than a few months.

It was always too easy, he reflected. He had never met a woman yet who had presented a challenge.

His eyes were drawn again to Emma's neat red-gold bob that curved around her face. There was nothing frivolous about her appearance. Her practical hairstyle was the ideal choice for a busy professional, yet there was something very sexy about her sleek, shiny hair that made him want to run his fingers through it.

Eliciting a smile from her could be an interesting challenge, he mused. His gaze lingered on her mouth, and the unbidden image came into his head of tasting her, of slanting his lips over hers and exploring their moist softness. She was sitting on the sofa, attending to Cordelia's hand, but she looked up at that moment and Rocco was startled to feel heat surge into his face.

Dio, the last time he'd felt embarrassed was when he had been fourteen and the housemaster at his boarding school had caught him looking at pictures of half-naked women in a magazine. Muttering an oath beneath his breath, he strode over to the window to close the curtains, grateful for the excuse to turn his back on his grandmother's nurse while he fought to bring his libido under control.

Emma finished re-bandaging Cordelia's hand. 'The burn is healing slowly, but there's still a risk of infection so you need to keep it covered for another few days. I'll visit again on Monday to change the dressing,' she said as she stood up.

Her body tensed involuntarily when Rocco strolled across the room and halted beside her. Although she carefully did not look at him, she was supremely conscious of him towering over her, and to her disgust her hand shook slightly as she closed the zip of her medical bag.

'It's started snowing again,' he announced. 'The roads were treacherous on the way here, and they can only be worse now. I think it would be a good idea for you to spend the night here, Emma.'

His sexy accent lingered on each syllable of her name and sent a little quiver of reaction down Emma's spine. For heaven's sake! How could she be seduced by his *voice*? she berated herself silently.

Taking a deep breath, she flashed him a polite half smile. 'Thanks for the offer, but I must get back.'

Rocco frowned. In his mind he had pictured sitting by the fire with Emma after his grandmother had retired to bed, enjoying the particularly fine malt whisky Cordelia always kept for him and exerting his acknowledged easy charm to break through her barriers. Her crisp refusal shattered the cosy picture and aroused his curiosity.

'Is someone expecting you?' This blunt question was just about the most unsubtle way of discovering if she had a partner, he acknowledged sardonically.

'My three-year-old daughter.' Cool grey eyes briefly met his gaze before flicking to the clock on the mantelpiece. 'I was due to collect Holly half an hour ago. Fortunately her childminder was fine about it when I phoned to explain that I would be late. But now I really must go.'

'Can't your daughter's father collect her?'

Rocco did not know who was more surprised by his unguarded query—him or Emma. He couldn't understand what had got into him—or why, when he glanced at her left hand, the sight of the gold wedding band on her finger intensified his feeling of irritation.

'No.' Emma did not offer any further explanation. The mention of Holly had made her impatient to get home. She was aware of Rocco's frown, but she had no intention of appeasing his idle curiosity by discussing Holly's father. 'I'll just go and get my boots and jacket, and then I'll be off. Stay in the warm, Cordelia,' she added, when the elderly lady began to get to her feet. 'I'll see you after the weekend.'

'Don't forget your hat,' Cordelia called after her. 'It's lucky I knitted it for you. You need it in this weather.'

Emma stifled a sigh at the mention of the dreaded woollen hat that so resembled a tea cosy. But Cordelia had been so proud when she had presented it to her a few weeks ago that she'd felt she must wear it. As she passed Rocco she caught the glimmer of amusement in his eyes and flushed.

He was waiting by the front door when she walked back down the hall from the kitchen a few minutes later. She was desperately conscious of his appraisal and, although she knew she was being ridiculous, she wished she was wearing her elegant grey wool coat rather than the unflattering ski jacket.

'I'll see you out,' he said, opening the door so that a gust of icy air rushed into the hall. The snow falling from the inky black sky was light, but steady, and not for the first time that winter Emma was grateful to her father for giving her the four-by-four.

'There's no need for you to come out,' she told Rocco when he followed her down the front steps.

He ignored her and walked with her to where she was parked. 'I haven't thanked you for coming to my rescue.' His face was shadowed in the darkness, but his eyes glowed amber, reminding her once again of tiger's eyes.

'You're welcome.' Emma hesitated. 'To be honest, I'm relieved you're here. I worry about Cordelia living alone in such a remote place. How long do you plan to stay?'

'I'm not sure yet.' His original intention to visit his grandmother for a few days was no longer viable, Rocco acknowledged. But he could not remain in England indefinitely when he had a business empire in Italy to run.

Perhaps Emma recognised his quandary, because after

she had climbed into the four-by-four she gave him a sharp look. 'While you're here I'll need to arrange a meeting with Social Services so that we can decide on the best way to care for Cordelia.'

Her schoolmistress tone annoyed Rocco. Did she think he would simply disappear and abandon his grandmother? He was about to tell her that he did not need interference from her or anyone else, but then remembered that without Emma's help over the past weeks Cordelia might have come to serious harm.

He gave a brief nod. 'You had better get going before the snow gets worse. Will you phone to say you have arrived home safely, to put my grandmother's mind at rest?'

The journey back to Little Copton on the hazardous roads demanded Emma's full attention, and she pushed all thoughts of Rocco D'Angelo to the back of her mind.

'I'm sorry I'm so late,' she apologised to Holly's childminder when Karen opened the door of her bungalow and ushered her inside. 'The roads are like a skating rink.'

'Don't worry about it. Holly has been fine playing with the twins,' Karen reassured her. 'I gave her dinner with Lily and Sara, but she didn't eat much, and she looks tired now. That flu virus really knocked her out, didn't it? What the two of you need is a nice, relaxing holiday—somewhere abroad, where it's warm and sunny.'

'Some hope,' Emma said with a sigh. 'My finances simply won't stretch to a foreign holiday, and I can't plan anything while the owner of Primrose Cottage is considering putting it up for sale. I might have to start looking for somewhere else to live.' Her heart sank as the worry that had gnawed away at her for the past few weeks filled her mind, but her smile was determinedly bright when she walked into Karen's sitting room and Holly hurtled into her arms.

'Mummy, I missed you.'

'I missed you too, munchkin.' More than words could convey, Emma thought silently as she lifted her daughter into her arms and hugged her tight.

Leaving Holly every day was a wrench she had never grown used to, but she had no choice. She enjoyed her job as a nurse, but when she had fallen pregnant she had planned to take a career break for a few years to be a full-time mother. Fate had intervened, and the necessity to pay rent and bills meant that she had returned to work when Holly had been six months old. It also meant that the time she spent with her daughter was doubly precious, and her heart ached with love when Holly pressed a kiss to her cheek.

'Let's go home,' she said softly, trying not to think about the possibility that Primrose Cottage might not be their home for much longer.

Holly was half-asleep by the time Emma had driven through the village and parked outside the cottage. Deciding to forgo giving the little girl a bath, she quickly carried out the routine of pyjamas, teeth cleaning and bed-time story, and then tiptoed from Holly's bedroom. An omelette was not a substantial meal after a long day at work, but it was all she could be bothered to cook for her dinner. But first she needed to phone Nunstead Hall to let Cordelia know she was home.

It was ridiculous for her pulse-rate to quicken as she made the call, but to her annoyance she could not control it—nor prevent the lurch of her heart when a gravelly, accented voice greeted her.

'Emma—I assume you have arrived home safely?'

'Yes, thank you.' Was that breathy, girly voice really

hers? And why did the sexy way that Rocco drawled her name make her feel hot and flustered? A glance in the hall mirror revealed that her cheeks were pink, she noted disgustedly. Having successfully put him out of her head for the past hour, she was dismayed when the image of his arrogantly handsome face filled her mind.

Sexual awareness had taken her by surprise from the moment she had followed him into Nunstead Hall and seen him properly for the first time, she acknowledged ruefully. He had dismissed her at first, after a cursory glance. But later, when she had taken off her coat in the kitchen, he had trailed his mesmeric amber eyes over her in a lingering appraisal, the memory of which sent a quiver down her spine.

Oh, hell. She gripped the phone tighter and fought to control her rising panic. She had never expected to be physically attracted to any man ever again. It was just chemistry, she assured herself. A mysterious sexual alchemy that defied logical explanation. It was inconvenient and annoying, but she was a mature woman of twenty-eight, not a hormonal adolescent, and she refused to allow her equilibrium to be disturbed by a notorious playboy.

'I hope your daughter was not upset that you were late to collect her?'

Once again Rocco's deep voice made her think of rich, sensuous molten chocolate. She drew a ragged breath and by a miracle managed to sound briskly cheerful. 'No, Holly was fine. She's in bed now, and I'm just about to cook my dinner, so I'll say goodnight, Mr D'Angelo.'

'Rocco,' he insisted softly. 'My grandmother has been talking about you all evening. She is clearly very fond of you, and now that I feel I know everything about you it seems too formal to address you as Mrs Marchant.'

'Right…' The word emerged as a strangled croak.

What on earth had Cordelia said about her? Emma wondered, feeling highly uncomfortable with the idea that Rocco knew 'everything' about her. Her flush deepened, and she had a strange feeling that he sensed her discomposure and was amused. She pictured his mouth curving into a slow, sexy smile, and was shocked to feel her nipples harden.

It was suddenly imperative that she end the call. 'Well, goodnight…Rocco.'

'*Buonanotte*, Emma. And thank you again for your help tonight.'

Rocco's expression was thoughtful as he replaced the receiver and strolled back into the sitting room at Nunstead Hall. He could not deny that he was more intrigued by Emma Marchant now he had learned that she was a widow. According to Cordelia, Emma's husband had been dead for three years—yet she still wore a wedding ring. Three years was a long time to grieve, he mused.

His jaw tightened. Why was he thinking about her? Heaven knew he had enough to deal with—including the problem of how he could take care of his grandmother. He did not have the time or the inclination to pursue an inconvenient attraction to a woman who came with baggage that included a young child.

CHAPTER THREE

USUALLY Emma loved Saturday mornings, with their promise of two whole days that she could spend exclusively with her daughter. But the weekend started badly when she picked up the post from the doormat and opened a letter from her landlord, informing her that he had decided to put Primrose Cottage on the market. The two months' notice she had been given to move out was more than Mr Clarke was legally bound to offer, and she appreciated his consideration, but she felt sick at the prospect of uprooting Holly from her home and trying to find somewhere else to live.

'You promised we could make cakes, Mummy,' Holly reminded her over breakfast.

'So I did.' Her appetite non-existent, Emma crumbled her uneaten piece of toast onto her plate, ready to feed the birds, and smiled at Holly's eager face. There was no point in fretting and spoiling the weekend, she told herself.

But the arrival of the estate agent later in the morning to take measurements and photographs of the cottage emphasised the stark reality of the situation.

'There are no other properties to rent in Little Copton, but I have a couple of houses on my books that are up for sale,' the agent told her. 'They're both bigger than this place, though,' he added. 'Four bedrooms, couple of bathrooms and big gardens—they might be out of your price range.'

'I don't have a price range,' Emma said dismally. 'I can't afford the deposit necessary to secure a mortgage. If I could, I'd snap up Primrose Cottage.'

She sighed. Holly was so settled in the village; she attended the local nursery and her name was down for the primary school where all her little friends would go. But now it looked as if they would have to leave Little Copton and move to a town where there were more properties available to rent.

The peal of the doorbell drew a frown. She wasn't expecting any visitors, and her heart sank at the thought that it might be another estate agent come to take details of the cottage.

'You look as though you're having a bad morning.'

Yes, and it had just got a whole lot worse, Emma thought silently, feeling her heart jerk painfully beneath her ribs when she pulled open the door and stared at Rocco D'Angelo's stunningly handsome face. It should be illegal for a man to smile the way he was smiling, with a lazy, sexy charm and a bold gleam in his golden eyes as he subjected her to a leisurely appraisal. His gaze lingered rather longer than was appropriate on her breasts. Perversely, she wished she was wearing something more flattering than a long-sleeved grey jersey top that had shrunk in the wash.

'You seem to have something on your shirt.'

Following Rocco's gaze, Emma glanced down and discovered that her chest was spattered with fine white powder. 'It's flour,' she muttered, blushing as she attempted to brush the flour from her breasts. 'We're baking cakes, and Holly whisked the ingredients a little too enthusiastically.' To her horror she realised that her nipples were jutting provocatively beneath her clingy top. A glance at Rocco's face told her he had noticed, and she quickly crossed her arms in front of her, feeling thoroughly flustered. 'Are you here for a reason, Mr D'Angelo? Because I'm rather busy.'

Dark eyebrows winged upwards at her sharp tone. 'I thought last night that we had agreed on Rocco?' he drawled. 'And, yes, there *is* a reason for my visit. Perhaps you could invite me in so that we can discuss it?'

Rocco glanced over Emma's shoulder into the narrow hallway of the cottage and tensed when a man emerged from a room at the back of the house. Was she busy entertaining a boyfriend at ten o'clock in the morning—or had the guy spent the night with her? For some reason the idea darkened his mood, and that in itself was irritating. He had convinced himself last night that he wasn't interested in his grandmother's nurse. But he had changed his mind when Emma had opened the door, looking delectably gorgeous with her red-gold hair framing her pretty face. Her fitted jeans skimmed the soft curves of her hips, and her too-tight top moulded her full breasts, evoking a hot throb of lust in his groin as he imagined pushing the stretch material aside and cradling the bounteous mounds of flesh beneath.

The last thing Emma wanted to do was invite Rocco into her home, but good manners prevented her from saying so and she reluctantly moved to one side, so that he could step into the hall. He immediately dominated the small space, the top of his head brushing against the wooden ceiling beams that were a feature of the old cottage. He was too big, too dominant and way too overwhelming, she thought, hiding her irritation as the estate agent walked towards them, making the hallway feel even more cramped.

'I've taken all the photos I need.' The agent cast a curious look towards Rocco before focusing his attention on

Emma. 'I like the way you've done the place up. It's fresh and bright and I believe it will sell pretty quickly.'

'I'm in no rush for it to be sold,' Emma said heavily, 'but I expect the landlord will be pleased.' She opened the front door again, to allow the agent to leave, and then turned to face Rocco. He was intruding on her precious time with Holly and she was impatient for him to go. 'What was it you wanted to discuss?'

'Where are you moving to?' Rocco parried her question with one of his own.

She shrugged. 'I don't know. I only heard this morning that the owner has decided to sell Primrose Cottage. I'd like to stay in the local area, but if I can't find somewhere affordable to rent I may have to consider moving closer to Newcastle.'

'Cordelia would miss you if you moved away.'

'I'd miss her, too.' Emma bit her lip at the prospect of having to leave the village she loved and the many friends she had made in the past three years, since she had moved into Primrose Cottage with her month-old daughter. She had built a life for herself and Holly here, away from all the painful memories of Jack.

'Why don't you buy the cottage yourself?' Rocco's voice interrupted her thoughts.

'I'd love to, but it's impossible. I'm a single mother, and my nurse's salary simply won't stretch to buying a house.'

The scent of Rocco's cologne teased her senses, and in the small hall she had nowhere to look but at his broad-shouldered figure. He was dressed in pale jeans and a thick oatmeal-coloured sweater, topped by a black leather jacket; the look was casual yet sophisticated—and heart-stoppingly sexy. Emma resented her fierce awareness of him. She wished he would explain the reason for his unexpected visit, but he seemed in no hurry to leave.

'Cordelia told me your husband died. Did he not leave some sort of provision for you and your daughter such as a life insurance policy?'

Emma almost laughed at the suggestion that Jack might have behaved with any degree of responsibility. In fact she had been awarded compensation from the fire service after his death, but the money had all gone on settling his huge credit card debts that she had been unaware of until she had sorted through his paperwork.

'Unfortunately not,' she said crisply, her tone warning Rocco that it was none of his business. She faced him square on, preventing him from walking down the hall. 'Look, I don't mean to be rude, but I have a lot to do this morning…'

'Mummy, I iced the cakes…'

Emma turned her head and stifled a groan when Holly trotted out of the kitchen, her hands coated in sticky white icing. Thank heavens she'd had the foresight to cover her daughter's clothes with an apron, she thought ruefully. She'd forgotten that she had left Holly stirring the icing while she dealt with the estate agent, and could not blame the little girl for becoming impatient.

'I can see you have, sweetheart,' she murmured, wondering if any icing had actually made it onto the cakes.

Holly stared curiously at Rocco. 'Are you a 'state agent?'

'You mean an *e*state agent,' Emma corrected, but Holly's attention was focused on the big man who dominated the narrow hall. Usually a shy child, she seemed unconcerned by the presence of a stranger in the cottage, and Emma understood why when she glanced back at Rocco and realised with a sinking heart that her little daughter had been charmed by his smile.

'Hello, Holly.' His deep voice was as soft as crushed

velvet. No, I'm not an estate agent. I am your mummy's friend.'

Since when? Emma wanted to demand. But Holly appeared happy with the explanation.

'What's your name?'

'Rocco.'

To Emma's surprise Holly gave Rocco a wide smile. 'Me and Mummy made cupcakes. You can have one if you like.'

The man could charm the birds from the trees—and obviously every female from the age of three to ninety-three, Emma thought irritably, adding the proviso *bar this one.* 'I don't think...Rocco...' she stumbled slightly over his name '...has time at the moment. He was just leaving,' she added pointedly, flicking him a sharp glance.

He returned it with a bland smile and an amused gleam in his eyes before turning his attention back to Holly. 'I would love to try one of your cakes—if Mummy doesn't mind?'

'She doesn't,' Holly assured him innocently. 'I'll get you one.'

'I think we'd better clean you up first,' Emma told her daughter. Determined to take charge of the situation, she pushed open the sitting room door and gave Rocco a cool look that did not disguise her annoyance. 'Perhaps you would like to wait in here?'

'Thank you.' As he stepped past her into the room he briefly brushed against her. The contact was fleeting, yet it sent an electrical current shooting through her body, making her skin tingle as if each of her nerve-endings was acutely sensitive. What would it feel like to be held against his broad chest? To have his arms curve around her and pull her close so that her thighs were pressed against his? Colour surged into Emma's cheeks and she jerked back from him so violently that she hit her head on the door frame.

'Easy,' he murmured gently, as if he were calming a nervous colt. His amber eyes rested speculatively on her flushed face. 'Coffee would be good with a cake—black, no sugar.'

Lord, what she wouldn't give to wipe that arrogant smile from his lips, Emma thought furiously as she stalked into the kitchen. She didn't understand why she was so wound up. Normally she was a calm, even-tempered person, but Rocco D'Angelo got under her skin. She would make him one cup of coffee and then insist that he leave—and too bad if he preferred proper coffee beans, because she only had cheap instant granules.

Holly finished washing her hands at the sink and climbed down from the chair she had been standing on to reach the taps. 'Can I take Rocco a cake now?' At Emma's nod she chose one smothered in icing. 'Rocco's nice,' she stated guilelessly.

Startled, Emma hesitated, torn by the need to gently introduce the notion of 'stranger danger' and at the same time not wanting to alarm her daughter. 'I'm sure he is, but you don't really know him,' she said carefully.

'He's got a nice smile.'

Holly raced out of the kitchen clutching the cake, and for a second Emma felt like rushing after her and snatching the little girl into her arms. *Don't*, she wanted to cry. *Don't be taken in by a charming smile or, when you're older, give your trusting heart to a man who can glibly say the words* I love you *without meaning it.* Smiles were easy and words were cheap—and Jack had had an abundance of both, she thought heavily.

It wasn't Rocco's fault that he reminded her so much of her husband. Not in appearance—Rocco's dark, devilish good-looks were a stark contrast to Jack's blond hair and disarming grin. But, like Rocco, Jack had been supremely self-confident and aware of his effect on the opposite sex. 'A babe-magnet'—that was how her brother had once scathingly described Jack, Emma recalled wryly. From all she knew about Rocco, he was no different. But how could she tell her three-year-old daughter that her mistrust of all men stemmed from the fact that Holly's father had been a deceitful cheat who had broken her heart?

In the sitting room, Rocco strolled over to the fireplace to study the collection of framed photographs displayed on the mantelpiece. The central picture was of a fair-haired man dressed in a fire officer's uniform whom he guessed was Emma's husband. Next to the photo was a silver medal displayed on a velvet cushion. There were several other pictures, including one of Holly as a baby held in her mother's arms, and a recent photo of the little girl standing in front of a Christmas tree in Primrose Cottage. Curiously there were no pictures of Emma with her husband, nor one of him with Holly.

Rocco focused on the photo of the late Jack Marchant. The guy had been undeniably good-looking, with overlong blond hair and brilliant blue eyes, but there was a cockiness about his smile that suggested he had been fully aware of his appeal to women. He would lay a bet that Marchant had been a womaniser before his marriage, Rocco brooded. He had deduced from his own observations the previous evening, and from conversation with his grandmother, that Emma was a rather serious, unassuming person, with a highly developed sense of responsibility. Brash-looking Jack Marchant seemed an unexpected choice of partner for her, but presumably the fact that she still wore her wedding ring three years after being widowed meant that the marriage had been happy and she had loved her husband.

Why did the thought rankle? Rocco wondered irritably, raking a hand through his hair. He didn't know what he was doing here, and if he had any sense he would leave immediately. Only the fact that he had been asked to give a message to Emma from his grandmother prevented him from letting himself out of the front door. But, as his eyes strayed to the photo of the young woman with red-gold hair and a shy smile who was clutching her baby in her arms, he knew he was not being completely honest with himself.

'My daddy was a hero.'

He glanced down to find that Holly had entered the room silently and was standing beside him. She was a pretty child, with hair a shade fairer than her mother's and the same dark grey eyes.

'That's his medal,' she explained, pointing towards the mantelpiece. 'He saved people from a fire. Didn't he, Mummy?' Holly turned to Emma, who had followed her into the room, for confirmation. 'But I never saw him because I was in Mummy's tummy,' she added, her little face becoming solemn for a moment.

'Jack died two months before Holly was born,' Emma told Rocco, seeing the puzzled look in his eyes. 'He rescued three children from a house fire, but was killed when the roof collapsed and he was trapped in the blaze. He was posthumously awarded the Queens Gallantry Medal.'

So her husband had been Superman. Rocco felt a flare of guilt for his uninformed and, as it turned out, unfair assessment of Jack Marchant. For some reason he could not bring himself to look at Emma, and instead smiled at Holly. 'Your *papa* was a brave man. You must be very proud of him.'

He was rewarded with a beaming grin as Holly offered him a sickly looking cake.

'I chose you one with lots of icing.'

Rocco disliked sweet foods, but there was no question of disappointing the child. He bit into the cake. 'Delicious,' he assured Holly, who was watching him anxiously.

She was apparently satisfied with his verdict. 'You'd better finish it before you drop crumbs on the carpet,' she advised him seriously.

'Did you say no sugar in your coffee?' Emma murmured.

Rocco caught the glimmer of amusement in her eyes and gave her a wry look. To his surprise her mouth curved into faint smile, and he felt something kick in his gut. His initial impression of her had been that she was averagely attractive, but he had spent a restless night wondering why he could not dismiss her from his mind and now he realised that she possessed an understated beauty that drew his eyes to her again and again.

'Grazie.' He took the mug of coffee she offered him, his keen gaze noting that her hand shook very slightly. It gave him a measure of satisfaction to see that she was not as composed as she would like him to believe. 'The cake has reminded me of why I'm here,' he murmured. 'I am taking Cordelia to have tea at the Royal Oak Hotel this afternoon, and we would both be delighted if you and Holly would join us.'

'Oh, no—that's very kind, but I don't think so.' Emma's response was immediate, and edged with a flare of panic she could not completely disguise. Spending an afternoon in the company of a devastatingly attractive Italian playboy was not her idea of fun—especially when she was not at all confident she would be able to hide her intense awareness of him. 'I…I have other plans, and I'm sure Cordelia would prefer to have you to herself—especially as she hasn't seen you for so long.'

Rocco chose to ignore the last barbed comment. 'My grandmother issued the invitation. She would very much like you to come.' He paused, his sensual mouth curving at the corners. 'And I am under strict instructions not to take no for an answer.' His smile held genuine warmth and a trace of amusement, as if he knew the reason for her refusal. 'I understand that the hotel has a collection of dolls' houses which children are permitted to play with. Do you like dolls' houses, Holly?' He turned his attention to the little girl, who had been listening to the conversation.

'That's unfair,' Emma muttered, in a voice meant for his ears only, as her daughter nodded enthusiastically.

'Unfair to want to give an elderly lady an enjoyable afternoon?' he countered quietly. 'Cordelia is excited about a trip out, and she is obviously very fond of Holly. Could you not postpone the plans you mentioned until tomorrow?'

He could not possibly know that her plans for the day amounted to watching a new children's DVD with Holly and then attacking the ironing pile.

'Can we have tea with Nonna? Please, Mummy?'

Faced with her daughter's hopeful expression, Emma stifled a sigh of resignation. Holly deserved a treat, and the Royal Oak was renowned for providing excellent play facilities for children and as well as superb food for adults.

She caught Rocco's surprised look and explained, 'Your grandmother suggested that Holly should call her Nonna because she found Cordelia difficult to say.'

It had been touching to witness the special friendship that had developed between her daughter and the elderly lady that was untroubled by the eighty year age gap between them. She forced herself to hold Rocco's gaze, silently cursing the way her heart skittered as she absorbed the masculine beauty of his chiselled features.

'Please tell Cordelia that we would love to accept her invitation.'

'I'll pick you up at three-thirty.'

'There's no need. I'll take my car and meet you at the hotel,' she said quickly. 'I assume your car wasn't seriously damaged last night?' Even if it was in perfect order she had no intention of allowing Holly to travel in a sports car on icy roads.

'Unfortunately the exhaust pipe was ripped from the chassis.' Rocco grimaced when he thought of the several thousand pounds' worth of damage that had been wrought to his Eleganza Classic. He could easily afford the repair bill, but the Classic had been one of the first cars produced by the company his grandfather had established fifty years ago. It was a personal favourite from his private collection of luxury cars—an exquisite piece of engineering which Rocco had lovingly restored. 'Specialist parts will have to be sent over from Italy for it to be repaired, but in the meantime I've hired a car better suited to the wintry conditions,' he explained, nodding towards the window.

Following his gaze, Emma saw a top-of-the-range four-by-four parked outside the cottage, its gleaming paintwork making her battered old vehicle look very much the poor cousin. What it was to have money, she thought wryly. Rocco was a multi-millionaire who lived a jet-setter's glamorous lifestyle very different from her life as a single mother in a quiet Northumberland village. But what did it matter? Soon he would return to Italy, and she would probably never see him again. Surely she could survive one afternoon in his company without making a fool of herself.

'We'll see you at three-thirty then,' she murmured, disguising her anxiety with a cool smile.

* * *

Holly was full of excitement at the prospect of having tea with Nonna and Rocco, and insisted on wearing her best dress that had been a Christmas present.

'Goodness, you've grown,' Emma said ruefully as she surveyed her daughter's skinny legs, where the hem of the dress stopped above her knees. 'Upwards, anyway—I wish you would grow outwards.' The flu virus had left Holly painfully thin and pale. If only she *could* afford a holiday abroad, Emma thought, recalling her conversation with the childminder, Karen. But it was out of the question now that she had to find somewhere else to live.

Determined not to make a big deal out of spending the afternoon with Rocco, she decided to wear her jeans. But at the last minute she changed into the beautiful heather-coloured cashmere jumper her mother had sent for Christmas and teamed it with a fitted grey skirt, sheer hose and her only pair of high-heeled shoes. The Royal Oak Hotel was an upmarket place, and if she was honest it was nice to have a reason to dress up, she admitted, slipping on her grey wool coat as the doorbell rang.

'We're ready,' Holly informed Rocco with a wide grin when Emma opened the door. 'I'm wearing my party dress.' She twirled around to show off her dress, clearly hoping for Rocco's approval.

Once again Emma was surprised by her daughter's eagerness to be friends with him. Holly had never known her father, and although both her grandfathers were alive she only saw them occasionally. Did her daughter wish she had a father, like her best friends the twins, Lily and Sara, had? she wondered. The thought had not occurred to her before, and it troubled her. She did her best to fulfil the role of two parents, but maybe it wasn't enough.

'You look very pretty,' Rocco assured Holly with a soft smile.

Emma was grateful for his gentle patience, which was all the more surprising when he presumably did not come into contact with small children very often, but her heart gave an annoying lurch when he turned his amber eyes on her.

'Both of you,' he murmured.

When they walked down the path she saw that Cordelia was sitting in the back of the car. Beside her was a child's booster seat. 'Up you come,' Rocco said, lifting Holly into the seat and securing the straps. 'You can sit in the front,' he told Emma.

She would rather have sat in the back than next to him, but she could not say so without revealing that he unnerved her and so slid into the front passenger seat without a word. Fortunately Holly chattered non-stop to Cordelia for the entire journey to the hotel, so Emma did not have to make conversation, but she was supremely conscious of Rocco, and could not prevent her eyes from straying to him. He was still wearing the black leather jacket, but had exchanged the jeans and sweater for tailored black trousers and a black shirt, and he looked so devastatingly good-looking that she felt a dull ache of longing in the pit of her stomach.

His hands on the steering wheel were a dark olive colour, and she wondered if the rest of his body was as tanned. A series of erotic images filled her mind and she quickly turned her head and stared out of the window, her cheeks burning. It was going to be a long afternoon, she thought ruefully, and the most annoying thing was that her tension was self-inflicted. She did not *want* to feel this fierce attraction to Cordelia's playboy grandson, but she did not seem to have a choice.

* * *

It was almost six o'clock when they returned to Primrose Cottage.

'Thank you for a lovely afternoon.' Emma's smile briefly encompassed Rocco, before she turned her head to Cordelia in the back of the car. 'Holly had a wonderful time. I'm not surprised she's fallen asleep. I've never known her to talk so much.'

Despite her reservations, the afternoon had been enjoyable. Holly had been in heaven playing with the dolls' houses in the charming family room of the hotel, where tea—comprising an extensive selection of sandwiches and cakes—had been served. Kept busy trying to persuade Holly to eat, and chatting to Cordelia, Emma had been distracted from her intense awareness of Rocco, and apart from a conversation when she had asked about his company and he had given her a brief history of Eleganza, there had been little verbal contact between them.

There had been eye contact, though, she remembered. Throughout the afternoon she had been conscious of his gaze resting on her, and on several occasions she had darted him a quick glance and blushed when her eyes had collided with his. His expression had been speculative, and when she had walked back to the table after playing with Holly he had subjected her to a bold appraisal which had made her breasts feel heavy and caused her nipples to harden into tight buds which mercifully could not be seen through her woollen jumper.

The memory of the predatory gleam in his amber gaze made her feel edgy, and she quickly released her seat belt and opened the car door.

'There's no need for you to get out,' she told him. 'You should take Cordelia home before she gets cold.'

'I'll leave the engine and the heater running while I carry Holly inside,' he replied equably. 'Go and open the front door, Emma,' he bade her, in a tone that brooked no argument when she opened her mouth to do just that.

Irritating man, she thought as she marched up the front path and fitted her key in the lock. She had cared for Holly on her own for three years and she did not need his help. She glanced over her shoulder and saw that Holly had half woken, but instead of being alarmed to find herself in Rocco's arms the little girl contentedly rested her head on his shoulder.

She didn't feel *jealous*, Emma reassured herself. But it was hard to watch her daughter instinctively snuggle up to Rocco, as if he had already become a part of their lives. He wasn't—and never would be. She certainly did not want Holly to become attached to him only to be upset when he returned to Italy.

She watched him carefully deposit the sleepy child on the sofa in the sitting room, and then followed him back into the hall. 'Thank you again for a pleasant afternoon.' She flushed, realising how stilted she sounded. 'Holly… *we*,' she corrected, 'really enjoyed it.'

'I'm glad you did not find an afternoon in my company *too* much of an ordeal,' Rocco murmured dryly.

In the narrow hallway he was too close for comfort: six feet plus of big, dark, broad-shouldered male towering over her, emphasising the fact that she was slightly below average height. Emma closed her eyes in a vain attempt to lessen her awareness of him, but her other senses immediately became more acute, so that the scent of his aftershave and the warmth emanating from his body stole around her.

Her lashes flew open when she felt something brush her cheek, her eyes widening in shock when he gently tucked a strand of her hair behind her ear. The gesture was unacceptable from a man she barely knew. It was an intrusion on her personal space and she knew she should tell him to back off. Yet the feather-light touch of his fingertips against her skin was beguiling. It was so long since she had been touched by a man.

Since she had discovered the truth about Jack's infidelity—or rather infidelities, she thought bleakly—she had built a defensive wall around her emotions. Was she going to allow that wall to be breached by a notorious playboy—a man who, if the reports she had heard about him were true, was even more unreliable than her husband?

The vulnerability in Emma's storm-cloud-grey eyes took Rocco by surprise. His instincts told him that someone had hurt her in the past—what other reason could there be for her to shy away from him like a nervous colt whenever he came within a foot of her? But who had made her so defensive? He thought of the photograph on the mantelpiece of swaggering Jack Marchant, and his eyes strayed to her wedding ring, remembering how often she had unconsciously twisted it on her finger during the afternoon.

She must have loved her husband to still be wearing his ring three years after his death. But if not Marchant who was responsible for the haunted expression in her eyes? And why did he care? he asked himself irritably. For reasons he was damned if he could explain, he found himself wanting to slide his fingers into her shiny bell of hair and draw her close. Only the slight tremor of her lower lip held him back from dipping his head and slanting his mouth over hers. She intrigued and infuriated him in equal measure: one minute a brisk, ultra-efficient nurse, the next a sensual woman whose wary expression could not disguise her sexual awareness of him.

She stepped away from him and pulled open the front door. 'Goodnight.'

He detected the faint note of desperation in her voice

and took pity on her. *'Ciao, bella,'* he drawled softly, his eyes lingering on her flushed face before he turned and strode down the path.

CHAPTER FOUR

So he had called her beautiful! It meant nothing, Emma told herself impatiently. A man like Rocco probably called all his women *bella*, so that he did not have to bother remembering their names.

Not that *she* was one of his women, her brain pointed out, nor was she ever likely to be. She did not need a man in her life—certainly not a gorgeous, sexy Italian who changed his mistresses more often than most men changed their socks.

A faint smell of burning dragged her from her thoughts and she cursed as she lifted the iron and saw the singe marks on her new white blouse. This was ridiculous. For the sake of her sanity, not to mention the pile of clothes still waiting to be ironed, she *had* to put Rocco out of her mind. He had disrupted her day, but she was not going to allow him to disrupt her life.

After he had left to drive Cordelia home to Nunstead Hall, Emma had carried Holly upstairs to bed. For the second night in a row the little girl had been too weary for a bath and had fallen back to sleep within minutes of her head touching the pillow. As she'd watched Holly's long eyelashes settle on her pale cheeks Emma's heart had clenched with love. Her precious daughter was the centre of her life and there was no room for anyone else. How could there be after Jack? she thought bitterly.

The discovery of his betrayal had shattered all her illusions about love and trust, but he had died before she could confront him. She would never know if he had planned to stay and be a father to Holly, or walk out on his marriage and his child as his mistress had insisted had been his intention.

But, whatever Jack might have planned, fate had intervened, and Emma had given birth to her daughter alone. From the start of Holly's life it had been just the two of them. And that suited her fine, Emma reminded herself. She loved being a mother, she enjoyed a rewarding career and she had good friends and a supportive family. She was content with all that she had. So why tonight did she feel that something was missing?

The ironing had lost its limited appeal, and she stacked the board and the laundry basket in the utility room, promising herself she would finish it tomorrow. On Saturday nights after Holly was in bed she usually curled up on the sofa to watch a DVD and treated herself to a bar of chocolate. She duly slid a film into the player and settled down to watch it, determinedly ignoring the voice in her head that whispered insidiously that she was lonely.

The peal of the doorbell caused her to tense. Was it a sixth sense that warned the unexpected visitor was Rocco—or wishful thinking? But why would he have driven all the way back from Nunstead Hall through the sleety rain that had replaced yesterday's snowfall? Common sense told her to slide the security chain across before she opened the door, and her heart flipped at the sight of her nemesis leaning nonchalantly against the porch, looking devastatingly sexy with the collar of his leather jacket pulled up around his face and a lock of black hair falling across his brow.

He took her breath away. She did not trust herself to speak and instead arched her brows in silent query.

'I thought tonight would be a good time to discuss my grandmother's living arrangements,' he greeted her. His lazy smile did strange things to her insides. 'And to share this excellent Pinot Noir,' he added, holding out a bottle of red wine.

Emma shook her head. 'Not now—it's late—'

'It's half past eight on a Saturday evening,' he interrupted her. 'Admittedly Cordelia was going to bed when I left, but she's eighty-three.'

The amusement in his voice made her blush. 'Well, maybe I'm busy,' she said tightly. 'Or maybe I would prefer not to spend my leisure time dealing with work issues—had that occurred to you?'

'I didn't realise you considered Cordelia's welfare to be a work issue.' His voice hardened. 'I believed you thought of her as a friend.'

'I do—of course I do.' She flushed uncomfortably. For weeks she had wanted to discuss her concerns about her patient with Cordelia's grandson. Now Rocco was here to do just that, and innate honesty forced her to admit that she had no good reason not to invite him in. Apart from the fact that he made her feel as edgy and awkward as a teenager with a severe crush on him, she acknowledged silently.

The thought had suddenly occurred to Rocco that perhaps Emma's reluctance to invite him in was because she already had a visitor—a male visitor. He frowned, startled by how strongly he disliked the idea.

'If you're entertaining, then I apologise for interrupting your evening,' he said stiffly.

Emma blinked in surprise. Did he think she spent her Saturday nights partying? *He* might lead a jet-set lifestyle, but her social life consisted of attending the monthly meeting of the village council in the church hall.

'Who on earth do you think I would be *entertaining* on a night like this?'

The temperature must be hovering just above freezing, because rain rather than snow was still falling. She suddenly realised that the porch offered him little protection from the weather. 'Just a minute.' She closed the door, released the security chain, and then opened it again, moving back so that he could step inside.

He smelled of rain and leather—and the musky scent of his aftershave that was already tantalisingly familiar to her. In the narrow hall she was immediately conscious of his size, and his raw masculinity seemed like an alien invasion of her cosy cottage with its pastel-coloured, feminine décor.

'Please come on through,' she mumbled, trying to ignore the erratic thud of her heart as she led the way into the sitting room.

'I thought you might have a boyfriend here.' He returned to the conversation he had begun on the doorstep. The gleam in his eyes was faintly challenging and openly curious.

Emma met his gaze levelly. 'I don't have a boyfriend,' she revealed, in a cool tone intended to deter further discussion on the subject.

Rocco did not seem to get the message. 'I guess it must be difficult to meet other men and pursue a relationship when you have a young child?'

She shrugged. 'I'm not interested in meeting men, so I wouldn't know.'

His eyes narrowed on her stony face. 'But you must

date occasionally. Your husband has been dead how long? Three years?'

'I really don't think my private life is any of your business.' She should have followed her first instinct and slammed the front door on him, she thought angrily, her tension mounting when he strolled across the room and studied the photographs on the mantelpiece.

'You don't date other men three years after your husband's death, yet you don't have any pictures of the two of you on display—not even a wedding photo,' he murmured. 'Why not?'

'I find it too painful to look at pictures of my wedding day.'

She had given the same excuse to Jack's parents, and it was the truth—although not for the reasons they believed. She could not bear to see the photos of herself smiling adoringly at the man she had loved, and Jack smiling adoringly at the camera.

He had been well aware that his blond good-looks made him extremely photogenic, and had loved being the centre of attention—unlike the bride, Emma thought ruefully. Never one to seek the spotlight, she had found their big white wedding an ordeal. But Jack had wanted it, and she had been so madly in love with him, and so amazed that he had chosen her for his wife when he could have had any woman he desired, that she would have flown to the moon to marry him if he had suggested it.

What a blind fool she had been. Her wedding photos were a painful reminder of her gullibility, for she had trusted Jack and believed him when he had told her she was the only woman he would ever want. But by the time she had discovered that he had had numerous affairs throughout the three years of their marriage he had been dead.

For the sake of his distraught parents she had kept the

truth to herself. Jack had died a hero, and it would have been cruel to taint Peter and Alison's image of their only son by revealing that he had been a lying cheat. She had struggled alone to come to terms with the two very different sides of her husband—one so admirable, and the other causing her so much heartache. She knew her parents had their suspicions that her marriage had not been as rosy as she pretended, but she had not even confided in them. Holly believed that the father who had died before she was born was a wonderful heroic figure, and Emma did not want anyone to shatter her daughter's illusion.

Rocco was watching her with a speculative look in his eyes that she found unnerving. 'I'm not in the mood to play a game of twenty questions,' she snapped. 'I thought the reason for your visit was to discuss what to do about your grandmother?'

'It is—and on that subject I have a suggestion to put to you.' Rocco stifled his impatience to learn more about Emma's relationship with her husband. He was good at reading body language, and her obvious tension when he had mentioned Jack Marchant fired his curiosity. But he could see she was regretting inviting him in. If she asked him to leave he would have no option but to comply, and so he masked his frustration with a smile.

Besides, the main purpose of his visit *was* with regard to Cordelia, he reminded himself. During tea at the hotel this afternoon he had witnessed the genuine friendship between his grandmother and Emma. Her kindness and compassion were traits distinctly lacking in the brittle socialites he usually associated with, and he readily admitted that he was impressed by her caring nature. His unexpected attraction to her was *not* the reason why he was here.

He waved the bottle of wine he was holding. 'Do you have a corkscrew? We'll have a drink while we talk.'

'There's one in the kitchen.' Emma took the wine bottle from him, wishing she had the nerve to tell him she had changed her mind and wanted him to go. Good manners insisted she play the role of hostess. 'Would you like me to take your jacket?'

'Grazie.' He shrugged out of the leather jacket and handed it to her.

The lining was still warm from his body. It seemed strangely intimate to hold something that seconds ago had sheathed his muscular torso. What would it feel like to be held against that broad chest, to press her cheek to his silk shirt and feel his arms close around her?

The image evoked a wistful pang of longing to feel protected, cherished. Her friends and family often commented on how well she coped as a single mother. She defined herself as being quietly confident, capable and independent. So why did the idea of being held safe in a pair of strong arms suddenly seem so enticing? And who was she kidding? she thought impatiently, as she walked out to the hall and hung Rocco's jacket over the stair banister. *Safe* was not a word she would equate with Rocco D'Angelo.

The corkscrew was hiding at the back of the cutlery drawer, which went to show how infrequently she drank wine. She was struggling to remove the cork from the bottle when he strolled into the kitchen.

'Allow me to do that.'

Rocco uncorked the wine with practised ease and watched Emma open a cupboard and retrieve two glasses. She had to stretch up to reach them, and in doing so her fine wool sweater was drawn taut across her breasts, emphasising their rounded fullness. Heat flared in his groin, prompting him to shift his position to ease the constriction of his suddenly tight trousers. The kitchen was built to the same minuscule proportions as the rest of the cottage. One step was all it would take to bring his body into contact with Emma's. But he fought the temptation to press himself against her soft curves and glanced around the room, feeling the top of his head brush against the ceiling beams.

'I hope the agent deters anyone tall from viewing this place. It's not much bigger than a dolls' house.'

'It's big enough for the two of us,' Emma said shortly, her heart sinking at the reminder that she would soon be forced to move out of the cottage which had been her home for the past three years.

'Did you live here when your husband was alive?'

'No—Jack was based at a fire station in the centre of Newcastle, and we lived in a flat nearby. I moved to Primrose Cottage after Holly was born.'

'What made you come out here to this isolated village? I would have thought Little Copton was too quiet for a young woman. It must be difficult to have a social life when you're so far from a decent sized town.'

'I don't want a social life—not in the way you mean… visiting nightclubs and bars,' Emma added, flushing when Rocco gave her a quizzical look. 'I did part of my nurse's training at Hexham Hospital, and used to spend my days off exploring the moors. My parents wanted me to move back to their farm in Scotland with Holly, but when I saw Primrose Cottage I fell in love with it.'

She knew her parents had been worried about her living on her own with a newborn baby, but she had craved isolation, wanting to be alone to grieve for Jack and come to terms with the knowledge that he hadn't loved her as she had loved him. The discovery of how he had betrayed her had decimated her sense of self-worth, and like a wounded animal she had gone to ground.

Three years on she was proud of the fact that she was in control of her life, and utterly determined never to relinquish her independence or risk her emotional stability. It would be easy to be dazzled by a man like Rocco, she brooded. The way her heart skittered at his sexy smile was annoying proof that she was not completely immune to his charisma. But she had fallen for a charmer once before and been bitterly hurt. She wasn't stupid enough to do so again.

Rocco skimmed his eyes over Emma's silky bob of hair and her creamy skin, noting the faint dusting of red-gold freckles on her nose and cheeks. 'So you're Scottish—I thought I detected an accent.'

She shook her head. 'Not technically—my family moved to Scotland from London when I was ten, so my Scots burr is not as strong as if I'd been born north of the border.'

'Are they your parents?' Rocco indicated the photo on the dresser of Holly with an older man and woman.

'My in-laws. They adore Holly.' Emma studied the picture of Jack's parents and saw the sadness in the eyes that their smiles could not disguise. They had been devastated by the loss of their son, and doted on their little granddaughter. For them and for Holly she would continue with the pretence that Jack had been a devoted husband, and never reveal that he had shattered her trust irrevocably.

She had joined Rocco by the dresser when he had asked about the photo, and now she was acutely conscious of how close they were standing. The fine hairs on her body stood on end, each of her senses alerted to his sheer maleness as she inhaled the subtle musk of aftershave and pheromones.

Why did he affect her so strongly? she wondered despairingly. And how had he drawn so much personal information from her without her even realising it. So much for keeping him at a distance!

She forced a cool smile. 'We seem to have diverted from

the subject of Cordelia. Let's go back to the other room and you can tell me about your plans for how best to care for her.'

She preceded him into the sitting room and offered him the sofa, but instead of sitting next to him she crossed to the armchair on the other side of the room.

He poured the wine and handed her a glass. 'Wouldn't you be more comfortable over here? Where you can put your drink on the coffee table?'

She felt herself blush at the amused gleam in his eyes. 'I'm fine where I am, thank you.' Determined not to show how much he rattled her, she settled back in the chair and took a long sip of wine. It was deliciously smooth and fruity, and she felt a relaxing warmth seep through her veins. 'So, what do you intend to do about Cordelia? I'm afraid the local health authority won't provide a live-in carer for her, but there are a number of private agencies who could arrange for staff to visit her every day.'

Rocco shook his head. 'I can see that Nonna needs more than that. She's too frail to continue living at Nunstead Hall—even with regular visits from carers. And employing live-in staff has not proved successful.'

'Then what do you propose? Cordelia is adamant that she won't move from Nunstead.'

'I've discovered that,' Rocco said with feeling, recalling his grandmother's stubbornness on the subject. 'As a temporary measure, while she is recovering from the hip operation and the burn to her hand, I've asked her to come and stay with me at my home in Portofino.'

Emma's eyebrows arched in surprise. 'And she's agreed?'

'No—not yet. But I've had an idea that I think will persuade her.' He looked across the room, his tiger-like amber eyes trapping her gaze. 'I've hinted that you might come to Italy to be her private nurse.'

She had been in the process of taking another sip of wine, but at his startling statement the sip became a gulp. The alcohol must have gone straight to her head, because for a second her brain felt fuzzy before his words sank in.

'Well, you'd better *un*-hint,' she said sharply. 'I have no intention of moving to Italy. The idea is ridiculous—and impossible.'

'Why?' Rocco queried calmly. 'I'm not suggesting a permanent arrangement. My suggestion to Cordelia is that she comes to my home for three months' convalescence. After that we will decide whether she is able to return to Nunstead, with the help of a live-in carer, or—as I'm secretly hoping—she will have settled in Italy and will agree to remain living with me. At first she point-blank refused to consider the idea, because she was worried she would be lonely and miss her friends here in Northumberland. But it's clear that *you* are her closest friend, Emma,' he said softly, and the husky way he murmured her name sent an involuntary quiver down Emma's spine. 'When I put forward the idea that you could come to Portofino for three months, Nonna was much happier to consider my plan.'

'You had no right to suggest that to Cordelia without asking me first,' Emma said tightly. What Rocco had done amounted to emotional blackmail, and she was furious with him. 'It doesn't seem to have crossed your mind that I have a life here in England—a job, *a child*. I can't simply take off for three months and abandon my responsibilities, and no way on earth would I ever leave Holly with my parents for that length of time. The most she's ever been away from me is a weekend, when Jack's parents took her to stay at their house in France.'

Rocco's dark brows drew together in a frown, his anger

mounting at her diatribe and the unspoken accusation that *he* had abandoned *his* responsibility for his grandmother over the past months.

'When did I say you would have to leave Holly?' he demanded. 'Naturally you would bring her with you. You say you have a life here that you don't wish to leave, but you're going to have to move out of this cottage. You've already told me there's no man around and you're not involved in a relationship—so what exactly is holding you back from taking a three month sabbatical from your job to help an old lady you insist you care about?'

'Dozens of things,' Emma muttered, infuriated by his casual attitude. 'For a start, I need to look for somewhere to live.'

'That's not a problem. I'll have one of my staff research suitable properties for you, and once you've chosen a place I'll arrange the move.'

He made it sound so simple, she thought irritably. But his wealth inured him to the mundane problems of day-to-day living that most people experienced. She was sure he had never had to worry about how much rent he could afford, or deal with unscrupulous landlords who demanded a huge deposit but failed to carry out vital repairs. She had been lucky that the owner of Primrose Cottage was a decent, kindly man; there was no guarantee that her next tenancy would be as trouble free.

But, as Rocco had pointed out, her life *was* going to change whether she liked it or not, she thought heavily. However, that did not mean that she should uproot her daughter and take her to live temporarily in another country.

'It's important for Holly to feel settled and secure.'

'I'm sure it is, and I am certain she will love my home in Portofino. The Villa Lucia has ten guest bedrooms and there is plenty of space for a child to play inside, or outside in the four acres of gardens. Already there is plenty of spring sunshine, and in a month the weather will be warm enough for trips to the beach. You were only saying earlier today how you wished you could take Holly for a holiday to help her recuperate from the flu virus that has left her so pale and robbed her of her appetite,' he reminded her.

Emma could not deny she had said exactly that, when Holly had refused to eat more than half a sandwich at the hotel. 'But it won't *be* a holiday,' she pointed out. 'Who will look after Holly while I'm working?'

'It won't be work as such. Cordelia doesn't need nursing. I simply want you to act as a companion to her. And you know as well as I do that she loves having Holly around. I can't see why you have a problem with the idea,' he said, frustration edging into his voice. 'It seems the perfect solution—I'll know that my grandmother is safe and happy, and Holly will get to spend three months where the climate is a good deal warmer than in Northumberland.'

When he put it like that it was difficult see a problem with his plan, she admitted. But there *was* a problem—and he was it. Or rather, she had a problem with the idea of living in his home for three months. She could hide her attraction to him while he was staying at Nunstead Hall and she was only likely to meet him occasionally. But to stay with him at his villa and see him every day—that was something else.

She wished he didn't unsettle her. He was offering her a golden opportunity to give Holly a wonderful holiday and she was angry with herself for allowing him to affect her. But he stirred feelings inside her she had been sure she would never feel again—desires that she'd believed had died when she had learned how Jack had betrayed her. Even now her mind was only half concentrated on what he was saying, while the other half was swamped by her intense awareness of his smouldering virility.

'I'm sorry, but my answer is no,' she said stiffly.

'Why not?' Rocco struggled to contain his frustration. It hadn't occurred to him that Emma might refuse. In his position as CEO of Eleganza he was used to people doing his bidding without question, and in his personal life he had never yet failed to charm a woman around to his way of thinking.

'I have my reasons.'

'Which are *what*?' He could not think of one good reason why she would turn down a three month sojourn in a beautiful part of the world, for which she would get paid. 'If it's a question of money, obviously I will pay you the top rate for a live-in nurse. Nonna won't come without you,' he said harshly, glaring at Emma's mutinous expression. 'What am I going to do? We both know it's not safe for her to remain at Nunstead, but I have commitments in Italy that mean I have to return there next week.'

Emma tried to quash her pang of guilt. She could not deny that it would be best for Cordelia to go and stay with Rocco, but he would have to find another way of persuading his grandmother to accompany him to Portofino.

'I'm sorry if you have led Cordelia to think I would go to Italy with her, but I can't. And I don't see why I should have to explain my reasons to you—a man I met for the first time yesterday,' she added fiercely, her temper rising when she saw the angry gleam in his amber eyes. 'That's all I have to say on the subject.' She jumped to her feet. 'I think you should leave.'

She was throwing him out! No woman had ever asked Rocco to leave, and the novel experience was not one he relished. But he had stated his case—or rather his grandmother's case—and he was damned if he was going to plead with Emma to reconsider, he thought grimly. Without another word he stood up, and placed his glass on the coffee table at the same time as Emma set down her half-full glass. Their fingers brushed and she snatched her hand away, sending the glass flying so that red wine cascaded across the table and dripped over the edge.

'Blast!' She stared in horror at the spreading stain on the cream carpet. 'It had to happen now. The estate agent phoned earlier to say he's arranged for someone to view the cottage tomorrow.'

'I'll get a cloth.' Rocco was already striding from the room.

Emma hurried along to the kitchen after him, and while he grabbed the dishcloth she rummaged in a cupboard, looking for the carpet cleaning solution she was sure was stashed at the back—before remembering she had used the last of it to clean up a spill at Christmas.

'Is the stain very bad? I've brought another cloth.' She ran back into the sitting room just as he was emerging, and they collided in the doorway.

'It's fine. I've cleaned it up and you can't see a mark, so stop flapping.'

His impatient tone brought her up sharp. 'I never *flap*,' she said tightly, flushing as she realised she had been doing just that.

What the hell was wrong with her? she asked herself furiously. She had spent two years working in an A&E unit, often dealing with life-threatening emergencies, yet here she was getting in a stew about spilt wine.

Rocco set her nerves on edge, she acknowledged ruefully. Ever since she had invited him into the cottage she had been conscious of the undercurrent of sexual awareness. And now they were jammed in the doorway, with their bodies touching, and molten heat was coursing through her veins.

Her eyes were drawn against her will to his face, and her heart gave a violent thud when she watched his gaze narrow and become predatory. Time stood still and the air between them quivered. He stared down at her, as if he could see deep into her soul, before he slowly lowered his head.

He was going to kiss her. She knew she should move, break the spell he had cast on her, but it was too late. His warm breath whispered across her lips and involuntarily she parted them as he claimed her mouth. With practised ease he took possession of her, sliding a hand to her nape as he deepened the kiss, yet keeping the caress non-threatening, so that she slowly relaxed and allowed her body to settle against him while she responded to the gentle demands of his mouth.

She was drowning in a sea of sensation. There was nothing but Rocco's strong, hard body pressing against her, so that she could feel his powerful thigh muscles through her skirt. His hand slid from her nape to tangle in her hair, holding her still while he subtly increased the pressure of his lips on hers and took the kiss to another level that was blatantly erotic.

Without conscious thought she lifted her arms to his shoulders, a tremor running through her when he curled his arm around her waist and drew her even closer, so that she could feel the thud of his heart and, more enticingly, the solid ridge of his arousal straining beneath his trousers.

He delicately probed between her lips with his tongue before initiating a bold exploration that made her tremble. Reality had ceased to exist. All she was aware of was the faint abrasion of his jaw against her cheek and the softness of his hair as she curved her arms around his neck and slid her fingers into the dark mass of silk above his collar.

At first slow and sweet, the tenure of his kiss changed to hot and hungry, seducing her with its innate sensuality. Nothing had prepared her for the wild, almost primitive pleasure he evoked, and she responded with a feverish urgency as her defences crumbled.

From upstairs came the sound of Holly coughing. The sexually charged silence down in the hall immediately shattered, and Emma dragged her mouth from Rocco's, her chest heaving as she snatched oxygen into her lungs. Dear heaven, what if her daughter had got out of bed and discovered her kissing a virtual stranger? What if Holly hadn't coughed and she had continued to kiss Rocco with the wanton abandon that had overwhelmed her mere seconds ago?

'What are you doing?' she demanded shakily.

His dark brows rose quizzically. 'What am *I* doing? Surely you mean what are *we* doing? And I think the answer is pretty self-explanatory,' he drawled softly. He trailed a lazy hand down to her breast and brushed across the hard peak of her nipple jutting beneath her jumper.

'Don't!' Mortified by her response to him, she snatched her arms from around his neck and sidestepped him out of the doorway into the hall, struggling to control her erratic breathing. 'You took me by surprise.' Panic made her voice sharp as she felt a growing sense of horror at her behaviour. 'You had no right to come on to me.'

Rocco raked a hand through his hair, surprised by the strength of his desire for Emma, and his fierce urge to pull her back into his arms and kiss her into submission. 'It was just a kiss.' He managed to sound coolly dismissive, even though his heart was pounding in his chest. 'There's no need to get worked up about it.'

He sounded faintly bored, as if he was used to kissing women he barely knew on a passing whim—which he probably was, she conceded sickly. No doubt he had confidently expected her to invite him up to her bedroom, or maybe he would have led her back into the sitting room and removed her clothes—*his*—before making love to her on the sofa? Her face burned as erotic images of their naked, entwined limbs flooded her mind.

'You shouldn't have done it.' Her voice sounded thick, almost guttural, as she fought the shockingly fierce pull of sexual desire that throbbed low in her pelvis. 'I told you, I'm not looking for a…' She faltered on the word *relationship*, certain that Rocco wanted nothing more than casual sex. 'I don't want a man in my life.'

As she looked through the doorway into the sitting room, the photograph of Jack's grinning face seemed to mock her. Rocco followed her gaze and his face hardened.

'He's been dead for three years. He might have been a hero, but you can't grieve for him for ever,' he said harshly. His eyes narrowed on her face as a startling realisation dawned. 'You're not telling me I'm the first man you've kissed since you were widowed?'

'I'm not telling you anything.' Her marriage was not open to discussion. Holly coughed again. 'Our voices are disturbing her,' she muttered, glancing towards the stairs. The maternal instinct to go and check on her daughter finally released her from Rocco's magnetic spell. *'Please go.'*

Arguing with her was not going to get him anywhere, Rocco realised frustratedly as he snatched up his jacket and yanked open the front door. And, when it came down to it, what *did* he actually want? He hadn't meant for things to get so out of hand. Hell, he hadn't meant to kiss her. But when he had stared into her soft grey eyes he had felt compelled by a force he'd had no control over to slant his mouth over hers.

The uncomfortable throb of his erection was a mocking reminder that Emma turned him on more than any woman had done for a long time. But it was patently obvious that she was still in love with her dead husband—and, although Rocco eschewed any degree of emotional attachment with his mistresses, he balked at the idea of making love to a woman who wished he was someone else.

CHAPTER FIVE

THE weather on Sunday mimicked Emma's mood: grey, gloomy and unsettled. Holly refused to eat breakfast or lunch, and the cough that had developed during the night racked her fragile frame.

'When will the sun come out?' She sighed, her nose pressed to the window as she watched the rain falling relentlessly from a leaden sky. 'I want to play in the garden.'

'Spring will soon be here,' Emma promised. But she was assailed by guilt when she recalled Rocco's suggestion that she should accompany Cordelia to his home in Portofino and give her daughter a three-month holiday in the Italian sunshine. It was out of the question now, she thought grimly. She had proved last night that she could not trust herself to resist her sexual attraction to him.

She determinedly pushed him to the back of her mind and concentrated on finishing the household chores so that she could play with Holly, eventually slotting a favourite DVD into the player when it became clear that the little girl was weary.

During the afternoon, a retired couple came to view the cottage, and enthused over its quaint charm. A phone call from her landlord a few hours later, to inform her that the couple had offered the full asking price and were eager for the sale to go through quickly, rounded off a bad day and preceded a second restless night when Rocco invaded her thoughts until the early hours.

On Monday Holly woke with a high temperature which, together with her worsening cough, warranted a trip to the doctor. He diagnosed a chest infection.

'I wish I could prescribe fresh air and a dose of sunshine rather than antibiotics,' he said ruefully.

Luckily Emma managed to reschedule most of her day's visits, and a colleague agreed to cover her more serious cases. 'It's just Mrs Symmonds that I'll have trouble fitting in,' Sandra explained. 'She lives so far out on the moors.'

'I'll go and see her, and take Holly with me.' She had to face Rocco some time, so she might as well get it over with, Emma brooded as the four-by-four splashed through deep puddles made by the rain and melting snow on the road leading to Nunstead Hall.

Her knock on the door brought no response. Assuming that Rocco was busy somewhere in the huge house, she used the key Cordelia had given her. But as she stepped into the hall she immediately realised that for some reason the central heating wasn't on. It was almost as cold inside as out in the bitter wind blowing across the moors.

Cordelia was in the living room, sitting in an armchair pulled up close to the fire that was smouldering in the grate. She looked unusually pale, and her eyes were closed. For a second Emma's heart stopped, and she drew a relieved breath when the elderly lady stirred.

'Why is the heating off—?' She broke off and stared at Cordelia's hands—one bandaged to cover her burn, the other purple and bruised, with the fingers swollen to twice their normal size. 'What on earth has happened to your hand?'

'I opened the back door to call Thomas, and a gust of wind blew it shut and trapped my fingers,' Cordelia explained in a shaky voice. 'Rocco doesn't think they're broken because I can move them.' She winced as she wiggled her bruised fingers a fraction.

'They must be agony.' Emma felt physically sick as she inspected the elderly lady's injured fingers. Desperately worried about her patient, she repeated her first question. 'Why is the house so cold?'

'The heating has broken down. Something to do with the boiler, I think Rocco said.' As she finished speaking, Cordelia closed her eyes once more. She looked heart-wrenchingly fragile, and was probably suffering from mild shock, Emma realised.

'Where *is* Rocco?'

'Oh, he went to Paris to meet one of his lady friends… today…or was it yesterday?' Cordelia shook her head. 'I'm a bit muddled.' She smiled faintly. 'He's such a Lothario—just like his father.'

For a few seconds Emma was too shocked to speak. 'You mean he's left you injured and alone in a freezing house to go on a *date*?' The sick feeling in the pit of her stomach intensified, and with it a growing sense of outrage that Rocco had so casually abandoned his grandmother. Professionalism held her back from voicing her opinion that he was the most heartless and irresponsible man she had ever met, but she could not dismiss the little voice in her head which taunted that his beautiful mistress Juliette Pascal lived in Paris. Clearly kissing *her* on Saturday night had been an aberration which he had probably already forgotten about, Emma thought grimly.

She needed to focus on her job, she reminded herself. Her priority was to arrange temporary accommodation for Cordelia in a nursing home, where she could be properly cared for. Stubborn as the old lady was, she would surely understand that she could not remain on her own at Nunstead Hall.

Emma glanced at Holly, who was coughing again. 'Keep your coat on, munchkin, and stay in here, where it's a bit warmer than the rest of the house. I'm going to go and make Cordelia a cup of tea.'

The little girl nodded and patted Cordelia gently. 'I'll look after you, Nonna. Shall I tell you the story about the three little pigs?'

The weariness in Cordelia's eyes faded, and she smiled. 'That would be lovely, darling.'

The special bond between her daughter and her elderly patient was so poignant, Emma brooded as she hurried down to the kitchen. She knew the two of them would enjoy spending time together in Italy, and once again she felt guilty that she had refused to accept the position as Cordelia's private nurse. The truth was she could not bear the idea of staying at Rocco's villa, where he no doubt entertained an ever-changing parade of gorgeous women. It would be torture, she thought dismally. And it would be all the worse because she bitterly resented her attraction to a man she disliked.

She was suddenly jolted from her thoughts when she felt a blast of cold air rush into the kitchen, and as she glanced towards the back door her eyes widened in shock.

'I thought you were in Paris?'

Rocco frowned at the accusatory tone of Emma's voice, but he was intrigued when she blushed and quickly looked away from him. 'I was there yesterday,' he told her with a shrug.

One half of Emma's brain was busy registering that he looked unbelievably gorgeous in faded jeans and the big sheepskin jacket that emphasised the width of his broad shoulders, his damp hair brushed back from his brow to reveal the stark beauty of his features. But the other half of her brain was clinically assessing his words. So it was true—after he had made a pass at her he had gone straight to visit his French mistress. It was utterly ridiculous to feel so betrayed, she told herself fiercely. She was aware of his playboy reputation. And his kiss had meant as little to her as it clearly had to him, she assured herself.

She thought of Jack, who—although she had not known it at the time—had sometimes made love to her only hours after he had spent the afternoon having sex with his mistress. Since his death she had supressed the anger that simmered inside her, but now it rose up in an unstoppable tide. She wanted to lash out at her husband, who had hurt her so badly, but Jack was dead. It was Rocco standing in front of her—Rocco, who for a few breathless moments on Saturday night had made her feel like an attractive woman. For all she knew he might have been thinking about Juliette Pascal while he had been kissing her, she thought sickly.

She launched into a furious attack. 'I can't believe you went to Paris and left Cordelia when you *knew* the central heating was broken, and after she had injured her hand so badly. It was utterly *despicable* of you. Good God—couldn't you have controlled your sexual urges? Or is your grandmother's welfare unimportant compared to you getting it on with Juliette What's-Her-Name?'

For thirty seconds after her tirade silence trembled in the kitchen before Rocco demanded in an icy voice, 'What the hell are you talking about?'

'*You* scurrying off to meet your mistress the day after you had kissed me. That's what I'm talking about.' Emma's voice rose several notches. 'I don't give a damn what you do, or who you do it with,' she assured him scathingly. 'But to leave Cordelia alone in a freezing cold house was unforgivable.'

'I did not leave her on her own.' His tenuous control on his temper exploded. '*Dio*, woman—it's a pity you don't check your facts before making wild and totally unjust accusations.'

'You don't deny that you went to Paris?' Emma snapped.

'No, I don't deny it. But Cordelia spent the whole of Sunday with Jim and Nora Yaxley at their farm. I took her over in the morning, flew to Paris on my private jet, and spent a few hours there before I returned in the evening to collect her. This morning I woke to find that the central heating had packed up,' he explained curtly. 'I called an engineer, and while I was showing him the boiler Cordelia injured her hand in the door. I checked to make sure she hadn't broken any bones, and then lit a fire in the sitting room to keep her warm while I went to chop some logs.' He glared at her coldly, with no hint of the friendliness he had shown her when he had taken her to tea at the Royal Oak Hotel on his haughty features.

'At no time did I abandon my grandmother.'

Emma stared at the floor and wished she could sink through it. Once again she had jumped to conclusions and judged Rocco unfairly. 'I had the impression from Cordelia that you had gone to Paris *after* her accident,' she mumbled. 'But she's in shock, and it's not surprising she's confused. I'm sorry,' she finished in a low tone.

She bit her lip. She might have misjudged him over Cordelia, but the fact remained that he *had* hot-footed it off to Paris to see his mistress, and had probably spent Sunday afternoon… She frantically tried to block out the image of him and the beautiful Mademoiselle Pascal naked on a bed, making love.

Acid burned in the pit of her stomach—indigestion, she reassured herself, not jealousy. Desperate to avoid looking at him, she busied herself with making a pot of tea.

'Well, anyway, you're back now.' She strove to sound brisk and efficient. 'When will the central heating be working again?'

'It won't,' Rocco informed her tersely. 'The problem is with the boiler, but the whole system is antiquated and needs replacing—which in a house this size could take weeks, if not months.'

Emma gave him a startled look. 'Cordelia can't stay here when there is no heating.'

'Of course not. I'm sure you agree that it is imperative I persuade her to come and stay at my home in Italy—by whatever means I can,' Rocco added obliquely as he picked up the tea tray and strode out of the kitchen.

Back in the sitting room, it became clear, when Emma poured the tea, that Cordelia was unable to hold a cup with her bruised fingers, and was struggling with her bandaged hand.

'Let me help you,' she said gently, feeling a wave of compassion for the elderly lady. Cordelia was so determined to hang on to her independence, but this latest accident had left her looking painfully frail.

Rocco stoked the fire and added another log, glad of the excuse to turn away from his grandmother for a few moments. It struck him forcibly that Nonna was in the twilight years of her life. For a moment his eyes stung, and he blinked hard, telling himself it was because of the smoke.

His mind drifted back to the past. It had been Nonna who had comforted him in the dark days after Gio's death, and who had insisted that the accident hadn't been his fault. He had overheard her telling his mother to stop blaming him, that Flora should have been responsible for her younger son rather than handing his care over to a teenage boy. His grandmother had been his friend and ally when he had needed her most. Now she needed him—and he would not fail her.

He stood and walked back across the room, his eyes drawn to Emma, who was patiently helping Cordelia to sip her tea. She might be a termagant with him, but the gentle compassion she showed his grandmother was a rare quality that moved him deeply.

Cordelia glanced at her injured hands and gave him a resigned look. 'This is a pretty kettle of fish, isn't it?'

'It is indeed, Nonna. But fortunately I have the ideal solution.' Rocco spoke firmly and without hesitation. 'Emma has agreed to come to Portofino to be your nurse while you are recovering from your various injuries. Naturally she will be bringing Holly with her,' he added, quickly reassuring the little girl, who had looked momentarily worried.

He saw Emma stiffen, but before she could say a word Cordelia gave her a beaming smile tinged with tangible relief. 'Oh, my dear—I can't tell you how delighted I am. Rocco has been trying to persuade me to go and stay with him, but he leads a busy life, and I was afraid I would be lonely. But if you and Holly are going to be with me we'll have a *lovely* holiday—before I come back to live at Nunstead,' she said, her tone as firm as Rocco's had been.

'We'll discuss that once you are fully recovered.' Rocco deemed it wise not to push his luck with his stubborn grandmother. Conscious that if the look in Emma's stormy eyes could kill, he would be dead by now, he focused on her daughter. 'Would you like to come to Italy and stay in my house by the sea?'

Holly nodded, her eyes as wide as saucers. 'Can we go in the sea?'

'The sun will soon be warm enough for us to go to

the beach, and you can play in the garden with Bobbo, my dog.'

Wonderful, Emma thought bitterly. If the promise of trips to the beach wasn't enough, Rocco had a dog. Holly would be in seventh heaven. She stared at her daughter's excited face and her heart sank. How could she disappoint an elderly lady and a small child by refusing to go to Italy? She glared at Rocco—who knew quite well that she could not.

'Can I have a private word with you, to discuss arrangements?' she murmured in a saccharine tone, so that Cordelia would not realise she wanted to murder her grandson.

'Of course.' Rocco gave her a bland smile. 'Why don't we step into the hall?'

'You are *unbelievable*,' she breathed, the moment she shut the sitting room door behind them.

'I'm not certain you mean that as a compliment, but thank you.'

Her fingers itched to wipe the amusement from his face. 'You know damn well it wasn't a compliment—just as you know my feelings about this trip to Portofino. I made my reasons clear as to why I can't go.'

'Actually, you failed to give any good reason for wanting to upset my grandmother and spoil Holly's excitement.'

'You had *no* right to use my daughter to try and get your own way. Emotional blackmail is unforgivable.'

He shrugged. 'In business, I'll use any means at my disposal to win a deal, and the same goes for my private life. I want you to look after Cordelia, and if I have to use a little coercion to get what I want, so be it.'

Beneath his charming façade there was a ruthless side to Rocco. He would make a dangerous adversary, Emma realised. But at the same time his loyalty and love for his grandmother were undeniable.

'If you are worried about your job here in Northumberland, it's fine. I've squared it for you,' he told her.

'What do you mean, you've *squared* it?'

'I spoke to the head of the trust you work for and arranged for you to have three months' unpaid leave. Mr Donaldson was most obliging—especially after I made a donation to the local cottage hospital.'

Far from being grateful that he had resolved a significant reason for her decision not to go to Portofino, Emma was furious at his interference. 'You treat people like puppets, don't you?' she snapped. 'You think your money gives you the right to arrange my life to suit you. If you want the truth, I don't *want* Holly to stay at your villa. A playboy's love nest is *not* a suitable environment for a child.'

While Rocco was absorbing this startling statement, she demanded, 'Will Juliette Pascal be there? Or another of your *lady friends*, as Cordelia euphemistically describes them? Maybe you plan to entertain more than one? From what I've heard, you frequently juggle multiple mistresses.'

'What an eye-watering vision you present,' Rocco drawled. He studied her flushed face speculatively. 'Juliette won't be visiting the Villa Lucia because I ended our affair yesterday. It wasn't really even an affair. We both lead busy lives and met up occasionally whenever we happened to be in the same city. It was an arrangement that suited both of us.'

After Rosalinda he had made sure any woman he dated understood unequivocally that there was no chance he would ever want more than a casual affair. He noted Emma's scathing expression and his jaw hardened.

'Despite what you may have read in the tabloid newspapers, I only ever have mistresses in multiples of one.

After kissing you on Saturday night, it was only right that I should end my relationship with Juliette. But I certainly wouldn't have done so with a phone call.'

Emma was struck dumb by his revelation. She felt a grudging respect that he had had the decency to end his affair in person. But had he slept with the beautiful model yesterday—enjoyed a final sex session for old times' sake? she wondered, feeling acid burn in the pit of her stomach.

'Why did you end your affair because of one kiss?' She strove to sound uninterested, not knowing that Rocco could see the uncertainty in her eyes. 'You said yourself there was no need to get worked up about it.' Unconsciously she worried the tender flesh of her lower lip with her teeth. 'It meant nothing to either of us.'

'Let's see, shall we?'

The sudden deepening of his voice should have triggered alarm bells, but he moved so quickly that she had no time to react. One arm snaked around her waist and pulled her hard up against him, while his other hand cupped her jaw as he covered her mouth with his.

This time his kiss was no gentle seduction. This time it was urgent and demanding, born of a sense of frustration—not only at Emma's stubbornness, but from the fact that ever since he had kissed her two nights ago all he had been able to think about was how soon he could repeat the experience. The feel of her soft curves pressed up against him heated his blood. Desire thundered through his veins, and he slid his hand from her jaw to tangle in her hair, tugging her head back so that he could plunder her soft, moist mouth.

Desperately, Emma fought the temptation to sink into him and lose herself in the mastery of his kiss. The logical part of her brain reminded her that she did not want this. She functioned perfectly well without passion and desire in her life. Those emotions had brought her nothing but heartache in the past and she would be a fool to be seduced by their sorcery. So *why*, instead of pushing Rocco away, did she slowly uncurl her clenched fists and lay her hands flat against his chest?

The determined probing of his tongue between her lips demolished her pitiful resistance and she gave a low moan as she opened her mouth for him, a tremor running through her when he explored her with devastating eroticism. Driven by a need she barely understood, she responded to him mindlessly.

Sensing her capitulation, he changed the tenure of the kiss so that it became a flagrant seduction of her senses. She shivered when she felt him slide his hand beneath the edge of her jumper to stroke her bare flesh lightly above the waistband of her jeans. Her skin felt acutely sensitised, so that the brush of his fingertips caused needle-darts of pleasure to shoot through her. Silently she willed him to skim his hand higher, to slip it beneath her bra and touch her naked breasts. Her nipples felt hot and swollen, and she was conscious of the moist secretion between her legs, the ache that could only be relieved by pressing her pelvis against his thighs.

She was utterly unprepared when he suddenly broke the kiss and lifted his head to stare down into her wide, stunned eyes. Realisation slowly dawned that she was clinging to him, and she snatched her hands from his body, scarlet colour flooding her face.

Attack was her only form of defence. *'How dare you?'*

He gave her a mocking look. 'Your outrage would have a little more impact if you had not responded to me so ardently.'

Rocco watched Emma pull the edge of her jumper firmly into place, feeling a curious tug on his heart when he saw that her hands were shaking. Her usually neat golden bob was mussed and had fallen forward across her cheek. He wanted to stroke her hair back from her face, but knew she would react like a wildcat if he attempted to touch her.

Fool, Emma berated herself furiously, closing her eyes as shame swept over her. It was bad enough that she had allowed him to kiss her, but to compound her stupidity she had kissed him back with embarrassing eagerness—until *he* had pulled back. She hadn't just responded to him ardently—she had practically eaten him alive!

Through the sitting room door she could hear Holly singing 'Twinkle Twinkle Little Star', her sweet voice joined by Cordelia's slightly wavering one. How could she walk back in and announce that she was *not* prepared to go to Italy as Cordelia's private nurse? The thought of the disappointment her words would cause made her wince. But how could she stay at Rocco's home after she had all but begged him to make love to her on the hall carpet? she wondered despairingly.

Taking a deep breath, she forced herself to meet his gaze. 'For Cordelia's sake I will come to Portofino.' Somehow she had to regain her dignity. 'I'll be happy to act as her nurse and companion, but I will *not* put up with you manhandling me.'

'If I had manhandled you, I promise you would not be standing there fully dressed, *cara*,' Rocco said dulcetly. Ignoring the daggers in her eyes, he reached into the pocket of his jeans and withdrew a slip of paper.

Frowning, Emma took the cheque from him, stared at it for a moment, and then back at him. 'I don't understand what this is for.'

'It's your salary for the next three months.'

'Don't be ridiculous. I earn this amount in a year.'

He shrugged. 'I want the best care for my grandmother. I know you will do everything possible to ensure she is comfortable and happy, and in return I am prepared to pay you well.'

'Not this well.' She shook her head briskly and tore the cheque in half. 'You don't have to offer me a bribe. I'm very fond of Cordelia and I want to look after her. All I require is the usual monthly salary I earn as a district nurse.'

Rocco stared at her in frustration. And he had thought his grandmother was strong-willed! Nonna was a push-over compared to Emma. 'But you could use the money as a deposit to buy Primrose Cottage.'

'No.' It was not even a consideration. 'Anyway, the cottage has already been sold. One day I'll have saved enough for a deposit on a house, but I'll pay my own way in life,' Emma said firmly. 'I don't want to feel indebted to anyone.' She hesitated. 'Neither do I want an affair with you. So if you were thinking you could pay me to…'

'Madre de Dio!' Rocco said harshly, his anger searing him like a white-hot branding iron. 'That is one insult too far, Emma. I have never *paid* for a woman in my life.' He stared at her haughtily, his skin stretched taut over his razor-sharp cheekbones, giving him a coldly autocratic appearance. 'I don't deny that I desire you, but when you come to my bed it will be of your own accord.'

His arrogance infuriated her, but she was even angrier with herself for the damning flare of excitement his words evoked.

'That's never going to happen.'

'Because you are still in love with your husband?' he speculated. Once again he struggled to contain his frustration—with him, with her, and most of all with the primitive need to possess her that made his gut ache. The world was full of attractive blondes who would be happy to share his bed. Why was he bothering with this feisty, stubborn woman who constantly challenged him?

Emma bit her lip, feeling an inexplicable urge to confide the truth about her marriage to Rocco. She could not, she reminded herself. For Holly's sake, Jack's duplicity must remain a secret. But her love for Jack had died with the discovery of how he had betrayed her. During the past three years she had come to terms with the hurt he had caused her, but her wariness and mistrust remained. Never again would she put herself in a position where her heart could be broken. She did not want any man in her life—certainly not a sexy Italian who regarded women as playthings.

'Jack is the reason why I refuse to get involved with you—or with any other man,' she said quietly.

'Do you think he would have wanted you to condemn yourself to a life alone?' Rocco demanded harshly.

'Maybe not, but I have Holly to consider. What do you suggest I do? Indulge in casual affairs, introduce her to a series of "uncles" who she may become close to, only to see her upset when they move on?'

'Of course not.' He raked a hand through his hair, appalled by the image she presented.

During his childhood his parents had both been openly unfaithful, and on the rare occasions when his mother had promised to visit him at his boarding school he had never been sure whether she would turn up with his father or one of her sleazeball boyfriends.

But, while he had taken scant interest in his parents' various lovers, it was likely that Holly, who had never known her own father, would welcome a father figure. Any man who became involved with Emma would need to recognise that he had a level of responsibility towards her child. A casual affair was out of the question—but that was all *he* could ever offer, Rocco thought grimly, all he would ever want.

His parents' volatile relationship had shown him that marriage was a gamble, with low odds of success. He was still haunted by Rosalinda's suicide attempt after he had ended their affair, and since then had made it clear at the outset with the women he dated that he was not looking for commitment or a long-term relationship. That meant that Emma was off-limits. She would not consider indulging in a brief sexual fling, and he could not help but respect her for her decision. Unlike his mother, Emma put the welfare of her child before her own desires.

The sitting room door suddenly opened and Holly appeared, happily oblivious to the tense atmosphere in the hall. 'Nonna and me want to know when we are going to stay at your house,' she asked Rocco.

'Tomorrow.' He ignored Emma's sharply indrawn breath and smiled at the little girl.

Big grey eyes, so like her mother's, studied him anxiously. 'Is Thomas coming too?'

'No. Cats don't like travelling on aeroplanes, so he is going to stay at Yaxley Farm.'

When Holly trotted off to relay this information to Cordelia, Emma glared at Rocco. Panic gripped her. She was backtracking fast, bitterly regretting the moment of insanity that had seen her agree to go to Italy with him. 'I can't possibly be ready to leave tomorrow. There are dozens of things to do, arrangements to be made…'

'All you have to do is pack yours and Holly's things. Make a list of anything else that needs to be done and my PA will take care of everything. Stop looking for difficulties that don't exist,' Rocco told her tersely. 'Because of the broken heating system I'm taking Cordelia to spend the night at the Royal Oak Hotel. But it's not ideal. I want to take her to Portofino as soon as possible.'

'But…' Emma found she was speaking to thin air as he strode past her into the sitting room.

Irritating man, she fumed. All her instincts were screaming at her to tell him she had changed her mind. But it was too late now; she could not upset Cordelia and Holly. It was only for three months, she reminded herself. Three months of living in Rocco's villa and seeing him every day, taunted a little voice inside her head. She could only pray she survived with her emotions unscathed.

CHAPTER SIX

'Look, Mummy. The sea!' Holly burst through the connecting door between her bedroom and Emma's at the Villa Lucia, and pointed excitedly towards the window. 'It's blue,' she observed, pressing her nose to the glass.

'It certainly is—almost as blue as the sky. Isn't it beautiful?' As Emma joined her daughter at the window she could not help but compare the sparkling cobalt waters in the Bay of Tigullio with the steel-grey surf that had pounded the shore on the coast of Northumberland the last time she had taken Holly for a trip to the beach.

Rocco's villa was built on a hillside, affording a panoramic view of picturesque Portofino, the wide sweep of the bay and the surrounding mountains, which were densely covered with pine trees and other foliage so that the landscape was a lush, verdant green. Directly in front of the house was a series of terraced gardens, and on the lower level was a huge pool which sparkled invitingly in the bright sunshine. Lower still could be seen Portofino's port, where dozens of boats were moored in neat rows. Pretty, pastel-coloured buildings ringed the harbour, the shopfronts shaded by striped awnings which fluttered in the breeze.

'Shall we go swimming now?'

Emma smiled at Holly's hopeful expression. 'Not for

a few days—at least not in the sea,' she said gently. 'Remember, Rocco said the sea will be too cold to swim in yet? But when your cough is better you can go in the pool, because the water is heated.'

'There's Bobbo!' Holly was distracted from the subject of swimming when she spied a chocolate-coloured Labrador hurtling across the lawn. 'Rocco said I can give Bobbo his breakfast,' she said joyfully.

'After you've eaten all *your* breakfast,' Emma told her firmly.

She sighed. Holly had fallen in love with Rocco's dog within five minutes of their arrival at the Villa Lucia the previous evening. Added to that, the little girl seemed to hero-worship Rocco, and Emma was already worried about how upset her daughter was going to be when it was time for them to return to England. But there was no point in thinking about that now, she told herself as she stared out of the window, her gaze focused not on the dog but on the tall, athletic man who was throwing a ball for the animal.

She guessed from Rocco's attire of shorts, vest top and trainers that he had been running. His sports clothes revealed his superb physique: broad shoulders, rippling biceps and muscular thighs. His satiny skin was tanned a deep olive colour, and his hair gleamed jet-black, like a raven's wing in the sunlight.

He was a work of art, she acknowledged ruefully. But, unlike any marble statue sculpted by Michelangelo, Rocco was a flesh-and-blood man. Not for the first time Emma found herself remembering how it had felt when he had pulled her into his arms and ravaged her mouth with his own. He had demanded a response she had been helpless to deny, and the memory of his kiss caused her nipples to harden, so that they rubbed uncomfortably against her lacy bra.

To her horror he suddenly glanced up at the house and lifted his hand in greeting. Holly waved excitedly back at him, but Emma hurriedly stepped away from the window, feeling horribly embarrassed that she had been caught ogling him. Rocco could not possibly have known that she had been imagining him stripping out of his running gear and stepping naked beneath a shower, sliding a bar of soap over the hard muscles of his abdomen and then lower…

'Come on, we must go and see if Cordelia needs any help, and then we'll all go down for breakfast,' she told Holly briskly. With any luck Rocco would take some time to shower and dress, and there was a good chance she would be able to avoid meeting him before he left for work.

So far, her plan to have as little contact with him as possible had been surprisingly successful. She even had a niggling suspicion that he was equally keen to keep their relationship to a strictly employer/employee basis. During the flight to Genoa aboard his private jet he had been exquisitely polite towards her, but distinctly aloof. There had been no hint of his sexy charm, no flirtatious glances, and his warm smile had been reserved for his grandmother and Holly.

It was exactly what she wanted, Emma assured herself. She had come to the Villa Lucia in a purely professional role, to act as Cordelia's nurse, and she was glad Rocco recognised that fact. The flat feeling inside her was probably a reaction to the previous twenty-four hours, when she had been busy packing everything she'd thought Holly would need for their stay in Italy, plus a small suitcase containing her own few belongings.

Holding Holly by the hand, she led the way along the corridor to Cordelia's room where she discovered that the elderly lady needed help fastening the buttons on her dress.

'Your burn looks so much better this morning that I

should be able to remove the dressing tomorrow,' Emma told her. 'Without the bandages you'll have more mobility in your fingers, but I'm afraid the fingers on your other hand are still very swollen, and it's going to take a while for the bruising to fade.'

'That's what comes of being a foolish old woman,' Cordelia said despondently. 'I've made such a nuisance of myself to everyone—especially Rocco.'

'No one could ever accuse you of being foolish,' Emma reassured her gently. 'And Rocco is delighted you've come to stay with him.'

His love for his grandmother had been evident in the tender way he had taken care of her during the flight to Italy the previous day. This softer side to his commanding personality was unexpected, and Emma was still embarrassed that she had accused him of being uncaring the first time she had met him.

They took the lift down to the ground floor. The villa was built on four levels, and it was doubtful Cordelia would have managed so many stairs. Rocco had confided to Emma that he had had the lift installed a couple of years ago, when he had realised that his grandmother could not continue to live alone at Nunstead Hall. Far from shirking his responsibility, he had clearly planned to take care of Cordelia in the last years of her life.

They were greeted by the cook, Beatrice, who chatted volubly in a mixture of Italian and broken English as she ushered them into the breakfast room, which overlooked the gardens and the sapphire sea sparkling in the distance.

'I bake rolls fresh this morning, and there is fruit and yogurt. If you need anything else for the *bambina* you ask Beatrice, *si*?' she said earnestly.

'*Grazie.* I'm sure we have everything we need,' Emma replied, taken aback by the wonderful selection of fresh fruit set out on the table. She was even more surprised when Holly and Cordelia both ate hearty breakfasts. It was probably the result of the antibiotics, but Holly was not coughing nearly as much, and for the first time in weeks there was a faint tinge of pink on her cheeks.

'*Buongiorno*, ladies.' Rocco strolled into the room and bent his head to kiss his grandmother's cheek. 'Nonna, Holly...Emma.' Was it her imagination, or had his voice cooled fractionally as he had spoken her name? 'I am glad you are here in my home.'

To her self-disgust the sight of him made her heart-rate quicken, and she busied herself with wiping yogurt from Holly's face while she struggled to regain her composure. It did not help that Rocco looked devastatingly gorgeous in beige chinos and a black polo shirt, his damp hair an indication that he had recently showered. She had assumed that as the CEO of a world-famous company he would wear a suit to work, and Cordelia must have shared her thoughts.

The elderly lady studied her grandson. 'Don't tell me you are one of those trendy executives who chooses not to wear a tie to the office, Rocco?'

'Certainly not,' he murmured, his lazy smile doing strange things to Emma's insides. 'But I'm not going to work today. I want to make sure my guests settle in to the Villa Lucia.' His golden eyes trapped Emma's gaze. 'Did you sleep well?'

Her cool smile disguised her intense awareness of him. 'Very, thank you.' He could not know that she had spent another restless night during which she had been unable to dismiss him from her mind.

'If you've finished eating, I'd like a word with you.'

Without waiting for her to reply he turned and strode out of the door, leaving her with little option but to follow him out to the hall and across to his study.

'Why are you wearing your nurse's uniform?' he demanded, the moment she entered the room.

Emma's brows lifted fractionally at the abruptness of his tone. 'Because I am your grandmother's nurse.'

'Your role here is to act as Cordelia's companion. I hardly think that necessitates wearing a uniform. I would prefer you to wear normal clothes.'

She compressed her lips. 'But *I* would prefer to wear the uniform which denotes that I am your employee.' It was vital to her peace of mind that she distance herself from him. Her uniform signified that she was staying at his home in a professional capacity, and in some strange way she felt safe and in control when she was dressed in her work clothes. 'I think it is important to establish boundaries. I have accepted a contract to work for you, and I believe I should dress appropriately.'

Rocco trailed his eyes over Emma's plain blue dress, adorned only with an elasticated belt which showed off her slim waist and emphasised the delightful curves of her bust and hips, before lowering his gaze to her shapely legs, covered in sheer black hose and her sensible black shoes. No one could accuse her of dressing like a *femme fatale*, yet he was consumed with an extremely inappropriate urge to wrench open the front of her dress and feast his eyes on her bountiful breasts.

He shifted in his seat in an effort to ease the lustful throb in his groin. 'It doesn't seem to have occurred to you that Cordelia might not want people to know she has a nurse. My grandmother is fiercely proud. She has accepted the idea of having a companion, but she would hate people to think she is unable to care for herself.'

Emma bit her lip as Rocco's words struck a chord. It was true she had been so busy thinking about herself that she had not considered her patient's feelings. 'I appreciate what you're saying,' she mumbled. 'But Cordelia doesn't actually know anyone in Portofino, so who are all these people whose opinion she might worry about?'

'That's the other reason I asked to speak to you. I'm thinking of hosting a cocktail party and inviting friends and neighbours, perhaps a few colleagues from Eleganza, to welcome Nonna to Italy. Do you think it would be too much for her?' He exhaled heavily. 'She looks so frail, and I don't want to overtire her.'

'I think Cordelia would love a party in her honour,' Emma assured him. 'She often talks about the parties she and her husband used to give at Nunstead Hall years ago. She would enjoy the chance to dress up, and I can help her to get ready.'

'You will, of course, accompany her to the party.'

The prospect of socialising with Rocco's glamorous friends made Emma's heart sink. It had struck her yesterday, when she had stepped onto his luxurious private jet, that their lives were light years apart, and she did not belong in his rarefied world of the super-rich. 'Surely that won't be necessary? I'll be on hand, of course, but—as you said yourself—Cordelia doesn't need a nurse in constant attendance.'

'*Dio*, Emma, why is everything a battle with you?' Rocco's patience snapped. 'You are a guest in my home and naturally you are included in my invitation to the party. Why are you so determined to reject any overtures of friendship from me?' His eyes narrowed on her startled face. 'You seem to be afraid to trust. But why? Who caused you to be so wary?'

'No one.' Her tone was defensive, and she flushed when he gave her a sardonic look. Emma took a deep breath. 'I'm sure we can establish a cordial friendship for the duration of my stay at the Villa Lucia.'

What was she thinking behind her cool grey gaze? Rocco wondered frustratedly. He was tempted to spread her across his desk, shove her starched nurse's dress up to her waist and prove emphatically that she no more wanted a *cordial friendship* than he did.

'Were you happy with Jack?' he asked abruptly, his sharp gaze noting how she tensed at the mention of her husband.

'Yes, of course.'

It was a partial truth, Emma acknowledged silently. Blissfully unaware that Jack had been unfaithful from the first weeks of their marriage, she had believed they were happy. There had been a few issues that had caused her concern—mainly his irresponsibility with money. She had quickly learned to put her wages away to pay the rent and bills, because Jack could blow his month's salary in a single shopping trip. He could not help his impulsive nature, she had told herself. Blinded by her love for him, she had made excuses for his selfishness—even in the bedroom, when he had often taken his own pleasure without any consideration for hers. He was tired after working a long shift, she had told herself, not knowing that he had been with his mistress, rather than on duty at the fire station.

Looking back, she despised herself for having been such a naive fool. It was not only other people that she now found hard to trust, but her faith in her own judgement had been shattered. She stared at Rocco's impossibly handsome face and felt her stomach dip. He had awoken her libido and made her long for the warmth and closeness of making love. But that closeness had been an illusion with Jack, and it could not exist with Rocco, who was the ultimate playboy.

'Getting back to the party,' she said quickly, desperate to steer the conversation away from her marriage. 'I don't have anything suitable to wear. I don't get invited to many cocktail parties in Little Copton,' she added dryly.

Rocco shrugged. 'That's not a problem. Portofino is renowned for its designer boutiques. We'll go shopping this afternoon, and I'll look after Holly while you try on dresses. Don't argue, Emma,' he warned, seeing the glint of battle in her eyes. 'Holly will enjoy a trip to the harbour. I've already asked Cordelia if she would like to come, but she says she's weary today and so she'll stay here with Beatrice.'

'You seem to have arranged everything—as usual.' Struggling to control her temper, Emma turned on her heels to march out of his study, but in her haste she banged her hip against the desk and knocked a framed photograph to the floor. 'Sorry,' she muttered as she stooped to retrieve it, thankful to see that the glass had not broken.

She studied the picture of two dark-haired boys. The older was clearly Rocco—even as a teenager he had been stunningly good-looking, she noted. The younger boy bore a strong resemblance to Rocco, and Emma suddenly remembered that he had mentioned he had a sibling.

'Will your brother be at the party?'

'No.'

Startled by his curt response, she looked at him and glimpsed a sudden bleakness in his eyes.

'Giovanni died a week after that picture was taken.'

Shocked, she stared back at the photo. 'I'm sorry. He was just a child.'

'Seven years old,' Rocco revealed emotionlessly.

Emma wanted to ask more, but Rocco's closed expression warned her he did not want to discuss his brother's death. He jerked to his feet and strode across the room to open the door. 'I need to work for a couple of hours, so I'll have to ask you to go back to my grandmother.'

'Yes, of course.' Summarily dismissed, she had no option but to stifle her curiosity and walk out of the study.

Rocco closed the study door and leaned against it, his eyes focused on the photograph Emma had handed to him. Even after twenty years he still felt an ache in his heart when he thought of Gio, and the guilt that he was partly responsible for his brother's death would always be with him. But fate worked in mysterious ways, he brooded. He had lost Gio, but now he had a brother again.

Marco was the image of Gio. And Marco needed him—just as Gio had. Although at the moment his little half-brother—his father's illegitimate son—was full of anger and confusion, and defiantly resistant to Rocco's attempts to build a relationship with him. But slowly, with patience, he would do his best to win the little boy round. Marco needed a father figure, and Rocco had vowed to give his brother the guidance and love that he would have given Gio.

For the time being, though, he had decided to keep Marco's identity hidden. There would be huge interest once it became known that Enrico D'Angelo had had a secret son, and Rocco was determined to protect his brother from the media sharks who would circle once the story broke.

'This is pointless,' Emma muttered that afternoon, as she trailed after Rocco along Portofino's main street and halted next to him outside another boutique. She glanced at the window display and her eyebrows shot up when she saw the price tag attached to the exquisite gown draped on the mannequin. 'I can't afford designer clothes.'

The Via Roma was lined with exclusive boutiques and jewellers, interspersed with local shops selling beautiful handmade goods, and art galleries stacked with paintings depicting the stunning scenery of the bay of Tigullio.

Portofino was known as the Italian Riviera—a mecca for the rich and beautiful—and Emma, wearing old jeans and a sweatshirt, which were the only clothes she possessed other than her nurse's uniform, felt decidedly out of place.

'I'm not going to find a dress here,' she told Rocco, who looked every inch a multi-millionaire business tycoon in his expertly tailored clothes and designer shades. 'You and I come from different worlds, and I am very much a discount store girl. I'm going to take Holly to see the boats in the harbour. Come on, munchkin,' she said, resisting the urge to prise her daughter's fingers out of Rocco's grasp. She had felt a sharp pang when Holly had happily held Rocco's hand and skipped along beside him. She was worried her little girl would get too attached, and it would break her heart when the time came to leave.

'I think Mummy should try on that pink dress,' Rocco said to Holly. 'Princesses wear pink dresses, don't they?'

She nodded, big grey eyes sparkling with excitement. 'You can be a princess, Mummy—like Cinderella.'

'Doesn't it bother your conscience to know you are manipulating a small child?' Emma hissed, giving him a glare that would have floored a lesser man.

'I don't have a conscience, *cara.*' Rocco grinned unrepentantly as he pushed open the shop door and ushered her inside. He spoke in Italian to the elegant assistant, while Emma hovered, feeling horribly conscious that her faded jeans were hardly couture. She had no idea what he said, but within minutes the assistant had brought out a selection of dresses for her to try on.

'I'll take Holly to buy an ice cream,' he murmured. 'Here's my credit card. Choose a couple of dresses and charge them to my account.'

'You must be joking. You're not going to pay for my clothes.'

'Think of it as a requirement for your job,' he advised smoothly. 'I want you at Cordelia's party, so don't leave here without something to wear.'

'*Signorina* does not like it?' the assistant queried ten minutes later, as Emma handed back the dress that she had seen displayed in the window.

'It's absolutely beautiful,' she assured the woman. 'But I can't afford it.' Made of pale pink chiffon, with narrow diamanté shoulder straps, the dress was a masterpiece of understated elegance. Emma had fallen in love with it the moment she had slipped it over her head, but it cost a fortune, and whatever Rocco said she was not going to allow him to buy it for her. Instead, she hurried out of the designer boutique and walked back to a shop which stocked clothes closer to her price range. The navy blue dress in the window was smart and practical. She would probably get years of wear out of it, she consoled herself as she handed the assistant her own credit card.

To Emma's relief, Rocco went to work for the rest of the week, driving to Eleganza's head office in the city of Genoa, some fifteen miles from Portofino. He left the Villa Lucia early each morning, and returned to dine with his grandmother in the evening. He insisted that Emma ate with them, dismissing her argument that Cordelia might want to spend time alone with her grandson.

'Anyone would think you are reluctant to be in my company,' he had taunted softly on that first evening, when he'd demanded her presence in the dining room. 'What are you afraid of, Emma? How can we become friends if you constantly avoid me?'

'I'm not afraid of you,' she denied sharply, the sultry gleam in his golden eyes making her feel hot and flustered.

She looked at him uncertainly. 'Is that what you want—for us to be friends?'

His sensual smile stole her breath. 'I would be lying if I said that was *all* I wanted, *cara*. But it's a start.'

In truth, Rocco did not know what he wanted. The simple answer was Emma—in his bed. His desire for her was like a ravenous beast, eating away at him, distracting his mind during the day and keeping him awake at night as he fantasised about the many and varied ways he would enjoy possessing her delectable body.

If she had been any other woman he would have wasted no time seducing her. But Emma was unlike any woman he had ever met. For one thing she was a widow who still mourned the husband she had loved—which made the vulnerable expression in her eyes whenever Jack Marchant's name was mentioned puzzling, Rocco brooded.

Now, at the end of the week, he felt as wound up as a coiled spring. Sexual frustration was not conducive to a good mood, he'd discovered. There were several women he could call—casual mistresses who would be happy to join him for dinner at an exclusive restaurant followed by a night of mutually enjoyable sex, with no strings attached. So why wasn't he tempted to pick up the phone? Why did he feel jaded by a diet of sophisticated lovers and meaningless physical encounters?

The answer could be found in a pair of grey eyes that regarded him coolly across the dinner table every evening. Sometimes the expression in those eyes was not as dismissive as he suspected their owner wished. Emma was fighting the sexual chemistry between them. But it was there, simmering beneath the surface of their polite conversation, and blazing in the stolen glances they shared. He heard her swiftly indrawn breath when he leaned close to refill her wine glass, and he knew they both felt a tingle of electricity if their hands accidentally brushed.

Their attraction to one another was undeniable, but for the first time in his life Rocco could not simply take what he wanted. Beneath Emma's crisp, no-nonsense exterior he had glimpsed a woman of deep emotions, gentle, compassionate, and possessing an air of vulnerability that tugged on his insides. And there was her daughter to consider. Holly was an enchanting child, who looked at him with such innocent trust in her eyes that he already felt fiercely protective of her. He would do anything to avoid hurting her, or her mother.

Rocco's staff had become used to him leaving the office early on Friday afternoons. There was much speculation as to where he went, the general consensus being that he must go to meet a mistress, but the gossipers were careful to keep their thoughts to themselves whenever Eleganza's CEO was in earshot.

As he drove through the heavy traffic to the other side of Genoa, the last thing on Rocco's mind was office tittle-tattle about his private life. When he pulled up outside Marco's school there were only a few kids hanging around, including a small boy with jet-black hair and unusual amber-coloured eyes, who trudged over to the car with obvious reluctance and a dark scowl on his face.

'I'm sorry I'm late. There was a snarl-up on the Via Serra.' Rocco stifled a sigh when his brother climbed into the front passenger seat and flicked him a glance of supreme indifference. The way the boy folded his arms across his chest was instinctively defensive, and revealed a vulnerability that made Rocco want to reach out to him.

'I told you—you don't have to come. I walk home every

other day.' Marco darted him a quick glance. 'I thought you weren't coming—and I wouldn't have cared.'

Beneath the belligerence Rocco caught a note of uncertainty in the little boy's voice and his heart clenched. 'I'll always come on Fridays. I would never let you down,' he promised quietly.

Golden eyes glared at him from beneath the untidy mop of hair—eyes that were shadowed with hurt that should not be borne by a seven-year-old. It was hardly surprising, Rocco thought heavily. Up until four months ago Marco had not known that he was the son of Enrico D'Angelo, or that he had an older half-brother. What had induced Enrico to ask to meet his illegitimate son as he lay dying Rocco did not understand. Possibly his father had felt remorseful that he had abandoned his one-time mistress when she had fallen pregnant with his child. But Marco had only seen his father once before Enrico had died. The boy was clearly traumatised, resentful and touchingly protective of his mother who had struggled to bring him up without any financial support from her wealthy ex-lover.

'Why do you come?' Marco burst out. 'Me and Mamma didn't need Enrico, and we don't need you.'

'You are my brother, and I want to visit you,' Rocco said gently. 'It was wrong of our father to turn his back on you, and it is my duty to help your mother take care of you while you are growing up. But, more than that, I want us to be friends, Marco.'

He hesitated, thinking of his recent conversation with Inga Salveson, who had been his father's mistress. 'Your mother has told me she is thinking about moving back to Sweden, and of course you would go with her. But that will only happen if you decide that you do not want anything to do with me and your grandfather here in Italy. It's your choice whether or not you want to be a D'Angelo.'

For the first time there was a glimmer of curiosity in the wary golden eyes. 'Does my grandfather know about me?'

'No—not yet. Silvio is an old man, who has been ill recently. I don't want to tell him he has another grandson until you are sure you would like to meet him. It would be upsetting for him if you decided not to.'

Marco's lower lip wobbled betrayingly. 'I don't know what to do.' Tears clung perilously to his lower lashes. All his defiance suddenly disappeared, leaving behind a small, confused little boy. 'My *papà* is dead and I didn't even know him,' he choked. 'Don't tell my *nonno* about me yet...but maybe I will want to meet him one day. I will want to meet him.' A tear overspilled and slid down his cheek.

Rocco swallowed the constriction that had formed in his throat, his anger at Enrico's irresponsibility turning to compassion for this little boy who had met his father briefly and then lost him for ever. It was not surprising that Marco was so mistrustful.

Throwing aside his usual caution when dealing with his brother, he put his arm around Marco's shoulders. 'Whatever you want, Marco,' he said softly. 'I promise I won't tell anyone you are Enrico's son until you are happy for me to do so. Now...' he smiled, trying to break the tension '...how about we go and get some ice-cream?'

'Okay.' Marco scrubbed his wet face with a grubby hand. And for the first time he returned his brother's smile.

Preparations were in full swing when Rocco arrived back at the Villa Lucia that evening. He frequently hosted social events, and his staff, under Beatrice's command, could be trusted to ensure that the cocktail party in his grandmother's honour ran smoothly. He headed straight for his room to shower and change, before going back downstairs.

Beatrice had excelled herself, he noted. The Villa Lucia looked beautiful and welcoming. Huge vases of roses and lilies decorated the entrance hall and reception rooms, filling the air with their heady fragrance, while dozens of flickering candles emitted a golden glow. In fifteen minutes the guests would begin to arrive. The champagne was on ice, and the kitchen staff would serve a selection of canapés.

It had been a good day—especially as he felt he had made a break-through with Marco. Feeling a pleasant sense of well-being, Rocco was about to join his grandmother in the sitting room when a terse voice stopped him in his tracks.

'Where are my clothes?'

He turned to see Emma marching down the wide staircase, and even across the distance of the hall he noted that her eyes were the colour of storm clouds.

'Don't even think about making one of your clever remarks,' she warned him as he subjected her to a leisurely inspection. 'This dress does not belong to me, and neither do any of the other designer clothes that have appeared in my wardrobe.'

Emma took a deep breath, trying to control the fury that had swiftly followed her shock when she had gone to change into the navy dress she had bought for the party and discovered that her own clothes had disappeared and been replaced with dozens of beautiful outfits—many of which she had tried on during her shopping trip with Rocco a few days ago. 'What are you playing at, Rocco?'

'I bought you the clothes because you can't spend the next three months wearing jeans and a sweatshirt,' he explained mildly. 'For one thing, you don't need winter clothes here. The temperature is likely to shoot up in the summer.' He trailed his eyes over her, from her silky strawberry-blonde bob down to her slim shoulders revealed by the narrow straps of the pink cocktail dress. 'Besides, it's a crime to hide your gorgeous figure beneath bulky, shapeless garments.'

The bodice of the dress was cleverly cut so that her breasts were lifted high, their creamy upper slopes displayed in all their bounteous glory. Rocco's mouth went dry as he pictured himself drawing the straps down until those firm mounds of flesh spilled into his hands. He dropped his gaze lower, noting how the delicate chiffon skirt skimmed the curve of her hips and stopped several inches above her knees. Strappy silver shoes with three-inch heels accentuated the slender length of her legs.

'Sei bella,' he said roughly, colour flaring along his cheekbones. Desire ripped through him, shocking in its intensity, and he was conscious of the erection straining uncomfortably beneath his trousers. 'I knew the dress would suit you, but you have surpassed all my expectations, *cara*.' So much so that he was gripped with a fierce urge to carry her upstairs to his room and peel the dress from her body before making hard, urgent love to her. But there was his grandmother, the party, his duty as host. However much he wished that he was alone with Emma, he had to control his hunger for her—not least because of the wariness in her eyes.

'The clothes are a measure of my appreciation for the way you cared for Cordelia in Northumberland, and my thanks that you agreed to accompany her to Italy.'

She shook her head. 'I can't accept them. It's enough that you pay me a salary.'

Emma could not disguise the note of panic in her voice. She did not want to feel indebted to Rocco. Ever since she had met him she had felt that her life was spinning out of control. As a single mother she had never had spare money to spend on herself, and she could only ever have dreamed of owning the exquisite creation she was wearing. But the dress did not belong to her—and she did not belong here in Rocco's luxurious home.

'Is it so hard for you to accept a gift?'

The gentle note in his voice undermined her defences and sudden tears stung her eyes. She felt an inexplicable urge to confide in him that Jack had ruined her pleasure in receiving gifts. He had frequently given her presents, and naively she had taken his generosity as a sign of his love for her. But after his death she had realised that the flowers and perfume he'd lavished on her had been a way of assuaging his conscience after he had slept with one of his many mistresses.

She closed her eyes, trying to block out the memory of the pain and hurt Jack had caused her. When she opened them again Rocco was still there, devastatingly handsome in superbly tailored black trousers and a white silk shirt, a lock of dark hair falling across his brow and his golden eyes watching her with the intentness of a tiger stalking its prey.

'What do you want from me?' she whispered despairingly.

He lifted his hand and smoothed her hair back from her cheek. His touch was as light as the brush of a butterfly's wing against her skin, yet she felt as though she had been branded by him.

It was no longer the truth to say that sexual satisfaction and the sating of desire was all he wanted. Perhaps it never had been with this woman, Rocco owned silently.

'A chance to try and win your trust,' he said steadily.

'Why?' A wealth of fear and confusion was in that one

word. Emma blinked back the tears that threatened to overspill, unaware that their shimmer made Rocco's gut clench. 'You can have any woman you want.' She had fallen for a handsome playboy once before. She could *not* make the same mistake again.

'I want you.' His voice was thick with need as he slid his hand to her nape. A warning voice inside Emma's head told her she should move—*now.* But Rocco's golden eyes were mesmerising, and she stared into them helplessly as his head descended.

The kiss was as gentle as thistledown, with an unexpected tenderness that tugged on her soul. Bewitching, beguiling, he moved his lips over hers with sensual deliberation, his hungry passion simmering but held in check—just.

Emma trembled as he drew her against him, silently acknowledging that she was losing the battle with herself. *This* was where she wanted to be—in his arms, his mouth warm on hers, eliciting a response she was powerless to withhold. Slowly she lifted her arms and linked them around his neck. The sound of his low groan as she parted her lips beneath his sent a shiver of sexual excitement down her spine.

The crunch of tyres on the gravel driveway at the front of the house, followed by car doors closing and the indistinct babble of voices, drove Rocco to break the kiss reluctantly. His timing was appalling, he thought grimly as he stared into Emma's smoke-soft eyes and watched them widen as panic replaced the sensual languor of a few seconds ago.

'Will you at least believe that I would never knowingly hurt you?' he said intently as he released her. He watched her unconsciously catch her lower lip with her teeth, and exhaled heavily. 'I must go and greet my guests.'

His words impelled her to action and she spun away from him towards the stairs. 'I'll go and check on Holly.' The little girl had fallen asleep soon after being tucked into bed, but the excuse would give Emma vital minutes to regain her composure.

The mirror on the first floor landing revealed the extent of the damage Rocco had wrought. Her eyes were over-bright, her mouth softly swollen. She took a tube of pale pink gloss from her purse and with a shaking hand reapplied it to her lips.

Trust! She gave a ragged laugh. Rocco did not know what he asked of her. After Jack, she had believed she would never have faith in any man ever again. But Rocco had sworn that he did not want to hurt her. He had offered her friendship, although the hungry desire in his eyes promised more.

For three years she had hidden away in a remote Northumberland village and focused all her attention on her daughter. It had been a safe existence, although sometimes a lonely one, she admitted. Rocco had forced her to see that she did not want to hide away for ever. But did she have the nerve to step out of her safety zone and risk her emotional stability by becoming involved with him?

CHAPTER SEVEN

To Emma's relief, the guests at Cordelia's party were not all glamorous and sophisticated. Rocco had invited friends and neighbours of a wide age range, including a retired English couple who had moved to Italy some years previously.

'We know Nunstead Hall. We saw it when we toured Northumbria a few years ago,' Barbara Harris exclaimed. 'We're actually just along the coast at Rapallo. There's quite a few of us ex-pats living there. Andrew and I hold a bridge evening once a week, and we'd love you to join us, Cordelia.'

'Thank you.' Rocco's grandmother looked delighted. 'I do enjoy playing card games. I used to belong to a bridge club in the village, but now that I don't drive I can no longer get there.' She smiled ruefully. 'It will be nice to have some company. Nunstead is rather remote.'

Coming to Portofino had been the best thing for Cordelia, Emma mused. The elderly lady already seemed less frail, after a week of sitting in the garden in the warm spring sunshine, and eating the wonderful meals served by Beatrice. She knew Rocco hoped to persuade his grandmother to stay at the Villa Lucia permanently, and Cordelia seemed to be settling in so quickly that perhaps she would not need a private nurse for much longer.

Once she returned to England she would probably never see Rocco again. The thought hurt Emma more than it should. *Don't*, her mind warned her. Don't dwell on that sweetly evocative kiss they had shared moments before the party. Rocco had kissed her because he wanted to sleep with her, and she could not deny that he had awoken her sensuality from a deep slumber. But if she did have an affair with him—and it was a big if—she must never forget that it would be a brief sexual adventure that could mean nothing to either of them.

He was standing on the other side of the room, chatting to neighbours who lived in a villa farther down the hill and their attractive young daughter. Perhaps he possessed a sixth sense which alerted him to Emma's scrutiny, for he suddenly turned his head and trapped her gaze. Colour flooded her face—embarrassment that he had caught her staring at him mixed with a fierce sexual awareness that sent a tremor of longing through her. His magnetism was so powerful that the other people in the room faded to the periphery of her vision and the murmur of voices, the clink of glasses on the silver trays carried by the villa staff, became muted.

How could she even contemplate an affair with him when he had the ability to decimate her composure with one look across a crowded room? she thought despairingly. The risk was too great. Perhaps it would be different if she only had herself to consider. But there was Holly, who already regarded Rocco as a friend. Her little daughter would be upset when he abruptly disappeared out of their lives, as he surely would when their relationship had run its course.

'Our host *is* gorgeous, isn't he?' drawled a voice.

Desperately trying to school her features to hide her inner turmoil, she glanced at the woman who had come to stand beside her and offered a polite smile. Shayna Manzzini's husband, Tino, was an executive at Eleganza, and a close friend of Rocco's. Emma had taken an instant liking to friendly Tino, but had not warmed to his Canadian wife. Shayna had given up a modelling career when she had married, but still retained a stunning figure. The elegant brunette was undeniably beautiful, but her hard features were set in an expression of permanent dissatisfaction, and there was a brittle quality about her.

'Poor little fool,' Shayna said mockingly. 'Any woman who hopes Rocco will fall in love with them is destined for disappointment. The tiger will never be tamed.'

For a moment Emma was mortified, thinking that Shayna was referring to *her*, before she realised that the Canadian woman was looking across the room at the daughter of Rocco's neighbours. The girl was probably seventeen or eighteen, incredibly pretty, and clearly overwhelmed by Rocco's charisma. Her eyes were fixed on his face and she frequently tossed her glossy black curls over her shoulders. Her flirting skills were not yet refined.

'Chiara doesn't have a hope,' Shayna continued in her derisive drawl. 'Rocco isn't interested in *bambini*. But give her a couple of years and she might capture his interest for a week or two.' She glanced at Emma, her scarlet-glossed lips forming a tight smile. 'We were lovers briefly—a few years ago. Rocco's affairs are always brief,' she added sardonically. 'I saw the end coming and decided to settle for Tino. Definitely a case of second-best.' She shrugged her narrow shoulders. 'But a modelling career doesn't last for ever, and although Tino isn't of multi-millionaire status, he's still loaded.'

Shocked by the other woman's calculating nature, Emma could not think of anything to say. Images of Shayna and Rocco as lovers filled her mind and her stomach churned. How many other women here tonight were his ex-mistresses? she wondered as she scanned the room and focused on several exceptionally beautiful female guests.

She remembered how at Jack's funeral she had looked around the church and tried to guess which women he had slept with during their marriage. Her grief at his death had been mixed with anger and humiliation and agonising hurt, and she had vowed never to lay herself open to that level of pain ever again.

'It's a pity Rosalinda Barinelli didn't understand Rocco's "no commitment at any price rule."' Shayna's voice once again broke into Emma's thoughts.

'What do you mean?' She could not disguise her curiosity, even though she had a horrible feeling she was not going to like the Canadian woman's reply. 'Who is Rosalinda Barinelli?'

'She is, or rather *was*, a talented Italian actress with a promising career ahead of her. That was until she met Rocco. A year ago they had an affair, and when Rocco ended the relationship Rosalinda took an overdose. She lived,' Shayna said, when Emma drew a sharp breath, 'but she hasn't worked since her suicide attempt. She maintains that he promised her they had a future together, although I actually find that hard to believe,' Shayna admitted. 'Rocco is the archetypal playboy and his allergy to commitment is well known. But possibly he spun Rosalinda a line in order to bed her.'

Emma swallowed the bile that had risen in her throat. 'You're saying he deliberately misled her into believing he cared for her?'

Shayna gave another careless shrug. 'I don't know anything for sure. But, despite his apparent charm, Rocco has a ruthless streak. It's hardly surprising, I suppose, when he is the grandson of Silvio D'Angelo—one of the most powerful businessmen in Italy. You don't get to build a company the size of Eleganza by being a pussycat, that's for sure. And of course Rocco's parents were both utterly selfish. He told me once that witnessing their turbulent relationship had put him off marriage for life.'

Emma spent the rest of the evening chatting and smiling until her jaw ached, while carefully avoiding Rocco. His frustration was evident in his narrowed stare, but he was unable to challenge her when she stuck faithfully to his grandmother's side.

It was after eleven by the time the last guests departed and she escorted a weary but happy Cordelia up to bed.

'It was so nice to meet Rocco's friends, and so good of him to arrange the party. He has always had a kind heart.' The elderly lady sighed, her face suddenly sad. 'He had a hard time when he was a teenager. Giovanni's death was a tragic accident, but Rocco blamed himself.'

'Giovanni was only young when he died, wasn't he?' Emma murmured, busying herself with hanging Cordelia's dress in the wardrobe.

'Yes, poor boy. Gio was a demanding child. He was diagnosed with a mild form of autism and my daughter couldn't cope with him. I'm afraid she left Rocco in charge of him much too often.'

'What actually happened?' Emma could not contain her curiosity. 'How did Giovanni die?'

'The boys were staying at Nunstead Hall for the Christmas holidays. It was bitterly cold that winter, and the lake had frozen over,' Cordelia recalled. 'Gio had been told a dozen times not to walk on the ice, but small boys don't recognise danger. Rocco almost lost his own life trying to save his brother. The gardener had to drag him out of the freezing water and physically restrain him from trying to swim to Gio. Because it was too late,' she said sombrely. 'Gio must have fallen through the ice some while before Rocco spotted him, and he was already dead.'

'How terrible.' Emma shivered as she imagined the horrific circumstances of Rocco's brother's death.

'Yes. And I'm not sure Rocco has ever come to terms with what he sees as his failure to save Gio.' Cordelia had been rummaging in her handbag and now gave a frustrated sigh. 'Emma, dear, I think I must have left my reading glasses downstairs.'

'I'll fetch them for you.'

Emma was glad to have a few moments alone to marshal her thoughts. In the space of one evening she had heard two conflicting stories about Rocco. According to his ex-mistress he had fooled Rosalinda Barinelli into believing he wanted a long-term relationship with her, and then heartlessly dumped her when he had tired of her and broken her heart. But from Cordelia she had heard that Rocco had been prepared to sacrifice his own life while attempting to save his younger brother. Who was the real Rocco? she wondered. A cruel deceiver, or a brave hero?

Perhaps he was both—just as Jack had been. Her mind whirled with jumbled emotions as painful memories resurfaced. Her husband had lost his life while heroically saving children from a burning house. But at the time of his death she had discovered that he had cheated on her and lied to her throughout their marriage. How could she trust any man after Jack? she thought bitterly. How could she trust Rocco after what she had heard about him from Shayna Manzzini?

Cordelia's glasses case was on a coffee table in the sitting room. Smiling at the maid who was tidying the room, Emma picked it up and retraced her steps back to the door. Rocco's voice made her halt.

'Running away again, Emma?' he drawled as he strolled through from the conservatory.

The electric lamps had been switched off, and in the soft, flickering light cast by the burned-down candles he appeared big and dark, his face in shadow so that she could not see his expression. But something in his hard voice warned her he was not in a good mood.

'I came down to find Cordelia's glasses,' she explained, waving the case she was holding.

'Maria will take them to her.' He addressed the maid in Italian, and the girl immediately hurried over to take the case from Emma before scurrying from the room, shutting the door behind her.

'Can I get you a drink?' Rocco walked over to the bar and refilled his own brandy glass.

'No, thank you.' Her nerves were as taut as an overstrung bow now that she was alone with Rocco. 'I'm tired and I'd like to go to bed.'

He gave her a sardonic look. 'Yes, I'm sure you've had an exhausting day, sitting in the garden with Cordelia, but nevertheless I would like a progress report on my grandmother. How is the burn on her hand?'

'Healing well—it doesn't need to be kept covered now that the risk of infection has passed. And Cordelia says it's not nearly so painful.'

He nodded. 'And how would you assess her general health?'

'She seems much less frail, which I am sure is down to the fact that she is eating properly. One of my main concerns when she was living at Nunstead Hall was that she didn't bother to cook for herself and seemed to survive on toast and cups of tea. She really enjoyed the party,' Emma told him, recalling Cordelia's pleasure at the evening.

'Good.' He stared at her speculatively. 'And how about

you? Did *you* enjoy tonight?' He hesitated for a heartbeat. 'I noticed you had a long conversation with Shayna.'

She flushed. 'Yes...she was very informative.'

'I don't doubt it,' Rocco murmured dryly. He swore silently. Shayna was a first-class gossip, and he would lay a bet that she was responsible for the expression of stark vulnerability in Emma's eyes.

'She said that the two of you were once lovers.'

'I have never professed to be a monk,' he said quietly. 'And it was a long time ago.'

Emma shrugged, determined to retain her dignity. 'It's really of no interest to me.'

'No?' he challenged softly. 'That's not the impression I received before the party. I got the impression that you were *very* interested, *cara*.'

Her flush deepened, but she forced herself to hold his gaze. 'My conversation with Shayna was a timely reminder of what kind of a man you are.'

Rocco's face darkened at her scathing tone. 'Explain that remark. What kind of a man am I?'

'One who deliberately allowed Rosalinda Barinelli to think you cared for her, and then dumped her when you were bored with her, leaving her so distraught that she attempted to take her own life.'

Anger surged inside him and he fought the temptation to drive his fist into the wall. 'Shayna really did a hatchet job, didn't she?' He took a deep breath. 'My relationship with Rosalinda is no secret. Every tabloid voiced an opinion on my culpability for the terrible events that took place soon after our affair ended. But only a handful of people are aware of the truth. My closest friends—the people who really know me—never doubted me,' he said harshly.

He drained his glass, slammed it down on the counter

and strode across to the door without another glance in her direction.

Emma bit her lip, remembering how she had initially misjudged him and accused him of not caring about his grandmother. She had been wrong about him then—could she have jumped to the wrong conclusions again now?

'Rocco!'

His hand was on the door handle. For a moment she thought he was going to ignore her, but then he slowly turned his head.

'What?'

His savage expression was not encouraging. 'There are always two sides to a story,' she said huskily.

'Yet you chose to believe the words of a woman you had only just met rather than ask for my side.' His jaw hardened. 'I'm beginning to think that friendship between us is impossible—especially when you are determined to believe the worst of me.'

She thought of the loving care he gave his grandmother, his gentle patience with Holly and the kindness he had shown her, and she felt ashamed that she had acted as judge and jury without allowing him to give his version of events. Shayna's revelation that she and Rocco had once been lovers had caused a flame of white-hot jealousy to sear her insides. He was right; she *had* wanted to believe the worst of him. But her reason for doing so had been an attempt at self-protection and a way of fighting her growing feelings for him.

'I'm sorry.'

Rocco stared at her downbent head and fought to control his frustration. He wished he could pull her into his arms and kiss away the doubt and insecurity that darkened her eyes. Even greater was his wish that he knew who had put those emotions there.

'I met Rosalinda when I was on a business trip in Rome and saw her performing in a play at the Teatro Nazional. We were introduced at an after-show party and there was an immediate attraction between us,' he revealed honestly. 'She was beautiful, ambitious and appeared to be extremely self-confident. Acting was her life, she assured me. She wasn't looking for a long-term relationship while she developed her career. If I had thought for one minute that she hoped I would make a commitment to her I would never have become involved with her. But she seemed content with a casual affair, and even when I ended the relationship a few months later she did not appear unduly upset.'

Rocco's expression became grim. 'I was horrified when I received a phone call from Rosalinda's parents to inform me that she had taken an overdose, and that I was the reason why. I swear I gave her no cause to think I was in love with her. The closeness she believed existed between us was in her imagination only. Her parents were very understanding. They explained that she had previously been diagnosed with bi-polar disorder and was prone to periods of depression, and also that she had unrealistic expectations about relationships. Without my knowledge she had been planning our wedding—even to the extent of buying a wedding dress.'

He looked away from Emma, not wanting to see the disbelief and disgust he was sure would be in her eyes. 'If you want the truth, not a day goes by when I don't feel guilty about Rosalinda,' he said harshly. 'Maybe I missed the signs of her emotional fragility, or maybe somehow I unwittingly led her to believe that I had deeper feelings for her.'

'I doubt it,' Emma said quietly. 'Bi-polar disorder is a complicated issue, but even without that being a factor it's not uncommon for people who are in love to see what they want to see.' And conversely to ignore warning signs that a relationship was not as perfect as they wished, she acknowledged silently. She had made excuses for Jack throughout their marriage because she had wanted to believe that he loved her as much as she loved him. She, more than anyone, could understand how Rosalinda might have kidded herself that Rocco cared for her.

She did not doubt that he had told her the truth. His remorse at what had happened was obviously genuine. He had not deliberately deceived Rosalinda, and he had been honest with *her*. He had made it clear that he wanted a sexual relationship with her, but that was *all* he wanted.

Why not take what he was offering and enjoy a few weeks of fun? she debated. Lord knew, she needed it. But to make love with him, to experience the seductive pleasure of his hands and his mouth caressing her naked flesh, would mean relinquishing her hold on her self-control. The prospect filled her with fear. What if sex wasn't enough for her? What if she wanted more than he could give? He had the power to hurt her. Not physically—her instincts told her he would be a skilled and considerate lover—but he had already undermined her defences and she was afraid he posed a very real threat to her heart.

She stiffened when he walked towards her, struggling for composure while her treacherous body trembled with fierce sexual awareness.

Rocco wondered if she was aware that he could read each fleeting thought that crossed her features. She was a volatile mixture of emotions, and if he had any sense he would end his pursuit and walk away from her. But his much lauded common sense seemed to fly out of the window when he looked into her grey eyes that reminded him of storm clouds or woodsmoke, depending on her mood.

'How old were you when you met Jack?'

Emma frowned at the unexpected question. 'I was twenty, and midway through my nurse's training.'

'Did you have other relationships before him?'

'Not really. I dated a couple of boys from school, but I studied hard to achieve the necessary grades for university and didn't have much time for boyfriends. Why do you ask?'

'It has occurred to me that if you haven't dated since your husband's death, and you weren't involved with any other guys before you married, that only leaves Jack as the person responsible for your deep sense of mistrust.' His eyes narrowed on her suddenly tense face. 'But that doesn't make sense, because you have led me to believe that it was a marriage made in heaven. So what is the truth about your relationship with Jack Marchant, Emma?'

What good would it do to admit that her marriage had been far from ideal? she thought dully. It would simply show what a gullible fool she had been. Jack was dead and no longer had the power to hurt her. But his parents and Holly would be hurt if she ever revealed that he had not been the perfect husband everyone believed.

'I'm not prepared to discuss my marriage,' she said stiffly.

He studied her intently for several moments, but to her relief did not pursue the subject. 'That is, of course, your prerogative.' He walked across to the door and this time opened it before glancing back at her. 'I have a series of business meetings scheduled in various European cities and I'll be leaving early tomorrow morning. If you have any concerns about my grandmother while I'm away you can contact me on my mobile phone.'

Emma's heart lurched at the news that he was leaving the villa. She wanted to ask him when he would be back.

Did he have a mistress—more than one—who he intended to visit while he was away?

She masked her disappointment with a cool smile. 'Fine, but I don't suppose I'll need you.'

Rocco's eyes glittered. He was tempted to haul her into his arms and prove that her need to assuage the sexual frustration which simmered between them was as great as his. He did not doubt that she would respond to him. After a week of stolen glances and intense awareness smouldering below the surface of their polite exchanges, their desire for each other was at combustion point. One spark would set it aflame. But would it be fair to light the fuse, knowing that for him the beginning of an affair always signalled its end?

For the first time in his life he found that his desire to protect Emma was stronger than his urgent need to take her to bed. Even more astonishingly, he was actually contemplating a relationship with her that he could envisage lasting longer than a few weeks. *Dio*, how had an averagely pretty English nurse brought him to the point where he was considering abandoning his long-held principles of never getting emotionally involved with any woman?

He tore his eyes from her. *'Buonanotte,'* he bade her harshly before he strode out of the door.

'I'm going to stay with Nanna and Grandpa,' Holly told Rocco, her big grey eyes glowing with excitement.

'That sounds like fun, *piccola*.' He smiled at the little girl and glanced enquiringly at her mother.

'Jack's parents have a holiday home in Nice and have invited Holly to spend a few days with them,' Emma explained, relieved that her voice sounded normal and did not give away the fact that her heart was thumping.

The past week that Rocco had been away had seemed

interminable. She'd had no idea when he would return, and although he had phoned her twice, their conversations had been stilted and exclusively about his grandmother. The unexpected sight of him at the breakfast table this morning had sent the air rushing from her lungs. 'Peter and Alison are flying into Genoa tomorrow. They plan to hire a car, collect Holly and drive along the coast into France.'

'Can I go and tell Bobbo?' Holly asked, seeing the dog run across the lawn.

At Emma's nod the little girl slipped off her chair and ran out into the garden. 'How do you feel about her being away from you?' Rocco murmured, noting the faintly wistful expression on her face.

'Fine.' She smiled ruefully when he arched his brows disbelievingly. 'It's only for a few days, and she'll have a wonderful time. Jack's parents dote on her, and I know they'll take good care of her.'

A necessary part of motherhood was learning to let go. She had no doubt that Holly would love spending time with her grandparents, but being parted from her little daughter *was* going to be a wrench, Emma acknowledged with a sigh.

'Cordelia tells me she is going to spend today with Barbara and Andrew Harris.'

'Yes, she's upstairs getting ready, and I'm going to drive her there.'

'How about we take Holly to the beach? We'll take Cordelia to Rapallo and on the way back stop off at Santa Margherita. It's a pretty seaside resort, and she'll be able to make sandcastles to her heart's content.'

Emma's first instinct was to refuse. The wild burst of pleasure she had felt when she had walked into the dining room and discovered that Rocco was home was ample proof that he affected her way too much. While he'd been away she had made the decision that she could not risk becoming involved with him. But his lazy smile undermined her defences. In faded jeans and a cream shirt open at the throat to reveal an expanse of olive gold skin and a sprinkling of dark chest hairs, he was irresistibly sexy. What harm would it do to spend one day with him? she argued with herself. After all, it would be purely for Holly's benefit.

She set down her coffee cup and gave him a composed smile. 'That sounds nice. Holly will love it.'

So cool, Rocco mused, his amusement mixed with an unexpected feeling of tenderness. The pulse beating erratically at the base of her throat told him she was not sure of herself, or of him, and once again her tangible vulnerability tugged on his insides.

Palm trees stood at regular intervals along the esplanade at Santa Margherita Ligure, which was lined with bars, restaurants and *gelaterie*, shaded by colourful striped awnings. The sea was crystal-clear beneath a cloudless blue sky, but Holly was more interested in the long sandy beach, and could barely contain her impatience as Rocco parked the car and lifted her out of her child seat.

Emma opened the boot and gathered up a plastic bucket and spade, a rug to sit on, towels and a bag containing all the paraphernalia required for one small child.

Her lips twitched when Rocco murmured, 'I thought we were spending the day here, not a week.'

Their eyes met and held, before she quickly glanced away and took hold of Holly's hand.

'You go and set up camp, and I'll get coffees for us.'

She watched him stride away, his height making him easy to spot among the crowd ambling along the esplanade, enjoying a leisurely Saturday. Dragging her gaze from his broad shoulders, she smiled at her excited daughter. 'Let's get building castles.'

Holly needed no persuading, and played happily in the sand while Emma spread out the rug. The sun was warm enough for her to remove her jacket. Rocco had been right; she would have been uncomfortably hot in the jeans and sweatshirts she had brought from England. The white pedal-pushers and blue-and-white checked shirt she had chosen from the selection of clothes he had bought her were stylish and elegant, and had no doubt cost a fortune, she thought ruefully.

'Mummy—a shell.' Holly held out her hand to reveal her find. 'I'm going to look for more.'

'Stay close,' Emma instructed. She kept her eyes on her daughter, but Holly did not wander far before she started to dig a hole in the sand.

A gull soared overhead, mewing plaintively, and gentle waves lapped rhythmically on the shore. Heavenly, Emma mused, lifting her face to the sun. It was hard to believe that only a couple of weeks ago she'd had to dress in umpteen layers to keep warm in the wintry conditions affecting Northumberland.

She glanced down the beach and squinted against the sunshine when she did not immediately see Holly. A bright pink bucket and spade were lying on the sand, but the little girl was no longer digging. Frowning, Emma looked along the beach to the left and right, sure she would spot Holly's distinctive yellow T-shirt. But there was no sign of her.

'Holly?' Feeling a faint flutter of concern, Emma stared towards the sea. A group of children were playing on the shoreline, but her daughter was not with them. *'Holly!'*

'What's the matter?'

She swung round at the sound of Rocco's voice. 'I can't see Holly. She was here a minute ago...' Once again she scanned the horizon, panic edging towards fear when there was no sight of the child.

'I'll look for her. She can't have gone far.' Rocco took his mobile from his pocket. 'Keep your phone to hand and I'll ring you as soon as I find her.'

Emma continued to scan along the beach, gnawing on her lip until she tasted blood. With every second that passed her tension went up a notch, but she forced herself to keep calm. Any minute now Rocco would walk back along the sand with Holly on his shoulders, she assured herself.

She spotted him striding towards her—alone. Terror swept through her and she ran across the beach to meet him

'I can't see her,' he revealed tautly.

'Oh, my God!' Her legs felt like jelly, and she clung to him when he slid a supporting arm around her waist. 'She *must* be here. I only took my eyes off her for a moment.' Guilt surged through her and she covered her mouth with a trembling hand, as if to hold back the anguished cry building inside her. 'Rocco…' She stared at him wildly as he activated his phone. 'What are you doing?'

'Calling the police.'

'The police!' A cold hand of dread squeezed her heart as the seriousness of the situation hit her hard. 'She *must* be on the beach somewhere,' she cried frantically. 'She must be.' Tears burned her eyes and she brushed them away impatiently. She needed to think, to stay calm in a crisis. But she wasn't dealing with an accident in the A&E unit; her precious daughter had disappeared and a multitude of terrible scenarios were swirling in her mind.

'We need to report that Holly is missing,' Rocco told her.

The quiet authority in his voice and the way he firmly

assumed control calmed Emma a little, and she took a shuddering breath.

'Of course she's here somewhere,' he reassured her. 'But the more people we have looking for her, the quicker we'll find her.'

CHAPTER EIGHT

'IT'S my fault. I didn't watch her properly.' Tears streamed down Emma's face as her tight control on her emotions gave way. 'What if something's happened to her?' She glanced fearfully towards the sea. 'Or someone has taken her?' she could barely voice her worst nightmare.

The utter devastation in her eyes caused Rocco's heart to clench. He, better than most, understood what she must be feeling, he acknowledged grimly. The realisation that a child was missing, the desperate search… It was twenty years since his brother had disappeared in the grounds of Nunstead Hall, but the memory of the sick fear he'd felt as he had searched for Gio would always haunt him. *Madre de Dio*, please make the outcome be different this time, he prayed.

He cradled Emma's head between his hands and stared into her eyes. 'Stop blaming yourself—you are the most devoted mother I have ever met. We'll find Holly, I promise you, *cara*.'

The following forty minutes were the worst of Emma's life. Not even when she had been told of Jack's death, or learned from his mistress how he had betrayed her, had she felt such raw anguish. Waiting for news was sheer torture. But all she could do was stay on the beach, in case Holly wandered back to the place where they had been sitting. Meanwhile, Rocco had called the staff from the Villa Lucia to join the search as they would easily recognise the little girl.

Every tragic story she had read in the newspapers about missing children circled in Emma's mind. The idea that she might never see her daughter again was too unbearable to contemplate, and she dropped her head in her hands and gave a keening moan.

'Emma…'

Rocco's voice sounded from some distance away. But something in his tone… She lowered her hands—and felt as though her heart had exploded in her chest when she saw him striding along the esplanade, holding Holly in his arms.

'Thank God—*thank God*!' Tears blinded her and her legs would barely support her, but she forced them to move as she stumbled up the beach.

That evening, Rocco knocked on the door of Emma's room. 'Is she asleep?' he murmured as she emerged from Holly's bedroom and quietly closed the interconnecting door.

'Yes. I'm not surprised she's worn out after chasing Bobbo round the garden all afternoon,' she replied, forcing a bright tone. 'And she's excited about seeing her grandparents tomorrow.'

She could not bring herself to refer to what had happened at the beach. Holly had eventually been found down by the harbour, where she had fallen asleep on a pile of fishing nets. Emma went cold at the thought that her daughter might have fallen into the deep water of the port and drowned. Thankfully, the little girl seemed unaffected by the drama of the morning, but they had cut short their beach trip and returned to the villa, where Emma had determinedly hidden the after-effects of her own shock and kept to Holly's normal routine.

'Are you still going to allow her to go to Nice with your in-laws?'

She nodded. 'I'd prefer not to let her out of my sight ever again, but it wouldn't be fair to disappoint her by cancelling the trip, and I've no doubt that Jack's parents will take great care of her.'

Without warning, her eyes filled with tears. All afternoon she had pushed thoughts of Holly's disappearance firmly to the back of her mind, but now agonising memories returned of the crippling fear and desperation she had felt. Earlier, a long soak in the bath had eased some of her tension, but the horror of losing her daughter was something she would never forget, and she sank down onto the bed, her shoulders shaking as sobs racked her.

'Cara.'

Rocco's deep voice sounded close to her ear. She felt his arms around her, felt him lift her, and she had no strength—either physically or mentally—to fight him.

It was some while before she finally brought her emotions under control. Feeling horribly self-conscious, she scrubbed her eyes with the tissues Rocco had pushed into her hand and lifted her head—to discover that he had carried her along the hall to his suite of rooms. They were in his private sitting room, a spacious room decorated in modern shades of taupe and cream. A door standing ajar led to his bedroom, where Emma could see a vast bed draped in burgundy silk.

'I thought you would not want to risk waking Holly,' he explained, correctly interpreting her questioning look.

Colour stained her cheeks at the thought of how she had broken down in front of him. 'I'm sorry,' she muttered, only now realising how close he was sitting next to her on the sofa. His arm was stretched along the back, and she had a horrible feeling that she had rested her head on his shoulder while she had been crying. She grimaced. ‘I’m sure you have better things to do than put up with me snivelling all over you.’

‘You’ve been through hell,’ he said quietly. ‘It’s better not to bottle up your emotions.’

Something in his voice drew her gaze to his face, and her heart turned over at the haunted expression in his eyes. ‘Is that what you did after your brother died?’ she asked softly. ‘Cordelia told me about Giovanni’s accident.’

‘Did my grandmother tell you that if I had looked after Gio properly there wouldn’t have been an accident?’ Rocco’s jaw clenched. ‘I can never escape the fact that my resentment at my mother leaving me to babysit yet again resulted in my brother’s death. I failed Gio,’ he said harshly. ‘He wasn’t an easy child, and he had a wild streak, but I loved him. He looked up to me and depended on me to look out for him. I will always live with the knowledge that I let him down.’

‘You were a teenager—just a boy.’ Her heart aching at his undisguised pain, Emma acted instinctively, leaning towards him and clasping his hand. ‘Cordelia said that your parents should have taken more responsibility for Gio. You almost lost your life trying to save him all those years ago. And as for today…’ Her voice broke. ‘When I realised Holly was missing, I was so scared. I couldn’t think. I didn’t know what to do. But you took charge and organised the search. While I was stupidly panicking, you did everything you could to find her, and I…’ She swallowed the lump in her throat and gave him a wobbly smile. ‘I’m so glad you were there.’

Emotions were hell, she thought ruefully as tears once again blurred her vision. The terror of losing Holly had stripped away her protective shell, leaving her feeling painfully vulnerable. For the past three years she had brought up her daughter on her own, and even though it had been hard sometimes she felt proud that she had not needed help from anyone. But today she had needed Rocco. He had been her rock, she acknowledged, her heart swelling with the intensity of her feelings.

'What happened to your brother was a tragic accident,' she told him softly. 'You didn't fail him, and today you didn't fail Holly or me.'

Her words were like healing balm on a wound that was still raw so many years after Gio's death. For the first time since he was fifteen Rocco felt a sense of release from the guilt that had weighed heavily on him. Since the day he had cradled his brother's lifeless body in his arms he had felt frozen inside. He had avoided relationships where his emotions might be involved. It was easier that way—safer not to care.

But with Emma it was different. She had crept under his guard, and without knowing how or when it had happened he found that he was concerned for her well-being. When her daughter had gone missing he had felt her agony, and he would have moved heaven and earth to reunite her with Holly.

Emma caught her breath when Rocco curled his fingers around hers and lifted her hand to his mouth, to graze his lips across her knuckles. His golden tiger's eyes burned into hers and she became conscious of the subtle shift in the atmosphere between them. Moments before he had provided comfort and a sense of security, but now the tiny hairs on her body stood on end as she felt the tangible quiver of their mutual sexual awareness.

He moved his hand from the back of the sofa to her shoulder and gently propelled her towards him. In the thick silence she was sure he would hear her thudding heart, just as she heard the sudden quickening of his breath as he slanted his mouth over hers.

There was no thought in her head to deny him, and her lips trembled a little with the intensity of emotions unfurling inside her. Trust—something she had been certain she could never feel again—enfolded her as Rocco tightened his arms around her. His kiss was tender, evocative and it tugged on her heart. She felt safe with him—confident to relax her guard and allow him to discover the innately sensual nature that she had tried so hard to hide.

What was it about this woman that drove him to the brink with a single kiss? Rocco asked himself. He slid his fingers into the silky bell of hair that framed her face and accepted that the answer did not matter. The moist softness of her lips beneath his, the feel of her parting them to welcome the bold sweep of his tongue blew his mind and his hunger for her overwhelmed him.

Her skin felt like satin as he pressed his mouth to her throat and found the pulse beating erratically at its base. He pushed her peach-coloured silk robe aside and bared her shoulder to trace the fragile line of her collarbone. *Dio*, in his past he had had more women than he could count, and his reputation as a playboy was well deserved, but at this moment he felt like a youth again—barely able to control his surging hormones or prevent his hands from shaking as he undressed a woman for the first time.

Slowly, he drew the narrow strap of her negligee down her arm, revealing inch by delicious inch the creamy slope of her breast, and his breath hissed between his teeth when at last he cupped her naked flesh in his palm. Shaking with the strength of his desire, he lowered his head and flicked his tongue across her rosy-pink nipple, back and forth, until it hardened and he took the engorged peak fully into his mouth.

Emma could not restrain a soft cry of pleasure when Rocco suckled her breast. Sensation arced down her body and pooled between her legs. The slow build of passion changed to a feverish need that demanded appeasement, and a tremor of fierce hunger shot through her as he removed her robe and tugged her negligee down to her waist, baring both her breasts to his heated gaze.

When he laved first one nipple and then its twin she arched her back in mute supplication. Her body had never felt more alive than it did at that moment, every nerve-ending acutely sensitive as she trembled beneath the erotic onslaught wrought by his hands and mouth.

He covered her lips with his own once again, and this time the kiss was hot and urgent, their tongues locked in a sensual duel. Their breathing was ragged when at last he lifted his head and stared down at her, with feral hunger blazing in his eyes.

'*Ti volglio*—I want you,' he said, his voice rough with need.

Rocco had never felt like this before—never felt such an intensity of desire that filled every cell in his body and drove everything from his mind but his desperate longing to make love to Emma. From the very beginning he had felt a connection with her that even now he did not fully understand. She was his woman. He felt it in his blood, in his bones, deep down in the centre of his soul. She belonged to him and he *would* claim her.

'Yes.' The single word whispered from Emma's lips, as fragile as gossamer yet strong with certainty. She knew beyond doubt that she wanted Rocco to make love to her. The past, and the pain Jack had caused her, no longer mattered, and the future was tomorrow. She could only focus on the present and seize this moment with this man, who had edged stealthily into her heart.

She met his gaze steadily when he stood up and drew her to her feet. He tugged her negligee over her hips so that the slip of silk slithered to the floor, and then with heart-stopping deliberation hooked his fingers into the edge of her panties and pulled them slowly down. She watched the convulsive movement of his throat as he swallowed, saw the predatory hunger blazing in his eyes, and caught her breath when he slid his fingers into the triangle of red-gold curls between her legs.

'*Sei bella*, Emma,' he growled as he swept her up into his arms and strode into his bedroom. 'I have to have you now. Feel how much I want you,' he demanded raggedly, setting her on the edge of the bed and pressing her hand against the rock-hard bulge beneath his trousers.

Her eyes widened; excitement and a faint flutter of trepidation filling her as she stroked the burgeoning proof of his arousal. It had been a long time since she had had sex. Jack had been dead for over three years, and in the months prior to his death he had seemed to be put off by her changing shape due to pregnancy.

Memories of how hurt she had felt pierced her, but she refused to live in the past any more. She was no longer the naive girl who had been so overwhelmed by her handsome, charming husband that she had overlooked his many faults. At twenty-eight, she was a strong, independent woman, capable of making her own choices, and right now she chose to be with Rocco.

The fierce desire burning in his eyes restored her confidence in her body. Emboldened in a way she had never felt before, she gave him a demure smile. But her eyes gleamed wickedly as she undid his zip.

'You seem to be experiencing massive pressure, *signor*. As a nurse, I feel it is my duty to relieve your symptoms.'

'Witch.' He gave a hoarse laugh, driven to the edge by her teasing tone. Now was not a good time to discover she was a sex kitten, he thought self-derisively. He wanted this first time with her to be a long, sensual seduction, but he was so turned on that he feared he was about to explode, and his need to possess her took on a new urgency.

Barely able to control his impatience, he ripped off his shirt and dropped his trousers. He pulled his boxers down and shuddered as he imagined sheathing himself in the silken embrace of Emma's body. But the slight shadow of wariness in her eyes forced him to exert control over his rampant libido. He was sure she hadn't been with a man since her husband, and he knew he must slow the pace and ensure she was fully aroused before he possessed her.

With a flick of his wrist he pulled back the bedspread and lifted her into his arms, to settle her on the pillows before stretching out next to her and drawing her to him. The contrast of her pale limbs with his darkly tanned body was intensely erotic. Her skin was velvet-soft, where he was all hard muscle and sinew, and he delighted in the feel of her firm, rounded breasts pressing against his chest. He caught her faint sigh with his lips and initiated a slow, languorous kiss that became a sensual feast as he took it to another level that was unashamedly erotic.

Lost in the mastery of Rocco's kiss, Emma gave a little shiver of anticipation when he skimmed his hand over her stomach and continued a tantalising path down her body to slip between her thighs. She offered no resistance when he gently pushed her legs apart. Sexual excitement flooded her, and she caught her breath as she felt him delicately stroke the swollen lips of her vagina before he parted her and slid a finger into her.

A gasp escaped her when he proceeded to explore her with an expertise that swiftly brought her to the brink. He held her there, trembling and eager, and then, to her shock, replaced his fingers with his mouth.

'Rocco…'

He heard the uncertainty in her voice and lifted his head. 'Don't you like it?'

'I don't know,' she revealed honestly.

So the Superman husband had never given her the pleasure of oral sex? Rocco felt a spurt of surprise at the man's selfishness, quickly followed by a surge of masculine triumph that he would be the first to bestow that gift.

'Let me show you, *cara*,' he murmured, dipping his head once more and applying himself to his appointed task with a thoroughness that soon had her writhing beneath him. His own excitement mounted when he flicked his tongue across the tight bud of her clitoris and she gave a guttural cry.

'Please…' She had never been so fiercely aroused, so desperate for him to possess her and assuage the restless ache of longing deep in her pelvis. Rocco was a sorcerer, and she was utterly enslaved in his sensual spell.

'I intend to please you, *cara*,' he assured her thickly.

Emma was caught up in the maelstrom of incredible sensations he was creating. Her eyes flew open when she felt Rocco move away from her. He smiled at the disappointment in her eyes and handed her the protective sheath he had retrieved from the drawer in the bedside table.

'You put it on for me.'

Colour stained her cheeks. She was a nurse, for heaven's sake, and this was certainly not the first time she had seen the male form, Emma reminded herself. But the size of Rocco's erection took her breath away and she fumbled to open the packet. He was iron-hard beneath her fingertips as she eased the sheath over him. Dear heaven, would she be able to take him? she wondered, feeling a flicker of doubt.

Her heart was thudding beneath her ribs as he pushed her flat on her back and knelt over her, one hair-roughened thigh firmly nudging her legs apart. He kissed her mouth and then trailed his lips down her throat to her breasts, sucking on one taut peak and then the other, until she whimpered with an intensity of pleasure that was almost more than she could withstand.

Only then, when she was trembling with need, did he ease forward and penetrate her with a deep thrust, pausing for a moment while her internal muscles stretched to accommodate his solid length, before he withdrew a little and thrust again.

'Okay?' he asked softly, resting his forehead lightly on hers so that their eyelashes almost tangled.

Passion mixed with tenderness was a potent combination, she thought shakily. She felt connected to him in a far more fundamental way than simply the joining of their bodies, and his gentle consideration touched her heart.

'I'm okay as long as you promise not to stop doing that,' she murmured—*that* being another thrust, and then another. Each rhythmic stroke was taking her higher, so that within minutes she was hovering on the edge of some mystical place that she had absolute faith he would lead her into.

'I wish this could last for ever, *cara*,' Rocco groaned. 'But I have desired you for so long that I'm afraid you will have to forgive my impatience this time.' Driven beyond the limits of his control, he increased his pace and his strokes became faster, harder and so intense that Emma clung to his shoulders while the waves of sensation built to a crescendo.

The explosion was violent, and yet drenchingly sweet—

spasms of exquisite pleasure radiating from her central core in an orgasm that was more mind-blowing than anything she had ever experienced in her life. She felt boneless, mindless, and her eyelashes drifted down so that her entire being was focused on the instinctive clenching and unclenching of internal muscles.

'Look at me, Emma,' Rocco demanded, aware that he was fighting a losing battle with his control. A degree of male pride made him want to be sure that in the climax of passion she knew it was *him* she was making love with, not a ghost from the past.

She opened her eyes and stared into his glittering golden gaze. For a few seconds he stilled, his big body shaking with the effort of holding back the tide. But he could not fight its relentless force and threw back his head, a harsh groan torn from his throat as his control shattered and he experienced the ecstasy of release.

His convulsive shudders evoked a feeling of fierce tenderness in Emma. This strong, powerful man could be vulnerable in her arms. Instinctively she hugged him close, stroking her fingers through his hair and gently pressing her lips to his cheek. *This* was what making love should be, she thought softly. A complete union of two bodies in perfect accord.

But for her it had been so much more. She could no longer deny the truth to herself. Love had crept into her heart and ensnared her soul, and that was why she had given her body to Rocco. He had restored her self-belief and healed the hurt Jack had caused. Making love with Rocco had been the most profound experience of her life, one that she would never regret or forget, and the beauty of what they had shared brought tears to her eyes.

Rocco's chest heaved as he lay lax on top of Emma, aftershocks of pleasure still rippling through him. He felt relaxed and sated, and strangely reluctant to withdraw from her. For the first time in his life he had felt a union that went beyond the physical joining of two bodies. It was almost as if their souls had meshed.

He lifted his face from her neck and sought her mouth, but the dampness on her cheek made him stiffen. The realisation that she was crying felt like a knife in his ribs. Had making love with him brought back memories of the husband she still grieved for? *Did she wish he was Jack?*

The unwelcome idea brought him to his senses and he rolled off her. What had he been thinking? There was no special union between them. His soul was untouched, inviolate. The sex had been good—more than good—mind-blowing—but that was all it was. There was no reason to dress it up and look for things that didn't exist—emotions that he did not want.

He turned his head just as Emma hastily brushed her hand across her face. Clearly she did not want him to see her tears, and he did not want to know the reason for them.

She gave a tiny yawn and looked mortified. 'I'm sorry—it's been quite a day,' she said huskily. Reaction to the day's events, its happy outcome and spectacular conclusion, was hitting Emma hard, and she was struggling against the waves of tiredness that threatened to engulf her.

Rocco knew she was thinking of those endless minutes on the beach, when her daughter had been missing, and despite his determination to ban emotions from his relationship with her he felt a tug of compassion. She looked exhausted and infinitely fragile, her eyes huge and dark with shadows.

'Come,' he said gently, and he gathered her close.

His body immediately stirred once more as he traced his hands over her tempting curves, but he ignored the siren song of desire and gave in to a deeper need simply to hold her while she fell asleep in his arms.

Emma was already at the breakfast table when Rocco strode into the dining room the following morning. Her cool smile did nothing to allay the annoyance he'd felt when he had woken to find that she had left his bed some time during the night, but the flush of colour that stained her cheeks and the way she hastily looked away from him as he sat down opposite her gave him some measure of satisfaction. He was used to being in control of his relationships and usually *he* was the one to leave his mistress's bed. The role reversal had left him with a distinct sense of pique.

But everything with this woman was different, he acknowledged ruefully as he poured himself coffee from the jug, added a spoonful of sugar and took a sip of the strong black liquid. Emma had never played by the rules—which made her capitulation the previous night all the sweeter—but he was insulted that she had crept back to her own room like a thief in the night. Particularly as he had been painfully aroused when he had reached for her in the early hours. His body was still throbbing with sexual frustration. He was going to have to set a few ground rules and let her know that *he* would call the shots during their affair, he decided.

'Nanna and Grandpa are coming soon.' A high-pitched, childish voice drew him from his thoughts, and he smiled at Holly, who was wriggling on her seat, barely able to contain her impatience at the prospect of seeing her grandparents. 'Very soon—aren't they, Mummy?'

'Yes, but if you don't eat some breakfast you're going to be too hungry to go on a trip with them. Now, please eat some yogurt,' Emma said firmly.

Catching her eye, Rocco murmured, 'Someone is very excited.'

'You wouldn't believe,' came the rueful reply. 'I knew she would be up early, but we've read a whole book of fairy tales since five o'clock this morning.'

He felt himself relax as the reason for her departure from his bed became clear. Emma would always put her daughter beyond any other consideration, and he respected her for that. Unlike his own mother who, when he had been a child, had frequently entertained her lovers at the family home, and had not cared about his confusion when he had walked into her room and found her in bed with a man who was not his father.

His parents had *not* been good role models for marriage. His childhood had been punctuated by their rows and affairs, their dramatic reunions, followed inevitably by bitter separations. No wonder he had vowed to steer clear of the outdated institution of holy matrimony, he thought sardonically. Why would he choose to tie himself to one woman when he knew he would grow bored with a relationship within weeks?

But lately he had found himself equally bored with meaningless sexual encounters. He had been aware of a vague sense that there had to be something more. But then he'd remember his parents' vipers pit of a relationship and realise that love was an illusion—wasn't it?

He raked a hand through his hair and ignored the dish of freshly baked rolls the maid had placed on the table, finding that his appetite had disappeared. Why did a snippy English nurse make him suddenly question everything? he wondered irritably.

Being introduced to Emma's in-laws when they arrived half an hour later was an uncomfortable experience for Rocco, considering that he had just slept with their dead son's wife, but he exerted his usual easy charm and welcomed them to the Villa Lucia.

It was immediately clear that the Marchants adored their granddaughter and shared a close bond with Emma—and that they had been devastated by the death of their son.

'Jack was our only child,' Alison told Rocco, while Emma went to check that she had packed Holly's favourite soft toy. 'Holly lives on through him.' Tears filled her eyes, and her grief was painful to witness. 'Emma is a lovely girl. Peter and I hope she'll marry again one day, but of course Jack was the love of her life.'

'I understand,' Rocco murmured.

What he did not understand was why Emma shied away from ever talking about her husband, and why the mention of his name caused her to withdraw into herself. Mystery surrounded her relationship with Jack Marchant, and he felt frustrated that even though they had shared the most intense sexual experience last night she did not trust him enough to confide in him.

Determined not to risk upsetting Holly by indulging in an extended farewell, Emma kept a tight hold on her emotions as she leaned into the car and gave the little girl a kiss and a brief hug. 'Be good for Nanna and Grandpa, won't you?'

'I will, Mummy. Love you.'

Dear, sweet Holly. So trusting and innocent and infinitely precious. She would willingly lay down her life for her child, Emma acknowledged, blinking back tears as her parents-in-law's car with its precious cargo rounded a bend and disappeared from view.

'She'll be back in a few days,' Rocco reminded her.

'I know.' She forced a smile. 'I don't know what to do with myself now that Cordelia has accepted the Harrises' invitation to stay in Rapallo with them for a couple of days and Holly has gone. I think I might be bored.'

'Assuredly not, *cara*,' Rocco drawled, the velvet-soft sensuality in his voice sending a quiver down Emma's spine. 'I can think of a number of ways to keep you occupied.'

His eyes roamed over her and he congratulated himself on his excellent sense of taste in female attire. The short denim skirt he'd bought her when she had first arrived in Portofino moulded her pert derrière and revealed a tantalising amount of slender, lightly tanned thighs, while the simple white T-shirt clung to her generous breasts like a second skin. An erotic fantasy filled his mind, of stripping her right there on the front lawn and tumbling her down onto the sweet-scented camomile.

Reality intruded as he remembered the report on his desk that required his urgent attention, and the several hours of work waiting on his laptop.

The glimmer of tears clinging to her lower lashes like tiny raindrops caused him to abandon both ideas. Work could wait, and he would have to control his sexual frustration for a while. Emma was putting on a brave face, but he could see what a wrench she found it to be parted from her daughter. Once again he was surprised to find that the desire to comfort and protect her was stronger than his desire to satisfy his sexual urges.

He looped his arms around her waist and could not resist dropping a light kiss on her mouth, smiling lazily at her startled look and the flush of pink that stained her cheeks. Last night she had been a passionate temptress in his bed, and her shyness this morning both amused and touched him.

'I want to spend the day with you,' he said softly. 'How about we take my boat out? We can sail along the coast to Camogli and have lunch there.' He drew her closer, so that their bodies were pressed together and she could be in no doubt of his state of arousal. 'And afterwards we'll have a siesta onboard the *Anna-Maria*.'

Emma caught her breath at the hungry gleam in Rocco's eyes, and felt the sweet seduction of sexual anticipation unfurl in the pit of her stomach.

'You want to spend the afternoon sleeping?' she queried demurely.

His rough laugh could not disguise his rampant desire. 'Let me put it another way, *cara*. You will be lying down, but do not expect to get much rest.'

CHAPTER NINE

CAMOGLI was a pretty coastal village with a busy harbour, where sleek motor yachts were moored next to brightly painted fishing boats. Emma had enjoyed the leisurely trip there on board Rocco's twenty-foot cruiser, which was the epitome of luxury. It was a perfect day, with a cloudless blue sky and the sun shimmering on the crystal clear sea. As she had stood on the deck, with his arm around her waist and the breeze playing with her hair, she had felt that she had stepped into another world.

It was a million miles away from her life with Holly in Northumberland, but in a few short weeks she would leave Italy and Rocco, she reminded herself. She was determined not to be overwhelmed by this peek into a multimillionaire's lifestyle. But when she looked into his golden tiger's eyes and saw the predatory hunger in their depths it was hard not to feel overwhelmed by him.

Along the way they had stopped at a famous landmark on the Ligurian coast, San Fruttuoso, and had spent an hour exploring the beautiful Benedictine monastery there, which had been built on the beach.

Now they were sitting outside a charming harbourside restaurant in Camogli. Lunch had consisted of scallops, followed by the local dish *brazino in tegare*—sea bass cooked with white wine and tomatoes—served with a bottle of Pinot Grigio. The deliciously crisp white wine had induced a pleasant lethargy in Emma, and she ruefully acknowledged that she needed the cup of strong black coffee Rocco had ordered at the end of the meal.

Her heart flipped in her chest when she looked across the table at him. In black jeans and polo shirt, his eyes hidden behind designer shades and his silky dark hair falling across his brow, he looked devastatingly sexy. From the numerous female glances cast in his direction, she was not the only woman to find him so, she noted.

They had spent a pleasant few hours discussing everything from politics to the arts, and had discovered a shared taste for a new author of complex thrillers, but now Rocco leaned back in his chair and sipped his coffee before asking, 'Did you always want to be a nurse?'

The question provided a welcome distraction from her fierce awareness of him and Emma nodded. 'Yes—as far back as I can remember. I grew up on my parents' farm and for a while I thought about training to be a vet, but by the time I left school I knew that nursing was my vocation.'

'I imagine it's not always an easy job? There must be occasions, incidents which you find upsetting.' Rocco had witnessed her compassion in her treatment of his grandmother, and he suspected that beneath her guise of brisk and efficient nurse she had a heart as soft as butter.

'Sometimes,' she admitted. 'The death of a patient is always hard, but the rewards of the job far outweigh the negatives. After I'd completed my training I worked for six months in Liberia. The country has been torn apart by years of civil war, and medical facilities are primitive, to say the least. It was so sad to see people—especially children—dying from preventable illnesses such as malaria and measles. But the trip was an amazingly uplifting experience. The people have suffered so much, but they are determined to improve their lives, and it was good to know that I was helping them in some small way. When Holly is older I'd like to work in Africa again.'

'So, after Africa you returned to England, married Jack and lived happily until his tragic death?'

'Yes.' She avoided Rocco's speculative stare, unaware that the sparkle in her eyes had suddenly faded.

Her happiness had been built on the illusion that Jack had loved her as she had loved him, and it still hurt to think of all the times he had been unfaithful. Sometimes she wondered if it would have been better to have found out about his infidelity sooner, so that at least she could have confronted him about it. But he had died on the same day that his mistress had revealed his true nature, and Emma's grief had been mixed with anger and bitterness that he had betrayed her trust so cruelly.

'How about you?' she said, desperate to steer the conversation away from her marriage. 'Did you ever want to become an actor like your parents?'

'*Dio*, no!' Rocco's reply was swift and succinct. 'There was quite enough artistic temperament in the family with the two of them,' he said sardonically.

'Flora and Enrico's life had been a continuous performance,' he explained, 'and, like a Shakespearian tragedy, full of drama. Neither of them had been able to cope with Gio's behavioural problems, but when he'd died they had played the role of grief-stricken parents.'

'They did consider sending me to a performing arts school, but fortunately my grandfather intervened. My father had never had any interest in joining the family company, but Silvio was determined that I would be his heir and one day take over as head of Eleganza.'

'Didn't you mind having your future mapped out by

your grandfather?' Emma asked curiously, thinking that Silvio D'Angelo sounded a formidable character.

Rocco shook his head. 'It was my choice to study engineering at university. I am interested in all aspects of the motor industry, but the development side—thinking of new ideas and using new technologies—excites me the most. The project I'm involved with at the moment is to design a high-performance hybrid sports car which uses an electrically powered engine as well as an internal combustion engine that will result in a reduction in the use of fossil fuels.' He grinned, his enthusiasm making him seem suddenly boyish. 'I'm probably boring you,' he said ruefully. 'Most women get a glazed look in their eyes when I talk about my work.'

'No, I think it's fascinating,' Emma told him honestly. 'I guess I'm not like the other women.'

'That is an understatement, *cara*,' he assured her gravely.

No other woman had ever made him feel this way, Rocco brooded. He had had more mistresses than he cared to admit, but his interest in them had never extended outside the bedroom door. He worked in a predominantly male environment, and although he might flirt with women, and charm them, he rarely talked to them about things that mattered to him. It was a new experience to be with a woman he valued as a friend as well as a lover. The sense of companionship he felt with Emma was something he hoped would continue for a long time. Which meant what? he asked himself, frowning. Did he envisage his affair with her lasting for longer than the three months she had agreed to stay in Italy as his grandmother's nurse?

He studied her beautiful face, framed by her golden bell of hair, and realised that the answer to his question was an unequivocal yes. He could not imagine a time when he would not want her. He dropped his gaze to her firm, full breasts and desire jackknifed through him as he imagined stripping off her T-shirt and bra and cradling her luscious flesh in his hands.

'I think it's time for that siesta,' he drawled softly. 'Are you sleepy, *mia bellezza*?'

Emma's stomach lurched with anticipation at the blatant sensuality in Rocco's voice. She had enjoyed the boat trip, and lunch, but all day she had been conscious of the sexual tension simmering between them. The idea that very soon he would spread her beneath him and make love to her with a wild passion that matched her own caused a flood of sticky heat to pool between her legs.

She met his gaze and gave him a demure smile. 'No, I'm not a bit tired.'

Her teasing tone inflamed his libido. 'We have to get out of here now—before I give in to temptation and make love to you on the table,' he growled, jerking to his feet and hustling her out of the restaurant.

He held her hand and they ran along the quay back to where the *Anna-Maria* was moored. Laughing and breathless, they stumbled onboard, and within minutes Rocco was steering the boat out of the harbour.

'We'll drop anchor a little way out from the shore, where we won't be disturbed,' he said, pulling her to him and claiming her mouth in a fiercely passionate kiss that left Emma in no doubt of his hunger for her.

The ringtone of his mobile phone drove them apart.

'I'll have to take this, *cara*,' he muttered reluctantly, 'it's Silvio.'

He spoke to his grandfather in Italian for a few moments, then ended the call and switched off his phone, before scooping Emma up into his arms and heading purposefully down the steps to the lower deck.

'The old man called to remind me that he's hosting a dinner party at his home tomorrow night, for a number of prestigious clients as well as Eleganza's top executives. I've told him I'll be bringing a guest.'

'Me?' Emma gave him a worried look. 'But what will your grandfather think? I mean, strictly speaking, I'm your employee. If I go to the party with you, won't he suspect there's something going on between us?'

'I don't give a damn what Silvio or anyone else thinks,' Rocco told her thickly as they reached the master cabin and he dropped her onto the bed. 'I want you with me. And if you are my employee I hope you are going to obey my every command, *cara*. Something is undoubtedly going on between us, and it's time you took your clothes *off*.'

The desire blazing in his eyes made Emma feel like a wanton seductress, and with a confidence she would never have imagined herself possessing she pulled her T-shirt over her head and wriggled out of her skirt. Liquid heat coursed through her veins as she watched Rocco dispense with his own clothes to reveal the broad, bronzed chest covered with wiry dark hairs. Her eyes followed a path over his powerful abdominal muscles and hard thighs, and she caught her breath at the sight of his proudly erect penis. She reached behind her to undo her bra and then, oh, so slowly, slid the straps down her arms.

'So you want to tease, do you?' He laughed raggedly as he pulled her to the edge of the bed and whipped her bra from her fingers, curling his hands possessively around her breasts. 'Do you know what happens to naughty nurses who like to tease? They have to suffer being kissed over every inch of their body.'

He started with her nipples, flicking his tongue across each taut bud until she whimpered. He relented and took one pebble-hard peak and then the other fully into his mouth. By the time he had peeled off her panties and continued her punishment with the most intimate caress of all Emma was gasping and desperate for him to take her.

She reached for him, and felt him shudder when she stroked him. With a groan he quickly donned a protective sheath and positioned himself between her thighs.

'Playtime's over, *cara*,' he growled, and he entered her with one deep thrust that filled her and gave her a sense of completeness that tugged on her heart.

Her man, her master. She welcomed each subsequent stroke and wrapped her legs around his back to increase the exquisite sensations that were building deep in her pelvis. The feeling of oneness she had with Rocco was like nothing she had ever experienced. It was as if their souls as well as their bodies had become a single entity: a circle that had no beginning and no end.

But there had to be an end, and it came in an explosive orgasm that caused her to rake her nails across his shoulders while her body pulsed with spasm after spasm of pleasure. He continued to drive into her, sending her over the edge for a second time, and as she tumbled he fell with her, uttering a savage groan in the ecstasy of their simultaneous release.

Afterward, Rocco settled her head on his shoulder and smiled when he saw her lashes flutter down to fan against her flushed cheeks. He would allow her a short siesta before he enjoyed her delectable body for a second time, and no doubt a third. He could not resist her, he acknowledged ruefully. But it was just good sex. He did not want a long-term relationship when experience had shown him that it might end in bitterness and acrimony, like his parents' hellish marriage and the marriages of so many of his contemporaries. But neither did he want to let her go, taunted a voice inside his head. At some point he was going to have to make a decision about where his affair with Emma would lead.

The following evening Rocco knocked on the door of Emma's bedroom, where she had gone to change for his grandfather's dinner party.

'Are you ready, *cara*?'

She spun round to face him, and he saw from her taut expression and the way she was twisting her hands together that she was as tense as a coiled spring.

'Just about. But, Rocco, I really don't think I should go with you. For one thing, Cordelia is tired after her trip to Rapallo—I think visiting three museums was a bit much for her. She seemed very frail when I collected her this afternoon, and I think I should stay here in case she needs me.'

'I've just been with Nonna, and she is delighted that you are going out for the evening.' He dismissed her argument. 'She says she's going to have an early night. And Beatrice is on hand should she require assistance.' He strolled across the room and slid his hand beneath her chin to tilt her face to his. 'What's the real issue here, Emma?'

'I won't fit in with your prestigious clients and top executives,' she mumbled. 'I'm not a glamorous socialite and I don't have anything interesting to say.'

Rocco gave her a quizzical look. 'You are the most interesting person I've ever met, and you have so much to say that is worthwhile. I would happily spend all evening talking with you rather than being bored to death by so-called "glamorous socialites", whose conversation is limited to gossip about celebrities or fashion.' He gave her an amused smile. 'You're one of the few women I know who fully understands the workings of the internal combustion engine.'

'I told you—I used to help my brother fix the farm tractors. But my experience as a grease-monkey is not an ideal topic for discussion at a posh dinner party,' she said dryly.

'You'll be fine, I promise. Silvio is looking forward to meeting you. And as for fitting in—in that dress you look elegant and sophisticated.' He ran his eyes over the floor-length black jersey-silk dress that moulded her curves and emphasised her slim waist. His voice thickened. 'And indescribably beautiful.'

Emma caught her breath at the sudden flare of emotion she glimpsed in his eyes, but it was gone before she could decipher it—hidden beneath the sweep of his dark lashes. In a black tuxedo and brilliant white shirt he looked mouth-wateringly sexy. She felt her heart rate quicken and gave a wry smile.

'So do you. Thank you for the flowers, by the way. They were a lovely surprise.' Her eyes lingered on the three dozen red roses that had been delivered to the villa during the day and were now arranged in a vase on her dressing table. Red roses were for love, she thought wistfully. But Rocco did not love her, and from all she had learned of him he would never give his heart to any woman.

'It's time to leave.'

His velvety voice drew her from her confused thoughts. Enjoy the present, and stop worrying about the future, she told herself as she slipped her hand in his and allowed him to lead her from the room.

'What do you think of my house, Mrs Marchant?'

Emma was standing by the window, gazing out at the night-time view of the city of Genoa, where graceful old buildings were illuminated by the golden glow emitted from the street lamps. She turned her head at the sound of the heavily accented voice to find that Silvio D'Angelo had joined her.

'It's incredible,' she replied honestly, recalling the tour Rocco had given her earlier of the five-storey house, whose elegant rooms were filled with priceless antiques. 'It's such a beautiful, historical building—as are so many of the other houses nearby.'

'This part of Genoa is known as the Old City, and is included on the World Heritage list,' Silvio told her.

Shorter and stockier than his grandson, he had a wrinkled face and grey hair that indicated that he must be well into his eighties, but there was a shrewd gleam in his dark eyes that Emma found unnerving.

She smiled hesitantly. 'Please—call me Emma.'

He dipped his head in acknowledgement. 'Rocco tells me you are a good friend of his?'

She felt herself blush. *Just good friends* was hardly an apt description of their relationship, she mused, recalling the numerous times he had made love to her the previous night. 'Yes. I'm staying at the Villa Lucia for a few weeks to act as a companion to Cordelia.'

Silvio's beady eyes seemed to bore into her. 'And after that you will return to England?'

Her stomach swooped at the prospect, but she hid her dismay and nodded. 'I'll be going back to my job as a district nurse.'

Her eyes were drawn across the room to where Rocco was chatting to a stunningly attractive woman who he had introduced earlier as Valentina Rosseti—the only female engineer on Eleganza's design team. From the way Valentina was batting her eyelashes at him she would lay a bet that the Italian woman wasn't thinking about hybrid engines now, Emma thought sourly.

Silvio followed her gaze and his expression became speculative. 'I am an old man,' he announced. 'I was ninety years old last month, and it is time I handed over control of Eleganza to my grandson.' He sighed heavily. 'But I have stipulated that Rocco must curb his playboy lifestyle before I assign full power of the company to him. He needs to marry a good Italian girl, and produce an heir to one day succeed him.'

Emma gave him a doubtful look. 'I don't think marriage is on Rocco's agenda.'

The elderly man snorted. 'My grandson knows his duty. Eleganza is his favourite mistress, and he will do whatever is required of him to take control of the company he loves.'

A gong sounded to call them to dinner, but her conversation with Silvio had unsettled Emma and she was unable to enjoy the five superb courses, each served with a different wine specially chosen to complement the food. It did not help that Rocco was seated at the far end of the table with his grandfather, Tino Manzzini and several of Eleganza's clients—presumably so that they could discuss business. Emma was seated next to one of Rocco's elderly uncles, who spoke little English, while to her other side was Shayna Manzzini.

'So Rocco decided to forgo his pretty young neighbour in favour of you,' the Canadian woman drawled towards the end of the meal, pushing away her dessert of Tiramisu untouched.

Emma had noted that she had barely eaten any dinner, and guessed that semi-starvation was how Shayna retained her model's figure. She was unsure how to respond to the comment, but Shayna did not seem to be waiting for a reply.

'I noticed at his grandmother's party that you couldn't take your eyes off him. But you do know it won't last, honey? Rocco doesn't do commitment.' She paused to ensure she had Emma's full attention and then said softly, 'Not even with the mother of his child.'

Trying to hide the fact that her hand was shaking, Emma put down her spoon, telling herself that it was the rich confection of mascarpone and cream in front of her that had made her feel sick. She had previous experience of Shayna's spiteful tongue, and was not inclined to believe a word she said. There was a lot of truth in the saying that hell knew no fury like a woman scorned, she thought wryly. But something in her expression must have revealed her uncertainty to Rocco's ex-mistress.

'I assume from your stricken look that he hasn't told you?' The model shrugged. 'Well, I'll grant you it is speculation rather than fact.'

'What is?' Emma demanded bluntly.

'That Rocco has a son by one of his mistresses. Rumour has it that the boy and his mother live here in Genoa, and that Rocco visits them every week. I guess that would explain why, according to my husband, no one can contact Eleganza's CEO after he leaves the office at midday every Friday.'

'There could be a dozen reasons why Rocco leaves work early,' Emma said tersely. In the past she had jumped to conclusions about him far too quickly and, as it had turned out, wrongly. She did not intend to make the same mistake again—especially at the words of an embittered woman who had had an affair with him years ago and clearly still resented the fact that he had dumped her.

She trusted Rocco.

The realisation settled like a warm glow around her heart. After having had her faith destroyed by Jack, she had never thought she would trust anyone ever again. But Rocco had always been honest with her—even to admitting that he did not want a long-term relationship. She had gone into their affair fully aware that it had no future, but she had no regrets. She would always treasure the time she had spent with him, she thought softly, conscious of the dull ache inside her when she envisaged returning to England without him. Her life would be a lot easier if she had not fallen in love with him, but that was her fault—not his.

'Rumours rarely amount to more than spiteful gossip,' she told Shayna coldly. 'And I certainly don't believe that Rocco has a secret child.' She thought of his gentle patience with her daughter, and was certain that if he ever had a child of his own he would be a devoted father. 'He's an honourable man.'

The model arched her finely plucked brows. 'Oh, dear, you're in love with him,' she drawled mockingly. 'Well, don't say I didn't warn you.'

Dinner finished soon after, and Emma managed to avoid Shayna for the rest of the party, but she was relieved when the evening drew to an end and Rocco escorted her out to his car. Doubts were like weeds, she thought dismally. They started out as a tiny seed but grew to smother rational thought as swiftly as Japanese knotweed left unchecked in a herbaceous border.

'You're very quiet, *cara*,' Rocco commented some twenty minutes later, as he turned the car onto the driveway in front of the Villa Lucia. He walked round to open the passenger door, frowning at her obvious reluctance to meet his gaze. 'Is anything wrong?'

'No,' Emma denied quickly. 'I was just thinking...about

things.' She hesitated, her heart drumming a warning tattoo beneath her ribs.

During her marriage she had never confronted Jack on the many occasions when he had arrived home from work hours later than she had been expecting him. The idea that he was seeing someone behind her back had hovered in her mind, but she had been scared to demand the truth and had pushed her suspicions away. Looking back, she regretted her lack of courage, and it made her determined to face problems head-on now.

She followed Rocco into the villa, but when he moved to draw her into his arms she stepped back from him, knowing that if he kissed her she would be lost. Sensing his frustration, she blurted out, 'Do you have any children?'

He stiffened, clearly shocked, and his eyes narrowed on her tense face. '*Dio*! What kind of question is that?' he demanded harshly. 'Of course I don't.'

'You admit that you have had numerous affairs,' Emma pushed on doggedly, despite his deepening frown. 'Surely it's possible that a woman from one of your past relationships could have given birth to your child?'

'No—it isn't,' Rocco told her curtly. 'I'm always careful, and there has never been any chance of an accidental pregnancy. What kind of a man do you think I am?' He gave a bitter laugh. 'On second thoughts, don't answer that. Past experience tells me that your reply won't be complimentary.'

He sounded hurt, Emma realised guiltily. His startled reaction had convinced her that she had made a big mistake in allowing Shayna's spiteful comments to take hold in her mind. She bit her lip. 'It was just a stupid thought,' she mumbled. 'Please forget I ever mentioned it.'

Rocco stared at her downcast face and was torn between wanting to shake some sense into her and kiss her senseless. '*If* I was a father, I would not be involved with you. I would be married to the mother of my child.'

Now it was her turn to look startled. 'I thought you didn't believe in marriage?'

'I admit that my parents' marriage was not a good advertisement. But a child's needs must take first priority, and although it might be old-fashioned I believe that children should grow up in a family unit with both their parents. Even though my mother and father argued frequently, I still had the sense that we were a family. When they split up I felt torn between them, and I wished they would get back together.'

The silence that fell prickled with tension. Certain that she had angered Rocco, and feeling uncertain of his mood, Emma studied the marble-tiled floor with apparent fascination.

'Let me ask *you* a question,' he said brusquely. 'Why don't you ever want to talk about Jack? I know you loved him,' he continued before she could reply, 'but it has been three years, and you can't keep your emotions locked away for ever.'

'What do you know of emotions?' she countered shakily. 'You're a playboy whose tally of ex-mistresses probably equals a cricket score. From the outset you've made it clear that our affair will be purely physical, and emotions will play no part in it.'

'Yes, I have,' Rocco agreed broodingly. 'And I was sure I meant it.' He stretched out his hand to tuck a lock of strawberry-blonde hair behind her ear and stared into her stormy grey eyes. 'Now I am not certain that my emotions are in my control. You have undermined the rules I have lived by all my adult life. I've discovered that I want a proper relationship with you, Emma,' he said softly, his smile a little rueful when she seemed to be struck dumb by his revelation.

Emma snatched a breath and tried desperately to steady her racing heart, but the expression in Rocco's eyes—a mixture of tenderness and sultry promise—was scrambling her brain. 'What kind of relationship?' she queried cautiously.

'One that involves us getting to know each other properly and sharing our thoughts…and feelings. I know there is Holly to consider, and that is why I think we should take things gradually, but I want you in my life, *cara*,' he said deeply.

He could no longer deny the truth to himself or to Emma. No other woman had ever made him feel this level of need, and with a muttered oath he pulled her into his arms. 'Is it so hard for you to trust me? I swear I don't want to hurt you. I'm prepared to take things one step at a time, but I need you to take that first step with me.' His voice dropped lower, his accent very pronounced as emotions he had never experienced before churned inside him. 'Will you, Emma?'

His face was so close to hers that his warm breath feathered across her lips, and she shook with longing for him to kiss her and seduce her with his sensual mastery. She had decided tonight, when she had chosen not to believe Shayna Manzzini's scurrilous accusations, that she *did* trust him, and she felt empowered that she had thrown off the shackles of her past.

'Yes,' she whispered, parting her lips eagerly beneath the pressure of his as he claimed her mouth in a kiss of pure possession.

CHAPTER TEN

SUNLIGHT slanting across her eyelids roused Emma from a deep sleep. She stretched, and smiled when a muscular arm immediately tightened around her. Cocooned in the relaxed state that preceded full wakefulness, she felt safe and totally secure, and her mouth curved into a soft smile when she lifted her lashes and met an enigmatic golden gaze.

'Buongiorno, cara.' Rocco brushed a kiss as light as thistledown over her lips.

'Were you watching me sleeping?' She could not disguise the faint note of vulnerability in her voice at the thought.

'It's a special part of my day—waking with you in my arms,' Rocco told her seriously. He traced the shape of her breasts and felt his body stir when her nipples hardened at his touch. 'Of course there are many other special moments,' he murmured huskily.

Emma caught her breath when he lowered his head and replaced his hands with his mouth, liquid heat pooling between her legs as he continued an erotic path across her stomach and down to tease the sensitive nub of her clitoris with his tongue. What followed was a slow, sensual loving that tugged on her soul as he positioned himself above her and entered her with exquisite care. His eyes locked with hers as he brought her to a shattering orgasm, and when their passion was finally spent he cradled her in his arms while their thundering hearts resumed a steady beat.

'I know why you're smiling,' Rocco said lazily, feeling a hand squeeze his heart as he studied her beautiful face. The silky bell of golden hair framed her flushed cheeks, and he thought that she had never looked lovelier. 'Holly is coming back today, isn't she?'

'Yes.' Emma had never imagined she could feel this happy. The past week that she and Rocco had been lovers had been filled with laughter and incredible passion, but she had missed her little daughter and ached to lift Holly into her arms and hug her close. 'Peter and Alison are flying home to England today, so I've arranged to meet them in Genoa. It's approximately a hundred-mile drive from Nice, so they should arrive about lunchtime.'

Unable to resist, she ran her hand lightly over his cheek, feeling the faint abrasion of stubble on his jaw. He was heart-stoppingly sexy first thing in the morning, she thought, feeling her stomach dip. 'You're welcome to join us for lunch.'

Rocco hesitated, thinking of the text message he had received from his half-brother a few moments before Emma had woken up: *See you after school today?*

It was the first time Marco had ever contacted him, and sensing the uncertainty behind the message Rocco had immediately texted back: *Of course.* The little boy was finally starting to trust him, and he could not let him down, he acknowledged heavily.

'I'd love to, *cara*, but I have an important appointment this afternoon. Tell Holly I'll see her when I get home from work tonight.' He glanced at his watch and threw back the sheet. 'Talking of work, my little temptress, I need to get moving. Fridays are always busy.'

He headed into the en-suite bathroom, and moments

later Emma heard the sound of the power shower. She tried to quash her disappointment that he could not meet them for lunch, reminding herself that he was the CEO of one of the biggest companies in Italy and could not rearrange his busy schedule for her.

Unbidden, Shayna Manzzini's comments slid insidiously into her head. *Rumour has it that the boy and his mother live here in Genoa, and that Rocco visits them every week.*

Rubbish, she thought firmly. Shayna was a nasty piece of work, and the rumour was nothing more than sheer bitchiness resulting from jealousy because the Canadian woman had realised that Emma and Rocco were lovers. Rocco had always been honest with her, and she felt confident that she could trust him. Yes, he had a reputation as a playboy, but he had stated that he wanted a meaningful relationship with her. He was not Jack, and it was not in his nature to deceive her.

Rocco stood beneath the powerful jet of water and tried to marshal his chaotic thoughts. Secrets were hell—and this wasn't even *his* secret, he brooded grimly. He wished he could tell Silvio about Marco. The old man was much stronger than a few months ago, when he had undergone major heart surgery. Back then the doctors had advised that he should not be subjected to any shocks, and telling him that he had an illegitimate grandson had been out of the question.

But the ultimate decision about whether he wanted to be part of the D'Angelo family had to be Marco's. Rocco had given his half-brother his word that he would tell no one of his true identity until Marco wanted it to be known. The little boy was coming round to the idea of meeting his grandfather, but until he made that choice Rocco felt he could not reveal the truth to anyone.

Damn Enrico for dumping this on him, Rocco thought bitterly. It was typical that he had been left to sort out the mess his father had left behind. He desperately wanted to confide in Emma, but he had worked hard to gain Marco's trust and he owed his little brother his loyalty. He could not break the promise he had made to a seven year-old child.

Reaching for a towel, Rocco rubbed his hair vigorously. There were a lot of things he wanted to tell Emma, he acknowledged, feeling his stomach clench with a nervous tension that was completely alien to him. He did not do nerves, or emotions, but both were churning in his gut—along with a feeling of vulnerability that he had never experienced before. All were the fault of an attractive English nurse with cool grey eyes and a smile that made his heart miss a beat.

So what was he going to do about it? he queried self-derisively. The situation demanded decisive action, but the possibility that for the first time in his life he might fail to achieve what he desired caused the cramping feeling in his stomach to intensify.

'Are we lost, Mummy?'

Emma glanced over her shoulder at Holly, who was sitting in her child seat in the back of the car, and gave what she hoped was a confident smile.

'Only a little bit, munchkin. I've stopped for a few minutes so that I can look at the map.'

The journey from Portofino to Genoa this morning had been relatively simple, and once she had left the main coast road and entered the city she had found the restaurant where she had arranged to meet her in-laws without any trouble. Trying to negotiate her way out of town, however, was proving more difficult. The roads were busy with Friday afternoon traffic, and although she felt reasonably confident driving on the right side of the road rather than the left, as was the law in England, she had been concentrating so hard on the flow of cars at a roundabout that she had missed the correct exit and ended up in a maze of narrow backstreets.

Map-reading had never been one of her strengths, Emma acknowledged with a sigh. She was tempted to ask for directions, but there were few people around, and her inability to speak Italian was likely to be a major stumbling block.

'Mummy, I'm hot.'

With the car's engine off, the lack of air-conditioning meant that the temperature inside the car was rising rapidly. Emma rubbed her brow, feeling the beginning of a headache. 'Okay,' she reassured Holly, 'we'll be moving in a minute.'

At the far end of the street a couple accompanied by a child riding a bike came into view. The gods might be kind and they would be able to speak English, she hoped, releasing her seat belt as the people drew nearer.

They were a striking couple, both tall—the man dark-haired and swarthy, the woman slender and elegant, with a mane of long platinum-blonde hair that suggested she was not a native Italian. Something about the man—his natural grace and air of supreme self-confidence—seemed curiously familiar. Frowning, Emma focused on the child—a boy of perhaps seven or eight years old—and her heart suddenly froze. The jet-black hair was not unusual for an Italian, but the perfect symmetry of his features, his eye-catching handsomeness even at a young age, bore an incredible resemblance to Rocco.

Don't be ridiculous, she told herself impatiently, angry for allowing the shadow of Shayna Manzzini's spite to hang over her. She was no longer the woman she had been after Jack's death, lacking in self-worth and terrified to trust her own judgement. She did not believe for one second that Rocco had a secret love child. But she could not tear her gaze from the boy on the bike. He was close to where she was parked now, and she saw that his eyes were an unusual amber colour—like tiger's eyes.

Bile rose in her throat, so acrid that she almost gagged. She felt as though she had been turned to stone and she watched, unable to move, as the boy leapt from his bike, stood it carefully against the wall and then hurtled back to the man who was drawing ever nearer. The man swung the boy high in the air, and they both laughed while the beautiful blonde woman looked on and smiled. The bond between the three of them was unmistakable—and now that he was close to the car so was the identity of the boy's father.

'Are we going now?'

'Yes, right now.' Spurred into action, Emma dragged her seat belt across her. She was terrified that Holly would spot Rocco, or that he would glance into the car. Why didn't she step out onto the pavement and confront him, as she should have done with Jack all those times when he'd arrived home late? a voice in her head demanded. The stark answer felt like a knife in her heart. It was because now, as during her marriage, she could not face the truth and see her pathetic dreams crumble to dust, she thought despairingly.

She had trusted Rocco. Dear heaven. She gave a bitter laugh. Had her blind faith in Jack taught her nothing? She had fallen in love with a playboy once and been cruelly betrayed. What kind of a fool was she to have made the exact same mistake a second time?

She started the engine and the sound drew the attention of the group on the pavement. Like a petrified rabbit caught in car headlights she stared at Rocco and saw him stiffen, watched the startled expression on his face turn to a frown. He took a step towards her and her instinct to flee kicked in. There was a horrible grinding noise as she clumsily selected a gear and the car shot down the road. She determinedly avoided looking into her rearview mirror for one last glimpse of Rocco, focused only on getting away from him.

Rocco gunned his sports car up the hill towards the Villa Lucia. The powerful V8 engine had eaten up the miles to Portofino, but it had been several hours since he had watched Emma race away down the road in Genoa and he was impatient to talk to her. Why had she shot off like that this afternoon? he brooded. He realised she must have been as surprised to see him as he had been to see her, and he did not understand why she had been in that part of the city. Recalling her tense face, he could not shake off a sense of grim foreboding.

It had turned out to be one hell of a day, he thought wearily. The new bike he had presented to Marco had finally won the little boy over. He had been shocked by the strong emotions that had surged through him when his half-brother had hugged him for the first time. It had brought back painful memories of Gio, and reinforced his determination to act as a father figure to Marco.

Emma's unexpected appearance and the disturbing, almost devastated expression he had glimpsed on her face had made him want to rush back to Portofino immediately. But Marco had fallen off the bike, and their subsequent trip to the hospital where he had been diagnosed with mild concussion meant that Rocco had been delayed in the city. Inga, Marco's mother, had been badly shaken by the accident, and even when Rocco had been assured that his brother would be fine he had felt duty-bound to stick around until Marco had been discharged.

At least Silvio had taken the news of his grandson better than expected. Marco had decided that he wanted to meet his grandfather, and Rocco had gone straight from the hospital to Silvio's house, to explain about the little boy. The old man had been shocked, and clearly dismayed that Enrico had kept his illegitimate son a secret for seven years. But Silvio was eager to meet Marco, and had agreed with Rocco that he should inherit a share of Eleganza.

Now, finally, he was free to tell Emma everything that was in his heart. Tension coiled in Rocco's gut and he gave a ragged laugh beneath his breath. Nerves were hell, and a new experience for him where a woman was concerned. But he had long ago realised that Emma was unique. He could only pray she shared his hopes for the future.

The discovery of a taxi parked outside the villa was puzzling. He drew up next to it just as Emma ran down the front steps with a suitcase in her hand. She stopped dead at the sight of him, and even from a distance of a few feet away Rocco could sense her tension.

She jerked back to life and threw the case into the boot of the taxi.

'What are you doing?' Emerging from his car, Rocco glanced into the taxi and saw Holly strapped into a child seat. The ominous feeling that his life was about to come crashing down intensified.

'Leaving,' Emma told him shortly.

Instinct warned him that her emotions were balanced on a knife-edge, and he resisted the temptation to grab her shoulders and demand to know what the hell was going on. 'I guessed that. But why? Your contract to work as Cordelia's private nurse is for three months.'

'Your grandmother no longer needs a nurse.' By a huge

effort of will Emma managed to keep her voice normal, hiding the fact that inside she was falling apart. Fate had a cruel sense of humour, she thought bitterly. If Rocco had arrived home five minutes later she would have already left, and been spared a confrontation with him.

Something was very wrong, Rocco realised. *'Cara...'* He took a step towards her, a hand outstretched.

'Don't,' she said violently, backing away from him. Her self-control cracked. 'Don't come near me.'

'*Madre de Dio!* What is going on, Emma?' Realising that she was about to climb into the taxi, Rocco caught hold of her arm and felt the tremor that ran through her.

'How can you ask me what's wrong?' she demanded, keeping her voice low for fear of upsetting Holly. 'I saw you today—*with your son.*'

Shock slowly turned to something cold and hard, like a lead weight in the pit of Rocco's stomach. When Emma snatched her arm out of his grasp he did not attempt to stop her. 'My *son*?'

'That boy you were with. Don't try to deny it,' Emma said wildly. 'Shayna told me about the rumour that you have a son by one of your mistresses and you visit them regularly.'

Nausea swept through her when she pictured the stunning blonde woman who had been with Rocco and the little boy. She had spent the past few hours thinking about it, and it all made perfect sense. Rocco knew his grandfather would not sign over full control of Eleganza to him unless he married an Italian woman, and so he had kept the fact that he had a son by his Nordic-looking mistress a secret. What other explanation could there be?

The dangerous gleam in Rocco's eyes sent a shiver through her. 'Naturally you would believe Shayna—

despite previous proof that she's a spiteful bitch,' he said sarcastically.

Stung by his icy disdain, she said fiercely, 'I didn't believe her at your grandfather's party. I trusted you. But you lied to me.' She held up her hand when he made to speak. 'You let me think that your afternoon's appointment was work-related, and that was why you couldn't meet me in Genoa. But I've seen the evidence that you were lying. The little boy you were with is the image of you.'

'So was Gio,' Rocco said harshly.

She frowned. 'What has that got to do with anything?'

'Think about it.'

She shook her head and reached once more for the taxi door. 'I don't want to think about anything. I just want to go.' Before the tears that felt like acid burning her eyes fell and he witnessed her utter devastation.

It would take a matter of minutes to explain about Marco—although whether Emma would believe him was open to question, Rocco thought grimly. Anger surged through him. If she had any faith in him he should not have to defend himself. Her readiness to believe Shayna proved that she had never trusted him.

She pulled open the car door and he felt a knife skewer his heart. 'You would walk away from what we have?' he asked in a raw tone. This was crazy. Hang his pride. He would explain, and then she would stop looking at him as though she hated his guts.

The huskiness in his voice made Emma hesitate. He sounded as if he cared, sounded as if he did not want her to leave. But maybe her ears were deceiving her, and hearing what she wanted to hear. Rocco had lied to her—just as Jack had lied throughout their marriage.

'What *do* we have, apart from good sex?' She could not bear to think of all the other things they had shared. The fun and laughter, the long conversations and lazy afternoons making love. Clearly those things had meant more to her than to him. He had destroyed her trust, but she refused to let him see that he had broken her heart. 'There's nothing to keep me here.'

'Then go,' he said savagely, stepping back so that she could climb into the taxi.

He could not force her to have faith in him, and he would not beg. What was the point? he thought bitterly. He knew her heart would belong for ever to her dead husband.

Hurt, pride and a pain more agonising than anything he had ever experienced, made his voice harsh. 'If you leave, Emma, I won't come after you. It's your choice if you decide to end our relationship right now. I will not give you a second chance.'

Spring had finally arrived in Northumberland, and the garden of Primrose Cottage was ablaze with daffodils waving their golden heads in the breeze. It was a perfect day for the nursery school's trip to a local farm to see the lambs, Emma thought, remembering Holly's excitement this morning. The little girl had adapted quite happily to their old life in Little Copton, and although she had mentioned Rocco and Cordelia a few times she'd loved seeing her friends again.

At least she did not have to worry about her daughter or, for the time being, finding somewhere to live. The sale of the cottage had fallen through, and the owner had told Emma she was welcome to stay until new buyers were found. Aware that that might be some months away, she had decided to get on with weeding the back garden. She had arranged to return to her nursing post next week, but until then it was imperative she kept busy so that she did not have time to think.

The image of Rocco's furious face as she had told the taxi driver to take her to Genoa airport seemed to be branded on her subconscious, and his final words, delivered with such deadly finality, haunted her dreams.

I will not give you a second chance.

Why would she want another chance with a deceitful cheat? she thought bleakly. Throughout her journey to the airport and the flight back to England she had assured herself that she had done the right thing. For the past five days settling back into Primrose Cottage and ensuring that Holly was happy had taken up all her time, and she had managed to push Rocco to the back of her mind—at least until she was alone in bed at night.

The long hours of darkness were unbearable, she acknowledged miserably, as she knelt in front of a garden bed and attacked a clump of dandelions with a trowel. She missed him so much that there was a permanent ache in her chest, and doubts, like stubborn weeds, refused to budge from her head. Maybe there was another explanation for the identity of the boy who bore such a striking resemblance to Rocco. The child had reminded her of someone else, and after days of racking her brain she'd realised that he looked very like Giovanni—Rocco's brother who had died twenty years ago.

But what did that tell her? she wondered wearily. Rocco's son was bound to share a family resemblance. There was no escaping the fact that Rocco had a secret life he had not told her about. He had deceived her and made her feel a fool. Tears slid down her face and dripped onto her jeans. Even after Jack's death she had not felt this level of raw agony—as if a serrated blade had slashed through her heart.

She heard the creak of the side gate and hastily scrubbed her cheeks with her sleeve. Gossip spread like wildfire through the village, and the postman would be curious if he saw her crying.

But instead of a cheerful good morning, there was silence—even the blackbird in the apple tree had stopped singing. The hairs on the back of Emma's neck stood on end and she stood up and turned round, catching her breath as the ground beneath her feet lurched like a ship's deck in a storm.

Her voice wouldn't work properly, and eventually emerged as a rusty croak. 'Why are you here…?'

Her nemesis, the keeper of her soul, gave a grim smile. Rocco had had a speech prepared, but the streaks of tears on Emma's face and her tangible unhappiness had made him forget his words and forced him to acknowledge a simple, stark truth.

'Because I've discovered that I can't live without you, *cara*.'

She closed her eyes, as if willing him to disappear. But Rocco wasn't going anywhere. He walked towards her, his eyes lingering on the rounded shape of her breasts beneath her soft grey wool jumper. His woman. He had endured five hellish nights before he'd accepted that pride was a lonely bedmate.

He halted in front of her. 'Marco is my half-brother—my father's illegitimate son. Enrico's three sons all inherited his unusual eye colour.'

Emma's eyes flew open, and she stared at him helplessly as guilt ripped through her. *His half-brother!* That was why Rocco had pointed out that the boy she had believed was his son looked like his brother Gio. There was no denying it. Once again she had misjudged him. This time so terribly that she knew he would never forgive her.

'My father abandoned his Swedish mistress when she fell pregnant, and he had no contact with Marco until he was dying and asked me to find the boy,' Rocco explained quietly. 'I could not tell my grandfather while he was recovering from heart surgery. He is fiercely proud of the D'Angelo name, and I feared the shock of learning about his son's reprehensible behaviour could kill him. For months I have worked to build a relationship with Marco and win his trust. I wanted to tell you about him, but I had promised him I would not reveal his identity to anyone until he felt ready for me to do so.'

Emma stared at his handsome hard-boned face and her heart clenched. He looked drawn, his olive skin stretched taut over his sharp cheekbones, and she had a feeling that, like her, he hadn't slept or eaten properly since their bitter parting.

She bit her lip. 'I refused to believe Shayna when she told me the rumour that you had a son. I told her you were an honourable man—and I meant it,' she insisted huskily when he gave her a wry look. 'I trusted you—and that was hard for me. A huge step that at one time I was sure I would never take. When I saw you in Genoa with a beautiful woman and a young boy I felt devastated.' The memory brought fresh tears to her eyes, but she owed Rocco the truth and she forced herself to go on. 'I felt like I did when I found out about Jack.'

Rocco tried to ignore the corrosive burn of jealousy in his gut. 'I understand how deeply you loved him, and how much you still grieve for him. Learning of his death must have been shattering.'

'It was,' she said slowly. 'But it was made worse because a few hours before the news came that he had died in a fire I found out that he had been unfaithful throughout our marriage.'

Rocco jerked his head back in shock. 'Did someone tell you that?'

'His mistress.' Emma gave a humourless laugh. 'Kelly was one of a long list of women he'd slept with, but she was also one of my friends—which made it worse. She said she was telling me about Jack's affairs out of loyalty to our friendship. But she also revealed that Jack was planning to leave me and our unborn baby and move in with her. Apparently he had told her she was "the one", but he said the same thing to me when he asked me to marry him.'

'I thought your marriage was made in heaven,' Rocco said roughly.

She gave another pained laugh. 'So did I. The revelations about Jack's infidelity destroyed my fantasy that we were happily married, but I never had an opportunity to ask him why he had betrayed me. I don't think he can have loved me—the only person Jack was in love with was himself. After his death I realised that I had been in love with the *idea* of love, rather than actually with him. He was good-looking and charming—the original Jack the Lad. I was flattered that he chose to marry me, and I ignored his many faults.'

She sighed. 'But nothing can alter the fact that he died a hero. At his funeral, part of me was proud of him and part of me hated him.'

'Dio!' Rocco interrupted explosively. 'All this time I thought you loved him. You allowed me to think your heart belonged to him,' he said accusingly. Pain tore in his chest. '*Why*, Emma?' he demanded roughly. 'Was it to push me away?'

She was startled by the raw emotion in his eyes. She had no idea where this conversation was leading, but after the way she had misjudged him she owed him her honesty.

'Jack's parents were utterly heartbroken when he died.

I couldn't damage their pride in him by revealing that he had been a lying cheat. They show Holly pictures of him and tell her how he was awarded a medal for his bravery. For her sake, as well as Peter and Alison's, I will always keep up the pretence that Jack was the perfect husband.'

She dropped her gaze from his and stared down at the lawn. 'And it was safer to allow you to believe I still loved him,' she admitted in a low tone. 'You are the ultimate playboy, and I was determined to keep my distance from you.'

'I noticed,' Rocco said dryly. 'I have never met a woman as prickly and distrustful of my motives. And I admit you had good reason. My sole aim *was* to get you into bed. I was certain I did not want commitment—why would I when I had seen the fall-out of bitterness and acrimony in my parents' failed marriage and those of several of my friends? Sex was a game, and mistresses are not hard to come by when you are wealthy,' he drawled sardonically.

'I was never interested in your money,' Emma said quickly, hating the idea that he lumped her in with women like mercenary Shayna Manzzini.

He laughed softly, and lifted his hand to brush her hair back from her cheek. 'I know that. You are different than any woman I've ever met. Compassionate, caring, fiercely independent and totally unaware of your sensual allure. Is it any wonder that I was out of my head with wanting you, *mia bella*?'

Emma's breath hitched in her throat as he traced his thumb over her lips, and her heart jerked painfully beneath her ribs when he lowered his head so close to hers that his words whispered across her skin.

'I still want you, Emma. I can't eat or sleep or function without you. Come back to Portofino with me? I know you want me,' he said raggedly. 'I can see the desire in your eyes, and your body tells its own message.' He curled his hand around her breast and gave a satisfied smile when her nipple instantly hardened beneath his touch. 'I can make you happy, and Holly will love living at the Villa Lucia.'

Fierce longing burned inside her so strong that her body shook with the force of it.

'I can't.' She jerked away from him, fighting the temptation to succumb to his velvet-soft voice.

It would be so easy to agree. She knew he would sweep her into his arms, where she longed to be, and kiss her with his sensual mastery until she was trembling with a desperate need that only he could assuage. But there was Holly. She knew it wouldn't be right for the little girl, and her daughter's needs would always come first.

Rocco paled beneath his tan. He had not anticipated her rejection, and he felt as though he was teetering on the edge of an abyss of eternal blackness. 'Why not?' he demanded savagely. 'You've told me you're not still in love with Jack. Is there someone else?'

'No.' There could never be anyone but him. 'But I can't be your mistress, Rocco. It wouldn't be fair to Holly. She needs long-term security, and I couldn't bear for her to regard your villa as her home only to be uprooted and upset when you grow bored with our affair—as you undoubtedly would,' she said painfully. It had been hard enough to walk away from him after a few weeks; it would destroy her to be forced to leave him some months in the future, when he no longer wanted her. 'You said yourself you don't want commitment.'

'I didn't think I did.' He caught hold of her shoulders and hauled her against him, holding her so tight that the air was forced from her lungs. 'Haven't you been listening to a word I've said?' He stared down at her, and Emma's heart turned over at the fierce emotion blazing in his eyes, the betraying, shocking glint of moisture that revealed his vulnerability.

'I love you, Emma,' he said in a driven tone. 'I don't want you to be my mistress—I want you to be my wife.'

She opened her mouth, but no words emerged, and he took advantage of her parted lips by covering them with his own and sliding his tongue between them in a kiss of hungry passion and fierce possession.

Emma clung to him and kissed him back, unable to hold back her frantic response or deny the emotions storming through her.

'Tesoro,' he said in a shaken voice when at last he lifted his head. '*Ti amo.* I will love you always and for ever. I never thought I would feel like this,' he admitted. 'I think I fell in love with you the first night we met—when I realised you were wearing that ghastly woollen hat Cordelia had knitted for you because you didn't want to hurt her feelings. I know you've been hurt, but I'm not Jack, and I swear I will love you and be faithful to you until the day I die.'

Icy fingers of fear gripped his heart when he saw the uncertainty in her eyes, and he crushed her tighter to him—as if by sheer force of will he could make her love him. 'I know I can be a good husband, and a good father to Holly. I can teach you to love me. Just give me a chance,' he pleaded.

Emma pressed her fingers to his lips, her heart aching as she realised that he wasn't sure of her. 'Of course I love you,' she assured him softly. 'I couldn't have made love with you if I hadn't felt it in my heart. But your grandfather told me he will only hand over control of Eleganza to you if you marry an Italian bride. I know how much the company means to you…'

'It means nothing compared to my love for you,' Rocco

told her passionately, relief seeping through his veins that she was truly his. 'You are my world, Emma. Silvio can do what he likes with his company—although I suspect he will be very happy with my choice of bride. Especially as he will gain a gorgeous little great-granddaughter, and hopefully more great-grandchildren very soon.'

As his words sank in, joy unfurled in Emma's heart. She felt as though she had travelled on a long journey but now she was home, safe and secure in the arms of the man who was the love of her life.

'How soon were you thinking of giving Silvio great-grandchildren?' she murmured as Rocco lifted her and strode into the cottage.

His tiger's eyes gleamed with a feral hunger as he headed purposefully up the stairs to her bedroom. 'I think we should practise making babies right away, *cara*.' His heart thudded when he stared down into her smoke-soft grey eyes. 'I love you,' he said raggedly.

Emma smiled. 'And I love you. And, as we seem to agree on everything, it's going to be a perfect marriage.'

* * * * *

The Italian's Blushing Gardener

CHRISTINA HOLLIS

Christina Hollis was born in Somerset and now lives in the idyllic Wye valley. She was born reading and her childhood dream was to become a writer. This was realised when she became a successful journalist and lecturer in organic horticulture. Then she gave it all up to become a full-time mother of two and run half an acre of productive country garden.

Writing Mills & Boon® romances is another ambition realised. It fills most of her time, in between complicated rural school runs. The rest of her life is divided between garden and kitchen, either growing fruit and vegetables or cooking with them. Her daughter's cat always closely supervises everything she does around the home, from typing to picking strawberries!

CHAPTER ONE

SHADOWS rippled over Kira's slight form. She stood on the lookout of ancient pine trees guarding the Bella Terra estate, all her attention focused on the other side of the valley. Far away across the rolling grassland a white streak scarred the distant hillside. It was a road, and Kira was waiting. She was watching for the telltale cloud of white Tuscan dust that meant the end of her solitude.

Her little patch of paradise was about to be changed for ever. The land surrounding her house was up for sale. And according to Bella Terra's estate agent, the most fantastic man in the world was interested in buying it.

Kira could not have cared less. She had moved to Italy to get away from all that. Everything she had heard so far about Signor Stefano Albani hadn't done anything to improve her general opinion of men. He had been due to view the Bella Terra villa and estate earlier that afternoon, but he hadn't shown up. The female estate agent had called in at Kira's cottage, looking for him. She had been breathless with excitement and full of this charming billionaire's flirty telephone manner, but Kira wasn't impressed. She guessed this rogue Albani was probably more interested in women than he was in buying a big country estate.

As time went on and he still never showed up, the estate agent's interest dwindled. She began to worry about missing her next appointment. Eventually, feeling sorry for her, Kira offered to take care of the villa's keys and details. Dealing with strangers tied her in knots, but it didn't look as though Signor Albani was coming, and her offer was only a ploy anyway. All she really wanted to do was get rid of the estate agent.

It worked. Her unwelcome visitor dashed off, leaving Kira alone once more.

That was exactly how she liked it.

And there were much worse ways of spending an afternoon than enjoying this view of the Bella Terra estate.

The scorching sun eventually slid behind a bank of clouds, heading for the wooded ridge on the western side of the valley. Kira began to relax. She felt more and more confident that Stefano the Seducer wouldn't come. That was a relief to her, in more ways than one. The fewer people who viewed the estate, the longer it would take to sell. Kira didn't care if the rambling old place stayed empty forever. Her small home was nicely isolated from the villa, although each building could see the other in the distance.

Bella Terra's last owner, Sir Ivan, had been as reserved as Kira. They had waved to each other across the valley every day, and she had looked after the estate gardens, but that was pretty much the extent of their friendship. It had suited them both, but now Sir Ivan was dead. It was odd: in the two years since she had bought La Ritirata Kira had rarely spoken to the man except on business, yet she missed him. And now she was faced with the unknown. Whoever bought La Bella Terra was unlikely to be as peaceful and unobtrusive as the old man. She hated that thought.

She wondered if the future would seem quite so threatening if she had someone to talk to. A letter had arrived from England the previous day. Kira knew she should have sent a curt reply by return, but couldn't bear to do it. The envelope lay where she had dropped it, unopened, on the kitchen table. She would have to release its tentacles of emotional blackmail sooner or later, but not just now.

With an effort, she tried to concentrate on the beautiful scene in front of her. The valley was a patchwork of flowery grassland and ancient woods. She strolled as far as the cool green shadows of the sweet chestnut wood. Thunderheads were forming over the hills. There would be a storm soon. That would cool everything down. She smiled. Rain would transform the single-track road leading to the Bella Terra villa into a quagmire. If Signor Albani was still on his way, that was almost guaranteed to put him off. The prospect of fighting a prestige sports car upstream like a salmon was sure to turn him back. Her little retreat would be safe for a while longer.

As Kira counted her blessings, she became aware of a subtle change in the air. All the birds fell silent. She looked around. The landscape was poised, waiting for something to happen. Then she felt a vibration. Faint at first, it rose from the ground beneath her feet like an earthquake. She started forward as a roe deer bounced through the trees behind her. With one bound it crossed the track and was gone. Still the shuddering increased, rising up through Kira's ribcage until she looked around for somewhere to run. Instinctively, she headed out into the summer-rich pasture. The trees surrounding it had been still in the oppressive heat. Now they swayed and bucked like a wild green sea. It wasn't an earthquake, but something even more alarming. A helicopter was sweeping in from above, and tearing Kira's peaceful valley apart.

'I'm going off-message for a couple of hours,' Stefano Albani announced into his hands-free phone. 'I've got the Milan project back on track, and if Murray's people ring, tell them the publishing tie-in is off, unless they come up with something that can really appeal to me.'

Closing the call, he sat back in his seat. There was no question of relaxing; his spine remained rigid. Flying a helicopter took a lot of concentration. He never inspected any property from ground level without making a low-level pass over it first. The Bella Terra estate looked perfect, and its aspect was a dream. Cool, shady woodlands offered sanctuary from the roasting heat of summer, while beautifully planned terraces around the house offered plenty of space for entertaining in the golden sunshine. Talking of which…

A movement at the edge of the trees caught his eye. It was a girl. She was flinging her arms about, and waving papers at him. Stefano's sensuous mouth lifted in a half-smile. He had only spoken to the estate agent by phone so far, but from where he was sitting she looked as good as she sounded.

His dark features eased as he thought back to that long, teasing telephone conversation with her. Taking up where they had left off would be a good way to wind down after a high-pressure day.

He gazed down on the pretty little ragazza, and gave her a wave. As he did so, a corresponding ripple of relief passed up his arm and across his shoulders. His muscles were tense from working for far too long without a break. What he needed was distraction. A few hours in a place like this would take his mind off all those boardroom battles and investment decisions. The company of a pretty girl was a bonus he had half forgotten in all the chaos.

Stefano smiled as he set his helicopter down on the far side of the house. His few precious hours of freedom were off to a great start.

Kira was in no mood for games. Bella Terra was supposed to be a private valley, and the helicopter's racket was shockingly intrusive among all that usually undisturbed beauty. Worst of all, it felt like an omen of things to come.

'I've seen pheasants fly higher than that!' she shouted after the helicopter as it swept overhead. Her voice was totally swamped by the thundering rumble of its rotors, but it hardly mattered. Simply putting her anger into words made Kira feel better.

As she watched, hands on hips, the machine swung its nose around and dropped down behind the beautiful old villa. If the pilot's antics hadn't made her so annoyed, she might have been nervous. Instead, she saw it as a chance to catch up with him. She sprinted along the track, heading for an overgrown entrance to the Bella Terra gardens. Squeezing in through a gap in its rusty ironwork, she marched up the path.

She found the helicopter parked as neatly as a saloon car, very close to the main house. It was deserted, and silent apart from the click of cooling metalwork. There was absolutely no sign of the pilot. Confused, she circled the villa buildings in the sultry heat. From every side, ornamental broom and gorse set off their exploding pods like gunfire. Anyone with any sense would have headed straight for shade. She made for the yew walk. Reaching the north end, she glimpsed a tall, masculine figure disappearing through a gap in the hedge that led into the fountain garden. She was about to call out to him, but something about the decided, athletic grace of his movements made her pause, and when she came out into the sunlit square of the fountain garden, it was empty.

Turning her head, she strained to hear any signs of life. Only the quiet rustle of air through pine trees and the constant sniper fire of genista seeds disturbed the peace. Then, as she listened, she heard something that might have been footsteps. It was only one tiny sound, and all the interconnecting yew hedges made it difficult to decide from which direction it came. She looked around, but there was no one.

Then two strong hands slipped around her waist, and in one smooth movement she was drawn into an inescapable embrace.

'We meet at last, Miss Barrett!' a deep, delicious Italian voice purred in perfect English. 'I have been searching for you. I felt sure you would be waiting for me at Bella Terra's front door!'

His teasing words reverberated into the curve of Kira's neck. She froze, shrinking from the whisper of warm breath against her skin. The movement only drew her closer to his hard, masculine body. He was holding her so perfectly, she could barely breathe.

'When we spoke on the phone you said you were looking forward to meeting me. Remind me—exactly where did you want to have dinner tonight?' There was a soft, low chuckle in his voice as he murmured, pulling her around to ravish her with a kiss.

Before he could make contact, Kira burst from his grasp with reflexes that astonished them both.

'I'm not Amanda Barrett, and I'm not very happy!' she confronted him, breathing fast. 'Please keep your hands to yourself!'

The visitor recoiled instantly, but he was far too professional to give his horror free rein. Instead, his features became a mask. With a slow, careful dip of his head, he addressed her gravely. 'Scusi, signora.'

Glaring, Kira took two steps backwards. His assault had been so swift and sure she hardly expected him to stop so suddenly. She had no idea what to do next. If this was Signor Stefano Albani, billionaire, then he was nothing like any of the rich men she had worked with in the past. They were predictable, humourless and would never have dreamed of such a stunt. In contrast, Stefano Albani looked ready for anything. He was fit and he was handsome in a tense, distracted way. Standing straight and tall before her, he seemed quite unfazed by her rebuff. He brushed his shirtsleeves down over his bare brown arms and fastened his unbuttoned cuffs.

'I mistook you for someone else, I'm sorry. It was arranged that I should meet the property agent here. Do you know where I can find her?' he asked in his softly accented English.

'She's probably at home by now, having dealt with

at least two more clients in the time it took you to get here,' Kira snapped, still unsettled by the unexpected embrace. Stefano's face remained expressionless, but his eyes glittered, and suddenly Kira regretted her rudeness to this rather formidable man. Then his mouth curled with sudden humour.

'Dio—it's been a long time since anyone spoke to me like that!'

In that puzzled instant, years fell away from his face and he looked much younger. Kira was momentarily thrown off balance. His beautiful eyes and quizzical expression were almost too much to bear. She had to swallow hard before she spoke again, but she'd be damned if she'd let him walk all over her just because she couldn't stop staring at his mouth.

'I'm sorry, *signore*, but you have turned up over three hours late—without any apology—and flown ridiculously low over this valley, terrifying the wildlife and ruining a beautiful evening,' she said firmly, quailing slightly inside as his expression turned stormy. Someone like this didn't hear enough straight talking in his working life. He had just said as much himself.

'If I have caused offence, I apologise,' he said, slightly stiffly. 'Not having the neighbours flying in overhead all the time is a big selling point as far as I am concerned.' Then his features softened. 'I am Stefano Albani, by the way. I'm interested in buying the Bella Terra estate. That's why I assumed you were Miss Barrett, the agent. I thought you were welcoming me with cries of delight!' he joked, searching her expression as he spoke, his mocking eyes somehow piercing her outraged manner and making it irritatingly difficult to stay angry.

'Well, I wasn't,' Kira said, biting back everything

else she felt like telling him. She had to tread carefully. Stefano Albani might have arrived late and lascivious, but there was, unfortunately, a chance he would become her new neighbour and there was no point in making it more difficult than it had to be.

Stefano compressed his lips at the note of accusation in her voice.

He has a really beautiful mouth, Kira caught herself thinking, before his frown dragged her attention back to the Mediterranean depths of his eyes.

'A delay put me behind schedule, and I wanted to get here as fast as I could. That meant flying. Besides, the disturbance was over in a few seconds. I'm sure the valley has recovered from much worse over the years. People always try to imprint themselves on the countryside. The land shakes them all off, sooner or later.'

Kira's alarm must have shown in her face. He quickly softened his tone and added, 'You have my promise that it won't happen again. There will be no low flying in this valley after I move in.'

His words were quite definite, but the essence of a smile still hovered around his lips. When he looked like that, it was impossible for Kira to look away. There was plenty to see. With the air cleared between them, his eyes were now the untroubled blue of a perfect Italian sky. His dark hair was a riot of soft curls, short enough to be neat but long enough to move slightly in the warm air rising from the parched earth at their feet. He was undoubtedly powerful, but it was the strength of steel hawsers rather than unsophisticated animal bulk. Unlike the millionaires Kira had worked for in the past, this man looked as though he used his body as hard as his brain. She could never imagine him parked behind a computer console. She wished she had paid more attention when Amanda Barrett had been rabbiting on about the wonderful Signor Albani. At the time, Kira had shut her ears. Thank goodness the estate agent wasn't here now. She would have fallen for this man like a lead weight.

It's all too easy to see how women must do that, Kira thought darkly. With bewildered fascination, she wondered why they didn't see him for what he must really be—a rich pleasure seeker with no thought for anyone but himself. She could tell exactly the sort of man he was, simply by the way he brimmed with self-assurance. Kira watched him looking up at the grand old building as though he already owned it. She tried to ignore a shiver of apprehension, and told herself looks meant nothing. He hadn't stepped over the villa's threshold yet. How could he be so sure this was the place for him?

'We'll see—if you move in,' she replied grimly, wondering if she held any influence over his purchase. Maybe it's time to forget what I think about Stefano Albani, and start wondering what he might be thinking about me, Kira told herself. Stefano seemed like the kind of man who might actually thrive on opposition rather than avoid it. She decided to try and muffle her objections, for as long as it took this man to make up his mind about the villa and estate. She told herself sharply that this had nothing to do with not wanting to appear like an angry shrew in front of such a gorgeous man.

'The fact is, *signore*, I was only waiting here with the estate details and keys, because I was confident you would never turn up,' she told him. 'I had my whole evening planned until you dropped out of the sky—'

'And wrecked all your plans?'

Kira's scowl returned. 'I was going to say you gave me the fright of my life and apologise for the way I reacted,' she replied frostily.

Stefano said nothing. Instead, he reached out his hand. Kira stared woodenly at his smooth, pale palm until she realised what he was after. She pushed the property details at him. They had been turned around in her nervous hands for too long, and he had to smooth out some creases before he could begin to read.

'What did I stop you doing this evening?' he asked after a few moments' study. His eyes never left the printed page, so the question caught Kira off guard.

'Nothing, as usual,' she replied instantly, before remembering what she had said to him in the heat of her anger.

He looked up from the brochure with a smile that glittered like pearl against his golden skin.

'In that case, why don't you show me around this old place?'

The offer was so unexpected, Kira replied without thinking. 'Oh, I'd love to!'

She regretted the words in an instant. This wasn't her job. She had no business here. She had simply offered to hand over the details and keys, before disappearing. That was the deal—nothing more. She tried to backtrack. 'Yes, I'd love to, Signor Albani, although I'm only a neighbour.' She looked up at the lovely old house and heaved a long, heartfelt sigh. 'I don't really know anything about the place. I've only seen inside one or two rooms before—'

'"It has been owned by an Englishman for many years,"' Stefano read aloud from the notes. 'Do you know him?'

'Sir Ivan was my client. I was his landscape consultant. That's all,' she added hurriedly.

'I suppose you two English people both "kept yourselves to yourselves," in that well-worn phrase?' Stefano's wry smile made Kira feel defensive. However right he may be, she didn't like that he assumed so much about her. Piqued, she ignored her impulse to refuse him.

'I'll gladly show you around outside, *signore*. There's no one who knows more than I do about the estate and the gardens here, but you'll be better off with the brochure when it comes to viewing the house.'

'You're a landscape consultant, you say?' His smile dimmed as he looked her over with a different intensity. Kira reddened as he studied her working clothes of dusty jeans and simple white shirt. Seeing her reaction, his generous mouth lifted in a grin.

'But why are we wasting time out here talking, when we could be looking around this beautiful house? If I know English women—which I do,' he said in a way that needed absolutely no explanation, 'I'm sure you are as keen as I am to get inside the villa and have a good look around. So come with me now. What do you say?'

There was nothing Kira could say. He was talking about a tour of the house she had spent two years dreaming and wondering about. She had been trying to pluck up the nerve to have a peek inside before he arrived, but couldn't bring herself to do it. Now he was inviting her in....

Without waiting for her answer, he started forward. Holding the Bella Terra brochure in one hand, he touched her waist lightly with the other. Kira found herself drawn gently towards the big old building. His pat of encouragement was enjoyable in a way she did not want it to be. Putting on a little more speed, she moved fractionally ahead of his hand. She reached the steps of the house just in front of him. Then there was a pause as Stefano used the great iron key to unlock the door. Standing aside, he let Kira enter first. Still she hesitated. She was desperate to poke around the villa, but on her own. Quite apart from him possibly becoming the villa's next owner, exploring such a beautiful place with Stefano Albani felt somehow much too intimate.

Stefano had none of her misgivings. His hand connected with her waist again, gently urging her to enter. A little sigh left Kira's lips. It felt dangerously like the sound of her scorn softening around the edges. He stayed where he was, but inclined his head politely. 'After you. I need to see everything, so I'm afraid this may take some time.'

He spoke softly, but with absolute authority. He was acting as though the house already belonged to him. Kira coloured guiltily. She had enjoyed the run of this valley for so long she considered it to be her own private haven. Now she finally had a chance to look around the villa at its heart, but the company of such a man added an extra frisson of excitement. If she was honest, it was the surprising intensity of this feeling which was making her hesitate.

What if she couldn't think of enough to say? She had got out of the habit of small talk. Flustered, she looked around wildly for help. Why, she had no idea. There was no one for miles. She had never felt so alone. This man scrambled her brains. He had totally blown away all her common sense. She looked into his eyes and saw things she recognised from the reflection in her bathroom mirror each morning. His blue eyes spoke words that never reached his lips, and she knew that look. Aside from his dangerously smooth assurance, there might be a deeper, darker reason to beware. He might have secrets like hers hiding beneath that sophisticated surface. Unaccountably, she felt the need to peel away his seductive veneer and find out the truth beneath the image.

The weight of Stefano's hand began to rest against her a little more noticeably. At first it had been the merest brush of his fingertips. Now his palm settled gently in the hollow of her back, like falling snow.

With terrifying clarity, Kira imagined it sliding around to encircle her waist again. It felt so good, it had to be wrong. Swallowing hard, she suppressed every wild, unfamiliar instinct and announced quietly, 'Please don't touch me, Signor Albani.'

His hand fell away. He stepped back, surprised.

'Are you sure?'

'I'm positive.'

He stared at her, trying to puzzle out her expression. Kira willed herself to return his look blandly.

'That's interesting,' he murmured at length.

After studying her face, he let his gaze drift at leisure over her body.

'First you answer me back, but now you're as nervous as a kitten,' he mused, his eyes hooded with thought. 'I came to look at property. It seems that's not the only thing around here that might be worth investigating.'

CHAPTER TWO

'DON'T flatter me, or yourself,' Kira muttered, beginning to fuss with the belt of her jeans. It felt wrong to be exploring such a place in her dusty work clothes; somehow she felt that the villa demanded a sense of occasion. He was standing so close to her that the temptation to study him was next to irresistible. Instead, she concentrated on brushing herself down, removing any stray grass seeds before she crossed the threshold of the grand house.

'Don't worry. It's a villa, not the Vatican!' He chuckled, again exhibiting a disquieting ability to read her thoughts. 'You look fine. You're one of those women who look good in anything.'

Kira glanced up sharply at his unexpected compliment. He laughed as their gazes connected. She couldn't stop staring at him, and when he caught her eye it sent a confusion of signals through her body.

'You're right. I'm only looking around a house, that's all. It's nothing more than that,' Kira murmured, trying to stake her claim to innocence. This Stefano Albani was strangely magnetic. Leaving him to investigate on his own might mean she never saw him again. If she followed him, she would delay the moment of parting and get to view the property of her dreams, too.

'So if you are ready, *signore*, shall we make a start?' she added with a bit more confidence.

He laughed again. 'Suddenly so businesslike! I'm making the effort to leave the world behind for a while. Why don't you do the same? I suspect it would do us both good to live a little, for once.' His gaze was uncomfortably direct and Kira shifted under it. 'In fact, it occurs to me that I don't even know your name. So, as we begin, why don't we start with some simple introductions? You know who I am, but who are you?'

Kira had often wondered that herself. 'That isn't important, Signor Albani.' She shook her shoulders irritably.

'Of course it is!'

'No, really. I'm nobody.'

'Don't be ridiculous.' His smile showed signs of fading. 'Everybody is somebody. Your name is your own. You can give it to me.'

Kira stopped. Ignoring this danger sign, Stefano didn't.

'Go on. You know you want to, and it won't hurt!' he teased her gently.

His question revived all Kira's pain. The isolation of Bella Terra meant she didn't have to introduce herself more than once or twice a year. That suited her. Every time she spoke her name, it reminded her of the shame she had left behind in England.

'It's Kira Banks,' she muttered. Head down, she tried to cross the threshold but Stefano blocked her retreat.

'You don't sound very happy about it.' His air

was light, but she saw interrogation in his relentless blue gaze.

Blast him, what was wrong with the man? Kira was used to people backing off, becoming bored when met with her reluctance to talk about herself. In her experience most people preferred to be talking about themselves in any case. It appeared Signor Albani was used to having his questions answered.

'Why is that?' Stefano persisted quietly in the face of her continued silence.

Kira wanted to stare him out but her features lost the struggle. They were moving of their own accord. Her lids would not obey. She lowered her lashes, unable to struggle against the depth of his gaze. Making up some excuse for any other person would have been easy enough, but Stefano Albani was looking down at her with a fiction-piercing stare that demanded nothing less than the truth.

She gritted her teeth and muttered, 'I came here to escape. I wanted to live in a place where no one knows my name.'

He drew back from her a little.

'Okay, I'll let it go at that…' he relented, although his face told a different story. 'For now…' he added with a smile.

Kira mastered her features and managed a bland smile.

'Don't say I have stumbled on a master criminal, living in her bolthole in Italy?'

He was teasing her again. She managed to lift her eyes to challenge him, but knew she couldn't afford to rise to his bait. Her pain hovered too close to the surface.

She didn't need him to aggravate her injuries. There were other people only too willing to do that.

'Why I'm here is nobody's business but my own.' She tried not to snap, but it was difficult. Only his steady gaze softened her reaction. 'In any case, the reasons would take far too long to explain, Signor Albani. Some things are best kept private. Why don't we stop wasting time, and start looking around this lovely house?'

Purposely keeping her voice casual, she jerked herself out of his grasp. She could not escape his expression so easily. It was like a caress. It took all her determination to break eye contact with him. She managed it by concentrating on the breathtaking photograph on the cover of the property brochure in his hand. It was the only sure way she could distract herself from the delicious dangers of this man. Stefano gestured for her to walk across the entrance hall first. It was large, cool, and it echoed with his slow footsteps as he followed her across the cracked marble tiles.

Kira took a good look around. She had only ever entered the villa by one of the back doors. This was her first time in the grand public areas, and she didn't want to miss a thing. While she was daydreaming, Stefano strolled past her. Pulling a pearl-handled penknife from his pocket, he pushed the blade against the woodwork of the nearest door. Kira gazed in wonder at the ornate plasterwork, and the beautifully worked banisters on the great double staircase, but he was busy with more practical things. He worked his way methodically around the entrance hall, testing, checking and inspecting.

'This is the most beautiful house I have ever seen,' she said wistfully. Stefano was not so easily impressed.

'My town house in Florence is more practical, and in

better condition,' he observed, before flashing another brilliant smile at her. 'But you're right. The setting and space here can't be beaten.'

Kira nodded. 'It's a lovely house. Oh, yes, there are bound to be things about it that must be altered, updated or replaced. It's old. But I'd like nothing better than the chance to give it some homely touches. Couldn't you just imagine the scene in December, with a fifteen-foot Christmas tree standing in that bay between the staircases?'

Stefano looked over to where she pointed. He studied the space, tipping his head first one way, and then the other.

'Yes, the proportions would be exactly right. That's important with these old houses. Everything must be in scale,' he said firmly.

Kira's heart gave a strange flutter. She had been half joking, hardly expecting the big-shot billionaire to consider Christmas trees with such seriousness. That might be a glimmer of hope. Even if he might fill the place with rowdy celebrity friends, he clearly had an eye for the important things in life.

'A tree like that in a place like this will need to hit exactly the right note. When I host my first Christmas party I want everyone to be speechless with delight—because I'm all for a quiet life.' He smiled, and gave her a look of undisguised interest. 'So that's the festive season sorted out. What do you suggest for my house-warming extravaganza?'

It was a totally unexpected question. Kira looked to see if he was trying to wind her up. He gazed back innocently. Smiling in spite of herself, she decided to answer in the same spirit.

'Actually, I'm the last person you should ask about entertaining. I'm a garden designer. I prefer to work with plants rather than people.'

'What is a Christmas tree, if it isn't a plant?' He shrugged. 'And I shall need all sorts of those. When we become neighbours I shall want your advice, sooner or later.'

Kira shot him a look of pure disbelief. 'You can have exactly what you like, *signore*. You don't need anyone to advise you, let alone me!'

'There are times when everyone can do with a little help,' he slung straight back at her. 'By employing skilled people, I can spend my time and effort on all the things I really want to do. In this instance, it gives me plenty of time to plan for Christmas.' He stopped inspecting the paintwork and turned an acute gaze on her. 'I know— you must have a good eye for colour. How would you like the task of co-ordinating all the decorations?'

Kira nearly laughed out loud. It felt truly bizarre to be standing in a vast Tuscan villa in the heat of summer, talking about something that was months away.

'Why on earth would you want someone else to decorate your Christmas tree? It's something I've looked forward to every year for as long as I can remember! It's the chance to be a child again, I suppose, without all the pressure.'

It was Stefano's turn to look askance. 'I know all about pressure.' His voice darkened with meaning.

Kira groaned under the weight of memory. 'That's why it's so good to get away from it all, to a place like this. I can enjoy Christmas my way. No rehearsing recitals in Gloucester cathedral, dashing between carol services and amateur dramatics, torturing tons of holly, ivy and mistletoe into wreaths and swags. When I was a child, it was never ending.'

He pursed his lips, and then said drily, 'It's a wonder you had any time to yourself.'

'I didn't. That's the penalty you pay for being a trophy child, isn't it?'

'I wouldn't know. I missed out on all that. I skipped it, and went straight from sleeping in a box under the table, to earning a living.'

'Gosh, you must have had a deprived childhood!' she joked.

He stared at her, unimpressed. His eyes were suddenly chill with all the hidden feelings she recognised from her own reflection. She stopped laughing.

'Yes. Yes, I did.' He grazed his lower lip with his teeth for a moment, and then added, 'But that's behind me now. The future is all that matters.'

There was iron-hard determination in his voice. His eyes were everywhere. She wondered what havoc he would wreak on this beautiful old house when he took possession of it. The thought worried her. A few moments ago, she had been annoyed by the way he talked as though the villa was already his. Now she was thinking about it in the same way. He was checking every inch of the building like the rightful owner. If ever a man was made to lord it over the Bella Terra valley, it's Stefano Albani, she thought, with a shiver of apprehension.

'You're cold. Why don't you step outside into the evening sun and warm up?' he murmured.

His words surprised her. She thought all his attention was riveted on the villa's sales brochure, and hadn't expected him to notice.

'No, I'm fine,' she said quickly, unwilling to miss this

chance to look over the grand villa she gazed at every day from her favourite viewpoint on the other side of the valley.

His eyes glittered with sudden fire. 'As long as you're sure.'

Kira began to feel uneasy. Every time he looked at her, he smiled as he spoke. It was an unusual expression, caressing the most secret parts of her. As she tried not to shrink beneath his gaze, she felt the peaks of her nipples push against the smooth profile of her thin shirt. They stiffened still more to know he was looking at her. It was no longer the chill of the cool marble hall affecting her body. He must have realised it, too, but looked away sharply as obvious appreciation flared for a moment in his eyes.

Kira didn't know what to do. Putting her head down, she scuttled off towards the nearest door.

'Let's see what's through here, shall we?' she said, bursting into the first room beyond the entrance hall. Within half a step she stopped. It was the reception room that time forgot. Sunlight streamed through tall, graceful windows but its beams danced with dust motes. The design of the room was in a typically grand Italian style, although its furnishings wouldn't have been out of place in an English country house.

'Oh, my goodness!' Kira exclaimed. 'A little bit of England overseas!'

Following close behind her, Stefano clicked his tongue when he saw her shudder.

'My stepparents have spent a lifetime collecting stuff like this. Cane-back chairs, chintz upholstery and Goss china. Sir Ivan must have shipped everything over here from England. Why on earth would you move to Italy, then recreate England in your new home?'

'I don't know.' Stefano was equally put out at the sight. His mouth was a stern line of disapproval. 'Some foreigners buy up these properties claiming to love Italy. In reality, Toscana is nothing more to them than England with better weather. They are more interested in worshipping their own land from a safe distance.'

'I'm not. I love it here,' Kira told him. 'I couldn't wait to leave England behind, decorations and all…' She paused, wondering whether to push her luck, and decided she had nothing to lose.

'If we're going to be neighbours, I'd feel happier if I knew you were going to treat this old place well,' she went on. 'It would be such a shame to see it spoilt.'

'It won't matter to you for a few weeks a year, surely?' He shrugged.

Kira was puzzled. 'So you're going to be away a lot?'

'No, but you'll be leaving with the summer, won't you?'

Kira coloured up angrily. 'Why should I?'

'So you won't be flitting between here and your home in England?' He looked surprised.

She shook her head defiantly. 'No! I thought I'd made it clear—I don't have a home in England any more. In any case, I couldn't bear to leave at the end of summer, as the holiday-home owners do. How could I abandon my home here? The Bella Terra valley is everything I want—peace and beauty.'

Stefano's dark brows lightened a little. 'I assume that means you could find no peace in England, so you brought your beauty here?'

His voice was low and melodious but his eyes shone with mischief. Drawn to look straight at him again, Kira could not help lifting her lips in the ghost of a smile, but she said nothing.

'I don't know of many people who would willingly hide away in such an isolated spot,' he murmured. 'You're not afraid to stand up for yourself, you work for your living and you love this place as much as I intend to. How could anything make such a forthright, independent woman leave England under a cloud?'

Kira lifted one hand and began to fiddle with a skein of her dark auburn hair.

'It was a combination of things,' she said, hoping to stop him asking any more awkward questions.

He lifted his brows still higher, encouraging her to unburden herself. She shifted from foot to foot. Her fingers moved from her hair to toy with the thin gold chain around her neck. Stefano watched her. He seemed genuinely interested, and ready to listen. Suddenly she was tired of bottling everything up, and keeping herself to herself. She wanted to talk. She needed someone who might sympathise, or at least answer back. It hardly mattered about the words. She had never seen Stefano Albani before today, and might never see him again. He had already proved himself to be sympathetic. If she explained the whole miserable business to him, as an impartial third party, it might make her feel better.

It was on the tip of her tongue to tell him the whole sorry story. She pushed the guilty words against her teeth, trying to force them out. It was no good. She had kept silent for so long, she didn't know where to begin. Finally, she shook her head.

'It's nothing.'

He considered her gravely. 'I think it is. Something is obviously weighing heavily on your mind.'

He took a step towards her. Kira knew he moved almost silently, but the brush of his leather-soled shoes sounded loud in the peace of the reception room. She stared at the floor. She winced when his feet appeared in her field of view, but it was still a shock to feel the gentle touch of his hand on her shoulder.

'There's no need to jump. I'm only offering a little support,' he said.

'I don't need it,' she said staunchly, but he took no notice and never moved. His touch was warm, reassuring...seductive. In spite of herself, Kira relished the feeling. Then he spoiled the effect. His touch vibrated slightly. She looked up, and saw laughter in his eyes.

'One day, I would really enjoy the chance to discuss sins with you, Miss Kira Banks. Whatever you may have done, I'm sure I can top it!'

With a sharp twist of her head, Kira looked away. She could not bear to let him see her misery. Squeezing her lids tightly closed, she battled to stop the tears falling. She was so lost in her own despair she was completely unprepared for what happened next. Stefano closed the gap between them. His arms glided around her. She was drawn into his body again, and it felt so natural she let it happen without a word. For a few heart-stopping seconds she leaned against him. The sensation of his shirt pressed against her cheek and the enveloping male fragrance of him closed her eyes.

'Is there anything I can do?' His voice echoed around the unloved caverns of the villa.

Kira shook her head. 'I'd be grateful if you could

just drop the subject,' she managed, with a trace of steel showing through her muttered words.

'Okay.'

He took his time in releasing her. Kira normally disliked physical contact, but this was different. Stefano seemed to specialise in the sort of touch she might like to experience again.

He obviously wasn't going to give up on her. Kira sensed he couldn't resist a challenge any more than she could. However, she also knew her fragile self-esteem couldn't stand too many questions. Her reaction to unwarranted attention was usually to snap first, and apologise later. It appeared that this hadn't dissuaded Stefano in the slightest. The most disconcerting thing about that was how ready she'd been to indulge in the comfort he offered. *Pull yourself together!* she ordered herself silently. This man was clearly used to getting his own way and she was embarrassed how easily she had mistaken his charm for anything more permanent.

A hint of her old defiance returned. It allowed her to face him calmly, but it didn't stop her cheeks flaming red at how much she had nearly revealed. 'I'm sorry, *signore*. That was a momentary lapse, but now you'll see that I really don't want to talk about it. So I'd be grateful if we could leave it at that. Okay?' she finished crisply.

Stefano's gaze ebbed away from her as she spoke. He said nothing. Instead, he tightened his lips, and bobbed his head once in silent agreement. In the pause that followed, he glanced around. His eyes, like his body, were restless.

'Everyone has parts of their lives they're not proud

of,' he conceded. 'I can relate to that. So if we agree on a truce, can we continue with the tour?'

He had been almost teasing as he tried to extract her secret, but now he had retreated again behind that impenetrable mask. Kira felt a strange pang of loss. She wondered if he ever experienced the sort of social unease that tortured her. It seemed unlikely. What could ever make such a man feel inadequate?

She nodded and gave him a fleeting smile. 'Of course.'

What would it feel like to unburden herself to him? She was certain he would listen. Really listen, and not simply humour her because he wanted something. Life would take on a different dimension. It was something she had never bothered about before, but a few seconds in Stefano's arms had opened up a whole new world of possibilities for her. It almost tempted her out of her shell, but not quite. If he couldn't be on time for a business appointment, he was hardly likely to treat a casual acquaintance any better. She gave up on the idea. At least when she was on the defensive, she couldn't be hurt.

'If you are really interested in buying the Bella Terra estate, Signor Albani, you should be making the most of your visit. You mustn't stand around here with me.'

Without waiting for his reply, she turned her back on him and walked out of the sunlit room. The vast, gloomy hall beyond was supposed to cool her feelings.

'There's no need to run away from me, Kira.'

She stopped.

'You might be surprised,' she said finally.

Her darkening attitude didn't bother Stefano at all.

He stuck one hand casually in his pocket, and grinned at her.

'So what are you waiting for, then? Surprise me.'

His words made her uncertain. Until a short time ago, endless surprises—none of them good—had been the story of her life. Then she had escaped, and moved to Italy. For a couple of years she had experienced wonderful freedom. And now, with the loss of Sir Ivan, her foremost client, she was faced with the threat that happiness might soon be snatched away from her again. Unconsciously, her shoulders began to sag. Then she sensed his gaze was still on her. She looked up. He was still quizzing her with his eyes.

She shrugged. 'I'm afraid there's nothing more to me than you see here, *signore*.'

His face was totally impassive but he went on watching her as he said quietly, 'Then it's a good job I came here to see the Bella Terra estate, rather than anything else. My journey won't have been entirely wasted,' he announced before setting off across the hall again. 'Now, down to business. I want to look around this house. Would you like to come with me?'

CHAPTER THREE

TOGETHER, they began to walk.

'Why did Bella Terra's owner—the English gentleman—leave you alone here?' Stefano was looking at her in a new way. Kira preferred the old one, but still felt her cheeks flare.

'He died.'

For the first time, the smile left Stefano's eyes. 'Then I'm sorry.'

His sympathy looked genuine. Kira decided to give him the benefit of the doubt. 'He was eighty-five, *signore*, so it was hardly unexpected.'

He shrugged. 'But it must have been a shock, all the same. Deaths are always tragic.' His last words grated uncomfortably in the marble-lined hall. Kira recognised a dangerous flash in his eyes. She couldn't help noticing the length and thickness of his soot-dark lashes. *He* probably knows they are one of his best features, she warned herself abruptly. It can be the only reason he keeps looking at me like that.

'I'm sorry you lost a friend, Kira. I know what that is like.' His voice was distant and regretful. Something about the tone hinted that he had his own secrets.

He shook his head suddenly, as if discarding old

memories and turned to her, a playful smile again curving the corners of his mouth, taking refuge in flirtation.

'Kira—that is a beautiful name for a lovely woman. Coupled with your shining auburn hair, jade-green eyes and magnolia skin, what more could any man want?'

That broke the spell.

'Nothing—until his wife finds out.' Sidestepping him smartly, Kira headed back across the shady hall towards the only parts of the house she had seen before. That way she could put a little distance between them, without losing contact entirely. People made her uneasy, and that feeling fed on itself. Every time she began to warm towards Stefano, she felt bound to pull herself back into line. Yet increasingly, his every move held her hypnotised. When he started sweet talking her, it was too tender a reminder of how things could turn sour all too soon.

'I have no worries on that score, Kira. I don't have a wife.'

She heard his footsteps fall in beside her, but did not look at him.

'That's what they all say—to begin with, Signor Albani.'

'Call me Stefano.'

'They all say that, too.'

Walking over to the glazed door at the rear of the building, she unlocked it. When open, it would give him a view into the courtyard garden beyond. The fresh air and perfume of flowers always soothed her. Kira had designed this entire quadrangle garden. Originally, it was nothing more than cracked concrete and stagnant slime. Now it was one of her triumphs. Stefano was sure to be distracted once he got out there. She was looking forward to seeing what he thought of her work. It would be good to get an unbiased opinion. She knew that would help take her mind off her troubles, more than anything else.

It had always been a struggle to free the warped woodwork of the garden door. Although the interior paintwork was smart brown gloss, Kira knew it was a different story on the other side. The Tuscan sun had roasted away the shine within months. Now sunburnt flakes speckled the steps and sills. She tugged at the door, but it was only when Stefano came to help that it could finally be dragged back over the uneven tiles.

The large rectangular courtyard was paved with local cream-coloured stone. Around its boundary ran a deep, shady colonnade. In the centre was a raised fish pool. The air beyond the hall was still and hot. It hung over the threshold like a heavy curtain. Kira stepped outside, and Stefano followed her into the stormy sunshine. His hair glittered like jet as he looked around the garden. A large ceanothus had been planted in one corner. It hummed with bees, their sound joining the quiet splash of water trickling over wet stones. Ornamental ferns grew in the shadiest areas. The ones with smooth, satiny leaves enjoyed the damp soil and mosses in deepest shadow. Those with leaflets like lace rippled in the slightest breeze, patterning the old riven flagstones with light and shade. The coping stones around the pool were wide and warm. Stefano strolled over, and sat down. Leaning on one hand, he looked into the water.

'This is spectacular. Come and join me,' he drawled, his voice languorous in the heat.

Kira took her time. She didn't want to seem too eager;

being close to him seemed to rob her of her usual self-composure. She walked over and perched on the opposite side of the pool.

'I love this place already. What a beautiful oasis!' For the first time since she'd met him, Stefano seemed to relax completely, breathing in the fragrant air and gazing around with unaffected pleasure.

'Thank you. I wanted to give old Sir Ivan somewhere on the ground floor that he could enjoy, whatever the weather.'

'You are responsible for this?' His brows lifted appreciatively.

'Yes—and all the other recent work you'll see when you inspect the grounds. Sir Ivan saw one of my garden designs on display at the Chelsea Flower Show, several years ago. He commissioned me to create a roof garden for his town house in London. After that, I did more and more projects for him and his friends, before relocating here permanently two years ago.'

Stefano's beautiful mouth twitched in appreciation. 'So you're a self-made woman? Congratulations.'

'I'm only doing my job.' Kira shrugged.

'Don't be so modest! Word of mouth may have brought you a long way in business so far, but with the death of your friend Sir Ivan, you must have lost a major client. You'll need to find a replacement. Have you got anyone lined up?' he asked suddenly.

Kira shook her head. She had been trying not to think about that. She really hated having to publicise her business. The more people who contacted her because they had seen and enjoyed her work through their friends, the better.

'If I'm honest, all I enjoy is the work. Dealing with people is a nightmare I wish I could avoid for ever.'

Stefano cleared his throat. Kira wondered if he was as surprised as she was by how honest she was being with him. At least he liked her garden, which was a good sign. Standing, she brushed off her memories of working in this peaceful sanctuary. Once Stefano Albani came to live here, she might never see inside this place again. She ought to make the most of this tour.

It was a poignant moment. As Stefano stepped out of the stark sunlight and back into the shadows, Kira hesitated. The shade should have been a wonderful relief from the hot afternoon. Instead, she felt the chill of abandonment, and not for the first time. It was the story of her life. She had been given up as a lost cause by her stepparents. Then her place on the sidelines of their life became permanent when their unexpected natural child arrived. Now she was doing much the same to the garden she had cherished. In a few weeks or months, she would have to turn her back on this place and leave it in the hands of others. She shuddered.

Stefano noticed, and smiled at her in a way calculated to immediately warm her up.

'It sounds as though you will be my perfect neighbour.'

Kira shot him a look that said she didn't share his view.

'I promise the experience will be an unforgettable one,' he added quietly.

She ignored that, and told him the simple truth. 'I'm afraid anyone who buys this house automatically gets on the wrong side of me. Sir Ivan and I used to co-exist in this valley very well. I can't imagine anyone else being a better neighbour than he was.'

She thought it would be safer to warn Stefano what she was like, right from the beginning. Instead of sympathising, he laughed.

'I'll try,' he said mischievously. 'Let's hope I can play the part as well as you act the role of estate agent!'

His refusal to take her statement seriously was infuriating. 'I'm not acting. I'm here to make sure nothing happens to the villa keys,' she said stiffly. 'You're here to view the place. We've got nothing in common, and we're never going to see each other again after today.'

Stefano said nothing, but smiled at her with an assessing look in his meltingly dark eyes. The dappled sunshine played on his clean, beautiful features and suddenly the thought of never seeing him again wasn't quite as comforting as she had expected.

As they continued their tour of the house, Kira began to wonder if she had misjudged the captivating Signor Stefano Albani. They did have one thing in common. It was obvious the moment they reached the first floor. He strode straight to the nearest window and looked out. Only when he had inspected the vista with its avenue of sweetly scented lime trees did he begin his careful study of the floors, walls and furnishings. Watching him, she noticed he carried out the same ritual with each new room they entered. He paid no attention to the high ceilings and airily beautiful rooms until he had studied what was on show outside. Finally, she couldn't stay silent any longer.

'I see you like the view,' she said with satisfaction.

There was a pause before he answered. It gave her

strange pleasure to see that he carried on drinking in the scenery before he replied. 'Is it so obvious?'

'You make a beeline for the windows each time we enter a room.'

He frowned, seeming uncomfortable that she had noticed his simple enjoyment of their beautiful surroundings.

'I'm simply checking to see where the nearest neighbours are. I value my privacy.'

Kira nodded, covering a smile. 'I understand. This valley is perfect for that. You won't be disturbed. Let's hope you don't disturb me!'

He gave her a sharp look, then paced on towards the next room. As he walked, he compared what he was seeing with the beautifully produced brochure. Kira decided to get a copy of the booklet for herself. It would be a permanent reminder of this day, and the house. She was seeing it for the first and last time, and that made her happy to wander along in Stefano's wake. He needed no commentary, and took his time. While he judged and estimated distances and sizes, Kira simply enjoyed herself. The old house was beautiful. Its corridors and great rooms had a quiet grace, despite all the grime and dust. Sir Ivan couldn't have visited the upper storeys of his house in years. There were worm-eaten long-case clocks on plinths, dusty carriage clocks on equally dusty coffee tables and delicate little china clocks on every mantelpiece. There wasn't so much as a tick or a tock between them. All were silent. All were sad. Only the sound of a golden oriole warbling from the lime trees outside and swifts screaming overhead broke the thick summer silence.

'Ah, perfetto,' Stefano breathed, with a look of total

satisfaction. Kira was entranced. As he strolled on into the final room on the top floor, she stopped. There was no point in going any further. The small, square box room was no competition for her last uninterrupted viewing of Stefano Albani. She watched as he finished inspecting the house that might become his own. He moved with the self-assured grace of a man who would be at home anywhere. His gestures were expansive as he waved the brochure in her direction, drawing her attention to some fact or another. He only became still when he returned to his favourite position, at the window. Kira felt somehow relieved to see him at rest, if only for a short while. He gave the impression of continuous movement, no matter how slight. She found that unsettling. When he was still like this, lost in thought, she could almost imagine he was at peace. Almost...but not quite. There was always a trace of tension lingering around those eyes. When he forgot to try and charm her, they held the thousand-mile stare of a troubled man.

She found herself drawn inexorably towards him. Silently, she moved across the bare floorboards, past anonymous, dust-sheeted furniture. The need to reach out and touch him again before he was lost to her forever was irresistible.

And then he moved. The moment was broken. He turned to her in surprise, but then a slow smile warmed his features, and she realised she had raised a hand as though to touch him.

'Go ahead. Be my guest. As we're going to be neighbours, it's a good idea for us to get to know each other better, wouldn't you say?'

Kira pulled her hand back as though she had been burned. 'I—I was going to brush a cobweb from your shoulder. You know how dusty these old houses can be…' She faltered, convincing neither of them.

Stefano was intrigued. Kira was full of contradictions. Half of her seemed to be yearning towards him, but something kept pulling her back. With another woman, he might have taken advantage of the situation straight away, but he wasn't about to push his luck with Miss Kira Banks—not for a while, at least. She interested him.

In the short time they had been together, he recognised the pain in her. It was too close to home. He wondered how deep the similarities ran between him and this privileged young Englishwoman. Once, when he was young, he had come face to face with tragedy. He could have let it crush him to powder. He dodged that, but paid a heavy price. From that moment, he had spent his whole life on the run. He was afraid of nothing but his conscience. This woman didn't need to draw pictures when she spoke to him. She had escaped from somewhere and ended up here. That was enough information for him—for the moment. He knew what it felt like to be goaded by guilt.

The fact we've both decided on this hidden valley is somehow comforting, he thought, and then cursed sharply. What did he need with comfort? All he wanted was somewhere he could withdraw from his hectic business life and enjoy some quality time. The Bella Terra estate offered everything he wanted. And it had the added advantage that at least one of the neighbours shared his love of solitude.

* * *

'I really enjoyed that,' Kira said as they reached the front doors again after the grand tour.

'You sound surprised?' He raised his eyebrows.

'I am! I only agreed to stand in for that estate agent because I was sure you wouldn't turn up this afternoon. I tend to try and avoid people, when I can.'

'You couldn't avoid me,' Stefano reminded her, stepping out of the house and striding off across the terrace. He was intent on seeing the grounds. That made Kira nervous. The bulky clouds rising up over the far ridge of hills were backlit by a blood-red sun. Despite that warning, he kept heading away from his helicopter, and towards the storm. Kira didn't share his confidence.

'Shouldn't you be going, Stefano?' she called, needing to draw his attention to the threatening sky.

He turned. 'Anyone would think you were trying to get rid of me! I like this place, Kira. I want to see the rest of it.'

'But it's going to rain!'

He was unimpressed. 'Get wet, get dry again. That's my motto. I'm going to be living in this beautiful villa, so I should start thinking like a country person. Maybe I can learn to look on the trees as nature's umbrella.'

Kira wasn't sure if he was joking. She hated uncertainty, and followed him to find out. A growl of thunder prowled into the valley, which was something else she didn't like. She stopped dead.

'You're going to walk around the grounds in this weather? You might get struck by lightning! Are you mad?'

He paused. 'I've been called many things in my time, but never that!' After another second's thought, he started towards her as rapidly as the storm. As he reached her side, he narrowed his eyes. 'Are you scared? Is that it?'

'Of course not,' Kira said, raising her chin defiantly and determined to shadow him whatever the weather might throw at them. 'Nothing scares me.'

He didn't look convinced, but swung away across the terrace again.

'Come on, then. I've seen enough of your landscape work from the upper floors to know that I want you to work for me,' he announced, leaving her to run and catch him up. 'After hearing about what you did for Sir Ivan, I've decided my town house in Florence needs a new designer. I want more greenery, and a roof garden. When you're not busy with that, you can act as consultant to some inner-city work I'm funding. Currently, it lacks focus. Community projects have been successful elsewhere. Your input may be exactly what I need. I'll want you to design something to appeal to everyone, and then organise working parties to—'

'Wait!' Kira tried to halt the imperious flow of instructions. 'That all sounds good and important, but I can't simply drop everything on your say-so!'

He stopped, as the sun went behind a cloud.

'Why not?' He stared at her, uncomprehending.

'Because…I'll have to consult my schedule,' Kira replied with dignity. She decided that Stefano was clearly far too used to getting everything his own way. Still, a chance to design the roof garden for a no doubt exceptionally beautiful town house in Florence…

'With the loss of the Bella Terra's owner, you're one client down. You've already said as much. I can fill that gap for you,' Stefano announced affably. 'You've already told me you hate canvassing for jobs and courting publicity. I've seen what you can do, and I'm offering you a valuable, long-term contract working for me. Where's the problem?'

The problem, Kira thought desperately, is you.

'I'm not sure I want to work for you, Signor Albani,' she said a little stiffly. 'We're so different. We might not get on.'

He trapped her gaze for a long time. 'What you mean is, you're afraid we might get on too well. And remember—my name is Stefano…' he added with a tempting smile.

Kira stared at him. His self-confidence was astonishing, and yet somehow she could not bring herself to resent it. He could read her mind—how could she criticise him for that?

'I appreciate your concerns, but you don't have to worry,' he went on. 'I have so many properties and projects, my contractors are dealt with mainly by email and text. I wouldn't be there in person to tempt you.' With that, his smile came dangerously close to laughter.

Kira had to look away. His body wasn't the only thing tempting her. She tried not to think of the begging letter, waiting for her on the table at home. There were so many calls on her slender finances. She needed money. The fabric of her house was so old there was always something that required repair. The security of a long-term contract appealed to her cautious nature. Her problem was, whenever she earned more than she actually needed she always felt bound to send any extra money back to England.

Her natural generosity might feel right, but she knew in her heart it was wrong. She would soon live to regret it, as she had done every single time in the past. What she earned ought to be hers to keep. She tried to harden her heart. It was difficult, and that was why she was such an easy target. Emotional blackmail was an ugly thing. Kira knew a steady contract to work for a billionaire like Stefano Albani would be a perfect new start. With that security behind her, maybe she could manage to make a stand. It would give her some badly needed confidence, and she could make sure that anything she did for Stefano would be strictly on her own terms. Yes, of that she was certain.

Well…almost certain…

'Your projects sound pretty interesting,' she told him carefully. 'When I get back home I'll check my diary, and see if I can fit you in somewhere.'

He gave her a calculating look. Then he dug a hand into his pocket and drew something out. 'Of course, I appreciate you can't give me an answer straight away. Here—take my card. I'll have my office draw up all the documents, and you can give them a call when you've come to a decision.'

His wallet was immaculate dark brown leather. The blue silk lining was no match for the intensity of his eyes as he pulled out a business card and handed it to her. Trying not to stare at it like a souvenir, Kira slid it into the pocket of her jeans.

'Thank you. I'll give it some serious thought.'

Lightning crackled. Kira braced herself, but the explosion of thunder still made her jump.

'It's getting closer.' She looked up at the sky, and then across at the horizon. It was as dark as an overripe plum. 'Are you sure you want to risk a tour of the estate in this weather, Stefano?'

'It will be fine.' He smiled. 'Trust me.'

That was the last thing Kira ever did. People always used that phrase as casually as they said 'to be honest.'

From that moment, she knew in her heart things would go wrong. She tensed, retreating into the role of observer as Stefano roamed around the formal gardens. Not content with admiring her work from the upper storeys of the house, he wanted information from ground level, too. He asked intelligent questions and paid her compliments about her work, but Kira could only let herself believe a fraction of his kind words. She moved uneasily under the shadow of his praise and flinched as the thunder grew closer. Finally, when they were at the furthest point of the tour, the rain began. Warm drops the size of pound coins darkened the dust, first in ones and twos, then in a downpour of tropical proportions.

'We'll head for there!' Stefano shouted over the torrents of rain. He was pointing at her cottage. 'It's the only blot on my landscape. We might as well make use of it before my men clear it away.'

'What?' Kira shrieked, but her horror was drowned by thunder roaring right overhead. They dashed for the house, but as they got closer Stefano faltered at the sight of garden flowers spilling through the woven hazel fencing.

'So someone lives here?' he shouted over the downpour.

'Yes—me!' Kira raced past him and flung open the door of her little retreat.

Breathless and soaked, they tumbled into the house.

'I didn't realise this estate came with a tenant,'

Stefano said as Kira kicked off her sandals and padded, dripping and barefoot, into the kitchen.

'It doesn't. I own La Ritirata outright,' Kira told him proudly as she returned, carrying a couple of hand towels.

'I wasn't aware of that. How much do you want for it?' Stefano looked at her quizzically.

'Oh, it's not for sale!' Kira laughed, running lightly up the wide stone stairs to fetch some larger towels from the airing cupboard. Stefano followed her for a few steps. Leaning back against the cream-painted stone wall, he looked up at her as she stood on the landing.

'Of course it is. Everything is for sale at the right price. You could find yourself a nice little hideaway in this valley, well away from La Bella Terra. Then we could each pretend we were totally alone in the landscape.'

'That's the point. There are no other houses—not for miles. That's partly why I love it here so much.'

'You could build yourself another paradise anywhere, Kira!' he went on. 'I've seen the proof, remember. Go on—name a figure. Anything you want, and it's yours.'

'All right, then—a million pounds!' Kira called down with a giggle.

'Done. I'll have my staff draw up the paperwork as soon as I get back to the office.'

Kira waited for him to laugh, but he didn't. He was in deadly earnest.

'You're joking!' she gasped. 'This place isn't worth a fraction of that sort of money!'

'My peace of mind is beyond price,' he announced.

Taken aback by the determination in his voice, Kira shook her head.

'Well, you may not have been joking, but I was. My house means the world to me,' she told him firmly. 'No amount of money would tempt me to give it up. La Ritirata gives me what I've always wanted—independence and contentment. I've worked hard for my little home, and I feel safe here.'

A tremendous blast of thunder rattled the windows. Stefano smiled.

'I notice you aren't so nervous, now we are within your own four walls,' he observed. 'You've obviously made a real commitment to this place.'

'I have.' She nodded, glad he appeared to have accepted she wouldn't be moving.

'In that case, I can't wait to benefit from the Bella Terra effect. I own a lot of investment properties around the globe, but I can't honestly call any of them home. If I see a place with potential, I buy it,' he told her, looking around her neat and compact little home appreciatively. 'Yet none of my houses have ever developed the comfortable, lived-in feeling of this place.'

'I spend as much time as I can here. Maybe that's the secret of my success.'

'It really works,' he said as she started back down the stairs towards him, holding out a huge fluffy towel. 'Living alone in a place like this, you must be as brave and resourceful as you are talented and beautiful.'

He reached out to her. As he took the towel from her hands, their fingers brushed against each other. His touch was light as an angel's kiss, but it sent lightning coursing straight through Kira's body. She gasped.

A thunderbolt crashed directly overhead, but neither noticed.

Stefano was looking deep into her eyes, and nothing else mattered.

CHAPTER FOUR

THE universe held its breath. Kira gazed at the gorgeous man standing just out of her reach. Her body ached to touch him. She could think of a million and one reasons why she should take that single step down into his arms. Only one thing stopped her. There was already a monumental mistake in her past. Kira was no longer the innocent girl she had once been, long ago and far away. She had forged a new life since then and almost learned to trust her instincts again, but she had never been faced by a choice like this before. Every fibre screamed at her to fall into Stefano's arms. At the same time, every cruel word and accusation she had suffered in the past kept her nailed to the spot.

Stefano came up a step to join her. Taking the towel from her hands, he draped it over her head. Very gently, he began massaging her hair dry. His light, sure touches made Kira wonder how many other women he had treated in this way. It was impossible to know. That was the danger. She knew what powerful men were like. They acted with confidence, and never left any room for refusal. She had the horrible fear that once she was in his arms he would give her no time to think. It would be bed, and then treachery. It might take a day, a week or a month before he deceived her, but the result would be the same. He would carry on as though nothing had happened. She would be totally crushed. It had happened to her once before, and Kira was not about to let herself become a victim again.

She put up her hands, shrinking back and trying to intercept his movements. His fingers closed over hers and gently pushed the towel back over her head. The clip securing her tumble of auburn hair fell away. It clattered down the staircase. Kira barely noticed. She was completely absorbed by the look in Stefano's eyes as he drew the towel away from her hair. The appreciation she saw was all for her. She began to tremble, but now it was with anticipation, not fear. She had never known such a wild yearning before.

She swallowed hard. There was nothing in her mouth but the taste of temptation. His eyes levelled a steady, questioning gaze, willing Kira to read what she wanted in them. It was mesmerising, but she could not escape the feeling of being confined in her own home. To take a step forward would lead straight into his arms. Kira refused to repeat her mistakes, and the irresistible Stefano Albani showed all the signs of being a disaster waiting to happen—to her.

She couldn't allow herself to fall under his spell.

'This is dangerous,' she said, forcing a laugh when he showed no sign of moving. 'Didn't you ever get told not to fool about on stairs?'

'No. But then, if I had I wouldn't be where I am today.'

Turning, he headed back down the stairs.

Kira was torn between relief and disappointment. When he walked away it was because he was unwilling to open up about himself. They had that in common, she recognised. It gave her enough courage to follow him downstairs. Although unable to take that one momentous step into his arms, she did not want to lose touch with him altogether.

'It's still pouring out there, Stefano. Why don't you stay for a coffee?' she ventured.

He did not look at her. Instead, he went over to the open front door. There he stood with one hand on either side of the door frame. When he spoke, his voice was as light and careless as hers.

'That would be great. And I meant what I said about wanting you to work for me.'

They might as well have still been discussing the weather. His attention was riveted on the curtains of rain rippling over her drenched and glittering garden.

'And I'm equally determined to take my time over considering your offer,' Kira said firmly, fixing him the macchiato he requested. She poured herself an identical drink, keen to keep a clear head while he was under her roof. 'I need to know what strings are attached, Stefano.'

'There won't be any. I like to keep my affairs simple.'

He was still watching the rain. As Kira reached his side with the coffee, the downpour wavered and began to ease. A final flurry of thunder rattled away into the distance.

'I like to keep my affairs completely separate from my work,' she said, handing him his cup.

He was silhouetted against the doorway, surveying the land beyond her garden fence as though it was already part of his very own kingdom. At last he turned his head and looked at her. A man who took control so naturally would never expect a woman to refuse him anything. That thought made Kira fizz with an illicit thrill. Stefano Albani might be about to buy the Bella Terra estate, but the power he had over her had nothing to do with territory. She felt the need for him growing within her. That desire was reflected in his beautiful blue eyes. His gaze was as tempting as evening sunshine. Kira knew she held the key to her own escape from solitude, and that made her powerful. She could choose to satisfy the cravings he was awakening in her body, or tighten her armour of self-reliance. The choice was hers and she was glad, but it disturbed her. It would be so easy to give in, right here and now. She was afraid that if she did, Stefano would turn out to be no better than the last man she had learned to trust.

Some dreams needed to be kept at arm's length. That way they could last for as long as she wanted.

As she passed Stefano the coffee, his fingers made contact with hers again. It was only for a fraction of a second, but it would linger in her memory for the rest of her life. Their eyes met as he drained the small cup in one movement. Then he walked over and placed it on the coffee table.

'The rain has stopped, so I must go. Thank you for being such a delightful hostess, Kira. I don't like to mix women and work, but as you aren't quite on my payroll yet…'

Before Kira knew what was happening she was in his arms. He took complete control as his body spoke for them both. His lips were cool and totally irresistible. She dissolved under the pressure, and he was there to catch her. Despite all her good intentions, she let herself reach out to him. She delighted in the delicacy of the thin, smooth skin stretched taut over his finely drawn cheekbones. Her fingers ran through the silkiness of his dark hair as she drew him ever closer to her, hungry to experience every nuance of him. In response, his fingers stroked lightly over her bare arms, forming a prison she never wanted to escape. When he began to draw away, she instinctively tried to follow. Gently, he detached her arms from his neck. Holding her hands between his, he squeezed them lightly.

'No. After what you have said to me today, Kira, I know you would never forgive yourself for mixing business with pleasure,' he said, his expression carefully innocent, but a wicked sparkle in his eyes belying his words. 'I'll tell my staff to get a draft contract out to you as soon as possible. Until then, goodbye.'

Lifting his hand to his lips, he blew her one final kiss, and then strode right out of her house.

It was all Kira could do not to rush after him. Fighting every instinct, she forced herself to stay exactly where she was. She wanted go out and wave him off, but a man like Stefano would see that as his right. Women were probably doing it every day of the week. It would do him good to think there was one woman who didn't keep him at the centre of her universe. The thought gave Kira a funny twist of pleasure, and she almost smiled. The racket his helicopter made as it roared into life was almost as hard to ignore as its pilot.

Kira only went out onto the veranda when the throbbing engine sound had dwindled away. Stefano's helicopter was high in the sky, reduced to the size of a child's toy. It made several slow circuits overhead like a bird of prey, and then headed off swiftly in the direction of Florence. This time she really did allow herself to smile.

Kira had run from romance for years. After that first disastrous affair with Hugh, she vowed never to get entangled again. And now Stefano Albani breezed into her life, attacking the walls of her reserve. She told herself it didn't matter, as the way she was feeling had nothing to do with love. Her heart was not involved. That meant there was no danger she could be hurt a second time. Her response to Stefano was on a purely physical level, and that was how she intended to keep it. He aroused her body to a pitch she had never before experienced. It was unprecedented, startling, but at least it was simple.

It was love that would complicate matters, and Kira had absolutely no intention of allowing that.

Stefano was a happy man as he flew back towards Florence. He hummed a snatch of Don Giovanni to himself, revelling in the comfort of his air-conditioned cockpit. The Bella Terra estate was what life was all about. That was why he worked so hard, and put up with all the long hours and pressure. His features sharpened with their usual hawklike intensity. Memory was a savage goad. Whatever he had to put up with, he could do it in luxurious surroundings waited on by dozens of staff. As a teenager he had heard English tourists talk of their villas in Tuscany and vowed he would live like them one day. Whatever they could do, he would do better. It had taken him nearly twenty years, but he had managed it. He was going to own the most beautiful valley in all Italy.

His blue eyes veiled. It contained the most beautiful woman in the country as well. The enigmatic Miss

Banks might well prove a bigger challenge than he had at first anticipated. Her failure to be swayed by his wealth or reputation made her unique, in his experience. A slow smile spread over his face the more he thought about her. Novelty wasn't the only reason why she leapt into his mind. Kissing her senseless had kindled a need for her within his body. The temptation to carry on softening her resistance beneath his lips and hands had been difficult to resist. It had threatened to overcome him, but he had conquered it. There was no shortage of sex in Stefano's life, but his reactions to Kira Banks felt somehow different. For once in his adult life, he was wondering less about her beautiful body, and more about the woman within.

He found himself wanting to see her again. That thought made him feel uneasy.

Miles away and far below, Kira shared his feelings. It had taken her so long to get over the horror that had been Hugh Taylor, she was determined never to be taken in by a man again. Yet Stefano Albani made her feel weak at the knees. And weak in the head, she told herself crossly, but it was impossible to think about him and frown. That was a revelation. Her only experience of men so far had ended in tears. Now, for the first time in years, a man was forcing her to reconsider. Stefano hadn't made her cry. In fact, every time she thought about him, she smiled. That will have to stop, she told herself sternly.

Memories usually knocked all the daydreams out of her head. Thoughts about Stefano didn't. Instead, she was filled with a wonderful warm feeling. It was such an unfamiliar sensation it took her a while to recognise it as lust. Shy amusement engulfed her in a wave of embarrassment, but that vanished when she caught sight of the envelope lying on her table. Stefano had stroked all thoughts of it from her mind. She picked it up. Meeting him put this letter from her stepparents into perspective. If she could cope so well with a man like that, what was to stop her dealing with a call from home? Full of unusual optimism, she tore the envelope open. It was the usual tissue-lined affair, drenched in her stepmother's trademark perfume. Unfolding the stiff sheet of handmade paper, Kira cut straight to the chase. Glancing at the foot of the letter, she read the words, 'All our love, Henrietta and Charles.'

She scowled. That was all she needed to know. Her stepparents only sent her their love when they wanted money. If things were going well, they conveniently forgot about the girl who had disappointed them in every way, except in her capacity as a cash cow.

She scanned the rest of the copperplate handwriting. Mr and Mrs Banks weren't stupid. They never came straight out with a request for cash. Hints were threaded through the glowing reports of their younger daughter Miranda's success as an actress, and her new romance with a millionaire. Of course, this meant the Banks family wanted to entertain on a grand scale. Kira chuckled, imagining her stepmother circling Miranda's boyfriend with canapés brought all the way from Fortnum and Mason. They were her preferred bait for a future son-in-law. The Bankses' mortgage was unpaid and their house was falling apart. Despite that, the expensive perfume was still on draft and hopes of coming into money from somewhere or another were still high. Some things never changed.

Kira's face fell again as she read the final paragraph of the letter: 'When you ring each week, could you make it a little earlier? Six o'clock is such an inconvenient time as we're nearly always on the way out.'

Their instructions usually made her feel nine years old again, but today was different. Stefano Albani was stronger than all Kira's bad memories put together. Impulsively, she screwed up the letter and lobbed it towards the waste bin. It missed, but Kira was in good spirits as she got up to retrieve it. It was amazing what a little boost to the self-esteem could do.

And a kiss from Stefano Albani worked like rocket fuel.

Next day, Stefano's legal team presented him with a contract for the landscaping and design work he wanted done on his town house in Florence. His PA scheduled a call for him, summoning Miss Kira Banks to his office. While Stefano held meetings, Kira was pushed to the back of his mind. However, the moment he pulled her file from his in-box to make the call, things changed. At the sight of her name, he paused. One look at the neatly printed contract catapulted her to the front of his consciousness again. This wasn't some run-of-the-mill conquest. This was Miss Kira Banks, who had been funny and spiky and brought back powerful memories of the last time someone stood up to him. He found himself going back over every second of the previous day.

He inhaled deeply, bringing to mind the sweet lavender and lemon fragrance of her. She was perfumed by soap and fresh air. He spent a few moments revelling in her image. It was a mystery why she hid behind such a prickly attitude. He knew it was only a front. The warm surrender of her body beneath his hands when he touched her assured him of that. Her reactions were perfect. It was her mind he needed to explore. That idea made him uncomfortable.

Suddenly he leaned forward and snapped a button on his office intercom.

'Cancel that call, and the contract in the name of Kira Banks,' he growled. 'I need to do some more research.'

Stefano believed in being the best, and having the best. To keep up his high standards, he used only the top people. He wanted to employ Kira Banks because she really was the best person for the job, not just because he wanted to bed her.

Slumping back in his seat he gnawed the side of his thumb, deep in thought. Work and women were totally separate compartments of his life. He had fancied Kira from the first moment he saw her, but that was the very worst reason for giving anyone a job. Her work was great, but he had only seen one of her projects. For her body and spirit to haunt him like this, it could only be a bad thing. Emotion mustn't be allowed to affect his judgement. He ought to distance himself from the process, and get some other opinions. He needed to be absolutely sure she was the right person for this project.

Picking up his pen, he drew two careful lines through the name and address on the cover of the file in front of him. He liked speed, but not at the expense of perfection. Besides, that faint air of mystery surrounding Miss Kira Banks might erupt into some sort of scandal for Albani International. It didn't matter how Stefano wanted her, nothing could be allowed to taint the name of his company.

Not even the most beautiful Englishwoman in Italy.

Kira looked at Stefano's stark-white business card every day. Her heart fluttered with excitement. She ran her finger over the engraved wording until his telephone number was burned into her brain, but she never rang it. That smooth, self-assured man must never be in any doubt that Kira was her own woman, with other projects and a lot of things on her mind.

Finally, exactly two weeks after Stefano had grabbed her by mistake in the garden, she couldn't resist any longer. She sat down, cleared her throat and picked up the receiver. Then she put it down again. Maybe she should get her laptop up and running in case he started talking business straight away. She wanted him to think she was calm and efficient, even though she didn't feel it as she lifted the phone to try once more. This time she paused to fetch a glass of water. It would be terrible if her mouth dried before she could speak to him.

Eventually, her heart rattling like a touch typist's fingertips, she dialled the number.

'Signor Albani's office. How may I help you?' a sunny female voice enquired.

Kira had no idea. Naively, she'd thought the number on Stefano's own business card would have been a direct line to his desk.

'Who is speaking, please?' the voice asked as though she was only one among thousands.

'Kira Banks.' Kira made herself answer in the friendly, confident tone she reserved for clients. 'I'm ringing to check on a contract that Signor Albani was going to arrange for me.'

'Ah.'

That single sound was enough to bring her back to earth. While the receptionist went off to check, Kira was left to imagine exactly how many other women rang this number each day. Silver-tongued Stefano must make a million similar promises.

She was on hold for ages. The silence was almost as painful as piped music would have been. It gave her a long time to reflect on her foolishness. Finally, the receptionist returned, and Kira's heart fell still further.

'I'm sorry, Miss Banks, we have no record of a contract being issued in that name. Perhaps if you could give me a reference from the letter we sent you?'

'No…no. It's okay. I must have made a mistake,' Kira muttered indistinctly. And not for the first time, she thought bitterly as she put down the receiver.

Kira stared at the telephone for a long, long time. She felt totally deflated. In her daydreams, Stefano Albani couldn't wait to get back to her side. He would have paid cash for the Bella Terra estate, simply so he could move in as soon as possible. Instead, he must have forgotten about her the moment he climbed back into his helicopter. He had turned out to be no different from any of the other rich men she had worked for. All of them could spin a fine yarn. They couldn't make and hang onto big money without being able to charm investors. And women, she thought ruefully, touching her lips. Remembering the rasp of Stefano's cheek against her skin sent a tingle coursing through her body. She smiled, recalling the wonderful experience of being held and kissed until her worries spun away. The man was a rat, but why had she expected anything else?

She would cope. She had survived a worse disaster—and at least her brush with Stefano had happened in private. Her life was her own, and from now on that was how it would stay. She smiled sadly. Her single, unforgettable contact with him was a total one-off. It was destined never to happen again. I should have known that from the start, she told herself briskly.

She tried to smile again, but it was impossible.

Kira's disappointment over the contract squashed all her fantasies flat. No one did anything for nothing. Mentally she shrugged her shoulders, but Stefano refused to be forgotten. He had set such an exciting fire into her soul. Long ago, life had taught her to expect nothing when it came to men. She knew in her bones Stefano could be no different, but it had been a lovely fantasy. Those sweet memories of him refused to leave her. Whether drifting through her dreams or sending shock waves through her day when she thought she glimpsed his familiar figure in the street, Stefano would not let her go.

She was putting the finishing touches to a very chic project on the outskirts of Florence when her mobile rang.

'Miss Kira Banks?'

Kira couldn't recognise either the woman's voice, or the number that flashed up on her phone's screen. The only people who used this number were clients. Instantly on her guard, she hesitated.

'Who wants to know?'

'I work for Signor Albani. We understand you are on the point of completing a project for Prince Alfonse.

Signor Albani wants you to leave it and travel straight to his office. A car will pick you up in approximately—'

'Wait a minute!' Kira interrupted angrily. 'When I rang your office to check about this, you didn't even have any knowledge of a contract in my name!'

'When was this?'

'The day before yesterday.'

'Then perhaps you were a little impatient, Miss Banks.' The voice was cool.

Kira was in no mood to be treated like an idiot.

'If Signor Albani is clever enough to have found out where I'm working, then he ought to know better than to interrupt me when I'm busy. I don't have time to waste on idle chit-chat with an unreliable man.'

She heard a little gasp at the other end of the line. The voice became a shocked whisper.

'Miss Banks, what are you saying? No one refuses Signor Albani!'

'Well, I'm very sorry, but no one disappoints the person I'm currently working for, either. Especially not me,' Kira said firmly. 'And if you aren't willing to tell him that, maybe you could put me through to Signor Albani, direct?'

The woman wasn't happy, but put her on hold to see if the boss was taking calls. It gave Kira plenty of time to decide she had gone too far. She was being too emotional about this. Much as she hated to back down in any situation, where work was concerned she was a realist. She needed contracts. This one had the delightfully infuriating Stefano Albani at the other end, and that might make it more of a liability than a blessing. Autocratic behaviour was part of every billionaire's job description, but this particular man had got right under her skin. She wanted to be known for the quality of her work, not for making a fool of herself over a man.

Suddenly a voice purred in her ear.

'Kira, it's Stefano.' The sound was so deliciously accented, those few words were enough to wipe all the arguments from her mind.

'Hello,' she said, unable to think of anything else.

'You wanted to speak to me, Kira?'

'Yes.' Everything sensible and businesslike seemed to have been swept out of her head. She gave herself a mental shake. 'Thank you for having your secretary ring me, but I'm working on a very important project,' she snapped, hoping her brisk tone would put some distance between them again. 'I can't simply drop everything and rush to your side.'

'I know. You're a woman of spirit.' The laughter in his voice was infuriatingly engaging. 'Alphonse tells me you're practically finished at his place,' Stefano continued. 'I'm going to be out of the country for a while, and I wanted to discuss your contract with you, face to face, before I leave. I thought this would be a good opportunity for both of us,' he added.

Kira needed this job. She was also desperate to see Stefano again. After all, it does make good business sense, she told herself. There couldn't be any harm in a formal discussion. It would be like gazing at temptation through the window of a locked cake shop. Work would form an invisible shield between them, keeping her from disaster.

'You could be right…' She tried to sound grudging. 'How do I find you?'

She could hear his lack of surprise at her decision. 'Don't worry. I found you, don't forget. A car will be arriving to collect you...' There was a brief pause. Kira visualised him glancing at the designer watch clamped to his beautiful bronzed wrist as he added, 'In exactly fifteen minutes.'

And it was.

As her chauffeur-driven limousine glided to a halt at the main entrance of Albani International, Kira looked up at the grand old building with a hint of anxiety. It was enormous, and a constant stream of people flowed in and out of the revolving glass doors. A commissionaire stepped forward to open the car door for her. Thanking him, Kira took a few moments to compose herself before walking into the reception area. She had worked in palaces, villas and condos, but this place had something extra—Stefano Albani. Taking a deep breath, she went in to meet him.

To Kira's relief, there was no hanging around. That would have shredded her nerves beyond repair. She had been desperate to see Stefano again from the moment he left her house. Now she realised dreams were one thing, but reality was terrifying. The moment he spoke, her insides would turn to jelly. Her instinctive reaction was to keep her head down and pretend she was invisible, but that wasn't the way contracts were won. Instead, she lifted her chin, ready to meet his gaze with an equally bold stare. It took a huge effort.

The man of her dreams was lounging back in a big black chair. His feet were on his desk. He was dictating into a voice recorder and although his eyes instantly locked onto hers he did not stop speaking into it as she walked towards his visitor's chair.

Stefano looked every bit as intimidating as she

remembered. Despite his casual attitude, he was dressed in a beautifully cut dark suit. The formality of classically designed business wear suited him so well it was hard not to stare. Kira gave in to the temptation.

Completing his letter, Stefano switched off the recorder and tossed it aside.

'We meet again, Miss Banks.'

'Indeed we do.' Kira purposely kept her voice light and professional, but couldn't resist a question that had been tormenting her since he left her side. 'Did you buy the Bella Terra estate, *signore*?'

'Yes, but I've been too busy to visit since then. I suppose you've been wondering where I've been?'

'No, not at all,' Kira said coolly, determined not to betray any trace of the embarrassingly large amount of time she had spent wondering what he was getting up to while he was out of her sight.

She saw from a subtle change in his expression that the stony nature of her reply had given him pause. His reaction gave her a little lift, and added some real amusement to her smile.

'In fact, Signor Albani, when your assistant rang it took me a little while to remember who you were.' She batted the words easily across the desk at him.

He parried with a wicked smile. 'I knew you were one in a million, Kira. Now it seems you are unique.'

He took his feet off the desk and sat up straight in his chair, his suddenly businesslike attitude making him even more imposing. Kira fought to keep her expression impassive.

Don't overdo the flip answers! she thought. I might not want him to think he means anything to me, but he is a man who managed to borrow me from Prince Alfonse!

'I want you to work for me, Kira. Name your price,' he drawled, glancing down as he threaded a pair of solid-gold cufflinks into his cuffs.

'I'd rather find out what I'm letting myself in for first.' Kira was proud of the careful neutrality of her tone. It was a shame the rest of her being was entirely focused on the man she had been fantasising about for the past few days. 'I want to make sure I'm the right person for the job. I'd rather you offered the position to someone else if I thought I couldn't give you exactly what you wanted.'

'I agree completely,' Stefano said. 'However, I wouldn't have asked you here today were I not already certain. You, Kira Banks, are capable of giving me *exactly* what I want.' His face remained expressionless but the ambiguity of his words made her cheeks flush red and her breathing catch.

In a quick, carefully judged gesture he spun the file across the desk at her. 'So why don't you read that, and tell me what you think?'

Kira did not move, but regarded him coolly.

'What? Now?'

Stefano raised an eyebrow. 'Unless you have some objection?'

Kira had spent too many restless hours since their first meeting. After her roller-coaster ride of hope, disappointment and surprise, she did not find his words at all funny.

'No. This is so important to me, and it deserves to be studied carefully. I take my work very seriously,' she said slowly, trying to gauge his reaction.

Stefano nodded appreciatively. 'That's exactly the sort of attitude I expect from the people I employ. It's why I want you on board. I had my staff check out some of the other projects you've completed. I needed to make sure I was offering you work for all the right reasons, not simply the wrong one.'

His smile became enigmatic and Kira had to look away. She transferred her gaze back to the cover of the file in front of her. If he paid such careful attention to detail, she wondered what else his people might have found out about her.

'Could you give me an overview?' she said eventually. 'Isn't it simply a contract to work on the gardens at Bella Terra?'

'That, and my Florentine town house as well…'

It had been at the back of Kira's mind, but she'd hardly dared hope he would remember his casual offer.

'Words are cheap. Nobody knows that better than I do, Stefano. Men often say things they don't mean,' she said quietly.

He stared at her. 'Not when it comes to business. Honesty is the only policy there,' he said firmly. 'Since we met and I've had such favourable reviews of your work, I thought I'd raise the stakes. This contract offers you employment not only at Bella Terra, and Florence, but also on my new property in the Caribbean.'

Kira could have bounced straight up to the ceiling in sheer delight. It sounded like her dream contract. Instead, she frowned and bit her lip. 'I've never worked in the Caribbean.'

'Then you're in for a treat. It will be a wonderful experience,' Stefano assured her. 'Silver Island has everything. One hundred hectares of tropical wilderness surrounded by beaches as fine as sugar, set in a warm blue sea.'

Despite her determination to play it cool, Kira's eyes sparkled.

'It sounds lovely already,' she said wistfully.

Stefano had no illusions. He frowned. 'I thought so, too, when I first bought it. But despite all the luxury there's still something lacking. It'll be your job to make the whole place more—' he grimaced, so used to total satisfaction that he couldn't find the words to identify the problem '—user-friendly,' he said eventually, but looked no happier with the phrase than Kira felt.

'That doesn't give me much of a clue.' She shrugged.

'Silver Island is a perfect hideaway. No expense was spared in setting it up, and yet—' he ran his fingertip pensively across his lips '—for all its qualities, it lacks something. I want to import the magic you have worked on the Bella Terra estate. In the same way that you can live in the town house here in Florence while you're working on it, you could stay in the Caribbean while you restructure Silver Island. You'll be on the spot, all the time.'

And where will you be? Kira was appalled to find herself thinking.

'I don't suppose you noticed exactly how interested I was in your garden?' Stefano continued.

'I did,' Kira said, trying to concentrate on their moments of light, insubstantial chit-chat and forget the instant he took her in his arms. It was hopeless. The way she felt about him surged into her mind again. The force of his presence overwhelmed every other memory. A tiny tremble in her voice betrayed her. He noticed, and suddenly his devastating mouth curled up at the corners.

'Yes, I can see....'

All Kira's worries about the Bella Terra valley faded. The intensity of his stare focused on her to the exclusion of everything else. He looked like a tiger ready to pounce. The tremble extended throughout her body and she felt her self-control slipping away into warm arousal. It gathered in all her most feminine places, waiting for one word, one movement from him, to unleash its power.

'Good...so as soon as you're happy with your contract, we'll be on our way.'

'Where?' Kira asked faintly.

Stefano put his elbows on the desk and netted his fingers. 'To Silver Island—you'll need to experience the place in all its glory before you can hope to do it justice. The computer hasn't been built that can give you the experience of warm sand between your toes, and swaying palms beneath a tropical sky.'

The words flowed from him like the tropical breezes he spoke of—warm, gentle and so very seductive.

CHAPTER FIVE

KIRA wanted this job more than anything else in the world, but if she was honest with herself, working so closely with Stefano would be dangerous. How was she supposed to keep her mind on her job? Travelling around the world with him would be torture. It wouldn't simply be a case of storming off down the road if she felt herself weakening. She would be a long way from home and completely at the mercy of a man who held her spellbound. It was the same old story from her university days. Kira couldn't face falling into that trap again. A man like Stefano could never commit to just one woman—that much was obvious from his easy smile and delicious kiss. No woman with any sense should trust him with her heart.

Kira didn't know what to do. Surely if she was aware of the danger, that would make it easier to avoid? And a business contract was legally binding. It meant security. She rated that highly. The problem was, working for Stefano was bound to be a temptation too far. She had no confidence in her ability to resist him, and the man was trouble with a capital T. Her heart had spent the past few days on a helter-skelter of hope and gloom, and it was all his fault. Even if she kept her distance from him, working together would mean seeing exactly how faithless he could be from day to day. That would be a thousand times worse.

'I know—let's leave business behind and I'll take you to lunch first. We can discuss it further there, if you like?'

Kira put her hands on her chair and shifted her weight back a little in the seat. Her feelings were all over the place. She needed to draw some boundaries between the two of them, make it clear that she wouldn't simply fall into line. Everything was moving so fast. She blurted out, 'I won't be rushed. Please don't take me and my feelings for granted.'

He drew back across his desk, and stared at her. It wasn't often possible to read his expression, but Kira thought she saw a brief flash of astonishment.

'Is that what you think I'm doing? Is that how it feels to you?'

She braced herself for an explosion of rage, and answered him defiantly.

'Yes. Yes, it does.'

The expected outburst never came. Stefano simply looked at her thoughtfully. Kira gained a little confidence from that.

'What else would you call it?' she added, more boldly. 'Before you left my home, you promised me great things. It was a good job I didn't believe you, because all I got was radio silence. When I finally rang your office to check on whether there was a contract in the name of Kira Banks, there was no trace—'

Stefano couldn't resist interrupting. 'That was only because I wanted time to double-check your work, and to be completely sure you were the right person to—'

'Please! Let me finish.'

Surprised into silence, he met her scowl with raised eyebrows. Then, with a nod, he raised both his hands as a sign she would be allowed to carry on without any more interruptions.

'You seem to be expecting me to obey you without question, Stefano, and I won't have it,' she said bluntly.

His clear blue eyes watched her steadily, and then he suddenly nodded.

'I'll take that into consideration.' He frowned a little before continuing. 'That took courage. So that we both know where we stand, Kira, maybe I should tell you that no employee has ever got away with speaking to me like that before.'

She opened her mouth to say something, but the way he began to smile stopped her.

'My relationship with contractors, on the other hand, can be rather more—' he lowered his lids slightly, hooding those beautiful eyes '—easy-going, shall we say?'

She stared at him. When he looked at her like that, she couldn't have gone on scolding him if her life depended on it.

'You don't have to make any allowances for me,' she murmured, suddenly and mysteriously short of breath.

Stefano shook his head sagely. 'I admire you for making a fresh start in a new country. A heart in pain is too often the cause of endless trouble.'

He was probing. Kira could tell. When she thought of the research he had done on her, it made her edgy. Had he stuck to her work, or had he delved into more personal areas? The uncertainty made her nervous, so she refused to be drawn any further.

'I bet you've created a fair few broken hearts yourself!' she parried with a laugh. She thought he would do the same, but his reaction was quite different. Instead, he stood and roamed over to the window.

'You could say that. When I was younger, I saw too much abuse to put any faith in human relationships. Instead, I turned my back on all the fine old Italian bonds of family. Escape cost me so much, I'm never going there again.'

Standing at the window, hands on hips, he stared out over the busy cityscape like an eagle searching for prey. His words hinted at an inner pain of his own. Kira's heart went out to him, but it would take a lot of nerve to approach a man who so obviously shunned sympathy.

'I'm sorry,' Kira said softly, after a pause. 'It's terrible to grow up where you aren't wanted.'

Stefano's answer shrugged off her concern.

'That's why I made sure I didn't.' He spoke to the pane of glass in front of him. 'I kept right out of everyone's way. From that moment I started working, and never stopped. It was around the clock, and all year long. It saved me from having to go back home.'

Suddenly he clapped his hands with a loud report that made her jump. 'But what are you doing to me, Kira?' His easy smile returned as he swivelled around and strode back to his desk. 'I didn't bring you here to dissect my private life! I brought you here to talk business, and enjoy a working lunch. Then we'll go and see my town house.'

Kira's own experience of a loveless childhood made her wonder about his past. Then Stefano's eyes connected with hers and wiped the thought clean out of her head. She recognised a heart-stopping shadow of the longing she had seen when he left her. Confused, she picked up the file containing her contract. She wanted to sign, and yet such close contact with the gorgeous Stefano was bound to put her self-control under impossible strain. To her, surrender meant dangerous dependency. She had seen her stepmother and her stepsister fall prey to it. Once a man took over their lives, they stopped seeing themselves as individuals. Kira could not bear to lose a part of herself like that.

'Did you take Amanda the estate agent out to dinner when you signed the final paperwork on Bella Terra?' Her question was as mild as mustard.

There was silence. Made brave by it, she looked up at him sharply. Expecting to find him looking guilty, she was disappointed.

'Would it make any difference to you, Kira?'

His face was impassive. It was another probe. That only made her wonder all the more. He hadn't denied a liaison with the woman, although if he had, Kira would have assumed he was lying.

'Maybe,' she mused, trying to look and sound casual as she studied the closely typed document for snares and pitfalls. 'I don't like men who use their position in life as a lever for their sexual conquests. I like to keep my work and my private life strictly separate.'

'You told me as much the other day. I'll bear it in mind,' he said gravely, but then his mouth twitched. 'So in future, there will be absolutely no business talk whenever I visit your house after moving into La Bella Terra.'

The thought of inviting Stefano over the threshold of her home raised Kira's temperature in a frighteningly exciting way. She cleared her throat, trying not to squirm in anticipation. Her lips became dry, and she had to moisten them with her tongue before announcing, 'I think we ought to get one thing straight right from the start, Stefano. I'm a genuine loner. I don't fancy the idea of you dropping into my home at odd hours while I'm off duty, distracting me with…talk,' she finished awkwardly.

His reply was so simple, it shocked her. 'That's a shame.'

She looked up, waiting for him to try and persuade her otherwise. His face was as poker fit as her own as he added, 'Now come on, let's have lunch.'

Kira stood, mentally preparing herself. Lunch with Stefano was sure to be the stuff of fairy tales. That worried her. Powerful people liked to create a good impression—to begin with. They showered you with pixie dust until you were dazzled into falling in with their plans.

'I'd be delighted, but don't expect me to sign this contract on the strength of it. I'd rather my legal people had a good look at it before I make a final decision,' she said airily.

Kira's only advisers were her cynical nature and a glass of pinot grigio, so she was rather looking forward to that consultation.

'Good. That leaves us free to discuss much more interesting things over lunch.' He smiled, pulling on his jacket as he led her to the door. 'Although I'm rather surprised a forthright woman like you doesn't go through her own paperwork!'

She smiled as he strode across his office and opened the door to let her out.

* * *

Kira's journey to the ground floor couldn't have been more different from her trip up to the executive suite. Then, she had spent every second checking her appearance. Now she kept her eyes riveted on the thick cream carpet. It wasn't that she didn't know where to look. She desperately wanted to gaze at Stefano, but somehow she couldn't do it. She had to be content with hints of his aftershave or the jingle of change in his pockets as he stood so close to her, yet so distant.

A limousine was waiting for them outside the revolving doors of the office block. Its driver opened the door for Kira. She slid in, glad of the excuse not to have to look at Stefano as he exchanged a few words with his driver.

He was every bit as good as her fantasies. His first words to her when she walked into his office had been absolutely right. The past few days had tortured, tormented and distracted her with thoughts of what he had been doing, and with whom. Stefano was the only man who had ever moved her like this. It made her certain he must have a new girl every night. Who could possibly resist that clear-eyed gaze? Kira was terribly afraid she couldn't. Her pulse increased to dizzying levels each time he looked at her. As he took his seat beside her in the car it felt as though her heart was trying to jump into her throat. Her mouth went dry, and she felt heat pool in the pit of her stomach.

It had been hard enough not to reach out to him when he had been standing alone and aloof in his office stronghold. How much more difficult would it be to resist him when they were at lunch together?

'When it comes to that contract, you'll have no worries,' Stefano said as their car pulled out into the stream of traffic outside the headquarters of Albani International. 'I'm ruthless in business, but I'm always fair. That agreement is simple, straightforward and totally unthreatening. Working for me will be the smartest move you ever make. I've seen the design work and planting you did on the Bella Terra estate, and I've heard brilliant reports from your other clients. Your touch is exactly what I need. You'll bring your talents to my properties around the world. In return, I'll reward you well and give you free advertising among all my contacts. That will save you all the tiresome brown-nosing for business you hate so much. Think of it—all the work you could ever want, but none of the socialising.'

He slid a smile towards her. Kira thought of the man she had seen silhouetted against the cityscape. His expression tangled her heartstrings before her brain had time to intercept it.

'You don't know what that would mean to me,' she said, the relief of getting work without having to pitch for it filtering through her words. Whenever she was in Stefano's presence, her body refused to behave. It ignored all the warning signs. Her brain screamed *danger* but her soft, warm feminine core heard only *temptation* and remembered only their kiss.

'We're here,' he said, sounding slightly husky, and Kira wondered if he was struggling with similar memories, but he leapt out of the car before she could see his face. By the time he had arrived to open her door, he was back to business.

'This is one of my favourite restaurants,' he explained as he escorted her into a beautiful old building in the heart of the city. Its glamorous receptionist was all teeth and talons. She greeted Stefano by name, and led them to a spacious table for two. It was like no business lunch Kira had ever attended. As a respected professional she was used to being treated well. Stefano's idea of entertaining was in an entirely different league. The Michelin-starred restaurant was as perfect as its extensive menu, and Kira felt entirely uncomfortable. She looked down the list of tempting dishes, studying the menu intently, but it was no good. Eventually, she had to swallow her pride. It stuck in her throat, but as a regular Stefano was the best person to ask for help. 'I'm sorry. This is a cordon bleu restaurant and I'm a cucina povera girl at heart. All these exotic things are way out of my zone. Which do you recommend?'

'Definitely the lamb. It's a favourite of mine.'

Her mind made up, Kira ordered and handed her menu to the waiter.

Stefano ordered the same for himself, and a bottle of wine to accompany their meal. When they were alone again, he leaned towards her. His eyes were keen with interest.

'I would have thought a woman such as yourself would be entertained in restaurants like this all the time,' he said quietly. 'You deserve the best.'

Kira withdrew from the intensity of his gaze. 'I've told you—I enjoy plain Italian food.'

Stefano smiled suddenly. 'You are very much an Englishwoman. None of them are any good at truly indulging themselves.'

Clearly, thought Kira wryly, *he's never met my mother.*

'There aren't any fish-and-chip shops in the Bella Terra valley, so I've learned to adapt a little!' she said, relaxing in spite of herself as she looked around at their luxurious surroundings. 'It makes it easier when you bring me to a wonderful place like this. Everything is so beautiful, especially that dessert trolley over there. Mmm, I do so love my puddings!' She laughed, suddenly overcome with amazement at where she was and who she was with.

The waiter delivered their main course, and the glorious scent helped to relax her further. She ate a forkful and almost moaned in pleasure. Stefano watched her appreciatively. There was something suspiciously predatory in his eyes, but, overwhelmed and exhausted from fighting her attraction to him, when he held her gaze Kira didn't look away. He smiled slowly and she felt her hunger change into a more immediate desire.

'I wonder if this is a good time to tell you I haven't thought about another woman since we met,' he murmured slowly, in a voice silken with charm.

'It wasn't the thinking I was worried about!' Kira sighed reflexively before snapping her mouth shut and blushing bright red. Too late, she corrected herself. 'If I was worried at all, which I'm not.'

His voice became a caress. 'That's good. I wouldn't want to worry you, Kira. The fact is, you intrigue me. I've spent the time since I left your side wondering about you, pure and simple.'

'I'll bet there was nothing remotely pure or simple about it,' she retorted, although it was hard to stay angry with a man who gazed into her eyes with such intensity.

Her tone had definitely mellowed. Stefano picked up on it. He put down his fork. For a moment his hands spoke for him. The fingers spread wide, his wrists rolled from side to side on the edge of the table.

'Why block me when I'm trying to tell you something,

Kira?' His words were quiet, but intense. 'Let me into your life a little. You won't regret it. I can do things for you that you would never dream were possible. With your skill and my backing, there is no limit to what can be achieved. I want to start finding my pleasure much closer to home, and you are the one who can make it happen.'

Transfixed by his expression, Kira let him slide his hand over hers as it lay on the table. Incapable of resisting him, her fingers went limp. He began to stroke the back of her hand. His movements teased her with thoughts of how he had held her willing body against his only two weeks before. From the second he swept out of her front door, he left a yawning void in her life. She had spent so little time with him, and yet over those long, lonely days she had missed him so much. Kira felt every moment she didn't spend gazing into his eyes must be wasted.

A rising tide of emotion stirred her restlessly in her chair. Fine dining was nothing to the thought of Stefano making love to her. Suddenly she wanted him as urgently as she had desired him that day in her house. The colour of his eyes mirrored her needs. Beneath the long, flowing tablecloth she felt the slight movement of his foot as it slipped between hers. It happened as easily as his bare limbs might caress and possess her own.

'The moment you agree to work for me and sign that contract, I shall take you to Silver Island and show you my new paradise. Sun, sand and warm blue waters. It is everything you deserve, *cara mia*…' he whispered. His voice slipped over the words like a lazy tide lapping over land. Kira felt the last vestiges of her common sense slipping away. It was the powerful seduction in his eyes....

She passed the tip of her tongue over her parched lips.

'Stefano...I...'

The yapping of a pocket dog at the reception desk broke the spell. Kira blinked as though waking from a dream. As she came to her senses she saw an unmistakable look pass across Stefano's face. He might be a master at hiding his feelings, but he wasn't quite quick enough to conceal them from her. He was anticipating something. She looked across the busy restaurant. An impossibly tall, thin blonde was handing over her designer shoulder bag. The head of a noisy chihuahua poked out of it like a ripe russet apple. Relieved of the sum total of her responsibilities, the blonde turned around and surveyed the restaurant as though she was at the end of a catwalk. After jiggling a hand at several acquaintances, her eyes fastened on the table where Kira and Stefano were sitting.

In a cacophony of sleek designer fabric and six-inch heels she sashayed towards them. Kira tensed. Unconsciously her fingers went to her hair, then her smart but simple jacket, smoothing down its creases and fiddling with the buttons.

'Ah, Chantal!' Stefano turned as the woman got nearer.

Kira couldn't see his face, but heard his smile and could imagine the rest.

'Darling Stefano!'

With a winning smile especially for her, Stefano abandoned his plate and stood up. Greeting the blonde as though he was used to interruptions like this, he showed more style than Kira's one and only lover had ever done. She wondered how many times a seasoned philanderer had to run through this routine before it became second nature. Stefano had obviously put in the hours. He had turned it into an art form. Grasping his friend Chantal by the elbows, he air-kissed her with great pleasure.

'It's been a while, Stefano!' The blonde returned his gesture, running cool blue eyes over Kira's clothes and hair in a way that didn't simply give Kira a hint, it dug her savagely in the ribs.

Stefano was totally unfazed. Taking Chantal's hand, he pulled her fingers towards his lips for a real kiss. 'How was Biarritz?'

Chantal sighed theatrically. 'Nothing without you, darling, of course! Aren't you going to introduce me to your new friend? I haven't seen you about before, have I?' she said, giving Kira a bright, shiny look.

'Kira is a business associate,' Stefano said with barely a flicker.

'Pleased to meet you.' Chantal sent her a vague smile which failed to reach her eyes, before turning her attention back to Stefano.

Kira wasn't fooled for a moment. There was sympathy in that look. It told her—loud and clear—that Chantal didn't see her as any sort of threat. That made her feel more alone than she had ever done in her life. Chantal and Stefano, two of the beautiful people, chatted easily about friends she knew only as employers. Several times, Stefano tried to include Kira in their conversation, but she was simply too self-conscious and had nothing to say. She sat in mortified silence until Chantal left. When Stefano turned his full attention back to her again, she couldn't meet his eyes. She looked down hurriedly at her meal.

He introduced me as his 'business associate,' she thought, catching sight of herself in the glittering silver cutlery. *That really puts me in my place. I suppose I should be glad—it saves me having to worry about getting jumped on at every opportunity.*

At least it meant she could sign that contract safe in the knowledge nothing more than work would be on offer.

Somehow, having seen Stefano in action as he charmed Chantal, that didn't feel like such a good thing any more.

He went back to his meal as though nothing had happened. Kira was left to burn with embarrassment in silence. She tried to console herself that an affair with Stefano would be like this all the time. There would be constant interruptions from glamorous women in designer dresses. It would be Kira's idea of hell on earth.

After savouring another mouthful of lamb, Stefano looked up and smiled at her again.

'Now, where were we?' he said in a confiding murmur.

Kira put her heart and soul into a dazzling smile. It was the only way she could speak without screaming.

'I was about to tell you I wasn't in the ego-massaging business, Stefano. I've been fooled by a plausible rogue once before and I've got no intention of being caught out a second time, thank you!'

A look came into his eyes that she could not name, but it definitely wasn't remorse.

'I never for one moment imagined you would be,'

he said, looking so serious that she knew straight away he was telling the truth. 'Although you've touched on something I've been unable to get out of my mind since I met you at Bella Terra. When we were talking the other evening, it sounded as though you left England under a cloud. If you feel able, I would like to know more about what happened.'

Kira stared at him. His eyes hadn't left her since he said goodbye to Chantal. He had never once looked over his shoulder to see what the other woman was doing. *Whatever she might have been to him in the past, he's gazing at me now,* she thought in a desperate attempt to steady her nerves. She thought of everything that had happened over the past two weeks. Throwing away that begging letter from her stepparents had been a wonderfully freeing gesture. She remembered how close she had come to unburdening herself upon their first meeting. It was so tempting to let him in, to give Stefano a tiny insight into her problems. She took a deep breath, trying to summon up the courage to shed a little more light onto her murky past.

'Yes, I did—but the cloud wasn't of my making,' she began, but the memory of Chantal's contemptuous gaze and how separate a world Stefano came from shook her, and at the last moment she could not bring herself to go into details. 'Although I helped make it into the thunderstorm that sent me scuttling over here. I was escaping a disastrous affair. I abandoned the rat, and started all over again. I found myself a new life, and made a new start.'

Realising she would go no further, Stefano nodded. 'I might have guessed. There are two sorts of people—

those who crumble at the first hint of disaster, and those who conquer it and thrive.'

'I didn't exactly bounce back the next day,' Kira said ruefully, waving away his concern. 'But you're right—drawing a line under my mistake was the best thing I did. It let me move on. I took stock of my life, and then decided to apply for a course in horticulture. I've always liked working with plants, and it turned out I had quite a talent for it. One thing led to another so fast I was exhibiting before the world at Chelsea within three years. Shortly after that I found my home in La Ritirata. I've been here ever since.'

'And achieved wonders.' Stefano leaned forward and quietly pushed a strand of hair behind her ear. Kira melted. It would be so easy just to lean forward and kiss him.… In less than an hour he had delighted, infuriated and confused her, sometimes all at once. She could hardly think straight. Then, from the other side of the room, she heard Chantal's laugh and suddenly tensed.

Maybe she's laughing at me, she thought, hopelessly hypnotised by a consummate seducer. If they're not laughing now, then surely it's only a matter of time.…

That was all it took. Her mind cleared, but her words were unsteady. 'I thought we came here to talk about work, Stefano?'

Lifting his glass of wine to her in a silent toast, he treated her to a devastating smile.

'Yes, but there's no need to restrict ourselves, Kira.'

Colour rushed into her cheeks. The days fell away and once again she was in his arms, her hands hungry for his perfectly formed body. The powerful bulk of him was so close she could have reached out and touched him.

Right now his body was hidden beneath the beautifully tailored lines of a white shirt and business suit, but the look in his eyes concealed nothing. He expected to take her to his bed. He demanded nothing less—and Kira wanted nothing more.

CHAPTER SIX

SHE fought to remain calm. Stefano wanted her, she wanted him—but she didn't need all the problems that would bring. He had affected her deeply from the moment they met. Bitter experience told her that was dangerous. She didn't want her illusions about him shattered by getting too close. He was bound to break her heart. She knew it. What happens when he dumps me—as he will, sooner or later? she asked herself. When he moved into La Bella Terra he would be living only a few hundred metres from her front door. Becoming the heartbroken doorstop of a faithless philanderer was definitely not on her 'to do' list.

Obviously deciding he'd let her suffer for long enough, Stefano seamlessly changed gear.

'How do you feel about house-hunting? With access to my contacts, the world really is your oyster. If you see anything that takes your fancy, let me know. There's no limit.'

Just as Kira felt herself taking off, Stefano's words brought her back to earth. Grateful for the chance to nail her feet back to the ground again, she interrupted him quickly.

'I hope you aren't trying to buy me out again. I'm

happy living right where I am, in the house I've made my own, in the perfect position.'

Stefano said nothing, but his slowly widening smile was enough to make her body move uneasily beneath its warmth.

'You are a stubborn woman. You have integrity and determination. Work with me and I can assure your future. It isn't only a matter of beautifying my own properties. My company, Albani International, has a charitable arm which is involved in all sorts of exciting projects. I was deeply impressed when I saw the work you have done at Bella Terra. Once you have finished working on my homes, you can start bringing your influence to bear in many other places.'

'I'm glad you've got such confidence in me.' Kira blushed, her clear skin for a moment matching the intricate strawberry meringue the waiter set before her.

Stefano's sensual lips parted in a half-smile as he saw Kira's delight in the summery confection of pinks and white on the dish laid in front of her.

'Look, why don't we visit my apartment after we finish here? You can see where you'll be working, if you decide to sign that contract. I told Prince Alfonse not to expect you back today.'

'Oh, you did, did you?' Kira said archly, inspired by a sugar rush. 'I hope you also told him we're out on business.'

Stefano didn't answer. His expression was telling Kira everything she didn't want to know, but her conscience was clear. For the moment, at least.

'As it happens, I think visiting the site is a very good idea,' she added coolly. 'I never accept a job until I have made a thorough study beforehand.'

'Good. I'm all for close scrutiny,' he said. With a nod of his head he summoned the head waiter, who brought a bottle of chilled champagne to their table. When it had been poured out, Stefano lifted his glass to her in another toast.

Kira remembered the last time he looked at her like that. It was in the split second before he kissed her. His eyes had a way of stripping away everything from her soul. She tried telling herself that he must size up every one of his female conquests like this, but a viper's nest of conflicting responses writhed within her body. His smile held out all sorts of possibilities. That was what made him so dangerous. At least she had no illusions, and could be on her guard.

'To our new partnership,' he said, his voice a sensual growl of anticipation which immediately created answering ripples in the pit of her stomach. Determined to quell them, she snapped

'Are you always so openly provocative?'

He broke the tension with a sudden laugh. 'I've never met another woman quite so woundingly honest! I can't help it, I'm afraid. Some men are born to it, while others need to be coaxed out of their shell by a loving, sensitive hand.'

Kira felt colour riot in her cheeks. Before she could explode, Stefano turned his statement into a warning.

'I am most definitely not one of those men.'

Stefano's town house was such a short distance from the restaurant he didn't bother calling up his driver. They walked. Kira had difficulty in keeping up with his long strides as he led her through the narrow streets. Without a word he fell back in step with her. Crossing a sunlit square, he directed her into a narrow canyon between two impossibly high and ancient stone walls. Kira looked around nervously as they left the sun-drenched crowds and plunged into shady solitude. Suddenly she realised he was no longer at her side. With a start, she swung around. He stood beside a pair of large wooden gates, let into the anonymous wall. With one hand he turned the wrought-iron handle in a small pass door and pushed it open.

'We're here. Go ahead.'

Kira cast one last apprehensive look up and down the narrow alley.

'Why are you so nervous? This is the best part of town.' He chuckled. 'Anyone would think I was trying to abduct you.'

A crazy vision of Stefano sweeping her away into the desert on a spirited Arab stallion flashed into Kira's mind. That threw her into confusion, but her mind cleared the instant she stepped into his courtyard. It was like standing at the bottom of a dry well. High walls irregularly perforated by small barred windows closed in on every side. This was a place the sun only reached when it was directly overhead. The building was ancient and beautiful, but putting a garden here would require imagination and skill. When he first mentioned a town house, Kira's mind had started playing with the idea of a private sun terrace. This place offered all the privacy anyone could want, but none of the rays.

'Good grief,' she whispered to herself, before adding aloud, 'This is going to be a challenge.'

He looked concerned. 'If you think it's going to be too much for you, tell me. I'll get someone to steam clean the whole place and leave it at that.'

'No!' Kira left his side and began pacing out the stark, stony area. 'There's nothing I enjoy more than a challenge. I'm not a quitter. If something can be imagined, it can be achieved.'

'Like a holiday home on Mars, maybe?'

Kira ignored him. Rummaging in her bag for a notebook and pencil, she began scribbling instead.

'I'll tell you what I like—' Stefano began, but she shook her head.

'This will only work if I tell you what is feasible first. Then you can choose which plants from my list you prefer.'

Stefano lodged his hands on his hips. 'What happened to "the client is always right"?'

Kira snapped her notebook shut, looked up and stared at him. He stared back. Despite her flinty expression, her mind was moving like quicksilver. This was one argument she could not afford to lose. Stefano could be infuriating, but he was offering her a series of lucrative contracts. He was also close to irresistible, and very easy on the eye. As long as she could harden her heart to stay out of his clutches, this would be a dream appointment. This site presented huge problems, but Kira would enjoy overcoming them. It gave her an unbeatable feeling to see a satisfied client, especially when it was a job other firms might consider too difficult. And she would be working for Stefano. The idea remained deliciously dangerous. She decided on a trial run.

'Fine. You're right—I'm not going to argue with you,' she announced. 'As long as you settle my bills, I'll do whatever you want. I can't guarantee you will be perfectly happy first time, though. The only plants that have a chance of surviving here are the sorts chosen specifically for these conditions. Unless you do as I say, you may end up with plants that have to be replaced every few weeks, because they die.'

'That's not a problem.' He shrugged.

'It is for me. I'm no tree hugger, but I can't stand the thought of all that waste. I'd rather we worked together as a team from the start and got this right straight away. Wouldn't you?'

'When you put it like that…' he reasoned.

Kira smiled. 'Great. My own website has a facility for choosing the right plant for the right place. I'll take you through the process, and then you'll be able to download the selection and spend as long as you like choosing what you want. The final decision will always be yours.'

His eyes narrowed. 'I know. That's why I'm looking forward to co-operating with you. Why don't we go inside? I can check out your suggestions, and try to soften a few of your rough edges at the same time.' He showed her towards the main door of his house.

Stefano ordered coffee and invited Kira into a stark, brightly lit office on the ground floor. It was full of the best and most expensive computing equipment, and the school-room stink of exam papers, solvents and printing ink. She recoiled. It was too sharp a reminder of the days when every exam success meant she was subject to more sneering at home.

With a computer logged in, Stefano stood to let her take his place at the keyboard. Kira called up her website. The moment he saw it, he looked impressed. That gave her confidence a big boost.

'I want to feel the same affection you have for your

own home,' he said, leaning over the back of her chair. 'I enjoy property, yet somehow it never turns out to be the pleasure I expect it to be. Whenever I buy anything, it is a rock-solid investment,' he said, but with an unusual lack of enthusiasm.

Kira was so surprised by the note in his voice, she swivelled her chair around to face him.

'You don't sound convinced, and I can't say I'm surprised. I don't care what my cottage on the Bella Terra estate is worth, but I suppose it will be a lot less than I paid for it.'

'You're right. For once, I don't seem to care about the money. It's something far more important that concerns me, Kira. I want Bella Terra to be much more than simply a run-of-the-mill investment.' He grimaced, and twitched a shoulder.

Kira turned back to the computer screen. He sounded like the typical spoiled billionaire, bemoaning his idle lifestyle.

'Ah, the curse of great wealth!' she muttered.

'I've told you—this isn't about money.' His retort was swift and sure. 'You are a case in point—the first time I looked across the valley from the Bella Terra villa I assumed your cottage would be nothing but a horrible reminder of everything I was trying to leave behind. And yet when you let me get closer, I got a different angle on your little garden and the homely touches inside. I envy you, Kira.' He stopped abruptly and straightened up. 'But maybe that was a case of giving you too much information.'

She felt the exact opposite. 'Why in the world would you envy me? I've got nothing, while you've got everything anyone could ever want!'

He modified his smile, and the angles of his fine face became acute. 'Is that what you think?'

Kira swung back to her screen. Tapping a few names over the keyboard, she accessed her file of planting suggestions for shady places. 'Pretty much.'

'Then I'll shut up. When I lived and worked on the streets, I spent too long listening to financiers and ex-pats moaning. I was a tour guide, not an agony aunt—not that you would have believed it.' He put his coffee cup down beside hers.

'I'll bet you only guided the women!' Kira said with sly humour.

'That depended on where they wanted to be led,' he replied with an equally wicked grin. 'I gave a top-class service to everyone, whoever they were—every time. And that is how I got here.' He gestured around the IT suite of his impressive house. 'I saw that tour guides were always in demand, and they were invariably a rip-off. There was a gap in the market for a first-class service. I set myself up with a second-hand suit and the right attitude, and cleaned up. The sky was my limit, and it still is. My firm has branches all over the world, publishes travel guides—'

He stopped abruptly and frowned. 'And to think—I've had all that success, yet so little satisfaction.'

He leaned against the table beside the keyboard. Kira kept her eyes on her hands as she tapped over the keys.

'I want to be as happy in my houses as you are in your home, Kira,' he announced, and then chuckled. 'That's a tall order, but I believe you can give me answers to all my problems.'

Kira looked into his blue eyes and trembled to think

how much she wanted to do that. Attempting to sound crisp and businesslike, she said, 'Rest assured, I've never disappointed a client yet. If I work for you, I'll do my best to make all your dreams come true.'

CHAPTER SEVEN

KIRA blushed as she realised her words could so easily hold another meaning. She held her breath. Once again she had said exactly what she thought, and that was the problem. Her words were intended to be a promise to make all his desires for his properties come true. Instead, she might as well have told him her deepest feelings. He was watching her intently. Surely it was only a matter of time before she betrayed herself to him? She wanted to give this her best, but felt the need to hide her true emotions. As usual, work came to her rescue. She hit Return on the keyboard with all the force she would have liked to use on herself. The screen leapt into life again. Simulated raindrops falling on the surface of water became a display of plant photographs.

'Almost as beautiful as you,' Stefano said.

Kira thanked him tersely. His words reminded her of Chantal's patronising smile, and the way he could take his pick from all the lovely women in the world.

'I'll key in the details of your courtyard—its aspect, an estimate of the hours of sunshine it can expect—'

'There won't be much of that, I suspect.'

'I have a few ideas that can help,' Kira rallied. She always felt more confident when she could bring the subject around to the plants she loved. Dwelling on her own thoughts and feelings, and speculating on the way he might respond, made her uncomfortable. 'Some discreetly placed mirrors will bounce light into the shadowy places.'

'It sounds like the effect you have on me.'

He was leaning over her, only inches from where her fingers played on the keyboard. The subtle fragrance of his nearness was intoxicating. It was totally impossible to ignore. Kira felt her temperature rising as she logged all the details she had taken down so carefully. She tried to keep her eyes riveted on the screen, but within moments the effort was too much. They were constantly drawn back to Stefano's face. As though to prove he was able to ignore the effect he was having on her, he kept watching the rapidly developing images on the computer screen. Anticipation rose in Kira like a column of mercury. When she was almost at the point of screaming with need for him, he turned his clear blue eyes on her with a smile of sheer innocence.

'So you are confident you can give me what I want?'

His words were warm drops in a dipping pool of desire. He had chosen them with care. Knowing they were calculated for effect was the only thing that made it possible for Kira to resist him.

'While I'm working for you, that's all I'm interested in.'

Her voice was faint and strangely unsteady. Stefano continued to watch her, waiting for more signs that her resistance was weakening. Kira willed herself to return his gaze with equal candour, but she was powerless to stop a blush rippling over her skin. It was a firestorm of feeling. She needed distraction, and looked for it in a new computer image.

'Here's a mock-up of your quadrangle, with the rough shapes of some suggested plant groupings added.'

With one final flourish on the keyboard, she sat back and steadied her nerves with a sip of coffee. Stefano had drawn away slightly while she was typing, but now he leaned forward again. This time, Kira was strangely disappointed to find he was intent on the screen, rather than her.

'That's impressive.' He nodded slowly, his clear blue eyes flicking back and forth between the sidebars of text and the interactive graphics of the screen.

'It's only my first thoughts.' She basked in his approval, but tried not to show it. 'The final version will take a lot more work. And this is only the courtyard. I seem to remember you mentioned a roof garden?'

He nodded. 'There are some stark, flat areas resulting from repairs and building work done in the sixties. I like the idea of a hidden sanctuary that no one else knows about but me.'

'And me, as your designer,' Kira reminded him.

'The best secrets are those we are willing to share.'

Picking up on his enthusiasm, Kira smiled. 'Why don't we go up and inspect what you've got to offer?'

'I thought you'd never ask,' he said, already heading for the door.

Stefano's town house rambled over several floors. It was a warren of unexpected twists and turns. Kira always enjoyed the thrill of seeing how successful people ran their lives. She took in every detail when she visited their workplaces. This satellite branch of Albani International was no exception. Despite her solitary nature, whenever she took on a grand new job Kira spent her time idly wondering what she would tell her grandchildren. Today was different. There was nothing remotely idle about her thoughts. This wasn't just any grand house, owned by a faceless billionaire. It was where Stefano Albani lived. He worked and walked about here, and today he was strolling along beside her. The sensation was so powerful it had an immediate effect on all her dreams. Her fantasy grandchildren gained names, parents and inherited their grandfather's beautiful blue eyes and dark, dashing curls.

As Stefano piloted her along corridors scented by cream polish and fresh flower arrangements, she was torn. Admiring the modern, minimalist surroundings meant tearing her attention away from the gorgeous man at her side. He introduced her to everyone they passed by name. That was impressive. She wasn't quite so happy with the way he spoke to all the women in the same flirty fashion that set her own heart hammering.

'You're very quiet, Kira.' He smiled as they left the busy offices behind. Only the gentle burr of air conditioning followed them beyond a stained-glass door into his private quarters.

'I've been resisting the temptation to contradict you,' Kira said primly. 'You've asked everyone we met to welcome me onto your team. That ignores the tiny fact that I haven't actually agreed to sign your contract yet.'

Stefano's self-confidence shone through his reply. 'You will. You're an intelligent woman.'

His voice was as smooth as the glass elevator that took them up the final two storeys. Letting her out onto the roof, Stefano stood back to let her take in the whole breathtaking panorama. At this distance, the circling shoals of traffic sounded very faint and far away. The click of Kira's heels on the flat cement roof was loud, so she tried to make them sound efficient as well by striding straight over to the nearest parapet.

'This view is astonishing,' she breathed. 'You can see to the hills in almost every direction! We're so high I feel as though I could reach out and touch the dome of the cathedral. The light over the city is so beautiful. What do you suppose gives it that lovely golden glow?'

Stefano strolled to her side. Resting one hand against an ancient wall, he surveyed the scene with obvious pleasure. 'It is the Tuscan sun. It has mingled with the inspiration of poets, and matured over centuries.'

Pleased by the image, she turned to him with an unguarded smile, and found that he had switched his attention from the city to her.

'Do you think you can improve my situation?'

Kira considered her reply. She looked from the spectacular view to the dreary surroundings of his rooftop eyrie. Her mind went into overdrive. 'The beauty of beginning with nothing is that you can try whatever you like. Nobody could top an aerial view of Florence—but I can give you a better backdrop to it, Stefano. When you bring a beautiful woman like Chantal up here, she deserves something a lot better than bare cement and these pigeon prickles…' Patting the metal tangle that stopped birds perching on the parapet, Kira leaned out over the low wall. She was tempted to look straight down. It was a big mistake. Suddenly the events and emotions of the past two weeks rolled over her in a wave of dizziness.

'Ohh…'

She swayed for a terrifying moment, until Stefano seized her with his strong hands and pulled her back from the brink. Her eyes flew open, and she found herself looking up into his lean, intelligent face.

'It is never a good idea to stray too close to the edge,' he said brusquely.

His voice was wonderfully resonant. Kira felt so safe, but it frightened her.

'I—I know. I'm sorry, Stefano. I don't know what came over me.'

'This place can have a very strange effect.' His words were quiet and almost hesitant. They were in complete contrast to his iron grip as it crushed her against the solid security of his body.

'I'm beginning to realise that…' Kira's whisper rose between them like a dream.

'It makes me want to tell you again how beautiful you are, Kira,' he whispered.

She slowly shook her head. To her amazement, she felt Stefano contradict her with a definite nod. Neither of them moved for a long time. Then, in complete harmony, they came together in a kiss that made the world stand still.

After a long, long time, Stefano's lips left hers and he pressed his cheek hard against her hair.

'Come with me. Now,' he urged.

'I can't.'

'Why not?'

'I don't want to be hurt again.'

He stood back a little and looked down at her with a calm, forthright gaze. 'I would never do that.'

'I can't take that risk.' Desperation tore the words from her lips.

'I'm offering you nothing but good things, Kira. How can that bring you pain? Nothing lasts forever. We both know that. As long as we never forget it, there can be nothing but pleasure for us.'

He had been drawing her closer and closer. As his whisper died away, he kissed her with a power that held her long after he had drawn back from her lips.

'So let's enjoy that pleasure while we can....'

Wicked thoughts ran crazily through her mind. It's not as though he's married—no one will ever know, and if they do find out, it won't be like last time....

Her defences dissolved with the intensity of his smile. It was focused directly on her. There could be no resistance. Mirroring his expression, she nodded her head.

Stefano slid one arm around her shoulder and drew her back inside to the elevator. It took only seconds to reach his suite, but his hands were already dancing over the thin fabric of her clothes. He led her into the sophisticated setting of his private lounge. There he slid the jacket from her shoulders and flung it onto a glass-topped table.

'I know what you said about mixing business and pleasure, tesoro, but you would be the first to remind me you haven't actually signed my contract yet,' he murmured.

Kira veered between nervous tension and excitement at the thought of taking a leap into the unknown. For the first time in her life, temptation felt good. There was no need to wonder why. It was an opportunity to indulge in the fantasy that had been teasing her from the moment she first set eyes on him. A throaty chuckle rose up from somewhere deep within her.

'I think that's the perfect reason to make an exception.' Despite a tingle of fear, she wanted to find how far her body would go to quench this overriding fire for Stefano. She already sensed he would give her the ultimate in satisfaction. A strange combination of daring and desire unleashed all sorts of feelings deep in her body.

I know what I'm doing, she told herself. It'll be all right this time, because I'm watching for the danger signs. I can't resist him any more, but it doesn't matter because I don't want to try. I'm going into this with my eyes wide open. I'll enjoy Stefano while he satisfies my every need, but if he dares to try and get inside my heart, that's the end—no more.

From that moment on, there was no more thinking. She was aware of nothing but his touch on her arm and the movement of his body as he drew her into the silent sanctuary of his bedroom. The curtains were drawn against the afternoon sun. It was as cool and shadowy as an oasis at dusk, lit only by a narrow strip where the floor-length curtains were not quite fully closed. A tiny fragment of goose down spiralled upwards in the single shaft of sunlight. It looks as light as my heart feels, Kira thought. It was the last thing she remembered before a surge of need carried away all her inhibitions.

He was more gentle than even her fantasies had promised. His fingertips had a delicacy of touch that sent shivers of delight dancing over her skin. When his cheek brushed her face the roughness of his incipient stubble released a little cry of desire from her lips. It no longer mattered that he had travelled this route with one girl or a thousand. While she was in his arms, Kira felt like the only woman in the world. As the silk and lace of her slip slithered away, she was filled with the exuberance of being. Standing in a pool of sunlight beneath the warm appreciation of Stefano's haunting gaze, she felt the life force thunder through her body. This was where she wanted to be, now and forever.

'Carissima mia,' he breathed in a way that drew Kira's whole attention right back to him.

With a flutter of delight she saw a subtle change come over him. It wasn't so much a new look in his eyes, as the sudden loss of something she had not wanted to acknowledge before. Playful amusement no longer danced in his expression. Stefano was a changed man. For once he was not the flippant lover of thousands. All his attention was devoted to her and her alone.

'You don't mean that,' she murmured, while hoping with all her heart that he did.

'Would you like to put me to the test?' his voice rasped through the drowsy silence. It was thick with an emotion she had never heard from him before. He took one, two steps across the soft rug. Now they were so close, she could feel the warmth of desire radiating from him. His heat transformed her. With a moan of anticipation, her head fell back.

'You are so lovely.'

His voice was a whisper. Kira felt fingertips dance lightly over her face, and then dive into the rippling luxuriance of her coppery hair. His kiss was a long, thoughtful expression of delight. Pressing his forehead against hers, he slid his arms around her body, drawing it close. 'I've said that so many times, to so many different girls, but this is the first time it has been from the core of my being, mia tesoro.'

Kira opened her eyes. Another transformation swept over his face, and with delight she put her hand up to touch the uncharacteristic colour flushing his cheeks. He was holding her with a possessive strength as they sank into the yielding luxury of his bed. Stefano kissed his way down the curve of her neck, before lifting her arm to tease the delicate skin beneath. His lips pleasured her breasts and belly, encouraging her to stretch out languorously across his silken sheets. It was such a lovely, leisurely feeling that when he pulled away from her she tried to follow him, jealous of every second he spent away from her arms.

Stefano had no intention of disappointing her. He had only knelt up to strip off his clothes and give her the full benefit of his magnificent body.

'I want to feel my naked skin against yours.'

His demand was husky but his movements were smooth and unhurried. Watching the relish in his beautiful eyes as he twined his lithe golden limbs around hers was the most wonderful aphrodisiac. As his body glided over and around hers, she floated in the clear blue of his admiring gaze. His hands and lips brought her to the peak of pleasure, time after time, and he left no room in her mind for any doubts. She was his, and she could not get enough of him. Only when she was almost faint from this glorious pleasure overload did he turn to his own satisfaction. With a wild cry his body convulsed in the sheer pleasure of orgasm.

The physical release was absolute, but a new kind of torment was about to begin. Kira had never known her mind and body meld in such a way, but it could not last.

As Stefano enfolded her gently in his arms, she knew things could never be the same between them.

'That was beyond even what I had hoped for,' he murmured.

As he drifted off to sleep, he took Kira's sense of proportion with him. She lay in the gloom, unable to put her fears into words and unwilling to wake him. She had never been in exactly this situation before, but something about it was frighteningly familiar. Her mind reeled back the years to her only other intimate encounter. She had been swept off her feet then, too. Before, during and after sex she had been suspended in a make-believe world which almost instantly unravelled. Her illusions vanished with the cold light of an Oxford morning. The tutor she once idolised had only used her to relieve his midlife crisis. How long would it be before the younger, more virile Stefano wrecked her dreams in a similar way?

She lay awake through all the long dark hours of the night. She knew exactly how this would end. The pain and humiliation were all too familiar. Listening to Stefano's soft, regular breathing as he slept, it was agonising to think he would start taking her for granted from the moment he woke. The infatuation she felt would not survive the death of his sweet words and sensuous touch. She couldn't bear to think he would never look at her in the same way again. What had she done? She had ruined all her own dreams by fulfilling his desires. From the moment she succumbed to his charm, the doomsday clock began marking time on their relationship.

She turned her head. Outside, dawn was breaking. She looked back at him. In sleep, his brow was smooth and untroubled. His finely carved features were heartbreakingly handsome. Such a man would never stay with someone like her. She could not endure the thought of never seeing him again, but what was the alternative? If she didn't run away now, he would dump her. It was as simple as that.

As the sun crept above the distant rim of hills she agonised over what she should do. If she bolted now, she would lose everything—Stefano's respect, any chance for another blissful coupling and all those wonderful opportunities he had promised her. Work seemed a million miles away when she was still being cradled in his arms, but she could not live without it. Her job was her reality. The rhythm and routine of it endured, although everything around her might be falling apart. Stefano's starry list of contacts could ensure the survival of her business.

It took a long time, but Kira had plenty of experience in teasing out the good points of a bad situation. Eventually, she worked out a restless compromise. While Stefano was busy in Florence, she would make sure she was working on his Bella Terra estate. When he retreated to his country hideaway, she would turn her attention to his town house. That way, accepting his offer of a contract would give her the excuse to keep in touch while staying out of his hands.

Holding onto that thought like a lucky charm, Kira eased her way out of bed and headed for the bathroom. Stepping into the shower, she tried to blast away all her regrets. It was impossible. She couldn't have any. Then, to compound her sin, she saw the bathroom door open. Stefano walked in.

He was naked, and joined her in the shower as though

it was the most natural thing in the world. Already shamed by her complete lack of guilt, Kira squeaked and tried to cover herself with her hands. It didn't impress him for a second.

'There isn't a single centimetre of your body that I haven't admired and kissed, *cara*,' he said as the water coursed over him.

'Stefano, this has got to stop,' Kira announced, with as much force as she could against the warm, relaxing water and the tempting sight of his naked body.

'Of course. But not for a little while.' His voice fell as softly as the water.

Squeezing shower gel over his hands, he stroked it expertly over her shoulders and back. The warmth of him in the confined space of the shower cubicle intensified the lemony fragrance of the bubbles he caressed across her skin. Despite her determination not to weaken, Kira could not resist. She closed her eyes, and let her head fall back as he worshipped her body with hands and lips. As they stood beneath the powering torrent of hot water, she felt the urgency of his desire match hers. She moved in close to the sheltering power of his body, pressing herself eagerly against the growing ridge of his manhood. Reaching around, he cupped her bottom in his hands and lifted her off the ground. Kira instinctively twined her legs around his waist. He entered her with a guttural sigh of satisfaction that echoed her own cry of need. Water coursed over their naked bodies as they coupled with a fierce, animal urgency. Kira's orgasm clenched him with a grip as hard as iron, and with a gasp he stopped the water and carried her out of the cubicle. Pulling all the towels from the hot rail, he made a soft nest on the marble floor and settled her down in it.

'Now I know exactly how to please you, I can delay my own pleasure for as long as I like.' Testosterone lowered his voice and made his smile wolflike.

Kira moaned with anticipation as his mouth dipped to nibble one nipple while the pads of his thumb and index finger rolled the other into a hard peak of anticipation. She lost count of the number of times he sent her sweeping over the edge. When she was sure her body could take no more she opened her mouth to beg him to stop, but he anticipated her cry.

'Now it's my turn,' he growled.

Stefano woke her with a kiss. Kira opened her eyes and realised that at some stage they had left the bathroom and moved on, in more ways than one. Stefano was standing beside the bed. He was fully dressed and ready for work. Kira smelled hot coffee and warm pastry, and saw he was holding a tray. She struggled to sit up, the sheet slipping away from her nakedness again. His business suit was beautifully cut, but could not conceal the sudden rise of his manhood as he looked down on her appreciatively.

She looked from him to the breakfast tray. It was set for one.

'Are you leaving, Stefano?'

He placed the tray on her lap. It was complete with fruit, cappuccino and brioche, fresh from his kitchens. Kira gazed at the beautiful display in wonder.

'I'm afraid I must.'

'Two weeks ago, I stopped you coming upstairs in my own home. Now I'm in your bed,' she said faintly. Kira couldn't believe her luck, but wasn't sure whether it would turn out to be the bad kind of fortune, or the good. A long shadow was lowering over the best, most exciting job prospect she had ever been offered. Any woman would be a fool to trust such a dedicated ladies' man. She would be doubly stupid: mixing work and a man had derailed her life once already. It would take a special sort of idiot to fall into that trap a second time. Kira was determined to stay independent. And yet, to resist such an opportunity…

There wasn't much time to decide. Stefano was already heading towards the door.

'I must go. Multi-billion-dollar enterprises don't run themselves, you know.' He smiled at her. 'Take your time to consider my contract, and let me know what you decide. If you make the sensible choice, I'll send a car to collect you later today—I want to take you to Silver Island.'

Kira made a snap decision. 'There's no need. I've made up my mind—I'll sign it.'

Stefano paused, one hand on the door frame. Genuine pleasure, but no real surprise, lit his eyes for a moment. 'I am glad. We have a lot in common, Kira.'

At his reminder of what they had so spectacularly shared, nervous defiance flared in Kira again. 'I can't always be relied on to do exactly as anyone says, Stefano, and once I'm working for you we can't carry on…'

He nodded, and his bright blue eyes became serious. 'Of course. You are your own woman…apart from those moments when I make you mine. So, until later…'

He reached over and kissed her hard, driving all thoughts of rebellion from her mind and leaving her gasping. When he drew back she only just stopped herself reaching for him again. Stefano gave her a look that made her blush. It said he knew exactly what she was feeling. A moment later, he was gone.

CHAPTER EIGHT

KIRA gazed after him, hardly able to believe what had happened. It was madness, she told herself over and over again. It didn't make a shred of difference. All she could think about was the look in Stefano's eyes as he left. His eyes had been dark and full of longing. The memory worked away at her, slowly chipping out a special place for him in her stony heart. Her ill-fated liaison with the lecturer who seduced her had never been anything like this. Hugh Taylor had lied and schemed to get her—and other women—into bed.

Stefano isn't like that, she thought, and then told herself the only difference was his honesty. She had thought of him as Stefano the Seducer before she met him, and that may be true, but at least he was truthful about it. He was quite happy to be the man of her dreams, as long as she woke up afterwards. He never made any pretence at being in this for the long haul. He was out for what he could get, but on their first night together, so was she. Once he sated her desires, Kira delighted in what she could give him.

It had never been like that with Hugh. She had been so upset by the whole business she had abandoned her university course and turned away from academic life altogether. Making love with Stefano made her think and feel in totally new ways. This wasn't some hole-in-the-corner affair. It was an awakening, and one she could dream of experiencing with him again.

She had total recall of every single second she spent with Stefano. It was all so special. She couldn't stop smiling. It had felt so perfect....

Suddenly a shiver ran over her skin. Her smile vanished. The spectre of her past reached out a cold bony finger and tapped her on the shoulder. She had known Stefano for only a few hours, yet her feelings had a cast-iron certainty about them. It made her look deep into her heart. She had never felt this way about Hugh. Never. The firework of that brief infatuation with her tutor had been hot and dangerous, but it had never reached this pitch of perfection. She ached for Stefano with a longing that scared her. He was bound to be as faithless as Hugh. How could she risk her heart and peace of mind again?

The answer was simple.

Because it is Stefano, she told herself, and this time I'm the one in control of the relationship. I won't sacrifice the most exciting job I've ever been offered because I'm afraid of pain. I'll throw my heart and soul into my projects for him. That will satisfy us both, she thought.

When the maid arrived, she found Kira still sitting where Stefano had left her. She was gazing over the rooftops of Florence, lost in thought. Her conscience might be clear, but her eyes were clouded.

Stefano leaned back in his chauffeur-driven Mercedes and breathed a long sigh of contentment. He was still relishing the details of his night of pleasure with Kira.

Soon he would be relaxing on Silver Island with the world's most passionate woman. When they eventually returned to Italy, the Bella Terra villa would be ready for him to move in. Life did not get any better than this.

He felt his brow pleat at the thought of going back to the office. The contrast between these past carefree hours and the urban jungle could not have been more marked. A scowl was as necessary a part of his office uniform as a designer suit and a Rolex. All his working life Stefano had been perfecting that image. Now he had the kingdom to go with it. Everything should have been worthwhile, at last. Today, he had it all—or so everyone kept telling him.

The creases accentuated his dark, beautifully arched brows. Deep in thought, he braced himself for re-entry into the business world of concrete and cut-throats. That was his domain during the working day. Nothing was ever allowed to distract him from it.

Then a faint, feminine perfume drifted through his limousine. He looked around. He had no idea where the scent could be coming from, until inspiration struck. Turning up the lapel of his jacket, he sniffed it appreciatively. He had leaned so close to Kira when he kissed her awake, some of her delicious fragrance had attached itself to his clothes. It brought back all those soft, sweet memories of the night he had spent with his lady of the flowers.

For a split second his frown disappeared again, and he smiled.

Kira's new project was the only thing that could stop her thinking about Stefano. Even that did not work for long. She was continually drawn back by the memory of his whispers through their one unforgettable night together. As she walked along the corridors of his big old town house, she let her thoughts dawdle deliciously over him and his body.

But the moment she crossed any threshold, work took first place again. Daydreams were put on hold until she had noted down a room's aspects and angles of light. It was only as she left that she took a moment to look back and appreciate it. The whole building, every nook and cranny, was filled with faded splendour. All the modern art and electronic offices could not hide its beauty. Every passage was full of interest. The rooms were absorbing. She really relished the chance to choose plants to soften and beautify the balconies and public areas. Most of all she wanted to see Stefano's pleasure—in her work, and in her.

As she was dreaming along an upper corridor, her mobile began to dance.

'Stefano!' To her shame, she almost dropped the phone.

'I never thought one single word could be charged with so much guilt,' he lilted. 'Don't say I caught you with your hand in a cookie jar?'

'No…no, I was busy thinking about something, that's all,' she muttered, her voice indistinct with embarrassment. She had been thinking about him, naked, and spreadeagled across her bed. 'You disturbed me when I was working,' she countered more sharply, as she managed to bring herself back to reality. There was much more truth in her words than he could ever imagine!

'I'm glad to hear you're taking things so seriously. Clearly, this will be a really good relationship—a really good *working* relationship,' he corrected himself carefully.

In spite of her misgivings, Kira blossomed under the warmth of his voice and his small slip-up. It felt as though she grew several inches. Not for the first time, she found that smiling was compulsory whenever Stefano was involved. She couldn't help herself, especially when she heard what he said next.

'Go home and throw a few things into a suitcase. A car will be round to collect you in a couple of hours' time, and take you to the airport,' he announced in a voice that made her tingle with anticipation. 'I'm taking you to see phase two of your commission to landscape my properties.'

The next few hours passed by in a blur. Kira was whisked to the airport and straight onto Stefano's private plane. He met her at the top of the steps and kissed her hand in greeting. She hesitated, not knowing how he wanted to play this reunion. His lips still pressing against her fingers, he gazed at her. The look in his blue eyes was watchful rather than seductive.

'Kira…' He made her name sound so beautiful she blushed. 'Welcome. In a few hours you'll see an entirely new kind of paradise.'

He seemed to be waiting for her reaction, so he could fine-tune his own. Kira decided to play it cool, although the mere sight of him threatened to send her temperature off the scale. She looked around appreciatively. The jet was new and smelled of luxury. Inside, the spacious cabin was an extension of his elegant furnished suite in Florence. It was thickly carpeted, and softly upholstered with linens and silks.

'Paradise? I think I've already arrived,' she breathed, wide-eyed.

* * *

Their trip to Silver Island was smooth and fast. Anything Kira could possibly want was to hand. There was a selection of magazines, several shelves of contemporary and classic novels, but she took her lead from Stefano. After his watchful greeting, he turned to his work. Surrounded by papers, he was riveted to his computer screen. Kira was almost relieved. She had packed her laptop case with plenty of work, and cautiously picked a workstation on the other side of the aeroplane. It kept her within reach, while maintaining the privacy she usually guarded so fiercely.

Unfortunately, it no longer felt quite so natural to keep her distance from him. Many times during the flight she felt her eyes drawn across the cabin to where he sat. To glance at him openly was to run the risk he might start a conversation. Kira had no idea what she could to say to him, outside the subjects of bed and the plans for his properties. She wasn't sure words would come easily on those subjects, either. With relief, she fell back on her plans for the Florence town house and its roof garden. Soon she was lost in her imagination, but it was still impossible to forget Stefano's presence. Every few moments a strange feeling crept over her, as though she was being bathed in a warm glow. The first few times it happened, she glanced up at him. He was always hard at work. With a shrug, she would turn back to her work, puzzled. It was odd. She could practically feel his eyes on her, but each time she checked he was gazing impassively at his paperwork.

Finally, the pilot announced that Silver Island was coming into view over the starboard wing. Kira instantly looked out of the window. A scatter of green islands rose softly from a sea that was almost as tranquil as Stefano's eyes.

'Oh, I've never seen anything so lovely!' she gasped.

'I have,' Stefano said quietly.

Kira looked over her shoulder, ready to make room for him if he joined her for a view from the window. He never moved. Instead, he sat back in his seat, watching her with a steady gaze.

'And if you think that is beautiful,' he murmured, 'wait until you are framed by orchids, set against a tropical moon and a sky scattered with stars.'

They flew in to a private airstrip. Unlike the sun trap of the Bella Terra estate, this land was cooled by sea breezes. The atmosphere was as clear as crystal. As she stepped down from the plane Kira stretched her arms up to the sun and revelled in the sharp salty tang in the air.

'This is wonderful,' she breathed, but the dream was just beginning. A car swept up to take them to a nearby quay. There, brightly painted fishing boats bobbed alongside the sun-warmed boardwalk, but Stefano led her towards a very different craft. Handing her down into a sleek black-and-gold speedboat, he took the controls and headed out towards a blue-green cloud low on the horizon.

'This is where I thought to make my base, until I discovered the Bella Terra estate,' he told her as the speedboat skipped across the clear blue sea like a flying fish. Kira watched indistinct shapes in the distance become a necklace of islands set in the warm, shallow sea. High, forested mountains rose up from shallow shelving beaches of flawless white sand. As they ran into the shallows, she saw the tension ease from Stefano's face once more. Boys playing football on the beach raced to greet them. As Stefano handed over the mooring rope, Kira was seized by a mad impulse. By the time he moved to help her from the boat she had slipped off her sandals and jumped barefoot into the water.

'Careful, the surf runs fast here!' Stefano called, but his warning was too late.

Dizzy with travel and excitement, Kira was pulled in two directions at once. Her feet went from under her and she promptly sat down in two feet of surging water. Stefano reached down and hauled her up. She surfaced, spluttering, to roars of laughter from the beach footballers.

'Are you all right?' Stefano's concern was obvious, but Kira was laughing as hard as anyone.

'It's wonderful!' She giggled, pushing her drenched hair back from her face. Her skirt was sodden, and wrapped itself in clinging folds around her slender legs.

'Take a seat and catch your breath.' He took her towards the treeline, where coconut palms draped cool shadows out over the sand. Kira sat down thankfully on a perfectly placed trunk. Instantly, a waiter appeared at her side. He was holding a tray with two tall glasses of passion-fruit cocktail, clinking with ice.

'This is heaven!' she gasped. Stefano laughed.

'Not yet, but it will be. I've gathered a world-class team to create an island paradise, and you're here to see how it can be made still more stunning.'

Kira took a long, slow sip of her drink. 'It'll be a challenge—' she smiled mischievously '—but I'm sure I'll think of something.'

'There's no hurry,' he said softly. 'No hurry at all. It's been a long flight. Shall I show you where you can freshen up?'

Kira bit her lip. She had spent the night with Stefano. There could be no secrets between them now, but that was what made her afraid. He was about to lead her to his suite. She wasn't ready for that and knew she should refuse, yet at the same it was everything she wanted. Stefano barely seemed to notice.

'I've had one of the guest suites made ready for you,' he said, taking her hand and leading her across the white, warm sand. Her sigh was a strange mixture of relief and disappointment, and he looked back with a laugh.

'Did you think I'd forget what you told me? You said there would be no repeat of our passionate night once you had signed my contract. I don't intend to blur the line between employer and employee.'

'Thank goodness for that,' Kira said determinedly, but with a heart that had suddenly plummeted. *Fool!* she berated herself. *Don't mistake his flirtation for serious intentions. It's good that he wants to keep this businesslike.* Tell herself what she would, however, the idea that she might never go to bed with Stefano again made her feel as though she'd lost something utterly precious. Caught up in her thoughts, she nearly missed his next words.

'Although I like to keep my staff happy,' he went on, and suddenly his eyes lit up with a dangerous spark. 'So I always make a special effort for new arrivals. That's why I'm inviting you to dinner at my apartment this evening.'

He moved closer. Kira felt it with every heartbeat. If

he was trying to test her, she was equal to it. 'Like you, I always mean what I say, Stefano.'

His eyes twinkled in the dancing sunlight. 'Fine. I wanted to see if you had changed your mind, that's all.'

With a wolfish smile he lifted her chin with his hand. She had been remembering his touch all day, but her memory was nowhere near as powerful as the real thing. His skin glided over hers like a kiss of fire, drawing a gasp from her lips.

'Second chances make life worth living, don't you think?'

His voice ended in a whisper of longing. Enfolding her in the curve of his arm, he drew her the last few inches towards his body. His kiss was a long, slow promise of all the things Kira knew he was so brilliant at. She could not help but respond. She was aware of all the dangers, but they were nothing when matched against his powers of seduction. Knowing she should pull back, she forced herself to do it.

At her first hesitation he let her go. His hands drifted regretfully from her body. She took a step back from him, struggling to catch her breath. Her common sense was marginally easier to manage.

'Last night was a mistake. One of those should be enough for both of us.'

His touch slid down her back, lingered around her ribs and then fell away. Pushing his hands deep into his pockets, he shrugged.

'I know—' he gave her an irrepressible smile '—but you surely can't blame me for trying?'

'I've told you. Now I'm officially on your payroll,

there can be nothing between us. I'm only interested in doing the best I can for you.'

He cocked his head on one side and regarded her with the keen look of a bush robin. 'Ah, but in what way?'

'You're my employer, nothing more,' Kira said firmly, desperately in need of the reminder. She had managed to keep her emotions out of it—until now. She could feel herself sliding out of control. Equally determined to call her bluff, Stefano wasn't about to give her a second chance to back down.

'Okay. If that's how you feel, follow me, and I shall show you to your room.'

He was already walking away. Kira was drawn along in his wake, trying to catch up.

'Isn't it lovely? Silver Island is the ideal refuge for me—and anyone I choose to invite here.'

Those last words were thrown casually over his shoulder as he walked into the treeline. Kira followed him. She caught him up as he breasted a little rise where palms gave way to lush, leafy shrubs. This oasis of cool shade was the perfect place for a collection of freshly whitewashed buildings. Each was roofed with yellow ochre tiles, patterned with age.

'That's my headquarters.' Stefano pointed out the largest building as they crossed a clearing. 'Like all my properties, the first thing I do is bring in office staff, so I can keep my finger on the pulse of business, day and night.'

Kira laughed at the picture he painted.

'It's no wonder you never feel at home! You make everywhere into an extension of your office.'

Stefano frowned and did not reply. They drew closer to the buildings. As they crossed the pine- and balsam-scented clearing, a cloud of brightly coloured parakeets exploded into the air from the eaves of an apartment building. It was twice the size of La Ritirata. Unlike Kira's ancient little home, its roof was supported by all the walls in all the right places. She was instantly impressed. As Stefano showed her up the steps of her temporary home, she was already wondering what design ideas she could take back with her.

'Well? What do you think?'

Kira had been too wrapped up in her own thoughts to realise Stefano was interested in her opinion. When she jumped at his light touch on her waist, he dropped his hand and stepped back. Hurriedly, she went in to discover her apartment's air-conditioned luxury—and stopped dead.

'It's amazing!' she breathed, and it was true. Her luggage stood in the centre of a large, cool room. There were big, squashy chairs and a matching settee for loafing. The floor covering was thick and plush. Beautiful art stood on every shelf, while woven hangings added splashes of colour against the sparkling white walls. Everything was brand new—and it was all oddly soulless, as though the wraps had been taken off this apartment especially for her.

'Am I your only guest, Stefano?'

'At the moment, yes.' He strolled over to where a reclining nude sculpted from rich red wood stood on a side table. Drawing his fingers over its glowing flanks, he gazed at her thoughtfully. 'At least, you're the first to stay in this particular building.'

Kira didn't say anything. Instead, she let him show her around the bland and beautiful apartment. Everything was absolutely right, from the wall hangings to the ethnic rugs and the huge gold-and-marble bathroom.

'I think it's wonderful,' Kira said as she strolled into her new bedroom. A genuine Victorian bed stood at its heart. The pillows and thick, soft mattress looked so inviting—but to her embarrassment her first thoughts at the sight of such a bed were certainly not of sleep.

'I'm impressed you haven't followed me in here,' she said airily.

Her words provoked a reaction in him, but too late she discovered it wasn't the one she wanted.

'You said you wanted me to stop all that,' he drawled, leaning against the door frame.

With a pang, she turned to face him. Her first rebuke had worked better than she expected. One look at his beautiful face and she knew he could see through her flinty manner to the real, pulsating woman within. She flushed with shame as he continued to watch her, his gaze feeling heavy as a caress on her skin.

'From now on,' he said softly, 'you're the one who makes the decisions. For example, whether you want to have dinner with me this evening at eight o'clock is entirely up to you.'

It was a statement, not a question. Before he finished speaking he pushed himself upright and strolled away through her apartment.

Stefano caught himself smiling as he headed for his own bungalow. That was a surprise. He had known Kira was a passionate woman beneath her reserve, but he hadn't expected such untapped depths of sensuality. She had been so determined not to fall for his charm that usually he would have looked elsewhere without a second thought, but she was different. Her hands put a stop to their kiss on the beach, but her lips told a different story. Stefano knew women and Kira Banks was definitely a girl worth waiting for. She would make such a change from the extrovert capers of his usual women. She needed much more careful handling, and Stefano knew he was the ideal man to conquer her fears. A few days of his company, together with the allure of this tropical island, would slowly melt her English reserve.

Like a stalking leopard, Stefano settled down for a long wait.

Kira watched him walk away. He never once looked back, although something told her he knew very well that her eyes were on him. She stayed motionless, until he disappeared inside his bungalow and closed the door. It was only then she took refuge inside her own rooms.

Leaning back against the closed door, she looked around. This place was paradise. A wand of fragrant orchids peeped over the nearest windowsill. Outside, the parakeets returned, tumbling over the eaves and squawking with delight. Silver Island had everything—including the only man she could ever want. This should be the project from heaven, and more holiday than work. Yet Kira already felt stressed. She might as well have been back in England, trying to sort out her stepparents' chaotic finances.

She knew she should ignore Stefano's invitation to dinner. Her willpower would be under pressure from the moment she crossed his threshold.

Somehow, that didn't feel like such a terrible threat any more. A small smile flitted across her face. When

Stefano wasn't with her, she missed him. That was a totally alien experience for Kira. It made her feel unsure of herself. She didn't like it, but she did like Stefano—in a way that encouraged all sorts of outrageous thoughts.

She was having a particularly wild idea right now. Any truly independent, intelligent person ought to be able to accept his invitation to dinner. She had come a long way over the past couple of years. She was a successful businesswoman. A perfectly respectable dinner with a man she fancied was exactly the treat she deserved for landing such a lucrative contract. It would also be an opportunity to put herself to the test. If she succeeded in resisting Stefano this evening, she would be unstoppable. There would be no limit to what she could achieve, if only she could show her new boss that not every woman would roll over and beg for his body straight away.

If she failed, the worst that could happen was that he would ravish her senseless. Her heart and mind would never be in danger. They were safely locked away, somewhere Stefano would never be allowed to find them.

Kira felt she couldn't lose.

CHAPTER NINE

ONE long, luxurious bath later, Kira slipped into the single evening dress she had packed. It was a silky little emerald number she had worn for the most recent Chelsea gala night.

I'll show Stefano that when it comes to his charms, I can be chilled steel. I can resist him, she told herself a hundred times.

The mirror told a different story. Her eyes were dark with arousal. The tip of her tongue rested against the glossy cushion of her lower lip as she pinned her mane of auburn hair up into a sophisticated coil. The sight made her smile. She looked good, and knew it. Loose tendrils danced over the creamy curves of her neck and shoulders. Her dress was a sumptuous slither of sequinned silk. Its opulent shade of green complemented the rich tawny of her hair. With every movement it shimmered like the sea.

As she twirled and swirled in front of the full-length mirror, Kira went on deceiving herself. Instead of trying to put Stefano off by dressing like a drudge, she would make this evening still more of a challenge by making herself irresistible. Then, when he tried to seduce her and failed, her triumph would be complete. After all, when we met I was only dressed in dusty jeans and look what happened then! It's not the clothes he should be interested in, but what is inside them, she told herself, managing to limit her self-delusion right at the end. There was absolutely no point in imagining he was only interested in her brain. To her horror, the reflection looking back from the glass smiled instead of frowned. Stefano Albani was all man. He had proved it to her any number of times during their fantastic night together.

She checked her appearance again. Her smile faltered, and then returned with added self-assurance. She loved this dress, and for once the torture of a social occasion was going to be sweet, sweet, sweet.

She added one last finishing touch. It was truly spectacular. With her first impressive pay cheque, Kira had spoiled herself with a real diamond necklace. It contained the smallest stones in captivity, brilliantly cut and cleverly set to make them look larger. Tiny they might be, but she was really proud of her necklace. It didn't matter to her that she never went anywhere she could wear it. That wasn't the point. It was beautiful, and it was hers.

She laid the galaxy of tiny stars against her skin and fastened the catch. Then she took the matching earrings from their royal-blue velvet bed. It had taken her a further two years of careful saving to add them to her collection, and this was the first time they had been out of the box. Finally, glittering like moonlight on the sea, she set off on the nerve-racking walk to Stefano's bungalow.

Her nerves were tuned to a high C of tension by the time she reached his apartment. They weren't helped by movement sensors switching on a battery of security lights. Startled by the sudden blaze, a deer shot away through the undergrowth. It leapt like her heart as it dived into cover. That close shave did nothing for Kira's nerves. Feeling like a prisoner on the run under all the lights, she started up the front steps. Raising her hand, she knocked hesitantly. Five…ten…fifteen seconds passed with no reply. Then she noticed the bell. The bungalow was so large, the chances were that Stefano hadn't heard her nervous tapping. She leaned on the bell, and heard it echoing through the building beyond. He must have heard it, but it still felt an awfully long time passed between pressing the button and seeing the bungalow door open.

'Kira.'

Stefano loomed in the doorway, dressed in an immaculate white shirt and dark trousers. He looked magnificent, but it was his expression that snatched her breath away. He was looking at her with the same illicit pleasure she had seen in her reflection only a few moments before. 'You look incredible.'

'Thank you!' she said breathlessly, relying on the glittering diamonds, sequins, lipgloss and nail polish to speak for her. It was a risky venture. There was a fine line between untouchable beauty and come-hither.

He stepped back from the door with an inviting gesture. 'Come in and make yourself comfortable.'

Kira followed him into the bungalow. The building smelled of new money and even newer paint. It was as tasteful as her own apartment, and just as soulless.

'I've given most of my staff the evening off.'

Kira stared at him. He returned her look with one that danced with silent amusement.

Escape was still not impossible. She could have reached out and touched the door from where she was standing. All it needed was a quick goodnight. She could make some excuse and slip out into the safety of darkness, beyond the security lighting.

She didn't do any of those things. Instead, she looked around. Rather than cowering by the door, she began to unfold like a flower. After all, she told herself, there's no triumph in running away. She had accepted Stefano's invitation. If she took up the challenge of treating him like a trustworthy employer rather than a casual lover, that was even better.

Stefano began moving around the room with careful deliberation. Under Kira's gaze, he shook sofa cushions and dragged scattered magazines into a pile.

'Now you've had time to settle into your own apartment, why don't you have a look around here, and tell me what you think?' he asked her as he prowled around.

'I think you have a beautiful house, on a lovely island. The peace and quiet here make it almost as perfect as the Bella Terra valley,' she said simply.

'Almost?' Stefano asked.

Kira didn't answer him. The large main room of his apartment had been painted pale ochre, with the woodwork a slightly lighter shade. It was sparsely furnished, with polished boards rather than carpet on the floor. They gave it a rather hollow feeling. The whole atmosphere was light and bright rather than warm and welcoming. It echoed the impersonal touch that seemed to follow Stefano around, but she didn't know how to explain it to him. Instead, she went to investigate two long leather couches and a beautiful large glass coffee table while he headed for the sound system.

'Make yourself comfortable while I set things in motion. We're dining on the mainland, so I'll alert the launch.' He walked towards the nearest telephone.

'Oh…I thought we'd be eating here?' Kira could not keep the disappointment from her voice. 'Leaving this paradise and plunging back into the chaos of city life doesn't appeal in the slightest.'

Stefano had been studying one of his works of art with a critical eye. When she said that, he stopped and looked straight at her instead. A slow smile spread across his face 'Squisita! You are an unusual woman, Kira. Not everyone would choose a simple dinner rather than air-conditioned luxury.'

'Well, I would,' said Kira firmly. 'You are so lucky, being able to escape from everyone and everything whenever you like.'

His art collection forgotten, Stefano's attention was now firmly riveted on Kira. One hand in his pocket he strolled towards her, his eyes intent on her face.

'Is that what you think?'

Kira looked askance. 'Why would I say something I didn't mean?'

'You'd be surprised how many people do. All of the women I speak to, as a matter of fact. With one notable exception.' He inclined his head to her, interest very obvious in his beautiful eyes.

'That's what living does for you.' Kira was hardly aware of what she was saying. Only one thing mattered, and that was the lovely warm feeling that came from basking in his appreciation. 'It's easy to forget what life is actually about.'

'And what do you think that is?' He was looking at

her with intensity and his expression demanded nothing less than the absolute truth.

'I'd love to be able to say home and family, but I've only got experience of half that equation. I've got the home. It's better than I ever dreamed it would be, but I've never known what a happy family feels like. My idea of what it must be like is hopelessly romantic. Please shoot all my delusions down in flames by telling me your Italian family background is full of fights and bad feeling, and not a bit like the cheerful stereotype!' Kira tried to joke past the pain, but she wasn't the only one with issues. For the first time in heart-stopping minutes, Stefano avoided her eyes. It was a painful reminder that she might not be the only person in the world hiding inner turmoil.

Walking over to the fully stocked bar that stood in a far corner of the room, he spooned ice cubes into two tall glasses. 'What would you like?'

To take back the last thing I said, Kira thought, wishing she hadn't rattled on so cheerfully. 'I'll have a St Clement's, please,' she muttered.

As a distraction, it worked perfectly. Stefano left the bar and stepped through a pair of French doors. Kira watched him reach out and select the ripest fruit from big old citrus trees shading the veranda. When he returned, so did his smile. In one hand he held a spray of polished, dark green leaves. Nestling at their heart was a cluster of waxy white blossoms and purple-stained buds. He held it out to her gallantly.

'This is for you, to make up for the bouquet that would have been waiting for you at the restaurant in town.'

'Thank you!' she whispered, glowing with pleasure.

The heavy, sweet fragrance stole through the warm evening air between them. 'It's lovely!'

'Then it is exactly the right gift for you,' he said quietly, moving in still closer. 'Let me see how it can be fixed...'

'No!' Kira leapt back in alarm. It was already hard enough keeping him at arm's length. When he lavished her with flowers and soft words, it was impossible. 'I mean, no, thank you. The perfume is so powerful I'd rather have them in a vase on the table.' *And I can pretend to be looking at them, when I'm really looking at you!* The words raced desperately through her mind as she watched him walk back to the bar. He halved all the fruit and extracted the juice with powerful but deft movements. Then he presented her with a perfect cocktail.

'That's really impressive. You handled that knife like a professional.'

'Call it the legacy of a wasted youth,' he said, mixing himself the driest of dry martinis.

'I know all about that,' she said with a shiver as the ice rattled enticingly in her glass.

Stefano's shoulders visibly relaxed, as though he had ordered them to. Until that moment Kira had assumed he was always perfectly at ease. Now she knew better. The change in him was noticeable. The mask was back in place.

'I doubt that very much, but we can discuss it over dinner. What would you like? Name it, and my chef will make it for you.'

He must have been through this routine with a thousand women. Kira heard the ring of fine crystal echoing again across the glade from his kitchens. No doubt they were getting ready to serve a meal fit for the latest princess of Silver Island. She had no intention of being a temporary attraction. The reason she was here was to stake her claim to something much more important than that. Caviar and champagne counted for nothing if it lacked one simple ingredient. She wanted Stefano's respect. That was more important than any amount of cordon bleu cookery, and she intended to get it. Leaving her drink on the bar she strolled away to admire a piece of glass sculpture so that he would not see her smile.

'Do you know what I'd really like, if it's not too much trouble?'

'Dressed in silk and diamonds? Do you want me to offend your sense of decency?'

Regarding him with a cool, steady gaze she said slowly, 'I'll tell you what would make my evening complete. Something utterly simple. No distractions.'

'No oysters or asparagus?'

'Aphrodisiacs? I don't need them,' she said simply.

He laughed, but for the first time the amusement never reached his eyes. As he phoned through to the kitchen, Kira watched him with intense interest. Moving restlessly beneath her gaze, he showed her into the dining room.

'I'll bet you can't remember the last time you shared such a simple meal with a girl,' she said idly.

There was nothing half-hearted about Stefano's reaction.

"On the contrary, I'll never forget it.'

His tone was so strange Kira shot a quick look at him. In profile he had a gaunt, distracted look she had never noticed before. As she watched, he collected himself and added, 'She was a girl who knew her own mind, too. That's the reason she's not here to share all this, tonight.' He pushed a hand out to indicate the luxury surrounding them. Kira could not help thinking of the svelte, glamorous Chantal.

'Someone else who wouldn't stand for your womanising ways?' she said slyly. 'So that makes two of us.'

'No, only one.'

That must mean she won't put up with it, but he thinks I will! Kira thought indignantly.

She was about to spring to her own defence, but the words died on her lips. Something about the way Stefano abruptly turned his back on her warned her to keep quiet. He walked over to the long, highly polished dining table. Closing his long sensitive fingers around one of the chairs, he pulled it out for her to sit down.

'And now, no more questions. You accepted my invitation to dine, so it's up to me to play the part of charming host.' The tension drained from his voice as he watched her shimmer into her seat. Candles set in silver candelabra stood in the centre of the table. Stefano lit them. Instantly, a million sparkles danced over the diamonds at Kira's throat. The same cold fire ran over her silken dress. It melted the frown creasing Stefano's brow. She actually saw him catch his breath, and it was wonderful.

'Kira...you have never looked lovelier,' he murmured.

She couldn't answer. Deep in her heart she hoped it was true, and wished she could believe him. While she was preening in front of her mirror, the thought of him had transformed her. Now he was working his magic on her in living, breathing reality. She felt fantastic, and he was telling her she looked it, too.

I have to put a stop to this. Right now, Kira told herself desperately. She was only here to prove to herself that she could resist him, that this was an adult, business relationship only....

But when Stefano looked at her in that way, only the first part of her brave statement was true. Business was the very last thing on her mind. The idea of a hot, very adult relationship with Stefano pushed everything else out into the cold.

Only a discreet knock at the door saved her. Swift, sure staff presented dinner on silver dishes and the finest china plates. Kira barely noticed the food. She could think of nothing but the tussle between her body's needs and her common sense. Stefano was trouble; she knew it.

'This is spectacular!' she laughed as the waiters poured her a chilled glass of pinot grigio.

'My guests always enjoy the best.'

'Is this how you entertain all your women?'

'No.'

Kira paused and looked along the table to where he was sitting. He looked up and met her eyes.

'What's the matter?'

'Then what do you do?'

His puzzled frown was exactly that—puzzled. However hard Kira tried to be suspicious, she couldn't spot anything shifty in his expression.

'Why this sudden obsession with other women?' His gaze was equally searching.

'You said I was only the second woman to stand up to you.'

He laughed. 'Yes...' He paused, clearly turning something over in his mind. 'If you must know, each time you answer back you remind me of my little sister, Maria.'

'Oh...I thought you were comparing me to...'

Kira's voice sounded very small suddenly, as she became aware of how little she really knew this man. His eyes burned with cold fire.

'No. Never.'

Kira's mind worked with the speed of light. She pieced together enough hints to know this was a delicate area.

'Were you very close to your sister?' she risked, pretending to be busy with her meal.

'We were inseparable. We had to be, on the streets. She had no one else to protect her.'

He dropped his fork with a clatter. Kira looked up sharply. Elbows on the table, his fingers were netted in front of his mouth as though to stop any more words escaping.

'Maria was very lucky to have a brother like you looking after her,' she said, hoping to sidestep the awkward subject. Stefano was not so tactful.

'It was people like me who made the streets dangerous in the first place,' he muttered.

'I don't think so.' Kira tried to pacify him, but she was desperate to hear more. 'You must have been different, even then. You told me how you started your own business.'

'Maria's death was the only reason I changed.'

He stopped talking, and looked up to meet her eyes. He saw only sympathy and willingness to listen. Taking a deep breath, he continued, his voice hoarse and seeming to force the words out. It was the first time he'd told anyone the truth for more than twenty years. 'She was killed when a raid on a shop went wrong. She hadn't wanted to go—I convinced her, saying it was "for the good of the family." It was my fault. From that moment on I vowed to turn my life around, and I did.'

'Maria would be really proud of you now.'

Stefano exhaled so heavily all the candle flames fluttered.

'I'm not so sure. When I decided to go straight, I made a clean break. Since her funeral, I haven't spoken to any members of my family. I turned my back on them all when I abandoned that way of life. It was the only way to get out. The last time I saw any of them was when I was acting as a witness for the prosecution.'

Oh, why did I have to open my big mouth? Kira thought desperately. She wanted to reach out and comfort him, but didn't dare. Where would that lead for either of them? Placing her knife and fork carefully on her plate she hoped for inspiration. None came. Instead, Stefano sprang to his feet when he saw she had finished. Collecting the remains of their meal, he carried it out to the kitchen. Kira fought the impulse to follow him. She desperately wanted to apologise for raising the subject, hold him, share his pain and tell him everything would be okay. It was impossible. Stefano wasn't that sort of man. Expecting an agonising wait, she was relieved when he came back almost immediately with a confection of tropical fruit sorbets. They glittered like jewels set in crystal dishes.

'There are sponge cakes and wafers, too, in case you share Maria's appetite as well as her temper,' he told her, sounding perfectly normal. There was no trace of the anguish she expected. All the self-control was back in place. Astonished, Kira looked up into his gaze. He was expressionless again, but something in her questioning face seemed to relax him.

'You're right, Kira. There are plenty of things about my life of which Maria would be proud. I'd never thought of that until you said it.'

'Wasn't it obvious?' she said as he placed the delicious dessert in front of her.

'No. I'd genuinely never considered it. All I focused on was losing her, and then the rest of my family. I knew there had to be more to life than crime and handouts. I made myself master of my own destiny. Working gave me an outlet, and an escape. I channelled all my frustrations into learning as much as I could about my own city, and then other places, as I climbed the ladder to success. That single-minded toil dulled the pain, but it left an awful void. Maybe that's why I'm never satisfied.'

He drew back from her suddenly. 'I've never told anyone that before,' he added, with such an air of surprise Kira couldn't help smiling.

'Then thank you,' she said softly.

On impulse, she stood. Before either of them knew what was happening, she kissed him on the cheek.

Coming to her senses like a sleepwalker waking from a dream, she dropped straight back into her seat. Until a moment before, she had been ready to resist him. Now she didn't know how she felt. In that same instant, Stefano made her confusion worse. He reached out and squeezed her hand.

'Let's live in the present and future, not the past, Kira.'

With a final pat he left her side and went back to his seat at the far end of the table.

* * *

Much later, Kira lay back on one of the long, cream leather couches and felt a huge smile creep across her face. A threatened disaster was turning into the best evening she had ever spent. The rest of the night had passed in a glorious blur of conversation—the best kind. Sharing true thoughts and ambitions and dreams. She felt filled with utter happiness.

A sound from the doorway made her sit up quickly. Stefano stood there, coffee in hand, looking at her.

'I didn't mean to wake you,' he said softly. Suddenly the sensual tension which had been disguised with words drew taut again. His gaze was serious, clouded and full of desire.

'It's okay. I wasn't asleep.'

She stretched into a sitting position as he came towards her.

'You don't have far to go,' he said simply.

Kira watched him placing things on the glass surface beside her. He wasn't looking at her any longer, but her body jangled from his nearness. He turned his head suddenly and she was caught in his gaze, almost trembling.

'Kira, tonight has been fantastic. In fact, I can't remember a night like it.'

'Nor me.' She sighed. 'Before I met you, I was uptight all the time. You're quite a role model.' Taking the cup and saucer from his hands, she looked reflective. 'I really wish I could be like you all the time, Stefano.'

He chuckled and sat down a little distance away from her, cradling his coffee. 'What—cold, calculating and immune to human feeling?'

'You need a little of those qualities to really succeed

in business. Loss, and an unhappy childhood, forces that tough shell onto people. I know all about that.'

'I do, too—although your background is still a mystery to me.' He watched her sip her drink. 'I've got every qualification the school of hard knocks can deliver, but what can have been wrong with your childhood? You told me it was full of Cotswold Christmases.'

'I was the big problem in my childhood,' she told him glumly. 'My adoptive parents wanted a porcelain doll, but they ended up with me instead. I've always liked doing things. They simply wanted me to *be*. I've never been happy, acting the part of a dim ornament.'

'I can imagine.' He smiled with a warmth that encouraged Kira to open up a little more.

'But that's all in the past. Now I'm earning a decent living, my stepparents can forgive me anything—as long as I keep sending the cheques home.'

He grimaced. 'Maybe you're lucky to have a family to spoil?'

She wriggled around to face him as they sat together on the settee. 'I wish that was all they wanted.'

He leaned forward and lifted the plate of sweet treats up from the coffee table. As he offered it to Kira, she got a tantalising hint of his evocative aftershave. She breathed deeply, but despite the distraction could not resist a piece of crystallised pineapple. Stefano selected a strawberry dipped in dark chocolate before putting the plate back on the table.

'The problem is, settling debts comes right at the bottom of my stepparents' list of priorities. I can't bear to think of them being without heat, light or transport so I bail them out—at least in theory. In reality, they use most of my money to send more invitations around the country club.'

Stefano made lazy circles in his coffee with a silver teaspoon. 'Why don't you offer to settle their debts direct?'

Kira was aghast. 'What—go behind their backs? I couldn't do that!'

'Then you'll have to be tough with them, Kira, and say "no more,"' Stefano said sharply. 'It will hurt in the short term, but will end up saving you a lot of grief. I should know,' he finished darkly.

Kira rolled her lip, wishing she could take his advice. 'It's all right for you. You're always so self-assured.'

He looked at her long and hard before replying. 'You don't do so badly. In fact, I would say you are an unusually forthright woman. You were certainly very decided about our plans tonight.'

Kira laughed. 'I've told you before. I like simple pleasures. You can have too much of a good thing!'

'I know, but I never expected to find anyone who agreed with me.' He sipped his coffee in silence, and then slowly and deliberately put it down on the table. 'Am I one of your simple pleasures, Kira? Or too much of a good thing?'

Her eyes remained on his hand. He drew it back from his cup, and rested it lightly on his thigh.

She bit her lip. 'I don't know. I can't decide.'

He hitched his shoulders in a casual gesture. 'You accepted my invitation and came for dinner.'

'Maybe I shouldn't have done.'

'Yes, you should, and I know you enjoyed the evening. I did, too,' he said, so quickly that she couldn't possibly doubt it. But worrying was a tough habit to break.

'Are you sure, Stefano?' she asked uncertainly.

'I'm positive.'

Her willpower started to wobble. Nothing had happened…so far. When Stefano seduced her the first time, it had simply been physical, if spectacular. Now, having spent the evening with such a sweet, funny, charming man, she was terribly worried. If he loved and left her after this, she would never be able to bear it.

'I'm not sure at all. I can't trust my own judgement any more, Stefano,' she confessed. Surely it was best to tell him the bad news straight out. 'I give money to lost causes. I made a fool of myself over a man and got my name all over the papers as a result. It was hell, and I'm so afraid of it happening again.'

The words escaped from her in a rush. She looked down at her lap, stunned to hear herself speak the words she had held back for so long. Beside her, she sensed Stefano tense. Her fingers twisted painfully as she waited for the questions to start.

'It's no wonder you send out mixed messages,' he said quietly. 'I wanted you from the moment I spotted you from the helicopter. When you put up barriers, I held back. Normally, I'd simply walk away, but something about you keeps me coming back. What happened? Tell me.'

His concern was so genuine. Kira was touched. Still staring at her hands, she spoke in the hope that sharing her pain might soften it somehow. 'I made an idiot of myself while I was at university. If I'm honest I knew there was something wrong about Hugh Taylor from the start. He only gave me his mobile number, saying he didn't have a landline at home. We never went back to his place, which should have been the decider. When I discovered he was married, I was too weak and stupid to drop him like the rat he was. To my shame I let the affair limp on, but I didn't know the half of it. It was left to his poor wife—or rather, one of them—to expose his double life. He was already a bigamist when he moved to Oxford, and started on me. The story was horrible enough to make the papers, and ruin me.'

There. She had said it. All the shame and embarrassment rushed over her again. She covered her face with her hands, unable to bear Stefano's gaze and sure she would never be able to look him in the eyes again after this.

'I was such a fool…' she went on through her fingers. 'I'd led such a sheltered life. I didn't know any better and took his bait. To know everyone was talking about me behind my back was awful. And my stepparents won't let it rest, even now…. There was no way on earth I could have carried on with my course after that. The shame was unendurable.'

Oblivious to everything but her pain, she had been rocking backwards and forwards. It was only when a light touch fell on her shoulder that she came to her senses. When Stefano spoke, she almost lost them again.

'How could anyone treat you like that?' he whispered.

'It's what people do. They use you, and then walk away,' she muttered, overwhelmed by the grubby scandal of it all.

'Yes. Life is hard for the weak.' Stefano's voice cut through the silence like a knife.

Kira dropped her hands and turned a simmering stare directly on him. If there was one thing she found more painful than self-hatred, it was someone else's pity.

'I am *not* weak,' she said, with absolute conviction.

'I know.' His reaction was equally unexpected. 'I was blaming myself for things I did, long ago. Seeing you like this has made me put my own past under the microscope. It isn't pretty,' he said grimly.

'You aren't a bit like Hugh!' She frowned.

'I was. I am,' he persisted. 'I may not have deceived my lovers—we had fun, but that was the extent of it. Sometimes I know I have left broken hearts behind me through not resisting temptation. You knew that when we slept together, didn't you?' he looked for her agreement.

'Yes. I'm under absolutely no illusions about you, Stefano,' she agreed. An odd expression flashed in his eyes for a moment, but then he continued.

'That's just as well. While I was on the streets I saw too many relationships driven apart by abuse and desperation. I was determined not to be like that, so I've never made any promises I can't keep. Giving a woman overwhelming pleasure is one thing. Promising to bind myself exclusively to her—never.'

'I understand.' Kira nodded. 'For me, you've always been Stefano the Seducer. Nothing more—and most definitely nothing less.'

The crease between his brows deepened a fraction.

'It almost sounds as though you approve of what happened between us, Kira.'

Unable to stop her memories warming her voice, she smiled. 'I can't help it. I do.'

Stefano's frown eased, and she corrected herself quickly.

'That is…I mean…I did.'

'You don't sound very sure?'

Slowly, almost hesitantly, his hand moved towards a curl of her hair that had strayed out of place. Coiling it over her shoulder, he smiled.

It was her turn to frown. 'I'm not.'

'Then let me help you to make up your mind. What you mean is, that as long as we are both completely honest with each other, no one will get hurt. Is that right?'

She nodded.

'I'm not sure I agree,' he said softly, shaking his head. Then his voice dropped to a whisper. 'For example, if I told you now that my deepest desire was to take you to bed, and you said that was the last thing you wanted to do, I would be crushed. Absolutely.'

His hand was still hovering near her hair. His eyes were very blue and clear.

Kira could barely breathe. She tried to speak. 'B-but then, if I said that, I would be lying…' she began, but could not finish.

Stefano anticipated what she was going to say. With the urgency she craved so much, he reached out and brought her within the circle of his arms. She could offer no resistance, and didn't want to. Stefano drew her towards him until their lips met in a kiss that swept away all her worries. She relaxed into the delicious warmth of his embrace. While his kiss held her captive, he drew his hand slowly up over her ribcage. As his fingers brushed the curve of her breast she shivered with anticipation.

'That is exactly the type of persuasion that can lead a girl astray,' she murmured.

'I know. Now, where would you like me to lead you—to your place, or mine?' he whispered, lifting her into his arms.

CHAPTER TEN

STEFANO undressed her right down to the diamonds. With a huge moon riding the velvet night outside, he worshipped his goddess of the flowers. 'I said you would be perfection, framed in honey orchids and silhouetted against the tropical sky,' he breathed, and it was true. He could not get enough of her, his lips sipping kisses from the yielding softness of her skin.

He made love to her the whole night long. No sensation was too divine. She fuelled feelings within him he had never experienced before. Each time she moved beneath his hands, a possessive need made him hold her ever more tightly to his body. He could not let her go. As their bodies entwined in a vibrant search for satisfaction, a truth began to slip in and out of the shadows shielding his mind. He had never before found such a perfect fit for his body, his mind and his senses. Kira had to be his for evermore. He wanted her—but his feelings ran far deeper than mere sex. He had wanted plenty of women in the past, and taken them all. But Kira was different. She was an experience he could not afford to lose.

Much, much later, Stefano swam back to consciousness through warm waves of satisfaction. Then the gravity of his feelings pulled him back to real life. Something incredible had happened last night. His seduction hadn't gone as planned; it had been spontaneous and reckless in a way he had never experienced before. The realisation opened his eyes wide. Then two words hurtled back at him and he shut them again, fast.

Love me.

Had he really said that? No, it wasn't possible. He wouldn't have—couldn't have—said it. He'd never done such a dangerous thing in his entire life. Although…he definitely remembered those words pulsating through the heat of his passion. Twice, in quick succession.

He must have imagined it. Yes, that was it.

With an exhalation of relief, he opened his eyes again. The room was still close and shadowy in the purple light before dawn. The sun outside had not risen high enough to penetrate the trees sheltering their refuge. He moved to check his wrist, but it was bare. He had tossed his watch aside in case it rubbed harshly against Kira's delicate skin. It was the first time he had ever done something like that, too. He wondered idly what time it was, but found he didn't care. Kira wouldn't mind, either. She liked it here on Silver Island as much as he did. They had lain awake for hours, listening to the mournful night birds outside, and wondering about the bright star that flickered down at them through the jalousie slats.

He tried to move, but couldn't. He had fallen asleep with Kira wrapped protectively in his arms. Until she wanted to escape, he was trapped.

Escape… The word rang through his head like an alarm.

Suddenly he stopped wanting Kira to wake. More

memories were racing back to taunt him. Before the wonderful abandon of bed, they had talked about her past last night—and his. That would mean she could never look at him in the same light again. Her image of him would be tainted by what she knew about his past. When she woke and gave him that lovely smile, what would be going on behind those beautiful eyes? His heart began to race. What exactly had they talked about last night, before words became unnecessary? He dimly remembered saying something about life being hard for the weak. Him? Weak? A hot wave of resentment washed over him, throwing more conversational flotsam back in his face. He had admitted turning his back on all his relatives. This, after Kira had been desperate to believe in some idealised dream of Italian family life. Well, he had shattered that illusion beyond repair!

Talking after sex, stargazing… Stefano was losing count of the number of firsts he had shared with Kira last night. There was no knowing where all this might lead, but he had his suspicions. Mercifully, another memory came back to him. He had stressed his independence again to her, hadn't he? She must understand that by now. Surely a man who could abandon his family couldn't be expected to be faithful to anyone else. In any case, where women were involved, Stefano considered himself a hunter, not a pet. Kira knew he was a lone wolf. Animals like that walked alone.

Beside him, she moved in her sleep. It was a luxurious movement, stretching out across the bed and freeing him.

A wolf walks alone, Stefano told himself. He hadn't been backed into a corner by anyone since he was a child.

Taking his chance, he began inching his way towards the edge of the bed. He had to escape. Last night, Kira had seen past his act of emotionally detached, successful businessman. She had captured some of his spirit. If he stayed by her side any longer, she would surely consume the rest.

He had to go. Now.

Peeling his body away from the last temptations of her touch, he eased his legs over the edge of the bed and inched into a sitting position. His clothes were scattered all over the place. As he reached for them, he tried not to think of the spectacular passion he had shared with Kira only hours earlier. Pulling his still-buttoned shirt on over his head, he stood, stifling a sigh of relief—but not well enough.

The rhythm of Kira's breathing changed. Stefano froze. So did she—and then she rolled over to greet him with that smile….

He swung away, unable to look her in the face.

'Stefano? What are you doing? It's too early to get up.'

Her voice was as velvet smooth as the touch he could never risk experiencing again. He shook his head.

'I'm sorry, Kira. I—I have to go. It's business. An urgent call. You know…' His voice disappeared. When Kira sat up and the silken sheet slipped away from her stunning nakedness, his willpower almost followed his voice.

'I never heard anything?'

'My phone was on vibrate. I really didn't want to wake you,' he added, with a sudden attack of the truth.

'So tell me—what is so important that it can pull you out of my arms?'

'You don't want to know.' Stefano went on dragging on his clothes.

'Yes, I do. Everything you do interests me, and I don't know the first thing about your work. All you've told me about so far is your past.'

He stopped and stared at her.

'Dio! Forget that. I shouldn't have said anything,' he muttered hurriedly. 'I—wanted to see how you'd react if I shot your dream of Italian family life down in flames. It was nothing. Forget everything I've told you.'

'No!' With a giggle she reached out to him, ready to tug him back into bed with her. 'First you try and sneak off without waking me, now you're backtracking on everything else as well. What's the matter, Stefano?'

He leapt back as though her touch was a threat. 'I've told you. It's nothing.' Making his face as bland as possible, he stared at her, daring her to contradict him. 'I must go.'

Kira had stopped laughing. The silence that fell between them now was deadly. There could be only one reason for his sudden coldness. He was leaving her. She gazed at him, unable to quite believe it.

'Why are you going? Tell me. I want to know.' Her voice crackled with emotion.

Stefano reached for his jacket and pulled it on. With short, sharp movements he checked that it contained his keys and wallet. 'All right—if you insist. I'm not going to lie to you, Kira. Have you thought you might not be the only one who could have second thoughts about all this?'

There was frostbite in his voice.

'It sounds like you're getting ready to abandon me.' Her voice barely trembled, but the tension was there.

'Of course that's what you must think.' Stefano's reply ricocheted back like a bullet. 'After what you've been through, it's only natural.'

Kira watched him brace himself, and take a step towards the bed. If kissing her goodbye took such a visible effort, she didn't want it. She sat back on her heels, distancing herself from him.

'Can you blame me, Stefano, when all men are so alike? I thought last night was something exceptional, but now it turns out every move you made, every word you spoke, was fiction,' she snapped.

Stefano drew back. The rising sun outside lit a shimmering aura around him. Despite the growing dawn, no bird or insect dared disturb the horrible silence as he formed his next argument. 'That's not true. But don't say you've never felt the need to nip a situation in the bud, before things get out of hand?'

She could hardly believe what she was hearing. Clutching the sheet against her body like a shield, she tried to make sense of this sudden change in him.

She was losing him. Unable to think of anything she had done or said to make him cool so abruptly, she began to panic.

'What is it? What can possibly have changed between us since last night, Stefano?' she implored.

'Nothing…and everything.'

His face was hard with an alien emotion. Kira gazed at him. The man who had seduced her with soft words and intoxicating caresses stared back at her in bitter disillusion.

'My US agent rang with details of an ideal investment property in upstate New York. That's where I'm going,' he said at last, each word drawn out and hesitant.

Kira's heart leapt. For a moment things didn't seem so bad. Looking around Sir Ivan's old house with Stefano had been wonderful. Maybe she could persuade him to include her in this next invitation? Her excitement was quashed by his next words.

'I'm leaving right away to go and view it. You can stay on here for as long as you like. Just tell one of my pilots when you want to go home.'

'So…you're flying to America alone?' Kira said slowly. With heart-rending effort, she managed to stop her smile sliding straight into despair.

He nodded. Grabbing his phone from the bedside table he dropped it into a pocket. Motionless with shock, Kira could not do or say a thing. It didn't matter. Stefano was perfectly prepared to do the talking for both of them.

'When I want to get away from people, I get right away from them. Once you've finished checking out Silver Island, you can go back to living in the grounds of Bella Terra, and working at my town house in Florence. While you're doing all that and flitting from one place to another, I'll keep well out of your way, until you've finished.'

'Why? There's nothing to stop you coming and going wherever you please. I'm won't be in your way,' Kira said, confused.

'I need space. I can't let you interfere with that.' Stefano's voice soared through the silence that fell between them.

It wasn't just a statement, it was a warning. Kira didn't need to be told twice. Gathering up her last reserves of courage, she stared him out.

'Don't worry on my account, Stefano. You know I'm

happier alone,' she said brusquely. 'I'll be fine. Once I leave here, I'll be totally absorbed by the Florence project. Go and find yourself another new house. Maybe you'll have better luck turning that one into a home, although I very much doubt it.'

'I can hope,' he said coolly.

'It won't take me more than a few hours to do my preliminary checks here. I'd be grateful if you'd arrange for me to be flown home this afternoon,' Kira countered, turning to hide her rage and shame as she got out of bed. Wrapping the sheet tightly around her body she stalked towards the bathroom. Ice-cold reserve was the only way she could deal with this situation. She expected Stefano to agree to her demand without question. His reaction came as a shock. As she strode past him, he grabbed her by the elbow.

'No. Stay here, on the island.'

'What?'

'That way I'll know where you are.'

'Now, wait a minute!' Kira flared. 'I may be on your payroll, but that doesn't mean you're in charge of my schedule. When it comes to my work, everything has to be done in the right order.'

And first on the list is getting you right out of my system, she thought painfully.

'I've got so much admin work to do back at home, I'll need to get started on it as soon as possible,' she went on, pulling her arm roughly from his grasp. 'Then there's the prince's project to sign off, and that's before I've even thought of starting work on your town house....'

Hugging the sheet tightly to her body, she started for the shower again. Hearing Stefano take some quick steps in pursuit and knowing that if he laid another hand on her she would be lost, she turned to confront him. She didn't want his touch clouding her judgement.

His expression gave her another jolt. He looked white-faced, almost lost, and as far from the smooth, composed Stefano as she had ever seen him. A moment later, and he was impenetrable once more.

'I'm glad you'll be keeping yourself busy,' he said, with all the passion of a diplomat.

Kira met his chilly good manners with a hard frost of her own. 'Don't talk about my work as though it is a hobby, Stefano. I signed that contract for you, don't forget.'

Her glare drew down shades over his expression. Any softening of his manner was instantly hidden from her, and from the world.

'How could I?' he said bitterly.

Stefano stormed away from Silver Island. He didn't need his newest employee lecturing him, even if her name was Kira Banks. Her anger worked away at his pride like a mountain stream running over rocks. An endless loop of her words went around and around in his head, and worse still, for the first time ever, Stefano could not settle to work on the plane journey. He hardly heard a word his agent said as they drove towards his latest dream property. His mind was a complete mess of regret and confusion. What did he want with another soulless palace? None of the others had brought him a moment's happiness or satisfaction. He had found both in Kira's arms, and then turned his back on her. Where was the sense in that? All he needed in his life was Kira, and her homely touch. Why had he ruined his only chance of happiness by letting slip his murky past, and the way he had abandoned his family? It would only reinforce her picture of him as a shallow pleasure seeker, flitting from one set of values to another. Kira deserved better than that, and she knew it.

She wouldn't want him now.

He barely noticed the colonial mansion he had travelled thousands of miles to inspect. Unable to make a decision on it, he retreated to Manhattan. His apartment on Fifth Avenue was as cheerless as any of his other homes. He roamed about, trying to put Kira out of his mind. It was hopeless. From the contrast between her cosy little home and his soulless apartment to the sight of lovers strolling hand in hand through Central Park, everything reminded him of her.

Finally, he went out, throwing himself into the surf of crowds and noise swirling through the city streets. It was supposed to block thoughts of Kira with the white noise of chaos. It didn't work. Each woman he saw was automatically matched against her memory, and found wanting.

Eventually, he washed up at an all-night club. The atmosphere was intended to stifle Kira's memory. Instead, her voice echoed in his brain. It cut straight through the racket, as he remembered how she had chosen to spend the evening with him on Silver Island—no distractions—rather than be wined and dined in the city. They wanted the same things out of life. Why didn't he trust himself to share them with her? The answer to that circled him like a shark but he didn't want to face it. Instead, he told himself that he'd done the right thing. She had been hurt before, and he'd only hurt her again—he had left her to protect her.

After a sleepless night, he went into the Manhattan

offices of Albani International. That was another disaster. He lasted twenty minutes. Unable to work, he spent the whole time resisting the urge to pick up the phone and ring Kira. In the end, he had to walk out and ask a secretary to order a car for him. He couldn't trust himself to make one simple, innocent business call. Once he lifted that receiver, he knew he would end up ringing Kira instead.

Kira tried to make a full and detailed assessment of Stefano's tropical paradise. It was impossible. She made some silly mistakes, and couldn't complete the simplest calculations. Her emotions were too raw. He had swept her up to heaven, and then dropped her the morning after. It was history repeating itself, and she felt empty, completely crushed. As soon as she had filled a few pages of her notebook, she made arrangements to board one of his private jets and leave the island chain.

The flight home was agonising. She did her best to make it look as though she was enjoying every second. She had a lifetime's experience of putting on a good show. She watched a romantic comedy, and took care to laugh in all the right places. She smiled and chatted to the cabin crew, and ate every meal and titbit they offered her. In contrast, she took only a solitary glass of white wine with her dinner, and most of that went back to the galley untouched. No way was she going to let anyone think Stefano Albani had driven her to drink!

One of his fleet of cars was waiting for her at the airport. The chauffeur said he had instructions to whisk her straight back home to La Ritirata. Kira had other ideas. She asked to be taken directly to Stefano's town house in Florence. That would put some distance between her and the valley she had left with such high hopes, only a couple of days before. Stefano had already infused the entire Bella Terra estate with so many memories for her. They had talked and laughed there. His new town house did not mean quite so much to her. As long as she kept well away from the place where he had seduced her, it had no hold over her. Stefano's offer to let her stay there while she worked on the project had seemed wildly overgenerous. Now she was glad of the opportunity. A break from La Ritirata was exactly what she needed. It would give her some time away from his memory.

Stefano suffered through another sleepless night, and that morning he knew he had to come to his senses. He couldn't think of anything but Kira and there could be only one outcome. He wanted her, and he would never get any rest until she was safely in his arms again. He didn't need to think any further than that. Summoning a car, he headed straight for the airport. Then he blazed a trail across the world. He hadn't thought beyond the fact that Kira had bewitched his mind and his body, and he could not live without her for a moment longer. All he wanted to do was reach her side. This was such a new sensation he had no idea what he was going to say, but right now, he didn't care. He needed her. The moment he saw her, the words would come. He knew it.

Driving towards the Bella Terra villa felt like coming home. It reinforced all his deepest feelings. This was where he wanted to spend the rest of his life. Now he was going to claim the woman he wanted by his side for all eternity. Leaping out of the car before his chauffeur had brought it to a standstill, he strode straight across the valley towards La Ritirata. He still hadn't worked out his argument, but words could wait. His first kiss would tell Kira all she needed to know.

He was so consumed by what he would do, it took him a while to realise something was wrong. The day was hot and the sky stormy, but all the windows of Kira's little home were tightly closed. As he registered that fact, he smelled smoke. The countryside was dry as dust. Fire was a constant threat, but now he saw it was a reality. Smoke was curling up from the back of La Ritirata. He started to run.

'Kira!'

Pulling out his phone as he ran, he summoned help from the villa but didn't wait for it to arrive. The woman he loved was in danger. Kicking down the front door, he burst into the living room. It was a furnace, centred on the burning kitchen door. A thick haze of smoke rose to fill the house, but Stefano never hesitated. Dropping to the floor where the atmosphere was clearest, he made straight for the burning room.

'Kira!'

There was no reply. He held his breath. The kitchen was well alight, but empty. His heart started to beat again. There was still hope. Calling her name, he quartered the living room, searching through the smoke and straining to hear the smallest noise. The crumble and crackle of feasting flames threatened to silence everything in its path.

Time was slipping away, dragging a suffocating chain ever tighter around his chest. He cast a desperate look at the fresh air outside, but could not waste a precious second. Reaching the staircase he went up on all fours. Keeping his head below the level of the smoke was good in theory, but the fire was sucking all the available oxygen from the air. If Kira was here, he had to get her out within the next couple of minutes. He ran into her bedroom, his movements now desperate Walking away from her was the worst mistake he had ever made, and if he had now lost her for ever…

The town house in Florence was every bit as tempting as Kira remembered from her first visit but the unfinished business with Stefano hung over her like a thundercloud. Nothing could distract her. Flipping on the TV, she tried to get interested in the news. Gazing out of the window, she was only half listening to the babbled headlines. The sky outside was crying. She stared out over the sodden rooftops of Florence. If only Stefano had not tried to shut her out of his life so abruptly. She might still be lying in his arms. The silver sand would be soft and warm beneath their skin, while sunlight danced in patterns overhead, sparkling through palm leaves.

Here in Italy, it was wet and Kira was miserable. She closed her eyes and inhaled, imagining the warm, fertile perfume of her garden back at La Ritirata after a shower. All it needed to make her fantasy complete was Stefano. He had broken her heart, but she could not stop yearning for him. Angry with herself for being so weak she reached over to switch off the useless distraction of the television when her hand froze in midair. Half a dozen words snatched her attention and held it, breathless.

'Mystery fire rages at billionaire's hideaway…'

The plasma screen was alive with flames and thick funnels of smoke. As the presenter droned on, the scene changed. A bird's-eye view showed again the frighteningly familiar landscape. The pictures were so huge and horrific she could practically feel the heat. The news report said only that a house on the estate of a reclusive billionaire had been destroyed, but Kira didn't need any more details. Despite the flickering flames and jagged camera work, she recognised La Ritirata.

Her home had been destroyed.

Alight with fear, she called a hire car and drove straight to the Bella Terra estate. The smell of smoke was almost overpowering as she drove up the track towards the villa. She had to close all the ventilators. It was impossible to miss the turning for La Ritirata. The TV item had been recorded earlier in the day, so the news crews and fire services had vanished. Only the mess remained, where all their vehicles had been stationed. Grass and bushes were flattened, and the recent rain had surrounded the blackened stinking ruins of her little house with mud.

Kira put a hand up to open her car door, but stopped before she made contact. She couldn't do it. She couldn't step out into this disaster. Unable to bear the horrible sight any longer, she turned the car around and headed for Stefano's villa. The sick feeling inside her was made a hundred times worse by the reek of smoke that crept into the vehicle. There could be no escape from the after-effects of the blaze. They would linger for a long time, and in her memory for ever.

She brought her car to a halt on the grand terrace where Stefano had once parked his helicopter. She got out of the car, and plodded up the steps to the great front doors. There she pulled on the bell, which echoed like an alarm through the rambling old house. She purposely kept her back to the wreckage of La Ritirata, unable to look at the damage.

When the villa door opened, the interior came as

a complete surprise to her. It had been transformed. Although Stefano had owned La Bella Terra for only a few days, an impressive desk and banks of telecommunications equipment had already been installed in the reception area. As Kira stepped inside, a woman rushed forward and grabbed her hands. Her face was tight with panic and stress and it took a few moments for Kira to recognise Stefano's senior PA beneath the smudges of mascara. That was a shock. Kira had last seen her arriving on Silver Island, and assumed she would have followed her boss to the USA.

'Is there any news, Miss Banks?'

'What about? And why are you here?' Kira stared at her, puzzled, the chaos surrounding her house momentarily pushed to one side. 'I thought you stuck to Stefano like a Post-it note?'

At the mention of her boss the woman went even whiter.

'Oh, I am so sorry, Miss Banks…'

Feeling panic rise, Kira prised herself out of the PA's grasp. To be clutched at by a stranger was almost as bad as seeing her house in ruins.

'It's only sticks and stones,' she muttered, embarrassed by such a show of emotion from someone she hardly knew. Stefano mustn't be allowed to see her fail. If she could walk away from him on Silver Island, she could carry on holding everything together now. She avoided thinking in too much detail about how much she had lost. All of her hard work over the years…

'It isn't as though there were lives at stake,' she went on, keeping a skin of ice over the turbulent depths of her true feelings. 'Could you send a message to Signor Albani, please?' she asked briskly. 'I was only going to be staying in Florence while I worked on his town house, but now I've lost my home, I've got nowhere to live. I'll need to stay in town on a permanent basis, until I can sort things out….'

The girl was looking at her in confusion.

'Miss Banks! You mean to say you don't know what happened? Signor Albani has been rushed to hospital!'

Kira's mind went completely blank. She fell back, aghast.

'He tried to save your house. He put his life on the line, looking for you, and for what? You hardly seem to care about him, or your home!' The PA was clearly fighting tears.

Kira was suddenly aware of the villa's entrance hall filling with faces. Builders, architects and members of staff poked their heads from doorways or looked over the banisters from the upper floors. Covered in shame, she wanted to run away and hide, but she was too thunderstruck to do anything but gawp at the collection of furious, accusing faces.

'Me? What have I done?' she said faintly. 'It's not my fault!' No answer came. The PA had turned away and Kira was left to her own thoughts. If Stefano had not gone looking for me—*why was he looking for me?*

'I had no idea he was in the country. I thought he was still in America,' she whispered to herself.

Kira's heart solidified inside her chest. Stefano had left her, that last fateful day on Silver Island. He had betrayed her, forcing mental and physical distance between them. Now she was expected to believe he had taken a pointless risk by searching for her in an empty house! It was too much to take on board.

Ignoring her audience, she marched straight back out to her car. On the way, she steeled herself to take another glance at the smoking ruin that had once been her home. It was terrifying. Stefano had been in there. She had to find out why.

CHAPTER ELEVEN

ONCE at the hospital, rules and regulations held her up for ages. Getting into Stefano's private suite took longer than the drive from La Bella Terra had done. When she was finally allowed to enter, her nerves were put to their stiffest test. Stefano lay motionless in the bed. His eyes were closed, and the only colour in his face came from a network of cuts, scratches and bruises. His natural colour had drained away to a deathly grey. Once the orderly had shown her into the room, he left. When she was completely alone with the patient, Kira could not contain herself any longer. She rushed forward and grabbed his hand, which was swathed in bandages.

'Stefano!' she gasped.

He flinched, scowled and opened his eyes, in that order. Kira instantly dropped his hand and stepped back, his cold eyes reminding her of the distance between them.

'What are you doing here? I gave express instructions that you, above all people, weren't to be allowed in.'

Digging both elbows into his bed, he struggled up into a sitting position. Once there, he reached for the alarm button on his side table.

'Stop! Don't blame the staff. It's nobody's fault but

mine,' Kira said. 'I waited until the shift changed on reception and then said I was one of your PAs, coming to consult you about some paperwork.'

Stefano let his hand fall back to the bed, winced and then managed a half-smile at her ingenuity.

'Why do you think I issued that order? I didn't want you to see me like this.' He wouldn't meet her eyes.

There was a silence. Scrabbling for words, Kira said with an awkward laugh, 'I did all that work making my house beautiful and comfortable, but never got around to fitting a sprinkler system!'

'Dio! It was a country cottage, not the Uffizi Gallery.' They both paused again.

'Are your burns very painful?'

He looked at her finally, but only for a moment. 'They're not too bad. I'm only in for observation.'

Kira poured him a glass of water, but he shook his head.

'Why did you risk going into a burning building?' she burst out, unable to wait any longer.

For a moment she thought he wasn't going to answer her, but then he sighed and spoke.

'I thought you were inside. I assumed you would shut yourself away in La Ritirata after getting back from Silver Island.'

Kira watched him intently. He brushed folds from his coverlet, picked up his watch from the bedside cabinet and put it on, but he did not look directly at her.

'So...you actually went looking for me?' she said at last.

'It was the least I could do,' he said, still avoiding her eyes. 'I realised that, however much you claimed to understand I wasn't offering you anything more than a good time, I had hurt you. I was determined to make up for that. I saw smoke, thought the worst and broke in. I thought maybe you were asleep, or unconscious, or…'

'You risked your life for me,' Kira said slowly. 'I never imagined anyone would do that.'

'I couldn't help myself.' Stefano evaded her eyes. 'The flames took hold very quickly. When I realised you weren't there I concentrated on getting as many of your belongings out as possible.'

'You saved some of my things!' Kira's heart leapt for a moment, before shock distracted her. 'You stayed and did all that when I wasn't even in the house, Stefano?'

'They were your things. You made a perfect home. You weren't going to lose anything, if I could help it,' he said simply. 'Things matter to you.'

And so do you, she thought painfully.

Shutting her eyes, she sank down in the nearest chair. When Stefano first abandoned her, she had been filled with anger. That evaporated the second she heard he had been injured. Now she felt weak, confused and resentful that he should force her through such an obstacle course of emotions.

'You might claim to know my mind, but you're a total mystery to me, Stefano Albani. I thought you didn't ever want to see me again. And then you go and do something like this,' she said quietly.

'I've told you. I couldn't help myself.' Stefano sounded as though he could hardly believe it himself.

Kira did not need to search his face to see that he was telling the simple truth.

'Did you buy that house in America?'

He shook his head. 'It didn't seem important any more. Once upon a time I had nothing, but now I can have what I like, and make a home anywhere I want. It's enough to know that. I don't need to follow through.'

'But you can't make yourself any kind of home, can you? That's what all this is about!' Her eyes flew open. 'On the day we first met, you spoke as though the Bella Terra estate was the answer to all your prayers. You were going to make your home there, and settle. But it wasn't good enough, was it? I should have seen the warning signs when you showed me around the town house in Florence—that must have been your previous "ideal home." It would have been the solution to all your problems—until you lit upon my valley. Before that, it must have been Silver Island. All these places have one thing in common, Stefano. You haven't been able to make a home out of any of them!'

Breathless, she ran out of words. Stefano had watched her in silence. Now he laced his fingers together, winced and straightened them carefully again before speaking.

'We're alike, you and I. Neither of us likes to be out of control. Neither of us appreciates surprises.' He paused before adding, 'But my existence has been anything but predictable since I met you.'

His calculated tone was in such contrast to her outburst, Kira sat back in surprise. He seemed to have somehow retreated from her, in spite of not having moved from his bed.

'I'm a free agent, Kira.' He spread his hands in a bleak gesture. 'I need to be able to come and go, in the same way you do. Work defines both our lives, doesn't it? We can't devote ourselves to our careers if we're always looking out for the other, can we?' he finished, with a hint of defiance.

Over the past few days Kira had begun to reassess her life. She was beginning to think work was playing too big a part in it. Her heart sank as she realised that Stefano had clearly done no such thing.

He grazed his teeth over his lower lip. 'What are you going to do about La Ritirata now? I doubt if it's habitable.'

'There isn't much left standing.'

Always restless, Stefano reached for the water Kira had poured him. After taking a sip, he slid the glass across his bedside table. He did not look at her as he spoke.

'Look—don't take this the wrong way, Kira, but why not consider selling what is left of your house to me? I can take it off your hands, give you a good price and you can start again. I can make everything all right for you again. You were never keen on a stranger moving into Bella Terra. This way, it won't matter to you.'

Kira stared at him, looking for any trace of the man she thought she loved. All she could see was the cold, hard exterior. She forced herself to ask, 'You—you'd like me to go back to England? '

'Well, it's obviously up to you,' he responded mildly. 'I'm simply offering to help you. That heap of rubble is nothing but a liability to you now.'

The truth hurt. Kira was so used to it, she only knew one defence. She squared up to him again.

'A liability? You know all about those, of course. Apparently, that's how you saw me on the morning you abandoned me on Silver Island.'

She rose from her seat, all the hurt rushing back as fresh and raw as that first moment when she saw him getting ready to leave her.

'I served your purpose, and then you left.'

'Oh, Kira…' For a moment she thought she saw a flash of something deeper in his eyes, but then it was gone, and when he spoke again, his voice was carefully controlled.

'That night on Silver Island, you seemed to understand me better than I knew myself. You know what I'm like now, which is more than anyone else in the world does. I didn't want you to get too fond of me, so I went to look at a property. That's all.'

Kira looked at him, really looked at him. His white face and guarded eyes. He was lying. She knew it. Somewhere deep inside, he must know it, too. Her sadness was suddenly gone, eclipsed by anger at his stubborn blindness. Her hands flexed in impotent rage. 'You are a coward, Stefano. We had something incredible between us—I know you felt it, too. Deny it all you want, but I hope one day you'll understand what you have thrown away. Property? You've already got more of that than you know what to do with! Why don't you start looking closer to home, Stefano? Oh, I'm sorry, you don't have one of those!' Grabbing her bag, she threw herself towards the door.

'Wait, Kira! Where are you going?'

'I'm going to show you how to make a home from absolutely nothing, Stefano. I'm going to rebuild La Ritirata stone by stone, if it takes me the rest of my life,' she finished, with steely resolve.

Swinging out of his room, she let the door slam shut behind her.

Shell-shocked, Stefano dragged himself out of bed. He didn't want things to end like this. They needed to finish on his terms—he needed the last word. He flung open the door of his private room. She was already gone, straight out of his life. It was too late.

It was almost dark by the time Kira reached her car. With a heavy heart she decided there was no point in going back to La Ritirata until the morning. Nothing could be done by night. Instead, she headed back to her guest suite in Stefano's Florentine town house.

Hours later, she wished she had returned to the Bella Terra valley anyway. Sleep was impossible. Inspecting the ruins of her home by torchlight would have been a better use of her time than tossing and turning in bed. She got up while it was still barely light, and went out for a short walk around town. It was supposed to clear her head, but her mind was too full for that. She thought about the home she had lost, and how much more terrible it could so easily have been. Stefano might have been killed. When it came to matters of life and death, possessions didn't matter. They could be replaced. People couldn't. When he left her on Silver Island, Stefano had torn a hole in her heart. While he was still alive, there was a chance it might be repaired. If he had died in the fire, he would have been lost to her forever.

At least today she still had hope, where there might have only been tragedy.

Kira was a perfectionist, but when it came to Stefano's town house her standards reached new heights. She went into overdrive. When she wasn't busy with her contract to beautify the house, its roof and courtyard, she sat in her borrowed suite and co-ordinated the rebuilding of her own home. It was so painful to be confronted by the ashes of her happy life, but she refused to be beaten. Her vow to recreate her home was written in smoke-blackened stones. She poured all her anger and disappointment into her project to rebuild it. Each day she concentrated on her work at Stefano's town house, determined to fulfil her contract impeccably. Each evening, she drove to La Ritirata and worked on until it was too dark to see. She did all the odd jobs that might otherwise eat into the builders' time: making phone calls, sweeping up and washing down. Everything had to run according to her plan. Nothing must go wrong. She wanted her house to stand as a monument to her iron will.

Her commitment to both jobs never wavered. Her self-control often did. She was so glad that this was something she could do alone. For anyone else to see her anguish would have been unbearable. Each time she walked out onto Stefano's new roof garden, she kept expecting him to appear. He never did. As she walked through the cool, beautifully designed rooms of his suite, she knew that other women would have the benefit of the emperor-size bed and the shower that was big enough for two. She had lost him. Her bridges were burned, along with her house.

She had turned out to be the architect of her own unhappiness, and that was the most painful thing of all.

Kira's punishing schedule began to take its toll. There were times when she could barely drag herself from one project to the other. Her body was numb with exhaustion. She kept her mind blank with the anaesthetic of work. If she let it wander for a moment, it homed straight in on Stefano.

Rebuilding La Ritirata would take a long time, and more money than she could bear to think about. Her beloved garden was wrecked. It sagged beneath the weight of disaster. Nothing had escaped. Plants had been scorched, crushed beneath falling masonry or trampled and drowned by the emergency services or the builders.

Her house could be replaced, but its heart and soul would take a lot longer to repair. Wandering around the site, Kira couldn't help wondering if it would feel as soulless as all Stefano's properties did. There would be no love in it. She had none left to give. The rebuilt La Ritirata would rattle with emptiness, and smell of nothing but new paint and plaster. They were nice smells, but as impersonal as a hospital. The place would be eerily silent, too. Kira had grown to love the little creaks and moans her old house made. All its imperfections would vanish, like the original building. None of the new windows would jam, and the front door would open first time, every time. The usual pantomime of wiggling the key and bumping her shoulder against one particular spot would be a thing of the past. This new house should be ideal in every way, but somehow she knew it never would be. Something would always be missing.

All she had ever craved was a quiet life, far away from strangers, in her old house with its funny little ways. Now she had lost everything. Looking out across the valley at the Bella Terra villa, all Kira saw now was the wrong sort of isolation. She wanted to carry on being alone—alone, together with Stefano.

It was the end of her wonderful dream. She had lost her home, and the only man she would ever love or need or want. Stefano had been on to something. She should have accepted his offer to buy the ruins of La Ritirata. Her contracted jobs were well on the way to being finished—they didn't need her any longer. There was nothing in the Bella Terra valley for her now. Sadly, regretfully, she pulled out her mobile phone.

He had been right all along. All she had to do was tell him.

It was ironic. Stefano's problem was that he could never be satisfied with what he had. Kira's problem was the exact opposite. She loved what she knew, and never wanted it to change.

Her message to him was a simple one: *You've won. I don't want to replace my home here after all. You can have it.*

It had been hard enough to begin. Finishing it took forever. Every ending she added felt desperate, so finally she put the single word *Kira* and pressed Send.

She had a long wait. Her time in Florence, which should have been spent packing, kept being interrupted by checking her email in-box. Each time she opened it and there was no reply from Stefano, it felt like another rejection. She usually spent her time avoiding office work and the computer. Today was different. Finally, eyes dry and gritty from staring at a screen that refused to come up with the only name she wanted to see, she flung herself away from the desk with a cry of desperation. Blindly, she dashed up onto the brand new roof garden she had designed and built for him.

For as long as she could remember, gardens had been Kira's sanctuary. That magic did not work today. Solitude could not help her. She drifted around, unseeing. Moving from the flower boxes of pelargoniums to the terracotta pots of lemon trees and back again, she was locked inside her own thoughts. It was not a happy place to be. The only thing that could distract her was the idea Stefano might have replied to her email, and she had missed it. Within minutes of escaping from the screen, her nerve broke and she fled back inside.

Inevitably, she discovered her message had been answered almost as soon as she abandoned her laptop. Excitement plummeted to despair as she opened Stefano's message to find only an automatic response. He was going off-message until further notice.

Kira put both hands on the edge of the table and pushed herself back from her computer. That made his feelings pretty clear.

The rest of her day went to waste. She could not eat, or settle to anything for more than a few moments. As evening approached she gave up and drove to the Bella Terra valley. The place had always healed her in the past. It didn't happen today. Gazing at the foundations of the new house, she wondered if the next person to live in it would be truly happy there.

A chill breeze ruffled her hair. High in a nearby pine, an owl quavered its mournful cry. Cold weather would soon be on its way. One of Kira's great pleasures had been to feed the creatures driven close to her old home in winter. When she left, she would lose that. It would be a terrible wrench. She might hate this new house, but she still loved the Bella Terra valley.

On impulse, she decided to recreate some of the best things about her life at La Ritirata. She shook out some biscuit crumbs onto an upturned oil drum. Within seconds a robin returned to investigate. Gathering up small branches from beneath the trees, she began rebuilding the wood pile. It would be ready for burning by next winter. The memories of the sound and fragrance of crackling wood might make this soulless new house feel a little bit more homely. The new owners would enjoy that.

She was kneeling on the ground, picking up pine cones, when a sound made her whirl around in alarm. What she saw almost stopped her heart.

'Stefano!'

Without waiting for her to say any more, he walked across what had once been her garden. She froze. As imposing as ever, his long shadow fell across her. Sitting back on her heels, Kira tried to push her tumble of coppery gold hair behind her ears.

'Yes,' he said mildly. Reaching down, he brushed a fragment of dried grass from the crown of her head. She held her breath. He leaned back, carefully under control, and she breathed again,

'You've lost weight,' she said faintly. He laughed.

'I've been too busy to eat. I've found a new purpose in life.'

'That American property tempted you after all?' She smiled, dying inside. He shook his head, but that gave her no cause to hope. Instead, she became defensive.

'I've gone beyond the point of playing games, Stefano. Did you get my email?'

'Yes. That's why I'm here.' He was equally forthright.

She watched him speculatively. 'Why hasn't your office answered any of my messages?'

He flipped his keys into his pocket. 'They had nothing to tell you. They couldn't contact me. I was on my way here.'

'Why? Of all the places in your empire, why visit here?' Kira asked, hearing her voice trembling slightly.

He paused for a long time before he answered. The only sound was the idle clink of coins in his pocket. It cranked up the tension to a point where Kira jumped when the lonely owl called again.

'I'm not visiting, Kira,' he said at last. 'I'm back in the valley for good.'

She stared at him, wondering what to ask and where to start. 'Until five minutes ago I knew exactly what I was going to do. I had everything planned. Now you've parachuted back into my life, and I don't know what to think.'

'So don't think anything.' He came towards her again with a huge, beautiful smile and she stood, legs wobbly, to meet him. 'Just feel. All you need to know is that your problems are over, tesoro.' He reached out for her and Kira took a hasty step back. Her body was already reacting to his presence, and she knew that if she let him take her in his arms all would be lost.

Anger bubbled up inside her. How dare he just return so casually? 'I don't think so, Stefano. I have a feeling they may only just be beginning. Do you think you can flit in and out of my life on a whim? You abandoned me once, remember? How do you expect me to trust that you won't suddenly change your mind again?'

Stefano's smile faded.

'I want to explain.'

'What is there to say? You deceived me!'

A lightning bolt of anger galvanised his body. 'That's not true, Kira, and you know it! We both said we wanted to resist mixing business and pleasure. When it happened and I made a move, you could have said no. I would have respected that. We are so alike, both wary of entanglement. We knew the dangers. That meant you were never under any pressure to respond, and neither was I.' He had started angrily, but the bitterness in his voice melted away as he added, 'But we did, and there can never be any doubt that you are a woman who knows exactly what she wants. I wanted the same thing,' he finished quietly. 'And I still want it.'

Kira bit her lip as her eyes threatened to fill with tears. His words had some truth to them. He had been cruel to her, but she had been naive. 'I always said I would never let myself be so vulnerable again,' she said eventually.

'I know, and that was why I had to leave!'

His words escaped in such an explosion, Kira's head jerked up.

'I told you too much about myself on our last night together, Kira. That's why you must have realised I'm not to be trusted.'

In the days they had been apart Kira had combed every magazine and newspaper, steeling herself to read about Stefano and a string of other women. There had been nothing.

'I don't know what you're talking about, Stefano,' she challenged him at last. 'And you can't possibly say something like that without following it up!'

'I don't know if I can,' he said, with difficulty. 'You learned more about me in those final hours than I have ever revealed to anyone else. Telling you about Maria and my family lifted a weight off my mind. At first it felt good. But next morning...' He shook his head wordlessly.

'I realised I had gone too far. I had to get away.'

Kira waited, hardly daring to breathe. It was a long time before he spoke again.

'I told you the darkest secret of my life—that in order to make myself a success, I turned my back on my birth family.'

'You also told me you chose honesty when you decided to leave them,' Kira said quietly.

He nodded, pushing a hand through his hair in a sharp, agitated gesture. 'But at the time…the thought of you discovering I couldn't be any more loyal than your faithless Hugh…it was too much to bear.' He exhaled in a rush. 'And knowing you knew my secrets, what my childhood was really like… I've never told anyone that since I escaped it. I kept imagining you looking at me with disgust or—far worse—pity.' He lowered his head for a moment, the sharp planes of his face tense and pale.

'Stefano,' Kira said softly. 'You must know your past could never make any difference to me. It made you the man you are now, the man I—' she stopped herself and swallowed hard before continuing '—I know. I understand exactly how you feel. I panicked after the first time we spent the night together. I couldn't believe how perfect it felt—there was no way I could trust it to last. I knew it would crush me when it fell, when you decided I wasn't good enough—or met someone else…'

'What changed your mind?'

Kira sighed. 'To be honest, I couldn't stay away from you! I wanted to keep my distance—but I didn't want to lose touch with you either. I think I was lost from the beginning, really. Ever since you gave me your business card, I've been treating it like a holy relic,' she finished ruefully.

'You wouldn't be the first,' he assured her.

They stood and looked at each other—and then they laughed.

Stefano reached out to her again, his touch gliding over her cheek. In that moment, Kira forgot all her fears. All she wanted to do was check that her body was still a perfect fit for his arms. Closing the gap between them, she looked up into his eyes. They were intense and totally focused on her face. His smile enclosed her in warm, honeyed security as his touch brushed like silk against her skin.

'I—I don't know what came over me when we made love on Silver Island, Kira. It was every bit as good—no, it was better than when we were in Florence. That was the problem. First I couldn't get you out of my mind, and then I didn't want to let you out of my bed. I'd never felt like that about any woman before. It was such an overwhelming experience, I had to get away. I thought I was lost. In fact, the exact opposite was true. Once we were apart I discovered you are my anchor in life, Kira. That's why I could never resist coming back to you. You're strong, and centred, and keep me grounded in real life. When I abandoned you on Silver Island, it was like leaving behind part of myself. It was the best part, but I knew it was safe with you because after we made love that night, something changed. I became one half of a couple. Do you realise what that means? Since then I've been lost without you, adrift. We are meant to be together, Kira. You make me whole. There can be no going back now—for either of us.'

She shook her head in disbelief. She had never dared

to hope that his feelings might run so close to hers. 'That's exactly the way I felt, after Florence,' she told him quietly. 'For the first time in my life, I didn't want to be alone any more. That scared me, because it felt so different.'

He nodded.

'The moment I left you on Silver Island, I discovered you were inescapable. I was carrying you everywhere. You were inside me—in my thoughts, and deep within my heart. I went back to find you in La Ritirata, but the fire got in the way. When you found me in the hospital, I couldn't find the words to tell you the truth—I was still scared. I drove you away again, stubborn fool that I am. When you left, I tried to convince myself it was what you wanted. That it was the right decision, and I tried again to let you go. But I was lying to myself. Kira, we need each other. Together, we can show the world what family really means. Together, we'll be unbeatable. That's why I came to find you. Kira, my only love, am I too late?'

He was gazing into her eyes, trying to read her thoughts. Kira feasted her eyes on him for a long time before replying, but there wasn't a doubt in her mind. 'Too late?' she said finally in a soft, slow voice. 'You can't be, for here I am.' Stefano's face lit up with blazing joy as he pulled Kira against him.

'And here you stay.' He cupped her face in his hands and passionately kissed her as she melted against him. 'With me, for ever.'

MILLS & BOON®

The Rising Stars Collection!

This fabulous four-book collection features 3-in-1 stories from some of our talented writers who are the stars of the future! Feel the temperature rise this summer with our ultra-sexy and powerful heroes. Don't miss this great offer—buy the collection today to get one book free!

Order yours at
www.millsandboon.co.uk/risingstars

0715_ST16

Don't miss Sarah Morgan's next Puffin Island story

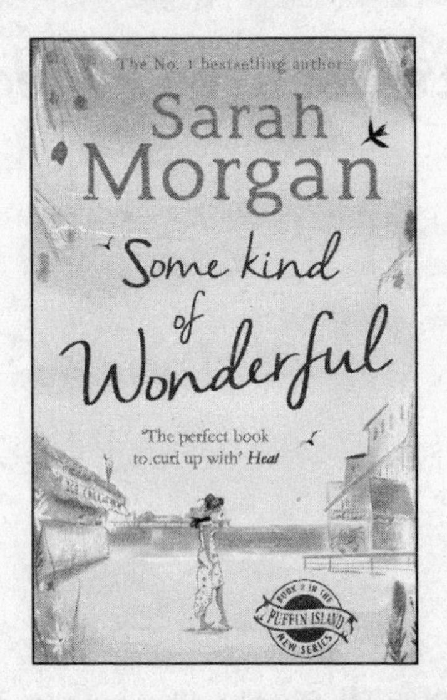

Brittany Forrest has stayed away from Puffin Island since her relationship with Zach Flynn went bad. They were married for ten days and only just managed not to kill each other by the end of the honeymoon.

But, when a broken arm means she must return, Brittany moves back to her Puffin Island home. Only to discover that Zach is there as well.

Will a summer together help two lovers reunite or will their stormy relationship crash on to the rocks of Puffin Island?

Some Kind of Wonderful
COMING JULY 2015
Pre-order your copy today

0315/MB507